THE PILOT FED FUEL TO THE ROTORS

"Go back! Go back!" James ordered into his radio, but McCarter wondered if it was too late. Even in the darkness of the night they saw the thick clouds of smoke billowing from the cargo hold. In moments the nerve gas would be released.

The Sea Hawk veered back, descending rapidly, sending the two men on the flexible ladder plummeting into the smoke. A hand reached out of the black cloud and grabbed the ladder.

It was Manning. He hauled Hawkins and Encizo, coughing violently, to the rope ladder.

"We're on. Go! Go!" James shouted into his mike.

As the others clambered aboard, McCarter watched the flaming, ruined hulk of the ship. Survivors staggered onto the deck, grabbing their throats, more victims of silent death.

D0822252

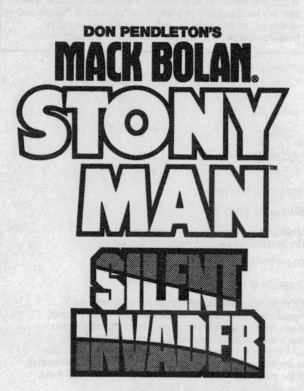

DON PENDLETON'S
MACK BOLAN®
STONY MAN™
SILENT INVADER

A GOLD EAGLE BOOK FROM
WORLDWIDE®

TORONTO • NEW YORK • LONDON
AMSTERDAM • PARIS • SYDNEY • HAMBURG
STOCKHOLM • ATHENS • TOKYO • MILAN
MADRID • WARSAW • BUDAPEST • AUCKLAND

First edition July 1999

ISBN 0-373-61925-1

Special thanks and acknowledgment to
Tim Somheil for his contribution to this work.

SILENT INVADER

Printed in U.S.A.

CHAPTER ONE

Al-Fallujah, Iraq

The brushed aluminum plaque at the door welcomed new arrivals to the Glorious Leader Hussein Hospital, and shellacked on the metal, yellowing with age, was a photograph of the glorious leader himself, standing in that very lobby when it was brand-new. He was surrounded by smiling doctors and four young girls in formal dress, raising gifts to him. Hussein beamed and smiled benevolently.

Dr. Taha Izzat was one of the doctors in the photo, but he found it difficult to remember that day. He'd been a different, happier man then. More importantly, he had been hopeful back in those days, more than fourteen years ago. Before the war with the Americans. Before the endless years of sanctions when he couldn't get medicine or supplies or even enough food. If he couldn't eat, he had wondered again and again, what were the less-than-privileged eating?

These days Hussein's fading smile mocked him when he arrived each day for work. But the image of the smiling, formally dressed girls was more painful. One of them was his daughter, an innocent ten-year-old when the picture was taken, beguiled by her par-

ents and by the contraband of the government to think
she was meeting a great man, a truly glorious leader,
at the hospital opening. Now she was a grown woman
and her husband was several years dead in the endless
battles the leader of the country waged—and she was
bitter, betrayed by Hussein. As they had all been betrayed.

Izzat stopped short at the door to his office.

"Colonel al-Duri," he said with civility, but without bothering to disguise his own bitterness.

Colonel Muhyi al-Duri nodded and watched the
doctor sit at the desk in the cramped office, waiting to
be asked his business. The doctor said nothing.

"There will again be activity at the hospital," the
colonel said.

The doctor nodded and shuffled among the tattered
folders on his desk. The scribbles of multiple names
crossed out showed how many times each of them had
been reused.

"Did you hear me, Doctor?"

"What do you wish me to say? Do I have a choice
here?" Izzat demanded. "You will do what you must.
You will shut down the east wing again, I assume?"

The colonel nodded.

"You will force me to displace thirty, maybe forty
patients. They will be sleeping in the halls tonight.
You will stay another two, three days, and you will
not hand over the supplies we agreed upon when we
first made this arrangement, to say nothing of making
amends for the past several times you have also come
without supplies. And if I protest, you will lecture me
about serving the glorious leader and make veiled
threats to my personal safety should I refuse to cooperate or should I attempt to seek some higher au-

thority's influence. Am I missing anything here, Colonel?''

Colonel al-Duri got to his feet. ''As long as you're clear on the procedure I suggest you start clearing out the east wing at once.''

IZZAT WAS RELIEVED that the operation in the east wing was surprisingly short this time. The colonel arrived with a smaller contingent than normal—just ten men—and four army transport trucks. Three battered steel, wheeled cases were assembled and sent through the halls of the now-abandoned east wing again and again, moving something either from the trucks to the storage or vice versa. The bodies had been removed from the morgue to the temporary facility in the west wing, and the steel cases were wheeled into the morgue. Izzat had realized long ago that some secret storage room had to exist beneath the morgue, and, in fact, that was the motive for the building of the hospital all along. The glorious leader was storing something that was so secret he had to sneak it in and out, keeping it concealed even from the eyes of his citizens. Which meant, the doctor had realized, the forces that monitored Iraq might very well learn about it someday. And, depending on the importance of the secret storage, might target the hospital when the next inevitable armed conflict came.

Throughout the war with the Americans he had expected the hospital to suddenly go up in a shattering explosion. He only hoped that he and the innocent patients in the hospital beds died quickly. He was truly surprised that they made it through unscathed.

Now he would have been relieved to know that the

secret storage chamber was being emptied, and that he was never going to see Colonel al-Duri again.

COLONEL MUHYI AL-DURI knew the most dangerous hours were those just ahead. A glance at his watch told him two hours remained until sundown. His driver gave him a quick sidelong glance, and al-Duri realized he looked nervous—fidgeting, looking at his watch, drumming his fingers. He'd have to act calm, even if he didn't feel calm. He had to act confident even though he wasn't at all confident they were going to make it out of Iraq alive.

Their method of transport assured them a certain measure of safety. The citizens didn't interfere with the army, especially when there was a colonel present. But al-Duri didn't know what kind of impromptu checkpoints were in place to keep valuable people and resources from leaving central Iraq. Members of Hussein's inner circle—even members of his family—had fled him, escaping overland into neighboring nations. He was loathe to allow anyone to leave his sphere of control.

The longer al-Duri considered it, the more he became convinced that he had made a gigantic mistake. He was a fool to think he could drive four army transport trucks right out of central Iraq. There was no way he wouldn't be noticed. They wouldn't escape Hussein's clutches.

Making no effort to be inconspicuous, they crossed directly through the urban sprawl of Habbaniyah, where the evening pedestrian traffic was still dense. Nothing aroused suspicion like furtive behavior. That had been the thinking, anyway. Now the colonel was convinced a guard had spotted them and was calling for an explanation of their presence, and very soon pursuit would be on its way.

Continuing west out of the city, they reached al-Ramadi a half hour later. A handful of soldiers on a street corner turned to watch the convoy pass, gripping their automatic weapons by the barrel, frankly curious. The colonel gave a brief wave. The soldiers didn't wave back, but one of them leaned into the others and spoke quickly. Then they were gone from sight.

Colonel al-Duri shifted in his seat and pressed his leg against the door, feeling the hard weight of the snub-nosed .38 revolver strapped there. It was Kuwaiti booty, a flashy rich man's toy, forgotten by its previous owner in the flight before the Iraqi invasion. But it functioned. Colonel al-Duri would fire it into his own brain if it was his final alternative to falling into Hussein's hands. That would be greatly preferred to the endless torture he would receive as a traitor.

The colonel had seen traitors tortured. In fact, tours of the torture chambers were SOP when serving on the staff of a paranoid dictator. Hussein wanted all his underlings to know what he did to those who even gave the impression of impropriety.

That fate wouldn't befall al-Duri. The .38 would see to it.

He couldn't help but check his watch again and almost swore out loud. Just an hour and forty-five minutes had passed since departing the hospital.

And they were still two hundred miles from Syria.

THE CONVOY WAS finally stopped just west of the city of Hit. The colonel rubbed his leg to check again for the .38, as if the weapon might have fallen from its calf strap somehow, and stepped out of the truck.

Three soldiers were getting out of an army sedan with Russian-made AKs. They saluted smartly when they spotted al-Duri's rank.

"We had not expected to see any army convoys moving through here this evening," one of them said apologetically.

"I am not surprised. My operation is supposed to be kept quiet. My direct superiors do not even know where I am. This letter should tell you all you need to know."

The colonel handed over the letter. It was stationery from the Office of the Vice Chairman of the Revolutionary Command Council. The soldiers grouped around it, struggling through the words as al-Duri took a few casual steps away from the vehicle and looked up and down the highway. They were at the edge of the Syrian Desert, which stretched for hundreds of miles from the arable land bordering the Euphrates River into Syria to the west and Saudi Arabia to the south. There were electric lights to the north and foot traffic a mile to the east. No one else was in the vicinity.

"We will radio this in. It will take just a moment, Colonel."

"That letter specifically calls for our unhindered passage," al-Duri spit.

"Still, we are under orders to radio in abnormal activity on this highway, Colonel," the solder protested.

"It is signed by army General Tariq Ramadan," al-Duri added.

The soldier was looking increasingly nervous. "I do not want to hold you up, Colonel, but I am under orders to radio in any activity on this highway."

"I understand." The colonel nodded. "Let me show you exactly what it is we are transporting. That will make it clear to you our need for radio silence."

He turned and waved for the soldiers to follow and briefly caught the eye of his driver, who would at once radio their approach to the rear truck in the caravan. But only two of the soldiers followed him. The driver would know what to do about the third.

The soldiers walked in silence as they followed the colonel to the last of the four stopped trucks. He banged on the rear door with his fist and it slid up into the ceiling, revealing stacks of metal cylinders and wooden crates—and four of al-Duri's soldiers aiming AK-47s. The colonel stepped into the back of the truck with his men as they fired simultaneously, and the soldiers crumpled, surprise on their faces.

The pop of a handgun sounded as the swift barrage ended. That would be the driver of the front truck taking out the third soldier, al-Duri knew, but just to be sure he sent out his four men. They jogged to the front of the convoy, where they found the driver dragging the third soldier's body behind the vehicles, out of view of any traffic that might happen by.

It took less than five minutes to stow the bodies in the trunk of the army sedan and move the car off the road into a depression where it was hidden from the highway. It wouldn't be found before morning.

The altercation, al-Duri decided when the convoy was moving again, had gone smoothly. If their luck continued, they would reach the safehouse in Syria before anybody even missed those soldiers.

They left the main road at the town of Fuhaymi and crossed the Euphrates, circled around the city of Rawah and headed west over the desert.

CHAPTER TWO

Aberdeen, Maryland

Truman Cie reached for the army-green field glasses hanging around his neck and put them to his eyes for the tenth time in the past half hour.

Finally there was activity around the ACADS building. Figures in hazardous materials suits began to emerge, one at a time. The last was a tall man who was studying a clipboard. He checked off items on his list, then stepped back into the building for a final look around. Cie saw him close the inner door, then the outer door, then check the seal on the outer door at least three times.

"Come on," Cie muttered.

"What's the matter?" Hedley asked, crouching beside him in the underbrush. They were stationed just seventy-five yards from the activity at the ACADS building.

"Nothing," Cie said. He disliked Hedley. The guy was too eager to please. But he seemed to know what he was doing with the equipment, and that was really all that mattered. "They're finally locking it down. We'll be moving within five minutes."

"Okay." Hedley crawled backward, deeper into the

trees, where the rest of the men had been hiding since they had cut the fence and bypassed the electronic perimeter system to the compound. Hedley relayed the update to the men, and Cie heard their faint rustling sounds. They were impatient too; the tension was palpable. A slipup during this operation would expose them to more than just the danger of getting caught. A mistake might result in the most horrible death imaginable.

The guy in the hazmat suit with the clipboard appeared to be overly cautious. He fiddled with the door seals and rechecked the small analog dials to the right of the door yet again. Then he shouldered the door, just in case, one last assurance that it was tight. He walked away a few paces, paused, looked back and finally walked around the building staring at his clipboard.

Cie didn't trust that guy. He was likely to have thought he had forgotten something. He gave him another few minutes before dialing the cellular phone headset he was wearing. The dialing went through and he heard an answer, then waited for the beep that indicated the scrambling procedure had been established. The computer-generated scrambling protocol was randomly developed for each call by the system. It wasn't unbreakable, but it would take hours to decode. That was if anybody happened to be listening and recording the conversation in the first place.

"What's our progress?" Cie asked.

"They're still in standby mode. What are they waiting for?"

"I couldn't tell you," Cie said. "They've got the building locked up. There's no staff in sight."

"Wait. Okay. They've started the procedure," Cie's

operator said, and his voice automatically shifted to a well-practiced monotone. "Stage 1 commences. Burners are firing up. Two minutes, thirteen seconds to Stage 2."

Cie spoke over his shoulder: "Let's move out."

There was nothing else said and almost no noise as the eight men crawled out of the trees and fanned out into a semicircle on the scrubby ground. There was no one else in sight. Who in their right mind would want to be in the vicinity now?

"One minute, fifty-five seconds," the operator stated in Cie's headphones.

They were cutting it close. In the trials they had anticipated a three-minute start-up time. Something had accelerated the process. Maybe the ACADS facility had determined they didn't need as much fire-up time on their burners, or maybe the Pollari team had screwed up. Cie thought the latter was probably the case, and he was going to raise some hell about it when this whole thing was done.

But he couldn't afford to let it distract him now. They'd pulled off practice runs in less than two minutes. They could do the real thing in two minutes—if no other unforeseen events occurred along the way.

He gestured to the building, and the eight men moved over the open ground, spacing out along the side of the building, three of them triangulating around Cie and Hedley as they took care of the door. Cie inserted a specially designed tool between the door and the jamb, at once completing the alarm circuit and popping the bolt. The analog dial jiggled slightly at the change, but not enough to alert anyone back at the control center. Cie raised the nail gun dangling on his belt and triggered a nail through the plastic tongue of the tool, holding it firmly in place, and yanked open the door.

"One minute, thirty-five seconds," said the voice in his headphones.

Hedley was wearing his stupid grin. He looked like an eager-to-please beagle, but he was hearing the same countdown Cie was. What was his problem?

Cie crossed the small vestibule in two steps, grabbing at the large hunting knife in his belt and stabbing at the plastic sealant tape around the interior door. The stuff was cheap and effective, and made a good fail-safe measure if all the other redundant measures somehow failed to contain one hundred percent of the fumes that would soon erupt inside the building.

"One minute, fifteen seconds."

"Not much time," Hedley commented. Cie stabbed at the calculator-sized electronic keypad on the door. There was a pause, then the small display blinked a red warning. Cie quickly overrode it with another code, and the red warning turned off.

"One minute."

"Jesus Christ!" Hedley said.

Cie was already reaching for the door, and there was a frozen second during which he could have stopped himself from opening it. But Hedley said nothing more, and Cie pushed open the door. It creaked on its huge stainless-steel hinges and opened into blackness.

The die was cast now. Hedley had less than one minute to take control of the system, or the burners would flare to life, and they'd be burned alive. If they tried to flee, they would be chased by an exploding cloud of catastrophically lethal gas. It would burn out their lungs, shut down their nervous systems, blind them, corrode the flesh from their bodies.

There were so many different types of so many lethal chemicals in that room, no one could even guess which would be the first to actually kill them.

Hedley pushed past Cie into the interior, and for a moment Cie saw him silhouetted against the grid of the wall- and ceiling-mounted gas burners. The burners mixed the oxygen and fuel like a rocket engine.

Hedley grabbed at the bundle of cables strapped by Velcro to his leg and feeding into the laptop strapped inside his backpack. He separated a single cable and popped the plastic cap off the plug with his thumb. The gold-plated connector glinted in the dim light as Hedley pushed it solidly into a wall-mounted thermosensor. The process seemed to Cie to be happening in slow motion.

"Forty seconds."

Hedley had a handful of those sensors to connect. There was no way he was going to attach them all in the time they had left....

For a fleeting second Cie felt the urge to break and run, an urge such as he hadn't experienced in two decades of mercenary work and in any number of dangerous, chaotic situations.

He didn't move. He was a professional, and they were paying him well to act like one.

Hedley had inserted another sensor, and another, and suddenly he was done. There had been another countdown announcement, and Cie had failed to hear it completely. Was it ten seconds or twenty? Were they out of time? Hedley's hands were shaking as he grabbed the last cable, this one with an SCSI connector, and his hands seemed to freeze in midair. Cie realized he wasn't seeing the SCSI port. It wasn't where it was supposed to be.

"There!" Cie shouted and pointed to the wall-mounted, all-steel port, a few feet to the right of its anticipated position. Hedley reached over and calmly inserted the connector and shrugged off the backpack in a single motion.

"Ten seconds."

Hedley unzipped the pack carefully and peeled back the nylon as if he were making a bed on a lazy Sunday afternoon, and he was grinning like a fool. Cie wanted to grab him by the neck, shake him and yell at him to get a move on. Time was running out!

"Seven seconds."

Hedley lifted the cover of the thin Toshiba notebook computer.

"Six seconds."

He depressed a single key.

"Five seconds."

The quartet of control panels on the notebook's screen jiggled, and the black bars moved nonsensically. Cie knew with all certainty that there was a horrible problem.

"Four seconds."

The electronics had failed. They had just heartbeats of life left....

The screen of Hedley's laptop was suddenly filled with a dialog box.

"We're in," he said. He moved the headset microphone to his mouth. "We're in, control."

"We confirm that. Readings are good."

Hedley turned to Cie with a grin. "We're in. Let's get started."

JAKE MERTAUGH PRESSED the enter key on his PC and watched a red box appear on his screen, with the white, slowly expanding word *proceeding*. He felt vaguely uneasy about the whole process.

Mertaugh was a computer whiz with a high degree of understanding of complex software protocols. He'd studied the new software as best he could and knew it was considered sound by PMCD. God only knew how many trials they'd put it through. It was built with every redundant system feasible. Any number of catastrophes were guarded against with multiple contingency subsystems. It was probably one of the most carefully engineered pieces of software on the site.

But the upshot was that it took control of the process. Mertaugh stared at the screen. The white words in the red box reversed out to red and white, then back to white and red, and a series of boxes began appearing on the screen to show him exactly what was happening. But the truth was, the computer was controlling it all. He was just a watcher, he had no input.

Mertaugh was a certified computer fanatic, but it still made him nervous to have nothing but electronics controlling something this potentially deadly.

Within seconds there were eight bar graphs growing on his screen. When he moved the mouse to expand the temperature monitor, the bar began to grow rapidly. That was normal. The process was underway.

THE ACTUAL HARDWARE of the Aberdeen Chemical Agent Disposal System—ACADS—was contained in a retention area several acres in size, a full three hundred yards from the nearest inhabited building. The walls and floor of the building were nonporous concrete, on top of a naturally contained area. If accidental runoff somehow got through the concrete, it would be contained in the ground directly below the system, without reaching any local aquifer. If it went anywhere, it was believed, it would sink far enough into the earth that eventually it would leech into Chesapeake Bay, by which time it would be too diluted to cause more than minor damage. That was the theory, anyway. That was what all the official reports on the site testified to.

The monstrous incinerator was a hulk of steel and prestressed concrete, arched over by a complex of pipes and filtering systems, and enclosed in a huge, virtually airtight building that looked like nothing but a gymnasium from the outside.

The theory here was that even if disaster struck inside the incinerator complex, such as broken pipes or other malfunctions resulting in major leaks, it would all stay inside the building to be bled into external holding tanks, without ever reaching the atmosphere.

That was what the head of the establishment explained to the reporters from the *Aberdeen Sentinel,* anyway, when they got nervous and nosy.

Mertaugh knew it was all true. The facility couldn't be safer.

Still, they were burning chemicals specifically designed to incapacitate and kill human beings. God help anyone who was exposed to them during the process.

Moving the mouse, he swung the cursor from one box to another, monitoring the specifications of the process. It was all he could do. A pressure sensor rose slightly toward its higher limits, and the software signaled a response in one of the natural-gas igniters, which reduced its BTUs to slow the process. Everything was as it should be. Everything was under control.

If the screen in front of him could be trusted.

"BRING IN THE TRUCK," Cie said into the headset microphone.

"Yeah," said Frank Crocell. With a shift of gears the Caterpillar bulldozer rumbled down the ramp from the rear of the flatbed semi and made a sharp left, coming to a halt at the base of the second ramp. Three men jumped forward to attach the massive chain. One of them gave a brief wave and Crocell started forward again, raising the blade on the front end of the bulldozer and steering it into the forest. The bed of what had once been a stone-hauling dump truck was dragged behind him.

The path had already been scouted and marked with raw cuts in the tree trunks—there was nothing in the way that the bulldozer's treads couldn't push through. The blade crashed into saplings and undergrowth, creating a trail of vegetative ruin, and the steel dump-truck bed further flattened the crushed forest.

Crocell slowed slightly as the edge of the forest appeared ahead of him, but there was nobody in sight other than Pollari's crew, hugging the face of the building. He accelerated again and dragged the dump-truck bed in a half circle that ripped at the sparse grass. It came to a halt three long paces from the entrance to the incinerator.

"Okay, let's get a move on," Crocell said and stood in his seat, pulling his Smith & Wesson revolver to his chest, keeping watch over the men as they jumped to do as they were told.

They yanked at the rear of the truck bed, sending

the makeshift gate flopping open. They grabbed at the dollies inside and wheeled them rapidly into the building.

"How we doing?" Cie asked Hedley as the first of them entered.

"We're doing fine, fine. No worries."

MERTAUGH STOOD AND CROSSED to a secondary monitor. The readouts there were fine. Normal. Some minor fluctuations, but nothing unexpected, and the software was reacting to each up and down perfectly, adjusting the process with impeccable timing, just as he would have been doing had the incineration process been running without the new software. Only it was doing the job better than he ever could. The software could make tiny adjustments in microseconds before he even would have noticed a fluctuation starting. And Mertaugh was one of the best operators in the field.

"Looks like I'm out of a job," he muttered.

"What's that, sir?" one of his National Research Council-supplied assistants asked.

"Nothing." Mertaugh leaned back at the hip to stretch the ache in his lower back. He glanced out the window, at the backside of the incinerator facility, and froze in position. He could have sworn he saw a faint movement in the air, like smoke—

He raced to the window and yanked the blinds out of the way and saw it clearly—smoke rising from the far side of the ACADS.

"Shit!"

"What's the matter?" the NRC man asked.

"Shut it down! Shut it down *now!*"

TWO OF POLLARI'S HIRED MEN wrestled the aluminum barrel by its rim onto the dolly, and Cie caught a glimpse of the red, leering skull on the label spinning crazily. They leaned it back onto its wheels, then rushed it to the entrance. That was twelve. Another five barrels to go. The other teams had removed fourteen of the twenty wooden crates. They would have been done ten minutes ago if they hadn't had to contend with the one narrow entrance.

"Uh-oh."

"What?"

"They're initiating emergency shutdown," Hedley said.

"What? Why would they do that?"

"I don't know."

"You said they would be getting nothing but safe readings!"

"They have been getting safe readings," Hedley protested.

"So why would they go to emergency shutdown?"

"Maybe they've got a hardware problem at their end."

"Not likely!"

"Maybe we've been spotted."

"Bullshit!"

Hedley turned on him with the first look of anger Cie had ever seen on his face. "I've done everything right! Don't give me shit!"

"Well, something's screwed up. Let's get out of here." Cie shouted to the workers. "Pack it up!"

"Give me a second," Hedley said and began tapping on the keyboard frantically.

"What're you doing?"

"Buying us time. They won't come anywhere near here yet—not until they are absolutely convinced of the safety of the facility. I'm going to make sure they don't think it's safe.''

Hedley's grin returned as he pulled up a new piece of software, one of his own devising, and started it with the tap of a key. At once the software took control of the false readings from the primary piece of software and began sending out a very different routine of commands.

MERTAUGH FELT A WAVE of nausea as virtually every digital readout suddenly went haywire. Half the temperature monitors started to climb uncontrollably while the rest of them dropped like rocks. The digital BTU gauges jumped into the redlines. No less than five red emergency windows appeared on the screen in the course of a few seconds and beeped angrily and repeatedly. Mertaugh's eyes were glued to the screens, trying to make sense of what was happening, trying to see it in his head. He had become one of the best incinerator controllers because he was able to keep a mental image of the incineration process and respond to its fluctuations and malfunctions intuitively. But none of this made sense. This couldn't be happening....

Then he heard the shriek of an alarm he had prayed he would never hear, and the large red panel above every workstation blazed to life.

The black letters on the illuminated panel read MA-JOR MALFUNCTION.

CHAPTER THREE

Caspian Sea

The flag of Azerbaijan—blue, red and green horizontal bands, a crescent and white star with eight points— was painted on the hull of the *Tuscany II,* along with the flags of at least ten other countries, including the U.S. and Canada. Yunus Akhmedov was proud to be on the vessel, proud to have his flag in the rich, strong company of the North Americans'. They were the real power players in the world. Now, at least in this one thing, Azerbaijan worked with the North Americans, side by side. In fact, the North Americans needed them. That, Akhmedov knew, was real power.

They were out of sight of land, but the Azerbaijan city of Lenkoran wasn't far over the western horizon. He squinted into the night and thought maybe he could even see lights from the city. But that couldn't be.

The Caspian was still. The air was clean to Akhmedov's nostrils, and he inhaled deeply. The North Americans said the sea stunk of chemical corruption. Akhmedov had lived most of his life in Baku, on the Abseron Peninsula, which was one of the most contaminated spots on earth, and he knew the entire Caspian was an environmental disaster. Maybe someday, when the oil companies started their operations and he and his people had real money, he would take a trip to the South Pacific or the Caribbean, and he would learn what a truly clean ocean was like.

He strolled once around the upper deck, waving to the captain's mate on the bridge, who was standing at the controls reading a book.

Akhmedov went to his own station, but he had little more to do than the idle captain's mate. They were at anchor. All the sea-bottom tests were done during the day. He glanced over the purring instruments and rested uneasily against the stainless-steel, controlled-humidity storage container. It held soil samples taken from the ocean floor. Akhmedov didn't understand exactly what the multinational crew was looking for, but if what they happened to discover was a better way to access the mainland oil field, Akhmedov's people would get none of the profits.

After all, they didn't own the ocean. But they did own, collectively, the vast tracts of Kur-Araz Lowland that, so far, had been designated the only easy-access point to what was being called one of the most extensive oil deposits located in decades.

Maybe there was a way to contaminate the samples.

The thought fluttered through his head and was dismissed as outlandish—just as he had dismissed it a hundred times before.

Besides, they weren't even looking for oil. That's what one of the Canadian geologists told him. They were looking for a way to *get at* the oil.

"Why not just dig a well at Azdan?" Akhmedov suggested, half-serious. "It is my hometown. My people will treat you very well."

"We just might end up doing that," the Canadian answered with a laugh.

Akhmedov liked the Canadian. He didn't treat him like a moron. Akhmedov knew he was uneducated, but he also knew he was a reasonably intelligent person. He'd come aboard the research vessel expecting to be treated like a stupid local. And his fears were realized when he met the Frenchman who seemed to be in charge of the operation. The Americans and especially the Canadian, however, had showed him the casual respect he had hoped for. The Canadian had even showed him how to operate some of the equipment, resulting in the nighttime assignment to monitor operations.

The watch said it was still five minutes before he was supposed to record the next list of readings from the analog instruments, but they weren't exactly fluctuating wildly. He decided to get a head start.

The glow on the horizon distracted him again. What was that? It simply couldn't be Lenkoran. They were too far out to sea. Was it actually getting brighter?

He turned off the lab lights to make the night darker and returned to the deck, squinting into the darkness. Sure enough, there was a light out there in the ocean, and as his eyes adjusted it focused into a single spot, coming closer. An aircraft of some kind.

"Iskander, check it out," he said, going into the bridge. "Are we expecting company?"

The first mate squinted out the window. The dot had grown so that it was now visible through the window. The mate shook his head. "Chopper," he muttered.

"Maybe there's some emergency."

"Why wouldn't they just call us?" the mate asked,

crossing to the radio. "I'll see if I can raise them. Maybe you ought to get the captain."

BY THE TIME Ali Jalaloglu had dragged on his trousers and shoes and stomped up the steps, he could hear the distant chop of the helicopter, and it worried him. There was no reason for them to be approached by a chopper in the middle of the Caspian in the dead of night. Unless there was something going on the researchers hadn't told him about.

Captain Jalaloglu knew he and his vessel had been chosen for this project because the multinational corporation behind the project wanted it to look as if they were truly partnering with the Azerbaijanis. He'd made it a point to prove to the researchers that he and his vessel were up to the task—and up to their standards. He didn't want trouble.

What could the chopper possibly be but trouble?

"Who are they?" he demanded as he entered the bridge.

"I can't raise them," the mate said.

"Is the radio equipment working?"

"Yes. I'm sure it is."

"Then switch channels!"

"I'm doing so."

The captain stomped onto the deck and was met with the heavy staccato thunder of the chopper. The extreme unlikelihood of its being a simple passerby was forgotten by the captain—the aircraft was headed right at them. He didn't know much about helicopters, but it sounded big.

"What's going on?" It was one of the Americans, Martini.

"I don't know. Would your people be expecting visitors you have not told me about?"

Martini wasn't fully awake, and the question fazed him for a moment as he watched the bright helicopter lights loom closer. "I don't think so. I mean, no—who would come? Why would anyone come?"

More questions were asked as the half-dozen researchers straggled to the deck. Captain Jalaloglu's crew was appearing as well, awakened by the rotor noise.

"Any response?" Jalaloglu demanded, sticking his head into the bridge.

"No, Captain," the mate said with a shrug of the headphones.

"Keep trying."

The helicopter slowed and came to a halt a hundred yards or so from the research vessel, and even less distance from the surface of the Caspian. As the crew and the researchers watched from the deck, the craft rotated slowly in place, showing its broadside to the observers.

"Iraqis. They're Iraqis!" Martini exclaimed.

"Have they answered?" Jalaloglu demanded, rushing back into the bridge. He didn't wait for the mate to do more than shake his head a little. "Then send a Mayday! We've been accosted by an Iraqi air force helicopter. Their intentions are unknown."

The mate blanched.

"Get on it!" Jalaloglu said.

The mate started shouting into the radio.

When the captain returned to the deck, the chopper was moving slowly to the front of the vessel, where it made a wide horseshoe and started back along the other side of the craft, keeping its distance.

"What are they up to?" the French operation supervisor demanded.

"Checking us out. Maybe they think we're Iranian, and they want to know what we're up to."

"We're better than five hundred miles from Iraq," one of the Americans retorted. "And the Iraqis don't exactly have free rein to go wandering around Central Asian airspace. This doesn't make sense."

"Let us hope they don't stop to introduce themselves," Jalaloglu muttered, and didn't care that he went unheard, because at that moment the Iraqi helicopter changed its behavior. It turned directly at the vessel and accelerated to a modest speed, passing over the vessel's stern, and Jalaloglu headed for the bridge.

"Look!" one of the Americans cried.

A small squarish object tumbled from the open hatch of the helicopter, and even before it hit the deck another followed it, then another as the helicopter covered the entire length of the vessel.

The first object hit the deck with a thump that sounded as if it were made of metal covered with canvas.

For a fraction of a second Jalaloglu considered that the chopper might be dropping them some type of supplies.

Then the gas began pouring out of the objects. One after another, the crew of the vessel began grabbing at their throats as if suddenly possessed of the need to choke out their own lives.

The mate spotted the activity and started shouting to his radio contact, somewhere safe in Lenkoran. "They're gassing us! The men are falling over! Save us, send help! In the name of God!"

Then the gas reached him, and he said nothing else intelligible.

Irkuk, Azerbaijan

THE VILLAGE, a couple of hundred miles northwest of Baku, was small and ramshackle, and on the verge of greatness. That was how Sardar Aydayev looked at things. The poor buildings, the empty plains—in a year or two there would be mansions. Because the people themselves now owned the land, and the land—to be more exact, the oil underneath it—was worth more than gold.

He had been drinking for hours. Every day was a celebration now of the wealth that was coming their way. Aydayev stopped at his doorway and leaned against it, breathing deeply of the night air. It would be best not to show his wife just how drunk he really was.

He heard the sound of a truck, which was very odd, since there was just a handful of trucks in the village—mostly Russian-built rattletraps dating from the Communist era and barely functional. Why one would be driving around town at this time of night Aydayev couldn't imagine. He walked a few paces down the gravel road and watched for the vehicle.

It wasn't a local truck, but a heavy diesel BMW, painted a glossy black. It came to a sudden halt, flinging up gravel, and the rear end swung open.

Aydayev crossed the street, trying to see with his hazy vision. He heard a whine from a stressed servomotor, and he watched two men standing on an elevator mechanism descend from the back of the truck. Between them stood a steel drum, topped off by some sort of machinery with electronic controls and glowing LED displays. While the machinery and controls looked new, the barrel itself seemed old. It was covered in dirt, and rust corroded the seams. The Arabic lettering painted on the side was so faded and chipped it was illegible.

The men hoisted the barrel a few feet from the truck, stabbed at the membrane switches on the controls and stepped back on the elevated mechanism. As the servomotors whined again Aydayev realized they were both armed with large rifles.

He wondered what they were up to, then the thought occurred to him that he might be in danger and he stepped quickly behind a neighbor's house. He listened to the truck accelerate and watched it drive past him, then he stepped out again and approached the abandoned barrel cautiously.

He peered at the electronic controls through his drunken haze. They were a mystery.

Bending at the waist, he brushed at the dirt on the barrel and tried to make out the characters. The words were gibberish, but when he saw the skull and crossbones he gasped and stepped away, realizing that, somehow, he *was* in danger. The entire village was. He had to get his wife and flee Irkuk.

Turning, Aydayev found one of the men standing in the street watching him, his rifle in his hands. Behind the man Aydayev saw that another barrel had already been set up. How many barrels of their poison were they going to position in his village? What exactly was the machinery designed to do with the poison?

"Let me go," he slurred quietly.

"No one goes," the man answered, triggering the

weapon. There was a slash in the air, but not so loud
as a real gunshot should be. Probably not loud enough
to wake the sleeping residents.

Aydayev clutched his chest, then looked at the
blood on his hands, too intoxicated to realize he was
dead until the pain cut through the alcohol. His killer
was already walking away. The ground rushed at Aydayev and slammed into him like a speeding car.

His killer helped station the third, fourth and fifth
barrels along the main street of the tiny village, then
the BMW accelerated into the night. It had another
village to visit and five more barrels to deliver.

Aydayev's body lay in the street undiscovered for
a full hour. Then, at 3:30 a.m., within seconds of one
another, the devices atop the barrels began to function.

CHAPTER FOUR

Stony Man Farm, Virginia

At least a half-dozen computer monitors were in the room, all apparently working with different types of software, but a close examination would have revealed that most of them were in the midst of various searches. The man in the wheelchair turned as one of the distinctive alarms alerted him to a completed operation.

His fingers danced on the keyboard, stepping him through search results. One after another he closed the results windows until he stared at a single paragraph of archived material, which he read through and quickly saved to a different hard drive on his local network.

"Aaron."

He'd been peripherally aware of her approach and looked up at the tall blond woman standing in the doorway to the Computer Room. She looked just-scrubbed, her honey-colored hair still damp from a shower, and the few traces of makeup she wore looked freshly applied. She was attractive and might have passed for a ranch foreman in her cowboy boots, blue Western shirt and clean but well-worn jeans.

She was in charge, all right, but not of a bunch of cowboys.

"You've been up all night," Barbara Price stated.

He grimaced. "What gave it away?"

"That's the same sweater you had on at dinner."

He shrugged. "I happened to catch some news on the net late last night. Before I knew it, I got caught up in the activity. I couldn't have slept."

"Why don't you tell me about it," Price said. "If we're lucky it'll be the same thing Hal just called me about."

Aaron Kurtzman nodded. "I have a feeling it is."

"Aberdeen?" she asked.

"Aberdeen."

"The Caspian Sea?"

"The Caspian Sea."

He looked at her expectantly.

"That's all I've got wind of," she said. "There's more?"

"Yeah, there's more." With a deft spin of the wheels his chair seemed to glide into position from one terminal to another. "Irkuk and Heydar, Azerbaijan."

"Never heard of them."

"Both strictly small-town Azerbaijan. Population just a couple of hundred, tops, between the two of them. At least, there used to be. Within hours after the attack on the research vessel *Tuscany II* in the Caspian, the people of Irkuk and Heydar were targeted to die. At least five fifty-five-gallon drums of hydrogen cyanide solution were erected in each town with some sort of mechanical dissipating device."

"Oh, God."

"A UN hazmat team and the U.S. Chemical-

Biological Incident Response Force are on the way. But the body count stands at 176 confirmed. And that's not all.''

His hands scrambled over the keyboard, and Price saw the windows swap themselves out at lightning speed. The document that now appeared was of Central Intelligence Agency origin and labeled for high-level security. It was the kind of document normally stored behind the highest level of software firewalls or preferably, for national security, in systems that weren't even accessible from outside the Pentagon intranet. Price was highly computer literate, but she didn't begin to understand how Kurtzman came to have access to some of the high-security systems he apparently waltzed through with impunity.

''Yesterday there was activity at the Glorious Leader Hussein Hospital in Al-Fallujah, Iraq. It was a suspected hiding facility for Iraqi chemical weapons in the 1980s, but was thought to have been cleared out years ago. Yesterday material was stolen from the hospital, and the Iraqis have placed a priority-one arrest command on one of their colonels, Muhyi al-Duri.''

''He defected?'' Price asked.

''He did something and went somewhere,'' Kurtzman said. ''I wish I could be a lot more specific. But he was known to visit the Glorious Leader Hussein Hospital, and the circumstantial evidence is that he took whatever was there and left the country with it. He probably fled over the desert into Syria. From there he could get anywhere he wanted to go, including into Azerbaijan without much trouble. The implication, according to the Pentagon, is that he took his shipment of nerve agent to Irkuk and Heydar, or delivered it to whoever took it to Azerbaijan.''

"I don't understand. Why would he want to wipe out a small town in Azerbaijan? And what ties does it have to the killing of the crew of the *Tuscany II?*"

"Other than the fact they were both wiped out with chemical weapons, nothing."

Kurtzman folded his arms across his chest and leaned back in his chair, shaking his head. He was a big man, barrel-chested, powerful enough to earn himself the nickname "The Bear." He had been a formidable man before a terrorist shot him in the spine and left him confined to the wheelchair. He still was formidable, and not just when riding the electronic communication nets.

But operating the electronic intelligence-gathering systems for the Stony Man Farm Sensitive Operations Group was where he excelled. He had been making maximum use of the Internet years before the public even knew the definition of the word. He kept the Farm's budget in flux by constantly updating and expanding the capabilities of its hardware. If there was an Information Age state-of-the-art at any given moment, Kurtzman was attempting to exceed it. He maximized his use of hardware with some of the most insidious hacker software in existence, most of which he had coded personally, and which he was constantly improving. The security clearance provided him by the U.S. government, combined with the security access he provided for himself, made Kurtzman's Computer Room a formidable information powerhouse.

"Now the big question," Price said, half-sitting on one of the computer desks. "Could the hydrogen cyanide used in Irkuk and Heydar and on the *Tuscany II* come from Aberdeen?"

"That's a definitive no," Kurtzman answered.

"The events at the Aberdeen Chemical Agent Disposal System facility took place within hours of the attacks in Central Asia. Hydrogen cyanide was among the chemicals stolen from Aberdeen, but getting it halfway around the globe that fast would be impossible."

There was an electronic buzz from the phone and he grabbed it, listened briefly and grunted an affirmation before hanging up. "Hal's chopper is coming in now. There's more to tell, but I might as well give it to you both when he's landed. That'll give me a few minutes to change my shirt."

HAL BROGNOLA SAT at the conference table in the War Room, chewing on an antacid tablet and staring at a white foam coffee cup on the table in front of him.

Yakov Katzenelenbogen entered and, by way of greeting, Brognola said, "Aaron didn't make that, did he?" He nodded toward the coffee station in the corner.

"It's mine," Katz assured him.

"Thank God," Brognola said as he took the cup, downing a third of it in a gulp. He had never understood how Kurtzman managed to produce such swill when anybody else at the Farm could make a halfway decent pot of coffee from the same can of grounds, the same pot of water and the same machine.

Katz took a seat at the table and dropped the morning edition of the *Washington Post* on the table. The two men said nothing. The headline for one of the front-page stories, Chemical Weapons Stolen from Aberdeen, said it all. Brognola hadn't stated what he was at the Farm to discuss, and he didn't need to. Katz didn't ask. Everybody's cards would be laid on the table, just like the paper, when the time came.

Katzenelenbogen had been in the operations center at the Farm for some time, but before that served in the field as leader of Phoenix Force. Prior to that, he spent time with the Israeli army. Now his frontline days were behind him. He'd been glad to put down the weapons of the warrior. He'd done his part; he'd carried far more than his share of the burden.

Not that he had retired. That would probably never happen. Since taking a desk at the Farm, Katz had proved his worth as a tactical adviser. It was clearly a better-running operation with Katz's presence.

Stony Man Farm had a highly ambitious mission: to keep the world's trouble spots from exploding and threatening the survival of Western civilization.

Time and again the Sensitive Operations Group's action teams had mitigated terror plaguing the people of almost every nation on earth. Men like Katz hadn't abandoned their birth nations to further a U.S. political agenda, but to chase the eternally elusive goal of true peace by cutting out the hearts of the madmen.

But the supply of madmen, Katz and Brognola contemplated separately and silently, as they stared at the *Post* headline, sometimes seemed inexhaustible.

PRICE WAS THE NEXT to arrive, and Kurtzman pushed through the door a minute behind her, in time to see Brognola taking the key from Price that would unlock the handcuff on his right wrist. The other cuff was around the handle of a briefcase the big Fed rested on his lap.

Inside were papers from the White House, some signed personally by the President of the United

States. Couched in cryptic and even coded language, some of the papers, if they fell into the wrong hands, might very well spell disaster for the President and for the Farm. Because the Farm wasn't supposed to exist.

Hal Brognola served a legitimate role as an official in the upper ranks of the Justice Department, where he was assigned as liaison to the White House. His true occupation was director of the SOG, directly above Barbara Price and the rest of the Stony Man Farm staff.

"I see you've been spoiling the surprise for yourselves," Brognola said with a glance at the newspaper. "This situation is getting out of hand. And quickly."

"So the President believes there's a connection between all these events?" Price asked.

Brognola raised an eyebrow as he opened the briefcase. "'All these events,' meaning what, precisely?"

"Aberdeen, the Caspian Sea, Azerbaijan, Iraq…"

"Iraq?" Brognola said with obvious alarm. "You're a step ahead of me, then. I wasn't aware of any Iraqi connection."

"You're at least three steps ahead of me," Katz said. "All I know is what I've read in the papers."

"All right, I think I had better start filling in everybody with what I know—get everybody up to speed," Kurtzman said. "Hal, you can fill in any gaps if there's information I'm not aware of."

"Fine."

Kurtzman started with a brief overview of the events in Aberdeen. The relatively low security of the Aberdeen operation meant there wasn't much the papers didn't know. They had even accurately guessed the makeup of the chemical weapons stores that were incinerated.

"There's only one fact that I consider important that was omitted from the *Post*," Kurtzman said. "The piece of earth-moving equipment used to haul out the chemicals was probably one reported stolen eight days earlier from a construction facility in Pennsylvania, where it was being used to grade new construction of a Pollari oil distribution facility."

"Is this relevant?" Price asked.

"Maybe," Kurtzman said. He continued with the report of the killings aboard the *Tuscany II* in the Caspian Sea and in the Azerbaijani towns. As he was speaking the door opened and an incongruous figure entered—an Asian man in his early twenties, dressed in tattered blue jeans and a black T-shirt with the garish artwork from the album cover of a popular alternative rock band. He smiled at the assemblage and placed a stapled printout in front of Kurtzman, who nodded briefly, then left without a word.

"Our intel on the Caspian situation is more or less identical," Brognola said, not at all surprised to find his Farm team so fully knowledgeable of a situation he hadn't even alluded to when he'd called to say he would be paying them a visit.

Next Kurtzman briefed them on the situation at the small Azerbaijani towns of Irkuk and Heydar. "Akira's latest report says the UN hazmat team and the U.S. Marine's Chemical-Biological Incident Response Force will be landing in Baku in time to get a team into the towns within an hour. As expected, there's not much left in the way of hazardous materials. It's all been mechanically dissipated into the atmosphere. Very little was sprayed into the soil, which would have resulted in a lingering hazard. The body count is pushing two hundred, but the team isn't expecting to find widespread casualties outside the villages. They were both pretty isolated.''

"Thank God for small favors," Price stated.

"The Iraqi link?" Brognola asked.

"The barrels used were all labeled as being of Iraqi manufacture," Kurtzman said, referring to his latest update. "Apparent age of the barrels indicate they might date from well before the Gulf War. They've been sitting around for a while."

"That makes sense," Brognola said. "Everybody's keeping a close eye on the Iraqis. It would be tough for them to start new production of hydrogen cyanide on a large scale. Now tell me what's happening in Iraq that you know about and I don't."

Again, Brognola wasn't surprised at the extent of Kurtzman's knowledge. In fact, he expected no less from the cybernetic expert. Kurtzman explained the Pentagon's recent intel on activity at the hospital once suspected of being a chemical weapons storage facility, and of the suspected defection of Colonel Muhyi al-Duri.

Brognola fished another antacid tablet from his pocket while Kurtzman spoke, the lines of worry on his face getting deeper. "This is the first I'm hearing about this. What the hell's the Pentagon sitting on this information for?" he demanded rhetorically.

"I'm not one for defending government agencies, Hal, but this information is fresh. They were probably still evaluating it when you were meeting with the Man."

"It changes things, I think."

"I'm not finished yet, Hal," Kurtzman said.

"Go on."

"As I said, the barrels used in Azerbaijan were

probably genuine Iraqi. The equipment used to dissipate it wasn't.''

''Explain that.''

''The barrels were set up in town with some sort of unique computerized vaporizing machinery. Somebody actually set these things up. They drove into the middle of town with the barrels and staged them for maximum effect. After the gas was dispersed, all but one of the units blew themselves up. That's not exactly how the Iraqis were known to use their chemical bombs.''

''Agreed. But we have to take into account that they weren't working in a wartime situation or bombing Kurds within their own borders,'' Katzenelenbogen suggested. ''They were working secretively on foreign soil.''

''The machinery traces to North America,'' Kurtzman added. ''There's some pretty highly sophisticated pieces involved in their manufacture. We're trying to track it down now. The CPUs are programmable units from a West Coast company. It's still too early there. At least one set of serial numbers on one of the components has been traced to a Toronto-based motor manufacturer. They were able to provide us with a list of buyers, and one of those buyers is a Pollari Corporation subsidiary.''

Brognola tapped the table with a ballpoint pen. ''Sounds like a stretch if you're trying to establish a link.''

''I know,'' Kurtzman admitted. ''We might have more when we can ID some of the buyers of the other components involved.''

''Until that happens let's stay with the Iraqi angle,'' Brognola suggested.

"What confuses me at this stage is motive," Katz said. "What does the President think is driving these attacks? Is it an issue of oil?"

"Probably," Brognola said with a nod. "The Iraqis are still struggling to get back into the oil business. Azerbaijan is in the preliminary stages of opening new oil fields. In fact, the villages are in the middle of what just might be the biggest untapped oil field to open since the crisis in the 1970s. The world's been getting along quite well without large infusions of Iraqi oil for years now. Once the Azerbaijani fields reach the yields they're expected to reach—Iraq's oil supply, its only bargaining chip, suddenly becomes that much less consequential."

"On the other hand, if the Azerbaijani potential has trouble becoming realized, there's the suggestion of crisis among the world's top oil-users and demand for Iraqi oil increases," Price suggested. "The mood will turn more favorably toward allowing Iraq to sell its oil."

"I don't like this scenario," Katzenelenbogen said, shaking his head and wrinkling his craggy forehead. "It's too easy to jump to these conclusions."

"Nevertheless, these are the conclusions the President is making," Brognola said.

"That's even more worrisome," Katz replied. "Aaron, you said the *Tuscany II* reported the Iraqi chopper circled the boat completely before bombing it. That's strange behavior, don't you think?"

Price agreed. "It did give the crew plenty of time to radio for help and report precisely who was about to hit them."

"And the barrels used in the Azerbaijani killings— left with the Iraqi markings intact?" Katz continued.

Brognola shrugged. "You're right, of course. If it is the Iraqis, they're sure not going to any effort to hide their identities."

"That, tied with what Aaron's learned about this Colonel al-Duri's flight from Iraq, makes me think we've got some sort of faction at work, using Iraqi equipment but with other goals," Price said.

"That's also too easy a conclusion, in my opinion," Katz said. "Maybe we are dealing with Iraqis who are trying to make us think it's some foreign faction at work."

"How do we make up our minds here?" Kurtzman asked with a grimace.

"We don't. We can't," Brognola said. "It's just not clear what—if any—entity can possibly benefit from these attacks and thefts." He laid out a photocopied map of the world, with scrawled red stars in the Caspian Sea, the middle of Azerbaijan, and Aberdeen, Maryland. With a flick of a pen he added a star in the center of Iraq and circled the three Eastern stars. "I have to be honest—I'm having my doubts about any connection between Aberdeen and these events." He tapped the circle.

"Do you have a mission for us, Hal?" Price asked.

"No, I don't. I didn't even come here with one, and, regardless, this new information is going to have to be taken into consideration before the President gives the go-ahead—"

"Striker is in the Commonwealth of Independent States," Price interrupted.

"What's he doing there?"

"Unknown. He's been following a private agenda for the past couple of weeks."

Brognola nodded. He had an idea what it meant when Mack Bolan went off on his own.

Bolan was unlike the other teams working out of the Farm. While Phoenix Force, the international strike team, and Able Team, the group that usually stuck to the North American theater of operations, took their orders from the Virginia-based headquarters, Bolan worked independently.

The truth was, Stony Man Farm was named after Bolan, and the soldier had been instrumental in establishing it and recruiting the members of its groups.

But it had been made clear that he was now on his own. He worked alone in the field, sometimes utterly independent for weeks at a time. He was under no obligation to take any mission Brognola offered him, and his activities were firmly outside the legal restrictions of all the nations in which he operated.

On the other hand, there wasn't a human being alive more devoted to true justice than the Executioner. He would always be there when the Farm needed him. Bolan didn't let them down. He was compelled with righting what he saw as moral wrongs.

"Where is he now?" Brognola asked.

Price glanced at a small gold watch on her wrist. "En route to Baku. He'll land within the hour," she said, adding, "He made the decision to go himself."

Brognola nodded. He didn't doubt that the Executioner would make the decision to investigate the events in Azerbaijan firsthand. It certainly wouldn't hurt to have him staged there if and when the President decided to act.

"Phoenix? Able?" he asked.

"I've called them in. They'll be standing by, unless

you've got something you'd like them to start on, Hal," Price said.

"Not now. Not yet. Let me get some direction from the President first." He looked at the map and chewed on his antacid. "At this stage, where would we even start?"

CHAPTER FIVE

Kurtzman pushed through the door to the Computer Room, followed by Price, in time to hear Akira Tokaido issue a crude expletive. The young cybernetics expert turned to see who was at the door, then blurted, "Check this *out!*"

Kurtzman rolled to the monitor Tokaido was using, and a quick glance showed him an electronic inventory system for a Silicon Valley company called Custom Twelve Cybernetics. The system was highlighting a line that showed delivery of six eight-megabyte, user-programmable electronic control systems to a Frederick Andershot of OS Systems Technologies, Toronto.

Kurtzman looked at Tokaido, who was grinning and nodding.

"This means what?" Kurtzman asked.

Tokaido tapped the glass over the name OS Systems Technologies. "That's the exact CPU used in the Irkuk machinery. Not exactly a high-tech item. I've got that much brain power in my HDTV. But OS is a Pollari Corporation subsidiary." He grabbed the mouse, bringing up a different window.

The screen showed another shipping order from another company. "This is a highly specialized gas dispersion component," Tokaido explained. "Some zoos use it to create specialized atmospheres in indoor rain forest environments—that kind of thing. Anyway, these were purchased by this guy." The name on the screen now was Willard Wilson, representing Jackson Innovating Enterprises in Jackson, Colorado. His finger hit the window accusingly. "Pollari subsid."

Kurtzman put down a third, fourth and fifth printout. Three more buyers of components from the surviving piece of machinery from Irkuk. Three more companies affiliated with Pollari Corporation.

"Five components. That's no longer a weak link. Somehow, somebody at Pollari is involved in the massacre at Irkuk and Heydar," Kurtzman said.

Price nodded. "Yes. But why kill all those people?" she demanded. "There's still no motive."

Kurtzman threw up his hands. "That I don't know. Pollari is an oil conglomerate. Petrodollars have got to have something to do with it."

"It still doesn't make sense," she declared, clearly exasperated.

"You're right, but is there any argument the link exists?"

She glared at the five pages of printouts. "No. Of course not, Aaron." She looked at him and was immediately on the same wavelength he was. "We need to investigate this. We need to get Able in the field on this ASAP."

"Yes, we do."

HERMANN "GADGETS" SCHWARZ presented his ID to the stone-faced "farm hand" at the entrance to the Farm. He'd seen the blacksuit many times, and this was the first time the man had said a word to him other than, "Proceed."

This time he said, "Proceed directly to the airfield, Mr. Schwarz."

"Sure." It was an unusual directive, but he didn't question it, taking the pleasant drive into the compound and parking at the front of what looked like a farm building. In fact, the facility was a working farm. This year it was growing corn, mostly, in addition to apples in the orchard. But a section of the cornfield, at the moment, contained an MD 600N light helicopter, emblazoned with the logo of a Washington, D.C.-based air tours company. The 250-C47 turboshaft engine had just been powered up, and Schwarz spotted Jack Grimaldi sitting at the controls.

Barbara Price stood conversing outside the chopper with Rosario Blancanales, and Schwarz left his keys in the car as he went to join them. It looked like they would be leaving immediately. Somebody would take care of his car later.

"Barb. Pol," he said in greeting. "What's up?"

Rosario Blancanales was also known as Politician, but none of those names rolled off the tongue easily in casual conversation. Schwarz tended to call him Pol for short, as did many of his friends. Blancanales was a stocky, powerful man, and his people-oriented personality, his techniques for understanding and manipulating his enemies, had earned him his nickname. But talking wasn't his finest quality—Blancanales was a highly experienced warrior, with a background that included service as a Black Beret in Vietnam.

"You guys are out of here right away," Price said. "We need you in the field at once."

"The field is where?" Schwarz asked.

"Denver, to start with. Tonight we'll video-conference and I can fill you in on more details, as well as give you an official go.''

"We're working without authorization?''

"We're working without the official sanction of the President. But you've got my authorization for this mission. Just don't make too many waves until Hal gets the word in writing from the Man, if possible.''

"Hey, I don't even know what we're doing yet.''

"I'll brief you en route to Denver," said a newcomer, approaching from the farmhouse. "Nice you could make it, Gadgets.'' The speaker was Carl "Ironman'' Lyons, leader of Able Team, which Blancanales and Schwarz completed. At his side was a large, powerful figure, John "Cowboy'' Kissinger, the Stony Man armorer.

"Hey, I didn't know there was a rush on,'' Schwarz protested.

"Well, there is,'' Price said. "Carl can give you more than enough intel for your activity this afternoon. Tonight we'll bring you fully up to speed and we'll have more targets for you to hit tomorrow. Now get going and good luck.''

Schwarz shrugged. "Sure thing.'' He stepped into the belly of the McDonnell Douglas helicopter with Blancanales. "This have anything to do with the trouble in Aberdeen?'' he called above the escalating roar of the turboshaft.

Price didn't even hear him, shouting a few last words to Lyons and patting him quickly on the shoulder before she and Kissinger hustled away from the vehicle. Aircraft never sat on the ground for very long at the Farm. They either took off again soon after landing or were hauled inside, out of sight of sky- and space-based surveillance systems.

Lyons entered the aircraft and one of the ground crew shut the door.

"We're set, Jack," Lyons shouted up to the pilot. Grimaldi nodded and spoke rapidly into the mike on his headset, then nodded and worked the controls. The helicopter grabbed at the air and ascended, leaving the cornfields of Stony Man Farm behind.

"What's going on?" Schwarz asked.

"You were right—the Aberdeen situation," Lyons said. "We'll have plenty of time for a briefing on the plane to Colorado where we can talk without shouting."

"Sure, whatever," Schwarz said. "Just point me in the right direction and give me a big gun." He cocked his hand into the shape of a pistol and blasted at the door of the helicopter.

Blancanales grinned; Lyons just nodded.

"Man, you can be one grim bastard," Schwarz muttered.

"I heard that," Lyons said.

Blancanales grinned even wider.

THEY TOOK THE CHOPPER only as far as their real ride to Colorado. Price had arranged for a ride in a leased corporate jet, a Cessna 750 Citation X, which waited on the tarmac, humming like a kitten.

Barbara Price was a logistics master. Those skills weren't just useful when it came to organizing inherently chaotic situations like firefights via radio—they also helped her keep the more mundane behavior of the staff of Stony Man Farm dynamic. She knew well that habits were noticed, and Stony Man Farm couldn't afford to be noticed. Only by remaining a secret could it survive. Like one of the warriors that served it, the

Farm had to stay alert, changing its patterns, keeping itself fresh, lest an enemy take advantage of a habit or pattern to undermine it.

Even the regular use of U.S. military transportation would arouse notice. Moving her men via the private sector was one way to avoid such attention.

"Sweet," Blancanales said as they entered the twelve-seater aircraft. The cabin was plush, with roomy leather seats equivalent to first-class seats on an international commercial flight. "Very sweet."

"She moves nicely, too," Jack Grimaldi added, entering behind him. "I mean, I wouldn't want to get in a dogfight in her, but she'll get us to Denver in a big hurry."

A figure in a formal flight uniform from the aircraft leasing company stepped out of the cockpit. "Good morning, gentlemen."

Grimaldi shook his hand. "Captain Greene. I'm Jack Grimaldi."

"Mr. Grimaldi. I've been told to serve as your co-pilot." He said it as if he couldn't believe it.

"Yes, that would be correct."

"This is a very unusual demand, I'll have to say. But the company commands and I obey."

Grimaldi nodded. "Good."

"I've also been informed that I'm not to ask questions." Greene looked pointedly at the long weapons packs being hoisted down the narrow aisle into the rear seats by Lyons and Schwarz.

"Why don't we go through the preflight, Captain Greene?" Grimaldi said, steering the uniformed man into the cockpit.

"Of course. How much flight experience do you have, anyway, Mr. Grimaldi?"

The cockpit door closed behind them, and a minute later the team had all their gear stowed. The supply of hardware would see them through a small war. Lyons didn't believe in traveling light.

"Where's the stewardess?" Schwarz asked.

"You're going to have to fetch your own peanuts," Blancanales said, sliding the hatch shut and locking it in place.

"That sucks." Schwarz poked his head into the cockpit. Greene was looking a little humble. Grimaldi had to have been rattling off some of his flying experience—everything from restored biplanes to the SR-71, the now-grounded Blackbird spy plane.

"We're ready when you are."

"Two minutes, Gadgets," Grimaldi said.

Gadgets Schwarz had earned his nickname from his ability with electronics. He could take apart and reconfigure electronic devices the way some guys instinctively worked with internal combustion engines. He was also highly trained in counterintelligence. He was younger than his teammates, with a trim build that he flopped into one of the spacious, well-cushioned passenger seats. The Citation X rolled across the tarmac and positioned itself at the end of a runway, the twin Allison AE 3007C turbofans rushing to life. The elegant aircraft spun forward suddenly and took to the air, banked slightly through a 180-degree turn, and aimed at the Rocky Mountains, twenty-five hundred miles away.

THE MAN WAVED a newspaper. "Have you seen *this?*"

It was a late edition of the *Washington Post.* "No, sir, I haven't," Hal Brognola replied.

"Take a look." The paper flapped into his lap and Brognola grabbed it, nearly losing the rest of the papers he had stacked carefully on his knees. The story about the theft of the Aberdeen chemical stores was still there, but the rest of the front page had been devoted to the attacks in Azerbaijan and on the Caspian Sea. Brognola wondered how the journalists could have coalesced all the information for the stories so quickly. Azerbaijan was an especially out-of-the-way locale. A quick skim of the text answered his question.

"'Reports from anonymous eyewitnesses,'" he read out loud. "There were no eyewitnesses. In either case. Not that we've heard about, sir."

"I know that, Hal," the Man said, "and you know that. But the media doesn't. They got turned on to a good story and they're running with it. And the story they are running with says the U.S. and/or Iraqis are to blame."

Brognola shook his head as he skimmed the remainder of the stories. "They're going on the evidence. You can't blame them. Assholes." He looked up suddenly, feeling like an idiot. He'd just said "assholes" in front of the President of the United States of America. In the Oval Office, no less. "Sorry, sir."

The Man ignored the language and the apology. "I'm staying noncommittal," he said. "Global opinion or not, I'm going only with this Iraqi plot theory at this point. There's too much evidence. The media was hand-fed these stories. The truth is never this neat and tidy. Do you agree?"

"I agree it looks that way."

"Do you believe the Iraqis have real motive for these attacks?"

"Yes, of course. Anything to scare off the competition."

"Do you believe they'd be capable of such bold attacks?"

"The Iraqis have never been politically sophisticated, sir."

The Man glared at him, and Brognola waited it out.

"No. I don't buy it," the Man said. "Not until I get evidence that it was the Iraqis. Real evidence, as in U.S. intelligence. Meanwhile, the Johnston start-up goes ahead as planned."

Brognola shifted gears in a hurry. "Johnston start-up, sir?"

Rhein-Main Air Base, Frankfurt, Germany

AIRMAN FIRST CLASS John Samuels put his girlfriend on the flight to Boston at 8:00 p.m. She was a ballet dancer, and Boston was her home. He knew he would never see her again, and he was feeling very sorry for himself.

He bought a bottle of German wine and went back to his apartment on the U.S. military base. His balcony looked out on the tarmac of the Frankfurt airport, and he watched a pair of Lufthansa 747s maneuver as he drank the wine and listened to his favorite Siouxsie and the Banshees disc. By midnight he was totally depressed and mildly drunk. He slumped into bed with music echoing through his head.

Two hours later the phone rang insistently. The voice on the other end sliced through his haze. It was his CO.

"Samuels, you trained with CBIRF?"

"Yes, sir. Two weeks." He hoped he sounded lucid, but he was full-blown confused. Why was his commanding officer calling him at two in the morning to inquire about his experience with the Chemical-Biological Incident Response Force?

"Good. Get your act together and get packed. You're heading out with a CBIRF team in twenty minutes."

"Yes, sir. Is this a drill of some sort, sir?"

"No way, Samuels. This is a response to a chemical emergency in Central Asia. We've got a transport plane on the airfield ready to lift off. We need you to go down with them and shoot footage of the operation. I have three half-inch videotape cameras, plus a hi-8, being delivered to the aircraft, plus a full travel kit."

"You want to feature footage of a chemical terrorist attack on armed forces news?"

"Your footage is going to get wider distribution than that. We need footage to prove this attack didn't use chemicals stolen from the U.S. We need you to prove we aren't to blame, Samuels."

CHAPTER SIX

Somewhere over southern Indiana

They noticed the change in the altitude of the Cessna 750 simultaneously. It slowed into a wide, miles-long turn to the northwest, and before they could get an explanation from Grimaldi he was on the intercom system from the cockpit. "Looks like our immediate plans have changed. Barbara's on the line."

"Lyons here," the Able Team leader said as he switched on the phone. A moment of furry static gave him the voice of the Stony Man mission controller.

"Can you conference on that equipment, Carl?"

"Just a second." He switched the equipment over and motioned for his teammates to join the conversation. They picked up their phones.

"Schwarz here."

"Blancanales."

"Good. I've just instructed Jack to alter course for Minneapolis. We've got a target there we need to hit immediately. After that we'll send you on your way again to Colorado."

"What's in Minneapolis?" Lyons asked.

"A software designer named Glenn Willott. He was primarily responsible for the design of the software

used by the new incinerators in four U.S. Chemical
Agent Disposal Systems or CADS. Aaron and Akira
have discovered a couple interesting facts that point to
his involvement in the Aberdeen fiasco.''

"Such as?" Schwarz asked.

"The software was almost certainly responsible for
giving the Aberdeen team the false readings. That
means it had to be designed to do so. Or, more likely,
had to be programmed to allow a temporary piece of
auxiliary code to be implemented over its operations.
While it fed highly detailed readings of an incineration
process that wasn't occurring, the infiltraters could
shut down the actual incineration and start loading the
chemical barrels and crates into their transport.''

"The robbers could have designed software themselves to enslave the CADS software," Schwarz suggested.

"We don't think so. It was designed to be a highly
secure system. It could have been broken into—Aaron
might have accomplished it, for instance—but even he
would have had to bypass several dynamic password
systems, and it would have taken hours of on-the-
scene tampering. Our thieves didn't have hours. They
probably had just minutes, in fact, to enter the building, plug into the system and simultaneously shut it
down and keep the simulation active. But that's not
the only clue pointing to our programmer.

"Mr. Willott has suddenly become a very wealthy
man, according to several new savings accounts he has
opened throughout the country," she said. "Far too
wealthy to be explained away by the fee he's getting
from Uncle Sam for the CADS software. Aaron thinks
we'll reach an even million dollars when all the accounts are located.''

"A million bucks? I should have gone into computer programming," Blancanales said.

"There's a sense of urgency here," Price said. "We've found there's another test of a new CADS scheduled for tomorrow."

"Seems foolhardy to go ahead with it, considering recent events," Lyons stated.

Price sighed. "Yes, it does. But the President is insisting that the U.S. chemical weapons storage facilities are secure. The media's getting a little wild with the news from the Middle East. He's in a high-pressure situation. But the only reason he's proceeding is because the CADS we're talking about is on the Johnston Atoll. Even a major malfunction won't endanger the U.S. public."

"The danger isn't from a major malfunction during the incineration. It's from what will be done with the weapons if they're stolen," Schwarz protested.

"That's why we need to learn the nature of the software used to break into the CADS," Price said. "Then we can protect the system."

Lyons nodded. "We'll see what we can come up with."

Edina, Minnesota

ON THE TARMAC at the airport in Edina they transferred enough gear into the Bronco for what was assumed to be a low-risk infiltration.

Schwarz drove them into the outskirts of Minneapolis proper and followed the map into a suburban area around a lake and country club. Although the homes were crammed together on small lots, they were large and expensive. They found their street and turned into it, driving slowly past the address they were looking for.

"Pretty ritzy neighborhood for a computer programmer, isn't it?" Blancanales asked. "I'm seeing a lot of Beamers and Lexuses in the driveways."

"Maybe not," Lyons answered. "He's obviously at the top of his field. Let's not prejudge him. I don't want us shooting up some innocent man or his house."

"I got that. Or his neighbors. There is a lot of civilian activity around here," Blancanales said as they passed a man shoveling in a garden. He waved at the Bronco and went back to his work.

"You're right. Let's walk softly. I don't want a round fired until we know we're in a dangerous situation," Lyons stated. "Ideally, I'd like these people to be able to go on with their lives without even knowing we were here."

"Got it," Blancanales answered.

"Yeah," Schwarz said. "We'll do our best."

BLANCANALES STROLLED UP the walk wearing the semipermanent polite smile of a religion salesman, carrying a slim briefcase. In a houndstooth sports jacket and an open-collar shirt, he had a clean-cut look that wouldn't arouse suspicion in this well-manicured suburb. His gaze was straight ahead, but out of the corner of his eye he spotted Lyons moving swiftly to the rear of the house and Schwarz waiting in the street at the bushes, ready to approach the front if and when the opportunity—and the need—presented itself.

Blancanales rang the bell, then waited with both hands holding the briefcase in front of him and listening to the barely perceptible sounds of movement inside. Someone walked to the door and paused, and he felt eyes checking him out through the peephole. He made the smile a little more polite and grinned broadly when the door opened.

"Good afternoon. It's a beautiful day!"

The man standing at the door was in his late thirties, frowning with almost exaggerated concern at Blancanales.

"I'm Eric Crone with the Plains All-Saints Mission. I'm wondering if I might have a few minutes of your time to talk to you about the state of your immortal soul?"

The door was open wide enough for Blancanales to see a neat front room with a lone man in a red-and-blue windbreaker sitting on the couch, ostensibly paying attention to a football game on the big-screen television. One glance was enough for Blancanales to determine why he wore the windbreaker—the bulging handle of a firearm strapped across his abdomen underneath it was plainly visible. Another man emerged halfway from a kitchen toward the back of the house. The one visible hand held a can of beer, but the other hand was carefully kept out of sight.

"Not interested," said the man at the door. He was in gray sweatpants and a T-shirt, and if he was concealing a weapon it was on his back.

"Would it be all right if I just left you some of our literature?" Blancanales asked, opening his briefcase and reaching into it.

That got their attention. The tension level in the house went up markedly. The man on the couch sat rigid and put his hand on his stomach, and the guy in the kitchen took a step forward, as if on the verge of yanking out the gun and blasting Blancanales where he stood. Only his hand, and whatever was in it, was hidden now behind the kitchen wall. The Able Team commando pushed the colorful glossy brochures at the man in the sweats, who took them and muttered, "Thanks." He closed the door quickly.

"Thank you, sir—bless you!"

Blancanales strolled to the sidewalk and rendezvoused with Schwarz behind a large, sculpted bush. "We've got at least two hardmen inside," he said. "The guy who answered the door didn't appear to be packing."

"Got that?" Schwarz said into his radio.

"Yeah. This must be the place," Lyons answered. "I'll create a distraction in ten seconds. That'll give you guys a chance to position yourselves in the front. We go in one minute."

"Affirmative," Schwarz said.

Blancanales shrugged out of the sports jacket and deposited the briefcase on the sidewalk, taking the suppressed Beretta 92-F his teammate handed him. Schwarz was going in with a 93-R, also silenced. Lyons had repeated that they were in a heavily populated civilian neighborhood, and the last thing they wanted was the panic that a firefight would cause. The suppressed weapons would go a long way toward that end, although they were still fairly audible. Both Able Team warriors carried high-powered, nonsuppressed alternative hardware should the situation demand it. Keeping the neighborhood peaceful wasn't a goal worth getting killed over.

LYONS BANGED on the aluminum siding along the rear of the house, nice and loud, then crab-walked under window level to the opposite side of the building and waited for a reaction. He, too, was armed with a Beretta 92-F, suppressed by Cowboy Kissinger back at the Farm. It was a fine weapon, firing a 9 mm Parabellum round, and would probably be up to the job required. But, just in case there were more players inside than those spotted by Blancanales, Lyons was sporting a Galil ARM rifle, as well.

There was movement at the miniblind over the rear kitchen window, although Lyons was too close to the wall to see who looked out. Then he heard the back door opening, and at that moment he estimated they had reached the sixty-second mark.

THEY RAN UP the driveway and crossed to the front of the house. A quick look through the gaps in the blinds showed them figures hurrying to the rear of the house to investigate Lyons's distraction. But it was impossible to tell if any of the players remained in the living room out of their sight. They kept low, under the door, and stood flat against the wall on either side of the front door.

"Pol," Schwarz said, gesturing across the street. A woman with a purse and car keys was stepping out of the house opposite. She spotted them and froze on her front porch. There was no mistaking the large handguns or the weapons on their shoulders.

"Shit," Blancanales said, gesturing with a finger across his lips for the woman to be quiet, then waved her back into her house. With a frightened noise she stepped back inside and slammed the door.

"I think we'll have the MPD joining us shortly."

"Let's try to get in and out by then." Blancanales glanced at his watch and nodded. "Let's go."

Blancanales aimed the Beretta 92-F once at the doorknob and triggered the weapon from just inches away, obliterating it, then sent another round into the dead bolt. The impact of the bullets into the wood and metal was louder than the discreet cough of the rounds. Schwarz's foot crashed into the door, then he jumped into the front room, sweeping it at eye level with the 93-R. Blancanales stepped in beside him, aiming low. There were no targets. They advanced in long strides across the living room, bringing the kitchen into view, and a man with a Glock automatic handgun stepped around the corner. He spotted the Able Team commandos and aimed the weapon. Blancanales and Schwarz triggered their guns in synchronicity, and a pair of 9 mm rounds slammed into the gunman before he had a chance to fire. A shout erupted from the kitchen, and another gunman appeared around the corner just long enough to panic-fire a police shotgun. The walls of the short walkway between the front room and the kitchen turned to tatters.

Blancanales went right and Schwarz left. Panicky or not, with a weapon like that the hardman's aim didn't have to be good. Blancanales snatched at the windbreaker he'd seen the TV-watcher wearing during his first visit and displayed it to Schwarz, who nodded. Blancanales tossed the jacket underhand into the hallway and with a sudden blast from the shotgun it was transformed into so much scrap polyester. Schwarz reached around the corner and triggered the 93-R at the shooter three times before withdrawing his hand in a hurry. They heard a grunt, the crash of the falling shotgun and the thump of a body.

LYONS SAW the back screen door start to open and then close again when activity erupted at the front of the house, right on time. He approached the screen door and peered through it, then fell back to avoid being seen. At that moment the afternoon peace was destroyed by a shotgun blast. Lyons's field of vision included just one man, who was backing toward the door. The programmer, he guessed. He looked scared to death and ready to flee. Another shotgun blast and the man in the sweats froze, then disappeared from the door.

The Able Team leader stepped inside just in time to see the man in sweats making a grab for the fallen shotgun, lying on the kitchen floor with two sprawled bodies. Lyons aimed the 92-F and fired, the round shattering the glass and slamming into the floor near the fallen shotgun. The man in the sweats froze.

"Don't shoot me! Don't shoot me!"

"Hands up."

He raised his hands slowly and turned to face Lyons with a quivering lip. Lyons stepped through the rear door and waved the man into the corner of the kitchen. "Clear!" he shouted. "Check upstairs."

By the time Lyons was finished putting plastic handcuffs on his prisoner, Blancanales and Schwarz finished their upstairs sweep, finding it empty.

"We need to get a move on," Blancanales said. "We were spotted by the neighbors coming in."

"Hell. Let's go."

SCHWARZ MADE A RUN for the Bronco and pulled it in front of the house as the piercing sound of sirens reached the neighborhood. They hustled their prisoner into the vehicle and screeched onto the street again, accelerating around a curve and pulling to the curb just seconds before a squad car with flashing lights roared around the corner. They sank low in their seats, and Blancanales pulled their prisoner to the floor of the back seat. He was too scared to put up a fight. The squad car sped past them and followed the curve of the street, out of sight. They pulled away and left the neighborhood behind them.

Schwarz got on the cellular phone. "Gadgets here. We've got our man and we're returning now."

"Good," Price said. "Casualties?"

"We took out two armed guards. We raised a racket, I'm afraid. The local law enforcement was arriving on the scene as we left."

"I'll give them a story," Price said. "We'll be sending in the FBI to investigate."

"Fine. Meanwhile we'll see what answers our man can provide us."

BLANCANALES, IN THE BACK SEAT with the prisoner, found the handcuffed man reluctant to leave his floor-hugging position. He dragged him onto the seat.

"Okay, Mr. Glenn Willott, let's have it."

The man's lower lip was trembling as he looked from one man to another. "Who are you?" he almost whispered.

"You've got it all wrong. We're not going to answer your questions, Mr. Willott. You're going to answer ours, and you're going to do it quickly."

"You're Americans."

"Well, you're a quick one."

"Americans can't treat other Americans like this. We have laws in this country. We have rights."

"Like the right to use chemical weapons on innocent people?" Schwarz demanded. "The right to start wars?"

"I had nothing to do with that."

"Mr. Willott," Blancanales said carefully, "as far as we are concerned, you're an accessory to mass murder. That makes you less than dirt."

"No! I had nothing to do with that! I was only involved in Aberdeen so far. None of those chemicals have been used yet!"

"They will be," Schwarz said, "eventually. On somebody. On some innocent family. Maybe on a whole innocent town. If it makes a difference to you, it might very well be used on an American town. Maybe on somebody you know. Then would it qualify as murder in your eyes, Willott?" The prisoner was on the verge of tears again, and he looked at Schwarz with red eyes. "Either way you're a murderer. A murderer of men, women and children."

Lyons had been silent as they drove, facing forward. Now he turned slowly, his eyes boring into the red eyes of their blubbering victim.

"He's not going to talk, is he?" Lyons said quietly.

"Doesn't look like it, Ironman," Blancanales said with a shrug, as if giving up.

Lyons nodded. "All right. We don't have time to torture him. Let's just kill him and dump him."

"Fine," Schwarz said, pulling the Bronco to a sudden halt on the shoulder of the road, flinging up gravel.

"Wait!" Willott cried in terror.

Lyons rested the Beretta 92-F on the back of his seat, finger on the trigger. "We do not have time to wait," he said quietly. "If you have something to say you have three seconds to start. One."

"Okay, okay, okay!" he blubbered. "I'll tell you everything! Everything!"

A CALL HAD the Citation X powered up and waiting for them on the tarmac, precleared for takeoff. Blancanales carefully draped his sport coat over the bound wrists of the prisoner and helped him out of the Bronco. Locals hanging around the airport didn't need to see a handcuffed man being forced at gunpoint into an unmarked jet. Discretion was by far the best policy.

"My friend will be very angry if you don't walk calmly from the car into the aircraft. Got it?"

Willott nodded, biting his lower lip, and Blancanales walked him across the brief span of asphalt separating them from the jet. The Stony Man pilot appeared in the door wearing his good-natured grin.

"Hi, J.G." Blancanales said warmly.

"Hey, Pol, who's your friend?"

Blancanales walked the prisoner up the short steps and inside, then gave him a seat at the back of the aircraft, adding a pair of steel restraints to his ankles. The restraints locked around the seat support.

"Hope you went to the bathroom before we left," he quipped. Willott was too busy feeling sorry for himself to respond.

THEY WERE LINKED with the Farm by the time they reached cruising altitude.

"Is he cooperative?" Price asked over the speaker. Able Team was making use of a small table that folded out of the wall of the aircraft.

"Yes. He decided it was in his best interest," Lyons said.

"So, what's the story?"

"He was approached by a man named Theodore Reibel," Lyons began. "He says he doesn't know who Reibel is or what organizations he might represent, but he was flashing around large sums of cash. He told Willott he had learned that he was organizing the software development for the CADS facilities and wanted to buy access to the software. Willott says he refused until they offered him the sum of two million dollars.''

"Hmm. Has it all been paid?'' Price asked. "We've found just under a million so far.''

"Right,'' Lyons said. "Half was paid on delivery. The other half would be paid in $250,000 increments—one payment each time Reibel completed a successful raid of a CADS facility.''

"So Aberdeen was just the start of a series of four raids?'' Price sounded incredulous. "How could they realistically expect to have four successful raids without drastic preventive measures being taken to stop them?''

"Willott apparently asked the same thing,'' Schwarz said. "Reibel said they planned to sabotage the facilities as they left, to point investigators in the wrong direction. Make it seem as if it were more of a standard break-in or an inside job.''

"So how do they actually accomplish it?'' Aaron Kurtzman asked over the speaker.

"Willott built an access module into the software,'' Schwarz said. "It was very small—just a few lines of code, he claims—but if you know how to find it, it can take you right past the security system into the heart of the programming. Then he designed another piece of software to make use of this access port. It gets inside and takes over control of one hundred percent of the software function. The first thing it does is enact a real-time simulation of the incineration process that is supposed to be happening for the benefit of the CADS controllers. It sounds pretty sophisticated. The simulation is designed to react realistically to any control adjustments the CADS people might make. Since they're essentially flying on controls only, they would never know the difference.''

"In Aberdeen, they did," Price said.

"Only because somebody happened to glance out the window and saw smoke from the bulldozer. That was a stupid mistake on the part of the thieves," Kurtzman explained. "The software was running perfectly."

"I think we can make use of him here," Kurtzman added.

Grimaldi, who had been listening from the cockpit, spoke up. "You want me to turn around?"

"What's your ETA to Denver?" the mission controller asked.

"Just over two hours."

There was a pause on the line, then Price said, "No. Keep going. I want Able in Colorado. Willott's apprehension doesn't begin to answer the questions we need answered. Lyons, you and Able have transportation waiting and your first target is still the one we discussed earlier."

"Got it."

"Jack, I'd like you to start back as soon as Able has deplaned. I'm sure we can make use of Mr. Willott's unique knowledge on this end."

"Is Johnston Atoll still planning on starting up its incineration program tomorrow?" Lyons asked.

"As far as we know, although the President has been urged by parties on all sides to call it off," Price said. "Now that we have Mr. Willott, the situation has changed dramatically."

"In fact, as soon as we're done here I'd like to get

on the phone with Willott," Kurtzman said. "I'd like to start investigating how to use his built-in software vulnerability against this threat."

When the call was wrapped up, Lyons walked back to Willott, who was slumped in his seat with his head in his cuffed hands. His lips started quivering again, and when Lyons brought the object in his hands toward him Willott made a noise that might have been the start of a scream. It died when he saw that the object was a headset.

"Willott, I'm not going to shoot you on the plane," Lyons said. "It might punch a hole in the cabin and cause us to depressurize. In fact, I might not have to shoot you at all. I have a friend in Washington who would like to talk with you. About your work. Will you cooperate with him fully?"

Willott nodded quickly. "Yes. Yes of course."

Lyons placed the headset on Willott and plugged the jack into the telecommunications panel on the armrest.

"Talk."

"Uh, hello?"

"Hello, Mr. Willott," Aaron Kurtzman said. "I have some questions to ask you about your ingenious CADS software...."

White House, Washington, D.C.

THE PRESIDENT of the United States pointed at the Secret Service agent standing at the door and gave him a wave. It was a less-than-polite dismissal.

"What have you got?" he said to the only man remaining in the Oval Office as the agent closed the door behind him.

Hal Brognola tapped his pages but didn't need to look at them. Although he always appeared before the President with full documentation, he always had the details firmly affixed in his mind before arrival. The last thing he wanted was to have less than all the facts when he was in the presence of the most powerful man on the planet. "We've just brought in one of the programmers from the CADS development project," Brognola said. "Glenn Willott. He's dirty."

"Oh, hell. How'd you track him down?"

"We found out he's very suddenly become a millionaire. We're pretty sure the government wasn't paying that well."

"Hell, no. You know what my salary is? What's the situation now?"

"We got him in Minneapolis at his home. The FBI is combing the place now, but their preliminary reports show no ID on the bodyguards my men took out. Willott himself came through unscathed."

"Why were your men on his trail without my authorization?"

Brognola bristled before continuing stepping softly. "We were simply performing some detective work. Nothing extralegal. We didn't go in firing, not until Willott's bodyguards fired on us. And we might have broken this thing open."

"Fine. Is Willott cooperating?"

"Yes, sir, he certainly is. He's been on the phone with my computer people for an hour. He's already explained how to find and bypass the encryption he planted in the CADS software. This code is what allows the perpetrators to shut down the incineration process before it begins, without alerting the operators.

Then they can get inside and clear the place out while everybody else is keeping their distance.''

The President nodded. "You know the Johnston Atoll CADS is supposed to perform its inaugural run tomorrow?''

Brognola nodded.

"Think your computer people can be ready to monitor and stop the situation should it go bad?''

"If we get the executive go-ahead, we can. We've already set the wheels in motion. We can set Willott up at a safehouse location in the D.C. metro area and tie him into the Farm. We'll have computer people at both the safehouse and the Farm tied into Johnston. We can have it done in just a few hours. We monitor the JACADS start-up from here. If we see evidence of tampering, we shut everything down at once.''

"That keeps us in control, but what about stopping the theft of more U.S. chemicals?''

"I can get one of our teams on-site before the scheduled start-up," Brognola explained. "How much good they will be able to do if and when a break-in occurs is unknown, because we do not know how the break-in will even happen. The JACADS is supposed to be the most secure of the new CADS.''

The Man nodded. "Fine. You have my go-ahead.'' He leaned back in his chair, glad there was a plan, feeling more secure, that he had some sort of an inside edge.

"There's another option," Brognola suggested. "We could just lock the bastards out.''

"How can we lock them out if we don't even know how they plan on getting in?''

"I mean lock them out electronically. Since we know how they are getting control of the software

that's operating the CADS, we can pretty simply dis-
mantle that access. Once they realize they cannot shut
the incineration process down, they'll get out in a huge
hurry.''

"But that gives us nothing," the President said.
"They leave without providing us with any information on who they are or what their targets are. We win
the battle but lose the war."

Brognola nodded. "More or less."

The Man was suddenly agitated, getting to his feet
and pacing behind his desk. "Have you been reading
the papers? I'm getting reamed on this one! *The Times
of London* called me ineffectual. The French papers
are saying I've lost total control of the nation's infrastructure. Even the Russians are on my case. Sure,
they can't handle their inventory of nuclear warheads,
but at least they haven't killed anybody yet."

"U.S. chemicals haven't killed anybody either,"
Brognola protested. "None of the inventory from Aberdeen was involved in any of the Azerbaijan massa-
cres."

"So what? It's still the same type of chemicals. We
still haven't recovered all the containers stolen from
Aberdeen. And there were Americans killed on the
Tuscany II. It's a foregone conclusion the U.S. chemicals will be used to kill more Americans or be used
to kill more innocent, poverty-stricken Azerbaijanis.
I'm going to get more bad press, and my credibility
with the American people will evaporate."

"What about the Iraqi connection?"

"Baghdad is steadfastly denying that they've lost
chemical weapons stores recently, and the media is
buying their story. They're playing up the U.S. thefts,

too. And they are pointing out that they simply don't have a motive for the attacks.''

"Nobody appears to.'' Brognola's eyes followed the President as he moved.

"I think the world is tired of seeing the Iraqis as scapegoats. They simply aren't the flavor of the day any longer. Nobody except Iran is seriously suspicious of Iraq's culpability here.''

"To be fair, sir, we aren't, either.''

The President stopped pacing and sat at his desk, looking tired. "Somebody is. Somebody is guilty.'' He sat up then and leaned over the desk, looking Brognola straight in the eye. "Find them.''

CHAPTER SEVEN

Denver, Colorado

The Jeep Grand Cherokee was loaded with enough gear to keep the combat team in the field and highly functional for weeks, then Able Team and Grimaldi pointed their vehicles in opposite directions and sped away. By the time the Stony Man pilot's jet was refueled and taxiing for takeoff, the Cherokee was speeding west on the interstate highway that eventually headed out of the Rocky Mountains and into Utah.

They didn't go nearly that far, turning off at Frisco, Colorado, a major ski town that was running at a much slower pace now that there was no snow on the ground. The road took them through the Hoosier Pass and shortly thereafter they headed off the highway.

"And what are we looking for, precisely?" Blancanales asked.

"A facility belonging to a Pollari Corporation subsidiary called Upgrade Systems."

"And we're going there because...?"

"Because the chemical stores taken at Aberdeen have to go somewhere," Lyons said. "They'll probably be processed in North America before they're taken to whatever field of operations they are needed in—for whatever they are needed for. This has been pinpointed as a likely place for that processing."

"Why here?"

"It was Carmen who located it," Lyons said, referring to Carmen Delahunt. She was an ex-FBI cybernetics expert on Kurtzman's team, and easy to pick out in the crowd because of her fiery red hair. "The entire Computer Room staff was combing the Pollari businesses, including those that are tenuously linked to the main corporation. Upgrade Systems was established and funded by a group of businessmen a year ago, but these guys never used any of their own money in the venture. They took low-interest loans from a banking group that Pollari owns, built the facility out in the middle of nowhere, ran the business for a month, then closed shop suddenly, claiming they couldn't make a go of it. They never paid off the loans, and the bank never tried to collect. So now the building is sitting there empty. Or it's supposed to be."

"We think not?" Blancanales asked.

"Carmen accessed the utility records on the place. For months it was using just enough heat and electricity to keep the place from freezing and the security system operational. Two days ago its energy use shot up to operational levels. Something's going on there."

THEY DROVE PAST the padlocked gates of Upgrade Systems, which was outside a small Colorado town sitting on a big patch of level ground. The drive-by showed them no sign of activity inside the building. They parked in a patch of pines on the side of the road a mile to the south and began to hike back, reaching the eight-foot chain link fence around the grounds as the sun was hiding behind the clouds. In the chilly shadows of the overcast sky they spotted lights glowing from the rear windows of the building and heard the hum of the heating and ventilating system.

The fence wasn't electrified, and they made quick work of locating a hidden corner and cutting an entrance. Then they crossed the scrubby ground to the side of the building, just briefly exposed in the cold light of the roof-mounted security lamp as the day grew darker. Now that they were at the building they heard voices and activity inside.

"Let's be sure we've got the chemicals inside before we start taking this place down," Lyons said. "And if we do find the chemicals, be damned careful. You guys know what that stuff can do."

The others nodded grimly.

"Pol, see if there's a point to scope out the place from above. Gadgets, you're with me."

Blancanales responded with a quick nod and draped the M-16 A-2/M-203 over his shoulder as he grabbed at the aluminum ladder bolted to the side of the building. The stocky commando ascended quickly and disappeared onto the roof twenty feet above them.

Lyons and Schwarz crept along the side of the building and peered around the corner, where they had glimpsed at least one truck and semitrailer parked. Now they made out a second vehicle, which they realized was running at idle. Lyons pointed to the vehicles, and Schwarz shot off across the open space, taking advantage of the deserted condition of the parking area.

Schwarz came to a halt against the far side of the first truck, where the front wheels of the semi hid his feet. He paused just long enough to listen for a reaction to his bold run, heard none, and a quick touch to the truck cowl told him the engine was cold. He stepped onto the stair into the cab and glanced inside, finding it empty.

He circled to the rear of the trailer and found the doors open and the trailer barren. He radioed a quick report to Lyons. "Still clear up front?"

"Go ahead."

Schwarz raced across the open space to the rear of the second truck. This time the doors were closed and padlocked. He stepped quickly around the driver's side of the trailer and made his way to the cab, his suppressed 93-R gripped at shoulder level, and stepped up for a look inside. It, too, was empty and locked. But a steaming cup of coffee sat in the cup holder.

"Ironman, they're moving this truck out soon, by the look of things. They'll probably come around your side of the building. Better clear yourself from sight."

"Affirmative. You're more vulnerable than me. Get out of there."

"I'm getting."

Schwarz crept back along the side of the trailer and paused at the rear set of tires, examining the ground, which was bare, light-colored dirt. Rain had soaked the ground, not long before the trucks had arrived. The dried tracks were clear behind both vehicles, and a third set of tracks pointed to another truck, now gone.

"Gadgets," Blancanales said over the radio, "you've got company."

Schwarz heard the building's doors opening a hundred feet away, and he raced away from the trucks, creeping behind a large, flat garbage receptacle surrounded by weeds.

Two men approached, both wearing shoulder holsters that they weren't bothering to conceal. Their manner was without urgency. Schwarz hadn't been spotted. That was a relief. Able Team needed to procure some serious intel before they started taking down the operators. They needed to get inside.

One of the men took out a screwdriver and quickly removed Colorado license plates from the trailer. Schwarz memorized the plate numbers quickly before they were taken off, then memorized the new set of Oregon plates that replaced them. With a brief goodbye one of the men jumped into the cab and put the truck in gear. Two more men emerged from the building and jogged around the side. Schwarz hoped Lyons had made it to concealment because they were within one yard of his last position.

ROSARIO BLANCANALES carefully moved over the roof, following the two newcomers. He couldn't see Lyons but the newcomers didn't, either. They jogged to the gate and unlocked it, untwisting the chain. One of them ran into the road, then shouted back to his companion, who waved to the slow-moving truck. It lurched forward and onto the highway, then accelerated from sight while the two men rewrapped the chain and locked the gate. They paced back to the rear of the facility and entered.

"Ironman?" Blancanales said into his radio.

"I'm in front, in the bushes." Blancanales leaned over the roof and watched the silent shadow of Lyons step out of the tangle of overgrown shrubbery, which had once been planted to decorate the front-office section of the building. Lyons looked up and gave him a wave. "Have you got a vantage point?" he asked.

"Yeah. I'm heading there now. Several sets of skylights have been covered to avoid alerting passersby to their activity. Give me a second.''

Blancanales crouched at the edge of one of the sky-lights, which had been covered with thick black plastic and black-painted canvas. The materials had been nailed into the roof. He made quick work of cutting a flap in the material with his knife.

Light burst out at him. Below, a vast manufacturing facility was in full operation. What it had been designed to produce was impossible to tell. Now the operation was largely manual. A dozen workers were standing on either side of a slow-moving conveyor belt, assembling components of small, football-sized devices. The conveyor disappeared into a tubular steel frame covered with thick, clear plastic. Inside was a pair of figures in plastic, full-body hazmat outfits. Blancanales couldn't make out what they were doing, but he could guess. Behind them were barrels and pallets of containers, each marked with skull and cross-bones and poison warnings in multiple languages.

''Eureka,'' Blancanales said into the radio.

''Can you tell how much of the material is still here?'' Schwarz asked.

''No. I'd guess all the original containers are here, but they're remaking bombs or some other dispersion devices out of them.''

''We can guess at least part of them were in the truck that just left,'' Lyons said.

''I've seen evidence of a third truck,'' Schwarz added.

''We'll deal with that later. Right now let's move in and shut this place down.''

''There's a complication,'' Blancanales said. ''The guys working the lines look like Mexican illegals. I'll bet they bussed them in for this." He adjusted his position somewhat. "I'm seeing bunks and eating areas. I wouldn't be surprised if these poor guys are being kept locked up in here for the duration to keep them out of contact with the locals."

"We'll have to be especially cautious until we know. If they're loyal to the Pollari group they might be armed. If they're not—"

"If they're not, we should consider them innocent bystanders," Blancanales stated. "Those guys probably have no clue who their employers are or what it is they're manufacturing in there."

"Pol's right," Lyons said.

Blancanales moved from one skylight to another, taking in the lay of the interior and describing it in detail to his teammates. "The only part of the interior I'm not seeing is the office," he concluded. "I think that's where the Pollari supervisors are housed. I haven't seen anywhere else they might have living quarters, and I seriously doubt they're bunking on the factory floor with the workers."

Lyons quickly strategized the probe, finishing up by saying, "Remember, no explosives. Not even a flash. No matter how removed you think you are from the chemical stores. If even one of those containers gets blown, this place could transform into a morgue in less than a minute. That means us, the workers, the bad guys, everybody. Got it?"

"I got it," Blancanales answered.

And he certainly did. He had witnessed human beings dying of exposure to nerve agents. He'd seen photographs of the holocaust the dictator in Iraq perpetrated against the Kurds with his chemical weapons. He had no interest in meeting death in that fashion.

"I GOT IT," Schwarz said. Damn right he was going to be careful around piles of that stuff. Give him a bullet over the impersonal agony of nerve-agent-induced death any day.

He stepped from behind his trash bin and crossed the back lot to the rear door, carrying his leathered 93-R and a Heckler & Koch MP-5 A-3 submachine gun, with a curved, 30-round magazine, as his primary entry weapon.

The lax level of security told him the inhabitants were confident they would go unmolested as long as nobody knew they were there. The door, he guessed, would be unlocked. The knob turned when he twisted it.

He shoved the door with his left shoulder and swept the loading bay right to left, finding it empty. Crossing to the door into the factory, he found it open an inch. He peered through, finding the scene matched the mental picture he already had of the place, and made his entry.

He leveled the MP-5 A-3 at the two nearest men. One of them spotted him and grabbed for a 9 mm pistol secured under his armpit. The move cost him his life. The H&K rattled in Schwarz's hands and cut across the player's abdomen, giving his companion incentive to dive to the ground. He rolled onto his back, dragging out a handgun of his own, a .40-caliber Smith & Wesson. But the moment it took him to drag it into position and thumb the decocking lever was more than enough time for Schwarz to pivot slightly and trigger the H&K in another brief burst. A trio of 9 mm rounds chopped the player in the rib cage.

Shouts erupted throughout the factory, and Schwarz headed for the cover of a five-foot tool cabinet, spotting three men on the opposite side of the factory coming his way. Caught in the middle, the workers at the conveyor belt cried out and dropped to the ground in terror.

Schwarz waited behind the tool chest for a three count, then stepped out just far enough to level the H&K at the spot he'd expected the new arrivals to fill—and just far enough from the workers to provide a margin of safety. One of the new arrivals raised an M-14 and fired wildly, running too fast to aim. The H&K spoke at the same instant, but Schwarz's shots were anything but wild. The hardman crumpled and the M-14 cracked to the concrete floor. Schwarz withdrew as the other two arrivals came to a halt behind the conveyor mechanicals cabinet and dropped to their knees. One leveled an Uzi on the tool chest and triggered a dozen rounds that rattled the box like an earthquake, but couldn't penetrate. As the barrage paused, Schwarz fired another volley from the H&K, timing it as the second hardman was getting to his feet to trigger a pump-action shotgun. The buckshot never flew. The 9 mm round hit him in the chin and pushed his head around. The second and third rounds downed him with tearing wounds to the chest and thorax.

Finding himself to be the last survivor unnerved the gunman with the Uzi, and he cut loose wildly, sending 9 mm rounds into the walls, the ceiling and the tool chest until its staccato chattering suddenly halted, empty. Schwarz took the opportunity to step into the open and trigger a controlled burst from the H&K. The gunman had already dropped behind the mechanical box and the fire was wasted, but he fired again as the gunman stood, now holding his dead partner's shotgun. It was a suicide move. Schwarz's next burst ripped through him and he fired the shotgun out of reflex, sending buckshot harmlessly into the air.

BLANCANALES WATCHED three more gunmen emerge from the front of the factory just as Schwarz took out the shotgunner, and one of them dropped into a firing stance with what looked like an AK. Schwarz's awareness of the newcomers was questionable, so Blancanales triggered the M-16 A-2/M-203 through the glass, shattering the skylight panels and cutting down the kneeling gunner.

His two companions recoiled in surprise and one of them aimed his own automatic weapon at the source of the fire. Blancanales found himself looking directly down the barrel of the gunman's rifle for a fraction of a second and triggered the M-16 A-2. The gunman collapsed to the floor.

The survivor had ducked back into the door from whence he'd come. Lyons would have to deal with him, and whoever else was still hidden in the front office section of the facility. Blancanales scanned the interior of the factory for other threatening figures. The only survivors were the cowering workers and Schwarz, who exited carefully from his shelter, nosing into a few hiding places with the muzzle of the H&K. Then he gave a thumbs-up in his teammate's direction.

Blancanales jogged to the ladder and headed down.

LYONS WAITED for the sounds of Schwarz making his back-door entrance, allowed for a few seconds of chaos to attract everyone's attention, then blasted at the front-door lock with the suppressed 92-F. He kicked at the door, then moved away from it, but no deadly barrage drilled through the panels. He pushed through and found an empty front reception area with a cheap-looking, black vinyl couch, still shiny with newness and littered with a pillow and a crumpled blanket. Lyons put his hand on the vinyl, which was still warm.

He advanced into the hallway, listening to a variety of shots from the factory. Two offices were located to the rear. He decided to check out those first—he didn't want anybody coming up behind him—and with two strides reached the first office door. It served as a kitchen, with a hot plate, a microwave oven and waist-high refrigerator. A figure in striped boxer shorts was bent over a table, pushing rounds into a large-caliber revolver.

"Don't move," Lyons advised.

The figure froze, and Lyons heard a rush of movement from the last office. He spun and triggered the Galil, and the faceless figure doubled over, cracking his spine into the wall.

With a click the man in the boxer shorts had closed the barrel on the six-shooter, but Lyons had anticipated the move and completed his circle, triggering the Galil again. The revolver hit the floor and its owner collapsed on top of it.

Lyons started back to the unexplored offices when a lone figure with an AK stumbled in from the factory, his eyes wild with fear. Lyons used the 92-F in his left hand, firing rounds into the newcomer's knees. The man screeched and dropped to the floor. Lyons ran forward and kicked at the man's hands as he tried to draw the AK to him and get up on his elbows. He cried out again as the bones in his hands crunched, and he hugged the carpet for the second time in a few seconds. Lyons pushed the AK away from the fallen figure and held the Galil over his head, so that when he peered up, eyes showing white like a terrified mongrel, the first thing he saw was the business end of the weapon.

Stony Man Farm, Virginia

BARBARA PRICE HAD JUST entered the War Room when the call came through.

"It's Carl. Able's secured its target," she said.

"Did they find the chemicals taken from Aberdeen?" David McCarter asked.

"Let's hear it from the horse's mouth," Price answered.

She pressed a button to put Lyons on the speaker. "You've got an audience, Carl," she said.

"Who's all there?" he asked.

"Phoenix. Plus Hal, Aaron and Katz."

"I guess I ought to feel honored. We've got this place locked up. There were several casualties among the enemy and one survivor. He might not walk again, however. There are also fourteen Mexican immigrant workers, who we think were bussed up from Southern California."

"Tell me they're all unharmed," Brognola said.

"Not a scratch, Hal. Rosario is questioning them now, but we're pretty sure they don't even know what they were doing here. I don't even think they realized they were working with dangerous chemicals. They were paid well to do the work on a no-questions-asked basis."

"The Aberdeen chemicals?" McCarter asked.

"Some of them are here. But as we were casing the place a semi left, we presume with another supply of the weapons they were preparing here. There's also evidence of a third semi that left here since the last rain.'' He read off the license plate numbers, the new and the old, that Schwarz had memorized. Kurtzman jotted them down.

''We'll try to track them down,'' Kurtzman said.

''You'll need the state police to help you with that,'' Lyons said. ''Can we trust the Colorado troopers to spread the word on this set of numbers without using radio? I'd bet those guys have scanners onboard.''

''Probably,'' Price said. ''Once we track down the truck we can keep an eye on it from the air. They'll never know we're watching.''

''And it will lead us right to their next distribution point,'' Lyons said, completing the line of reasoning.

''My thought exactly.''

''How long has it been since the truck left the facility?'' Kurtzman asked.

There was a pause. ''Forty-three minutes.''

Kurtzman turned to Carmen Delahunt, and they began a rapid-fire conversation that lasted just seconds, then the redhead was on her feet and heading for the cybernetics center.

''We're on it,'' Kurtzman stated.

''We're finishing up here,'' Lyons said. ''You've got Feds on the way?''

''Yeah, and a hazmat team. You'll want to be out of there in about twenty minutes.''

''Good. We will be. Then what?''

''I'll call you as soon as I know,'' Price said.

CHAPTER EIGHT

Dignified was the one word that best described Huntington "Hunt" Wethers. A tall, older black gentleman, he looked every inch the former professor that he truly was. He had been a cybernetics instructor, educating future cybernetics experts, when Aaron Kurtzman asked him to join the expanding SOG computer team. He had proved his value to the team on multiple occasions.

But everyone there had proved his or her worth. Each individual at the table had demonstrated abilities that at one time or another achieved the resolution of deadly situations. Every one of them, directly or indirectly, had at some point saved innocent lives around the world.

Barbara Price got a strange mix of feelings when she was in the room with these people. These meetings were always precipitated by a global crisis of a type that required the direct involvement of the SOG. Yet she almost welcomed the gathering of these people, as they were the closest thing to an extended family she knew.

Just like a true family, a gathering of all the members was rare. Even now there was a big gap in the ranks with Able Team in the field. Also highly conspicuous by his absence from the Farm was the Stony Man himself. The Executioner, at that moment, couldn't have been farther away from them.

Her emotional reverie lasted just long enough for her to hear the click of the phone as Lyons hung up. Then she looked directly at Hal Brognola at the other end of the table and demanded point-blank, "Do we have the word?"

Brognola had just returned from his latest meeting with the President. He wasn't at all surprised by Price's direct manner. "We have the word."

"Good—"

"The President is in a sticky spot," Brognola continued. "You've all seen the bashing he's been getting in the media. They've been calling him indecisive and worse. They're saying it's foolhardy to risk American lives in the inaugural run of the Johnston Atoll Chemical Agent Disposal System without having caught the people responsible for the Aberdeen fiasco. On the other side of the fence are those who are ready to pounce on the administration if it backs down to the terrorists."

"Isn't it, though? Foolhardy, I mean?" Thomas Jackson "T.J." Hawkins asked. Outside of Akira Tokaido, Hawkins was the youngest man on the Farm and the newest arrival. He was ex-Delta Force, a soldier who proved himself in Somalia when he saved a village from the murderous rampage of a local warlord—a rampage that Hawkins's Swedish UN commander had been prepared to allow. They needed men with the courageous fortitude Hawkins demonstrated in Somalia, and, indeed, throughout his career. When Yakov Katzenelenbogen retired from Phoenix Force, he and Bolan went to great lengths to recruit the disillusioned soldier. Only when Hawkins became convinced that the SOG wasn't subject to the manipulation of politicians did he agree to come on board. He'd become convinced during his short tenure that he had made the right decision. But now he was hearing another politician trying to keep himself in the good graces of the people, by whatever tactics.

"Not anymore, it isn't," Price said. "We've got an inside edge." She briefly outlined Able Team's activity over the past several hours in Minneapolis, concluding with the capture of the man responsible for the CADS software.

"Where's Willott now?" Calvin James asked. The black man managed to look tall and lanky even at ease in his chair. He was ex-SEAL, a formidable warrior.

"Ensconced in a safehouse in Arlington," Jack Grimaldi replied. "I put him there myself. He's well-guarded—we've got staff from the Farm on-site. But our security is so good I highly doubt anybody could determine where he was, let alone get at him if they found him."

"Is he skillful enough to try to make a break for it himself?" James asked.

"No. I think his spirit is pretty well broken. We've also got Akira there with him."

"That's because he's agreed to cooperate with us to undermine any sabotage attempts at tomorrow's JACADS inaugural run, and he's instructing Akira in the methods he used to compromise the incineration software," Price said. "By the time the start-up begins, the Farm should be on-line with JACADS. We'll be able to monitor and control all activity—including infiltration attempts."

"The plan is to have Phoenix Force on the atoll

when that happens," Brognola added. "To put a stop to it."

McCarter nodded. "Will the army cooperate?"

"Yes, they will," Brognola said firmly. "Their commander-in-chief is ordering them to."

"You'll have just about enough time to get there and get staged," Price said. "Any other questions?"

"Yeah. I've got one," said Rafael Encizo, the Cuban-born member of Phoenix Force. "I want to know what these people are up to. Why are they stealing these weapons? Why are they killing all these people?"

"That we can't answer," Price said, a little more quietly. She knew how Encizo was feeling. Mass murder without even knowing the maniac's motivation was dismaying. "I'm hoping we'll find out soon and can keep it from happening again."

IT WAS A RESTFUL NIGHT for some members of the Stony Man team. Barbara Price, for one. She had learned to rest when she could and as much as she could during a full-scale Stony Man alert. Now she had the opportunity. Tomorrow and the next day and the next day, who knew? She had left word to be awakened only when the truck IDed by Able Team was spotted.

That happened at 2:00 a.m., when the Colorado State Police tagged it near Fort Collins on the interstate. A few quick phone calls got the Wyoming State Police involved. They picked up the truck just across their border and put a surveillance chopper on it. They protested a little, but Price's authorization cajoled them into cooperating, and Price went back to bed.

When she got up in the morning her first order of

business was to get the Oregon State Police involved, because the truck had traveled into that state.

Others hadn't had as restful a night.

Akira Tokaido had been interfacing with Glenn Willott throughout the night at the Arlington Hilton. Their room was packed with PCs that were on-line to the Computer Room at Stony Man Farm. The Stony Man guard had changed twice, and room service had arrived with fresh pots of coffee every two hours.

Aaron Kurtzman spent the night with them, in a sense, tied in via an open phone line from the Farm and assisting them over a secure link. He, too, was consuming vast quantities of coffee until, by dawn, his head started to pound from too much caffeine. But by then, he was satisfied to note, Tokaido had a good handle on CADS and how to take control of it when the time came.

Jack Grimaldi was heading west yet again during the midnight hours. "Playing taxi driver," he commented wryly to himself. The pilot's seat of the Citation X, he was convinced, was starting to take on the shape of his rear end. Meanwhile Phoenix Force was sleeping in their reclined seats, lulled by the steady roar of the 3007C turbofans.

The slim Stony Man pilot off-loaded his passengers in Denver in the middle of the night, where they were catching a Delta red-eye to Oahu. Then he and his company-supplied copilot each grabbed one of the reclining seats in the Cessna's cabin and took advantage of the few hours they had until Able Team arrived in the morning.

ABLE TEAM ARRIVED before dawn, and Grimaldi had them in the air minutes later. They gathered around the front fold-out table and dialed up the Farm, getting on the speakerphone with Barbara Price as she was reading the overnight reports.

"The Oregon State Police reported in to us about five minutes ago."

"They manage to keep an eye on that truck for us?" Lyons asked.

"Yeah, and it was no easy task. It's a big state," she replied from the speaker. "And our truck driver crossed well over half of it. He left the interstates and headed into some depopulated country in the western middle of the state. The truck stopped on an isolated section of road about twenty miles southeast of a little town called Flatwillow."

"Is that as precise as they got?" Blancanales asked.

"That's as precise as we need," Price answered. "It took Carmen about a minute to determine that there's an old factory and landing field on that road, on property now owned by Pollari Oil."

"A landing field?" Schwarz asked.

"Supposedly abandoned," Price replied. "There hasn't been activity on that field since the 1970s, as far as any official records indicate. But it wouldn't have taken much effort to repave it and make it serviceable."

"We going into Portland?" Lyons asked.

"Yes," Price answered. "From there we've got a Black Hawk helicopter to transport you to the scene. Jack will pilot the chopper, but the Army has insisted on providing a copilot."

"Will the Oregon troopers be willing to pull out?" Lyons asked. The former Los Angeles Police Department detective knew how testy regional law enforcement could get when the federal agencies started nosing around in what they saw as their business.

"They've been instructed in no uncertain terms to stay out of your way," Price told him.

Lyons nodded, but wondered if that would truly be the case. If the state police knew something was going down at the Pollari facility, they would want to be involved. Their investment of time and resources throughout the night would give them a sense of ownership of the situation.

"How long until we land in Portland?" Blancanales asked.

"Half hour, tops," said Grimaldi, who was patched in from the pilot's seat.

"All right," Lyons said. "Let's be ready to move."

THE SIKORSKY UH-60L Black Hawk sat poised on the tarmac, its T700-GE-701C engines running. Jack had radioed ahead to the copilot provided by the Army, who had the helicopter ready for immediate takeoff. The dark, insectlike appearance of the helo contrasted starkly with the sleek, white lines of the Citation X as she came to a halt a stone's throw away.

As soon as the jet halted, Blancanales popped the hatch and, joined by Grimaldi, hustled across the asphalt with their packs to the waiting helo.

Grimaldi found himself trading off one less-than-trusting copilot for another. While he left Greene in the Cessna corporate jet to await their return, he found himself shaking hands with an unenthusiastic Army pilot.

"Captain Hassan," the man stated.

"Jack."

"Can't say I'm too happy to be turning my aircraft

over to some guy who's not even a military pilot. But I'm told you'll have a clue what to do in the cockpit.''

"Yeah, at least a clue," Grimaldi said and entered the cockpit without entertaining further discussion.

The members of Able Team strapped themselves in, and the Stony Man pilot had the rotors accelerating within minutes. The Black Hawk rose smoothly and swiftly, then Grimaldi aimed the chopper north for the flight into the big skies of Oregon.

GRIMALDI SOON HAD Captain Hassan appeased as to his capability, and when he had skirted the urban and suburban areas of Portland he increased his speed to 160 miles per hour. They hugged the treetops as they came to within a few miles of the Pollari compound, landing on a grassy plain in the middle of a long stretch of forest. Able Team hit the ground running, and the Stony Man pilot took the Black Hawk into the air again, heading out of the neighborhood at top speed.

The hope was that even if the sound of the helicopter did reach the Pollari compound, it would come and go quickly enough to give the impression of a passing chopper.

Lyons took the lead, taking his teammates through the dense forest. Their pace was steady and strong, meant to eat up the miles without taxing the commandos for the real work that would follow.

"Wings to Able One," Grimaldi said in their radio headsets.

"Go ahead, Wings," Lyons said.

"We're parked."

"Roger."

Grimaldi had planned to put down the Black Hawk

in a secluded area, well out of earshot but close enough to be able to provide rapid assistance should it be needed.

"I'm gonna get real bored here real fast," Grimaldi added.

"We'll keep you posted, Wings," Lyons retorted.

They came to a halt at a tree line, looking out over what had to be several thousand acres of gently rolling, grassy plain. A hundred yards from the trees was an eight-foot barbed-wire fence, with an added Y of barbed wire jutting another foot-and-a-half from the top. A collection of low buildings stood another hundred yards inside the fence.

"Check it out," Blancanales said, gesturing. He was indicating a section of the fence where the old, rusted wire had been replaced with new, shiny silver wire.

"Well, we know something is going on here," Schwarz commented.

"This way," Lyons said, leading them back into the cover of the trees. They marched along the tree line for another five minutes before finding what they judged would be the optimal approach point. Here, the bulging tree line allowed them to get an extra forty feet closer to the fence, in an area where they were visible from only a single window from the distant buildings.

They saw their first hint of activity as a garage door opened on one of the buildings. Inside, several people were moving around the rear end of a semi-truck trailer.

"There's our friend from Colorado, I'd bet," Lyons said.

A small cart was driven out of the loading dock,

towing a flatbed trailer. It was stacked with something but covered by a tarp. The driver steered directly for the nearby hangar and touched the button that opened a garage-sized section of multiple doors set side by side. The quick glance inside showed them a very large, low-set prop aircraft.

"They're loading up," Blancanales stated.

"Master of the obvious," Schwarz answered.

"But they're going to a lot of trouble to keep all their activity under cover."

"They'll have figured out something has gone wrong in Colorado by now," Lyons said. "My guess is they're trying to get this shipment onboard and out of here. Which means we need to get in there ASAP."

"First we need to prevent that aircraft from getting off the ground," Schwarz said. "I take the hangar."

"What's your intention?" Lyons asked.

"I'm not sure, yet. Hopefully I'll get inside and shoot up the controls. That would be the safest option."

Lyons looked at him a moment, then nodded. "All right. But be damn careful. One good blast and God knows what we'll be blowing into the air. Let's all keep that in mind. Any explosions or fires could blow one of whatever weapons they're making in there. If that stuff starts filling the atmosphere in the compound, well, we're all dead men. Good guys and bad guys both."

"I got it," Blancanales said.

Schwarz nodded.

"Pol," Lyons added, "you'll be with me."

They crouched and ran across the open scrub grass to the barbed-wire fence, where they fell flat, hiding behind the weeds and grass that clung to the wire.

Blancanales grabbed his wire cutters by the rubberized plastic handles and poked at the fence, finding it non-electrified. Then he made quick work of snipping out a low opening.

Now came the most dangerous segment of the approach. Once they were through the gate they were in the open, without a cover or a hiding place for a good hundred yards. They would have to run and trust to chance that no one would look out any of the windows or leave the buildings. Making the run together minimized those chances, yet left no one in hiding to cover the runners.

"Ready, Gadgets?" Lyons asked.

"Ready." Schwarz was lying at the mouth of the opening on his elbows, his Heckler & Koch MP-5 A-3 submachine gun in his hands.

Lyons stared at the buildings, watching for any sign of movement. "Go!" he said.

Schwarz slithered through the narrow opening and into the open field beyond, then shot to his feet, with Blancanales right behind him. By the time Lyons came through after them, Schwarz had reached the building and flattened against it, covering the others as they joined him. They waited for a few seconds for signs they'd been spotted, then Schwarz took off around the corner, crouching as he passed under the shaded window and the door window, which was covered with newspaper. Then he crossed the distance to the hangar, coming to a halt against the wall next to the door.

"I'm here," he said into the mike of his headset. "But I can't stay long. I'm still in the line of sight from the window of the other building. I think I'll try along the back way for another entrance."

"Go," Lyons answered. "Pol and I are going to find a way in here."

Schwarz jogged the length of the hangar, which was a solid brick building that wasn't letting out any sound. He would have heard if the aircraft had started up. He peered around the corner and found more empty scrubby grassland. There were two entrances, one sized for aircraft, one for humans, both of which were closed. He stepped to the smaller door and found its small window also covered in newspaper.

He heard nothing inside, and he twisted the knob slowly and applied steady pressure with his shoulder, forcing it open just an inch. He peered inside, trusting to chance that no one was watching the door or standing behind it, even now targeting him.

Inside, the abundant skylights illuminated the bulk of a C-130H Hercules. The heavyset, low-slung aircraft filled the hangar. The rear ramp was down, and the cart and its trailer had been backed into it.

Schwarz saw no evidence of activity in the hangar, which meant whoever was inside had to be either behind his door or inside the aircraft.

He shoved at the door and twisted around it, leveling the MP-5 A-3, but found no one there. He hurriedly shut the door and crossed to the aircraft.

"How you doing, Gadgets?" Lyons asked in his headset. Schwarz tapped the microphone twice, signaling that he wasn't in a place where conversation was possible.

"I got that. Pol and I are going in."

Schwarz sent back a one-tap affirmative and dragged off the headset to hear more clearly. There was movement inside the rear of the C-130H, but no voices. Schwarz estimated there was a single man, the driver of the cart, who was unloading the material from the trailer into the cargo hold.

Schwarz pondered waiting for the driver to finish his task, then rejected waiting as too risky. Who knew when another person might show up from the other building. And if Lyons and Blancanales caused a ruckus over there, the driver might very well hear it and grab for a weapon.

The Able Team commando crept to the end of the ramp and vaulted onto it quickly, leveling the MP-5 A-3 into the interior.

At that moment he realized he'd made a major error in judgment.

THE WINDOWS WORE heavy shades.

"We're going in blind, no matter what," Blancanales stated.

"Yeah," Lyons said distractedly, his mind whirling with ideas. But each plan was rejected before it had fully formed. There might be a dozen hardmen inside, heavily armed. They simply wouldn't be able to get inside without exposing themselves.

"We could blast the doors with something low-grade enough it wouldn't risk the weapons containers inside," Blancanales suggested. "Even set off a flash in the open just to draw them out."

Lyons shook his head slightly. "I don't like it."

"Got any better ideas?"

"No, I don't."

"Wait!" Blancanales whispered and held up a finger, hearing the creak of a door. Lyons pointed to the way they had just come, and Blancanales moved out in that direction, while Lyons circled the building the other way.

Blancanales found the side of the building clear and crept back to the front, his M-16 A-2 up and ready to defend him against all comers. When he reached the front of the building he spotted a group of three men, carrying automatic weapons, heading for the hangar.

"Gadgets, company's coming!" Lyons hissed over the radio. "Are you there?"

The group opened the hangar door and in that instant the sound of a handgun shot was plainly audible. The hardmen reacted at once, falling away from the open door and readying their weapons. There was a yell from inside and they grabbed for the door again.

Lyons and Blancanales joined the battle, both leveling their weapons and firing across the open ground at the hardmen as they entered the building. The first gunman was already inside as their twin blasts of autofire cut across the two stragglers. One of them dropped where he stood, while the other turned in their direction in surprise. The bullets cut across his abdomen and chest, sending him crashing to the earth.

THE DRIVER OF THE CART spun, with a canvas-wrapped cylinder hugged to his chest, and Schwarz froze where he stood, coming to the full realization of his error. So did his opponent, who grabbed at the .357 Magnum revolver tucked in the back of his trousers.

"You shoot and we all die," his opponent shouted.

Schwarz knew he was correct. If a single one of his rounds compromised the shell of that container, God knew what would seep out. Everyone in the hangar, everyone in the compound, might be dead in minutes. His opponent stepped quickly behind the stacks of containers he had already loaded into the C-130H, to protect the lower half of his body. Only his head and his gun hand were exposed.

"Drop it," he ordered.

Schwarz stood his ground.

"Drop it, asshole!" He raised the revolver, his finger quivering on the trigger.

The door opened, and Schwarz turned the MP-5 A-3 at the newcomers. His opponent fired. The .357 round drilled into his chest, stopped cold by his Kevlar vest but hitting him with the impact of a hammer blow. He grunted in pain and spun halfway around, then heard the second shot from the .357. For a fraction of a second he thought about the consequences of a shot to the head, then he found himself staggering backward and reeling under the impact of a second sledgehammer-like impact, this one to the abdomen.

He grabbed the MP-5 A-3 to his gut and tried to see through the blinding flashes of white pain; he heard the distant rattle of autofire. His backward motion was brought to a halt as he slammed into the garage door of the hangar. Then he spotted his assailant coming at him with the revolver raised in his hand like a club. Schwarz tried to bring up the Heckler & Koch to deflect the blow, but his system was slowed by pain and shock. A blast of pain stabbed into his face and head.

"POL, OVER HERE!"

Blancanales bolted across the front of the building. It was essential they get together if they were going to fend off the possibility of a two-pronged assault. The front door of the building opened as he made his break and a figure with a shotgun stepped out, looking in the direction of the building. Blancanales leveled his M-16 A-2 and triggered it. Four shockers crashed into the shotgunner and flung him into the door, and as he was falling Blancanales turned to face the interior of the building. Three men stared at the doorway, looking surprised. A fourth man raced out the rear door. Stacks of containers wrapped in canvas stood stacked next to the semi-truck and trailer. The Able Team commando resisted his urge to fire into the building and was past the door before those inside could target him. He ran to Lyons's side.

"Wings, get over here now!" Lyons shouted into the radio.

"Company's coming up behind you!" Blancanales said.

With his teammate there to watch the hangar and the front door, Lyons turned to the rear and spotted movement. He triggered his weapon and shattered bricks but scored no hits. He snatched at one of the grenades on his belt, a flash-bang.

"Cover your ears!" he shouted. "In five!"

"Got it!" Blancanales leveled the M-16 A-2 at the front door, which was wedged open by the body of the shotgunner, rattled off a few rounds and turned to the hangar's front door, chugging out a few more, then dropping into a crouch with the gun wedged between his knees. He dragged the headset onto his neck, jabbed his fingers into his ears and squeezed his eyes shut.

Lyons pitched the grenade toward the rear of the building and followed his teammate's example. There was a sudden flash of brilliance and a screech of explosive noise. Lyons made a run for the corner and found one man reeling on the grass, moaning and clawing at his eyes, while another figure staggered at the entrance to the rear door, where he'd received less than the full force of the blast.

He spotted Lyons through the assault to his vision and triggered his shotgun wildly into the air. The Able Team leader targeted him first, snapping out three quick bursts with the Galil that hit his adversary dead-on.

The man in the grass screamed, filled with terror, and scrambled to his knees, pushing to get to his feet. But Lyons took him out with a burst that punched into his abdomen and shut his organs down.

The door swung open again and another figure peered out, then retreated as Lyons triggered more rounds, which clanged into the steel fire door without penetrating. The enemy reached around without looking and fired a 9 mm automatic handgun, the rounds flying far to Lyons's right. The big ex-cop targeted his hand. There was a yelp, and the handgun sailed into the open with a splash of blood. Lyons raced to the entrance, cutting loose with a single round that brought down the wounded gunner.

He withdrew and the door was filled a half-second later with ricocheting autofire rounds.

"Ironman, I've got big trouble!"

Lyons backed to the corner, then jogged to Blancanales's side, the sound of a garage door reaching him.

"Check this out!" his teammate said.

Another cart was being wheeled out of the building, stacked high with the canvas-covered containers of toxic chemicals. The hardmen were behind it, pushing it over the grass in the direction of the hangar, their feet visible under the cart.

"Don't fire," Lyons stated.

"I'm not planning to," Blancanales assured him.

The two men stepped around the corner and moved across the front of the building. A quick look inside revealed that no one else was inside.

"What're we going to do?" Blancanales asked.

"You got me."

They heard the rumble of machinery and watched the wide hangar doors slowly rise, revealing the nose of the Hercules C-130H. Even as the door slid into position the four massive Alisson T56-A-15 turboprops rumbled to life.

The cart full of toxic containers maneuvered into the hangar, keeping as much distance as it could from the outside turboprop without exposing its manipulators to the Able Team warriors. As soon as the cart was inside, the aircraft started forward.

Lyons and Blancanales approached in a run and spotted the escapees running across the hangar for the open ramp at the rear of the aircraft. Lyons allowed himself just a second to evaluate the layout for the proximity to the containers of chemicals and make a decision; he triggered the Galil and targeted the fleeing men. Blancanales was a few steps ahead and to the left of him, and he targeted the aircraft itself as a figure appeared with an Uzi in one hand, hanging on to a structural support with his other hand. He targeted Lyons but couldn't get off a shot before Blancanales stitched him across the belly. The Uzi clattered to the concrete. At that moment the rear of the C-130H cleared the hangar, and the surviving gunner made a dive for the ramp. Lyons's final burst cut into him. The ramp started to rise, the wounded hardman clawed at it, but his legs were on the ground and he could no longer work them. He was dragged off the ramp and flopped to the ground with a crash.

Autofire erupted from inside the closing ramp.

"Don't return fire!" Lyons commanded, spotting the familiar stacks of canvas-bound containers in the hold around the shooter. He had just spotted something else—the limp body of Gadgets Schwarz draped over the containers.

"This way," Blancanales said, breaking into a run as the wild autofire sailed around them.

Lyons joined his teammate behind the protective brick wall and snatched at his radio as he heard the familiar thrum of the Black Hawk closing in.

"Wings, this is Able One. Do not fire. Repeat, do not fire."

"This is Wings, Able," Grimaldi said as the dark chopper came to a menacing hover over the compound. "We just gonna let them take off?"

"Affirmative," Lyons replied, feeling impotent as he heard the Allison turboprops roar to life. He and Pol Blancanales helplessly watched the plane accelerate down the runway and lift heavily into the air.

CHAPTER NINE

"This is Jack, and we've got trouble!"

"Go ahead, Wings," Barbara Price urged.

The radio crackled and Price heard shouting against the roar of the helicopters rotors, which was plainly rising. She heard "We're in! Let's go!" She was sure that was Lyons and he sounded agitated, to put it mildly.

"Report, Jack!" she radioed. "Are you guys in danger?"

"What? No, not us. Just a second!" There was a rising tide of noise as the Black Hawk took to the air. She heard another shout from Lyons and suddenly he was on the line.

"This is Able One."

"What's going on?"

"We took down the facility in Oregon, but Gadgets was taken prisoner. He's on their plane, and they're running with him."

Price swore softly under her breath. Kurtzman was entering the room and caught the tail end of it over the speakers.

"What are they in, Able One?" she asked.

"It's a Hercules. We're in pursuit, but we're losing them pretty fast. We need some air support up here."

"What's the plan?" she asked.

"I haven't thought of one yet!"

Her eyes locked with Kurtzman's as she talked, both of them easily reading the edge in Lyons's voice. Kurtzman was dialing up the Air Force at another communications center. "What's Gadgets's situation?" she asked.

"Can't we get this thing going any faster, Jack?" Lyons was saying. "They're leaving us! Base, are we getting air support?"

"Aaron's on it, Able One. We're not going to lose them. What's Gadgets's situation?"

"I don't know. I spotted him on board the Hercules before they closed it up. He was out cold. Gadgets could be dead already, for all I know, Base."

"Okay. We're on it," Price said. She looked to Kurtzman, who was talking hurriedly into his own headset. He gave her a thumbs-up.

"Able One, what's your position?"

Lyons gave her their position and she relayed it to Kurtzman, who passed it on to his Air Force contact. "Remember," he was saying, "we've got a friend in that aircraft."

"What's the situation at the facility?" she asked Lyons.

"No survivors, Base," he answered. "Plenty of chemical weapons were on-site and not all of it was successfully loaded before they took off."

"Right," Price said. "I'll get a hazmat team in there to clean it up."

"WHAT'S THE DEAL?" Lyons asked Grimaldi.

"I've got the pedal to the metal, Carl," the pilot

replied. In fact, the Army-assigned copilot was watching the controls nervously.

"I'll say," he added.

"Not good enough!" Lyons retorted, watching the disappearing speck that was the C-130H. "We're losing it."

"The Air Force will keep an eye on it," Grimaldi assured him. "We won't lose it."

"Think they can bring it down?"

Grimaldi didn't know how to answer that.

GADGETS SCHWARZ FELT PAIN before he felt true consciousness, then through his pain came the thrum of the engines. It took him a long moment to get his bearings, and he willed himself to stay motionless, eyes closed. Then he recalled his circumstances—the sledgehammer impacts from the .357 Magnum rounds slamming into his vest, then the sight of the gun descending on his head. The memory brought a new realization of the pounding in his skull.

He had been aboard the Hercules, and now he realized the thrum he was hearing had to be the engines. The movement he was feeling told him the aircraft was in flight, at a cruising altitude.

That didn't bode well for the success of the mission. For a moment he wondered what might have become of his teammates. Had they been taken out in the firefight? Was that how the Pollari team had managed to take off with him?

Not necessarily. They would never have fired on the plane once it was in motion. They wouldn't have risked compromising the integrity of any of the chemical containers. That would have been suicide. They might not even have realized he was on board the aircraft until it was gone.

So what now?

He heard voices and felt hands on his arms, which he now realized were tied behind his back. He was yanked to his feet, sending a rush of blood into his bruises and into his aching skull, and his legs started to give out beneath him. He gave into gravity, allowing it to pull him to the deck of the aircraft, cracking into the floor with his knees.

"Come on, asshole!"

Schwarz felt himself being lifted roughly to his feet, and he opened his eyes in a squint, moaning softly.

He was being walked to the front of the aircraft. He let his knees give out again, and his escort cursed as he fell.

The Able Team commando was thinking fast. He wasn't nearly as weak as he was making out to be. He was still in the cargo hold of the aircraft, and several men were busily reinforcing the straps on the chemical weapons containers.

He was walked to a door and leaned against the doorjamb as his caretaker opened it. He panted and swayed, his head lowered, and managed to peer around the passenger cabin they were entering. No one else was there. He allowed himself to be walked inside.

Schwarz didn't know what the situation was—how long he'd been on board the aircraft, how many men were on board with him, what his teammates knew about his situation. The only real fact he had was that he was going to get one good opportunity to make a bid for freedom, and that opportunity was right now.

The Hercules swayed slightly. Schwarz made a

frightened sound and staggered into one of the empty seats, pulling his captor along with him. His captor swore under his breath and yanked at Schwarz's shirt.

The Able Team electronics specialist had lowered himself into a stoop. In the next instant he pushed hard with his legs, propelling himself and his captor into the next aisle of seats. His captor hit the arm of the seat with a cry and fell back into the row as Schwarz yanked back, tearing his clothes out of his captor's grip. The man tumbled off the seat to the floor with a shout, and Schwarz slammed his foot into his adversary's gut. The guy's face became a twisted mask of pain.

Schwarz took a step forward and kicked his opponent in the temple. His head snapped in a half circle and his body went limp. The Able Team commando knelt quickly and began feeling with his tied hands in the man's pockets, coming up with nothing more than a set of keys and a cheap plastic lighter.

The lighter would have to do. He flicked the flame and gritted his teeth, doing his best to direct the flame into the rope that bound his hands. If he had had the time he would have tried to avoid burning his own flesh. But he did not have the time. He felt the rope and his wrists start to burn at the same time, and he flexed his arm furiously. The rope gave a little, and a streak of pain raced up his arm. His flesh screamed, and his biceps ached under the strain and the fire. Suddenly his wrists flew apart.

Schwarz grabbed at the armpit holster his former captive was wearing and came up with a 10 mm Glock 17 pistol. The clock in his head was ticking furiously. It had been less than a minute since he had entered the room with his captor. How long until the others joined them?

His time ran out. Someone opened the door at the front of the cabin, at the top of the stairs to the cockpit. The new arrival saw the legs and feet of the man stretched across the aisle. He charged down the stairs with a shout and Schwarz leveled the Glock. The charging man dived fearlessly from four steps up, knocking Schwarz's gun hand high as he fired, sending the 10 mm round into the ceiling of the cabin.

He brought his gun hand down hard, slamming it into the shoulder of his attacker, who reacted almost instantly with a blow to the ribs. Schwarz ignored it and rammed the Glock's butt across the man's skull, sending him crashing to the floor, amazingly still conscious, as the cockpit door swung open again.

The man who emerged at the top of the stairs was a giant who took up a shooter's stance without a second thought, aiming with two hands but too slow to beat Schwarz to the trigger. The Able Team commando stroked the Glock's trigger once, blasting his enemy in the face and covering the wall behind him with blood. The second round took him in the heart and sent him tumbling down the steps into the passenger cabin.

Schwarz's hand-to-hand attacker launched himself bodily from the floor. The Able Team warrior heard activity from the rear and knew his chances were getting slimmer. He fell backward, landing on the body of his original captor, and fired into his attacker as he stood above him. The figure froze, a strange look of calm taking over his fierce expression, then pitched forward. Schwarz found himself sandwiched between the two bodies. He kicked hard at the man on top of him and tried to propel himself to his feet. As he did, he saw men coming at him from the rear of the cabin. Before he could get into a standing position, the first man swung a four-foot section of two-by-four. Schwarz turned enough to take the blow on his back rather than his chest, but it pitched him into a metal seat. He staggered and leveled the Glock as he spun, only to feel and hear the crunching impact of the two-by-four slamming into his hand. The Glock flew into the far wall of the cabin, and the section of wood smacked into Schwarz's skull.

"HOLD ON, WINGS," Barbara Price said over the radio. "There's something going on."

Lyons stood behind Grimaldi, staring out over the wide horizon. As they passed over the coast and the wide Pacific Ocean filled the window of the Black Hawk, he was feeling more and more like a member of his team was lost, maybe irretrievably.

"What's up?" Grimaldi asked.

When Price didn't answer, Grimaldi waited patiently. There was nothing else he could do except keep the Black Hawk on course.

"Price here!"

"Go ahead, Base."

On the Black Hawk they heard, "I'm patching you in, Wings!"

"Patching me in to what?"

An unfamiliar voice filled the Stony Man pilot's headphones. "...I say again, we are ready to negotiate."

"Is this the pilot of the C-130H?" Price demanded.

Grimaldi gestured wildly over his head, and Lyons and Blancanales scrambled for their headphones.

"Our pilot is dead. I repeat, our pilot has just been killed."

"What about your copilot?" Price asked.

"Shot by your men before we even left the ground," the speaker replied angrily.

"What's your situation, then?" she prodded.

"We need somebody to talk us into a landing, what do you think? We've got about eight hundred pounds of explosive chemical weapons onboard."

"Exactly," Price said. "That's why we want you over the Pacific Ocean. Every minute takes you farther from human beings. You go down now, you'll only kill yourselves."

"We got your gunman, too. He'll go down with us."

"He's dead, already," Price said, exhibiting no emotion. "Not much of a bargaining chip there."

"He's alive, although we beat the crap out of him for killing the pilot."

"I don't believe you. If he's alive, put him on the radio."

There was a moment of silence on the other end. Then someone croaked out of the speaker, "Ironman, don't I have vacation time coming?"

Grimaldi laughed out loud, and Blancanales punched the air with his clenched fist. Gadgets was alive. Somehow, he was still alive. Lyons just exhaled long and low, nodding slightly.

"There you go," Schwarz's captor said. "He's still with us, but none of us on board this plane will be for long if we don't get help flying back to the mainland."

"Wings?" Price said.

"Here."

"What can you do for these guys?"

"Can you hear me, Hercules?"

"I read you."

"Listen to me if you want to get out of this mess. I'm a pilot and I have time in the C-130H."

"First we negotiate—"

"First we get you landed without killing everyone on board and spreading toxic chemicals across the West Coast of North America."

There was a moment of silence. Then, "Go ahead."

"First of all, I need to know your situation. I assume you're on autopilot or you'd have gone down a long time ago."

"I guess so."

Grimaldi described the autopilot system on the C-130H and took the readings. He then started the process of walking the man through a control deceleration of the craft, taking it to just a few miles an hour above its stall speed.

"What good is that going to do me?"

"It will give me a chance to catch up to you," Grimaldi said. "I'm in a Black Hawk helicopter about ten miles behind you. We'll be on top of you in a little while."

"And then what?"

"Then I'm coming on board. I'll fly you all back to the mainland myself."

Captain Hassan, who had been quietly enduring the operation from the copilot's seat, erupted. "What? Are you out of your mind? You expect me to transfer you to the Hercules in-flight?"

"Yeah, I do."

"No way. I'm going," Lyons said.

"You can't fly that aircraft," Grimaldi said. "I can."

"I have no intention of flying the aircraft. I intend to get on board and jettison myself and Schwarz. Then let them fall into the sea."

"No go, Able One," Price said. "The risk is too great. Number one, there are too many gunmen on board that aircraft. Getting past them and extracting Gadgets would probably be impossible. Number two, the environmental damage would be substantial should those chemicals get into the water. Plus, we might be able to get a lot of good intel from these guys once we get them on the ground."

Lyons was staring out to sea, where the tiny black dot of the Hercules was growing larger.

"That's how we're playing it," Price stated in a voice that said she would brook no further argument.

Lyons nodded.

"So what will you do when you get on board, Jack?" Blancanales asked.

"Just what I said. Fly them to the mainland. Land the Hercules safely."

"And then they'll have two hostages instead of one," Lyons pointed out.

"We'll deal with that later."

Grimaldi accelerated the Black Hawk to near its maximum, at 180 land miles per hour. The Hercules loomed closer, and Grimaldi kept in contact with the man at the controls of the large aircraft, making sure the readings stayed where they should be. Without bad weather, it might fly for hours without a pilot at the controls, until running out of fuel and plunging into the middle of the Pacific Ocean.

Grimaldi ordered the Hercules to lower its rear ramp as the Black Hawk homed in.

"Why can't you come in the side hatch?" the speaker demanded.

"No way. You know how close I'd be getting to the props when I rappelled down?" he retorted. "This isn't going to be an easy entrance, man. I need a little more margin for error. And I suggest that anybody in the rear cargo bay strap themselves in good when you open it."

The ramp on the Hercules opened a moment later, and the aircraft became erratic as its aerodynamics changed. Paper and other trash fluttered out. Grimaldi took the Black Hawk higher and slowed it to match speed with the Hercules, until it parked some ten yards above the tail of the aircraft. Then he handed the controls to Captain Hassan.

"This is crazy! I shouldn't be going along with this!" Hassan said.

"I talked to your boss and he says it's okay," Grimaldi said. He quickly moved into the troop cabin of the Black Hawk, where Blancanales was checking out a harness. Grimaldi shrugged himself into it, carefully checking all the straps and quick-release buckles. He snapped on a first-aid kit, which, under a wad of sterile, paper-wrapped bandages, included a Beretta 92-F. He buckled on a combat knife and put on a parachute, then attached the snap-on hook at the end of the winch cable. He gave Blancanales the thumbs-up.

They held on as Lyons opened the hatch and the 150 mph winds buffeted the inside of the Army helicopter. Grimaldi stepped to the open hatch and held on to the cable. The tail of the Hercules was silhouetted beneath him. He leaned back, over the rushing backdrop of the distant ocean, then he stepped into the open air and found himself dangling beneath the Black Hawk.

"Okay!" he yelled

Blancanales operated the winch, feeding out cable, and Grimaldi descended beneath the helicopter, the wind rushing around him. He hit a patch of errant air and found himself swinging momentarily like a swatted piñata. He watched the tail of the C-130H sweep erratically under him and shouted into his headset microphone. Above him, Blancanales stopped the winch.

"You okay down there, Wings?" Hassan asked.

"Just some bad air." He rode it out for another few seconds until the air became steadier. "Okay. Go, Pol."

The winch started again, and Grimaldi descended behind the C-130H, finding himself swinging wildly as he entered the slipstream of the aircraft.

"Hold it there," he called out as he found himself level with the entrance ramp to the aircraft. The winch stopped. Grimaldi could see the interior of the cargo bay.

"Okay, Captain, maneuver me in," he radioed.

"All right. Watch your head."

The Black Hawk accelerated easily, carrying Grimaldi closer to the rear of the C-130H, and he called out instructions over the radio. Hassan proved to be highly skilled at the controls of his aircraft, which the Stony Man pilot highly appreciated. A pilot with a heavy hand might easily have sent him crashing into some part of the Hercules. As it was, the erratic swaying in the high winds and changing slipstream made it tough enough to close in, a situation exacerbated by the design of the Hercules, with its tail extending farther than the ramp he was attempting to get onto. Grimaldi instructed Hassan to lower him to directly behind the ramp, then move the Black Hawk ahead so that the cable was flush against the tail of the aircraft.

"Okay, Pol, give me a little more slack," Grimaldi radioed.

He allowed Blancanales to feed out another five feet of cable before he called for a stop. He was swinging several feet behind and below the distended ramp.

"Okay, now swing me in, Captain," he radioed. And then he prepared for impact.

Hassan slowed the Black Hawk slightly, carrying Grimaldi away from the ramp, then accelerated quickly. Grimaldi flew at the rear end of the C-130H and the cable hit the rear wing. The Stony Man pilot continued to swing forward under his own momentum and found himself careening wildly toward the distended ramp. He spotted a handhold and made a quick grab for it as he sailed within a foot of the ramp. As his momentum gave out, he felt his full weight suddenly on his one hand and his body dangled below the ramp.

"Slack, Pol!" he shouted.

The cable fed out behind him as he slapped at the ramp, another handhold falling into his free hand, and he dragged himself over the edge. He scrambled onto the ramp and lay there spread-eagle for a moment, getting his bearings, then crawled forward out of the tearing wind into the rear cargo hold of the Hercules.

"I'm in," he radioed.

The Pollari team had wisely vacated the cabin, and it contained nothing but the large stack of cargo. Grimaldi examined it carefully, finding that the stack of chemical containers had been tightly secured to a pallet of two-by-four wood beams. It had been virtually cocooned inside a webbing of tight nylon strapping, and was lashed to the floor using at least ten heavy-duty cargo straps.

The idea snapped into Grimaldi's head in an instant and he radioed, "More slack."

"You okay, Wings?" Lyons asked.

"Yeah. Prepare to extract cargo, Captain."

"You kidding me?" Hassan demanded.

"What, me kid?" He made quick work of unhooking the cable and threading it through the webbing in the deadly cargo. He tied it in three places, then hooked the end of the cable to itself, making quick work of sawing at the cargo straps with his fighting knife. In a minute the eight hundred pounds of chemical weapons were sitting without restraint in the rear of the hold.

"Bring it up, Pol," he radioed.

The draping cable slowly straightened and drew tight, then the pallet of weapons tilted off the floor and was dragged to the rear of the aircraft. Grimaldi held on to the rail in the wall and prayed the bad guys had at least gone to the trouble of building weapons that held their integrity prior to deployment. If even one of those casings broke open now...

The Hercules lurched and descended suddenly and the nylon-wrapped pallet popped out of the rear of the aircraft and disappeared. Grimaldi gripped the rail as the aircraft righted itself—but not enough. It was descending.

"Wings!"

"Did you get it?"

"We've got it, but what's going on down there?"

"I don't know. Something's wrong with the aircraft.

I think we might have damaged the rear stabilizer with the cable.''

"I think you're right," Hassan radioed. "I'm behind you now. It looks a little out of whack. I suggest you do something about it."

"Good idea," Grimaldi replied. He was already dragging himself to the door to the passenger cabin, and his fist slammed into the large red ramp button as soon as it was within reach. No matter what the problem was, the aircraft would be easier to control with the ramp shut.

Four men craned their necks as he entered the passenger cabin. "What the hell is going on?" the closest man demanded, jumping to his feet and waving a handgun. Grimaldi had the distinct and unsettling feeling of having entered a lion's den.

"I don't know," he retorted, grabbing on to the seats as he made his way to the cockpit, past a row in which a pair of corpses had been unceremoniously dumped. The face he was looking for most eagerly was nowhere in the cabin.

Clambering up the steps, he yanked at the cockpit door and a man turned to face him, leveling a Browning .380. Grimaldi raised his hands. "I'm the pilot," he declared.

"We're losing control!" the man exclaimed.

"I noticed."

Grimaldi had also noticed Schwarz, propped like a rag doll against the wall, eyes open but unfocused. He looked up at Grimaldi and squinted. "Snafu," he forced out. A large bloody streak covered his jaw.

"I see that. Hang on, there, Gadgets."

Grimaldi took the pilot's seat and scanned the mass of analog meters. The plane was descending steadily, not at an alarming rate, but what was alarming was that it shouldn't be descending at all.

"What's the deal?" the gunman demanded.

"Give me a minute."

Grimaldi disabled the automatic pilot and wrestled to get better control of the Hercules. He fed more fuel to the Alisson turboprops and wrestled for height.

"You're pulling away from us, Jack," Lyons said.

"This bird is broken," Grimaldi answered. "The only way I'm going to stay out of the water is by overcompensating. I'm going to have to ride high back to the mainland."

He felt the headphones get torn from his head. "We're not going back to the mainland," the gunner with the Browning declared.

"You've got no choice," Grimaldi declared. "In case you haven't noticed, your transportation isn't working up to snuff." He reengaged the autopilot and watched the controls long enough to see that the craft was more or less stable, starting into a slow descent. He had some time to play with and jumped out of his seat.

"Where the hell are you going?"

"To help my friend," Grimaldi declared, kneeling at Schwarz's side and opening the kit bearing the large red cross. He pulled out a wad of bandage and ripped it open.

"We don't have time for this shit! Get back in the pilot's seat," the gunner ordered.

"I'm not flying anywhere until my friend is out of danger of bleeding to death," the pilot answered. He looked the gunman in the face. "It won't take long unless I have to sit here arguing about it with you."

The door at the rear of the cockpit opened. "Frank! He dumped the cargo!"

Frank plainly didn't believe what he'd heard. "What?"

"It's gone! He dumped it!"

Grimaldi extracted the Beretta 92-F from the first-aid kit as Frank turned on him again. "You mother-fuck—"

He made the mistake of bringing his Browning into play. Whether he would have actually made use of it on the only person who could fly the plane was a question Grimaldi didn't wait to have answered. He stroked the Beretta and fired a pair of rounds into the gunner's gut, cutting short his last eloquent statement. The second man raised his own handgun to cover himself and another pair of 9 mm rounds drilled into him, sending him staggering two steps back. He suddenly found himself on the stairs and his arms flew up to retrieve his balance, but he tumbled down the steps and out of sight.

Grimaldi reached out with his foot and kicked shut the cockpit door, and an instant later a series of gunshots sounded behind it. The rounds slammed into the door, three of them cutting through it and burying in the ceiling.

"What now?" Schwarz asked, his brow creased as he tried to think clearly. Grimaldi knew he no longer had the luxury of time to bandage the cut on the side of Schwarz's face. He just hoped Gadgets wasn't as bad off as he looked.

"We're leaving."

"Door's downstairs," Schwarz said through gritted teeth.

Schwarz was right about that. The side hatch for

passengers was in the passenger cabin below. Another series of rounds slammed into the cockpit door. Grimaldi crawled to the door and reached for the latch. The lock was a simple bolt, which he threw. Lot of good that was going to do them. He withdrew his hand quickly when more rounds slammed into the panel at a lower level, one piercing the metal. Locked or not, that door wasn't going to buy them much time.

He yanked at the small closet and extracted an emergency parachute, then returned to Schwarz and said, "We'll take the window."

The Able Team commando looked incredulous through his pain and shock. "Sure. Whatever."

Grimaldi grabbed at the headset and jammed it on his neck, then rolled on his back and aimed his Beretta at the left side window, triggering it until the magazine was emptied. The glass shattered into opaqueness. He snatched up the first-aid kit and used it to push the shattered glass out of the frame, then changed the mag in the Beretta.

The Stony Man pilot aimed at the cockpit door and fired 9 mm rounds into it until the magazine ran dry again. He had no hope of actually hitting any of the players downstairs. He was just buying precious time.

Schwarz looked at the ragged piece of scored and tattered metal that had once been the door and said, "You killed it."

"Come on." Grimaldi grabbed him by the arm and dragged him to his feet. Schwarz's brow became a mass of wrinkles as the pain screamed through his body from multiple injuries, but he made no sound as Grimaldi pulled the emergency chute harness over his arms and secured the straps tightly around his chest and abdomen. Grimaldi pushed him to the window.

The wind was billowing in at hurricane volume, which still couldn't muffle the roar of the massive Alisson turboprops.

"How are you expecting us to avoid those?" Schwarz called over the noise. "We'll be sliced and diced."

"Easy!" Grimaldi said. His hands moved quickly over the controls. There was a moment when nothing happened, then the engine sputtered. The whirling disks turned into individual rotors that sputtered and spun to a sudden stop.

"Problem solved!" Grimaldi shouted.

The two props on the other side of the aircraft continued to run. "They'll keep this thing in the air for a while," Grimaldi said. "You first."

Schwarz mustered his strength and stood on the pilot's seat. Grimaldi was changing the mag on the Beretta again and fired at the door as the passengers below saw the engines die and got desperate. They fired another barrage into the cockpit door, which swung open limply. Two men on the stairs were approaching—a suicide run, but maybe they knew they had nothing to lose at this stage, and maybe their lives to gain. Grimaldi fired three rounds, then pulled into the area behind the pilot's seat as they returned fire.

"You need help?" Schwarz called, stooping in the open window.

"Go!" Grimaldi gave him a shove. The pilot was a stronger man than his appearance belied, and he managed to eject Schwarz through the opening. Suddenly he was alone in the cockpit.

The Hercules gave a strange lurch and leaned on its side. The readouts were fluctuating. Grimaldi knew the autopilot wasn't able to compensate for two switched-off engines and the rear-end damage. Now, he determined, would be an excellent time to leave.

He stepped into the open again and triggered a burst at the man who was charging up the steps. Three rounds punched into his chest and sent him falling on top of the man behind him.

Grimaldi knew it was now or never, and he jumped on the pilot's seat and forced himself out the window. For a moment the wing loomed up over him, threatening to smash into him with the subtlety of a two hundred-mph brick wall, then it was gone and he was in open free fall. He tumbled end over end before spreading his limbs and establishing a controlled descent, the ocean racing at him at a furious pace. It was a low dive to start with. He yanked the cord the first moment he was able and the chute deployed in time to slow his descent to a steady plummet.

He crashed into the Pacific Ocean. The impact shocked his system, sending white bolts of lightning through his head, and all he could see was the foaming chaos of the ocean. He couldn't even tell which direction was up. Somehow he managed to detach the sodden mass of the chute and claw his way to the surface, gasping for air.

Schwarz! He was struggling inside his chute a hundred yards away, as if being attacked by a massive jellyfish. In his battered, weakened state, his movement seemed slow and drunken.

Grimaldi propelled himself through the five-foot waves as rapidly as he was able, pausing just long enough to rid himself of his boots, his gun and the first-aid kit. The only tool he kept was the fighting knife, and as he reached Schwarz he grabbed the slimy chute material and sliced into it. Within a minute he was able to cut and tear the material off him.

Schwarz sputtered and coughed up seawater.

"Check it out," he said weakly.

He was watching the Hercules, which had tilted on its side and was descending in a long, graceful arc that was miles long. Grimaldi couldn't tear his eyes from the sad spectacle of the aircraft's death. When its wing sliced into the water, its smooth flight disintegrated, bathed in fire. The remaining skeleton, twisted and smoking, flopped into the surface of the sea and sank in seconds.

By the time they had seen the last of it disappear beneath the waves, the Army Black Hawk helicopter was raising a maelstrom as it descended over them.

CHAPTER TEN

Heydar, Azerbaijan

The Land Rover Discovery XD wasn't a common sight in the coastal regions north of Baku, but the drab olive paint job helped it blend with the battered rattletraps that wheezed and lumbered in the streets. As it cruised onto the highway, it accelerated to a speed that allowed it to easily pass the rest of the traffic, mostly Communist-era automobiles.

Maybe some of the people of Azerbaijan looked back on the years of Soviet control as the good old days. Certainly there had been more security for the people then. And less war. The Russians had more or less kept the factions from fighting. Now there was nothing to stop the Nagorno-Karabakh separatists, and for years the nation had been practically split in two.

The man driving at the wheel of the Land Rover didn't know or care about the politics in this land. He made a deliberate attempt to remove himself from the endless verbal warfare of the ideologues, the politicians and the moralists.

Not that he didn't have a very sharply defined philosophy or moral code of his own. In fact, it was all he allowed to guide his actions, when push came to shove.

And in his world, the pushing and shoving were constant.

He steered the Land Rover onto a side road that appeared out of nowhere, and followed it for another mile in a northwest direction, moving farther from the Caspian Sea coast. But he could feel the Caspian pollution in the air, could even taste it.

He knew what he was smelling wasn't the lingering residue of the chemicals. If they remained in concentrations enough to smell, he would be dead.

He knew he was getting close and spotted the dirt highway he was looking for—the road to Heydar. At the edge of town a young Air Force MP, pale and wide-eyed, brought the Land Rover to a halt, looked at the ID that was presented to him and waved the vehicle through.

The Land Rover came to a halt at the outskirts of the chaos that just eighteen hours ago had been a peaceful Azerbaijani village. The driver stepped out of the four-wheel-drive and looked at the carnage.

Mack Bolan had seen death before, more death than he cared to look back on, but this was shocking even to him.

Heydar had been the last of three major hits that occurred in the middle of the night in the vicinity of Azerbaijan. The first had been the Caspian Sea attack on the *Tuscany II,* the next in the village of Irkuk, thirty miles from Heydar. At least thirty bodies lay on stretchers covered in bright orange plastic tarps on one side of the village square. The Air Force had just begun its work of clearing the area. Bolan could still see figures slumped in windows, in cars, against walls.

A young airman came out of a nearby building with a video camera and set it up a few paces from Bolan's vehicle. He glanced at Bolan curiously, surprised to see a civilian on the premises.

"Why does the Air Force think it's necessary to take video footage of this tragedy?" Bolan asked.

The airman had haunted eyes. "It's news," he said with a shrug. "The ulterior motive is to prove to the world that the U.S. military isn't at fault. Maybe you didn't hear there was a theft of chemical weapons from a base in Maryland yesterday."

"There wasn't enough time to get those materials here for these attacks," Bolan said.

The airman nodded. "I know that. You know that. The trouble is convincing the people of the world of that." The airman finished his adjustment and flipped a switch on his camera, then crossed to Bolan, extending a hand. "John Samuels. I'm a reporter for Armed Forces TV and radio out of Frankfurt."

"You're not with CBIRF?"

The airman shrugged and grimaced. "I just happened to do a half-hour feature for the news on the Chemical-Biological Incident Response Force a few months ago, which included some training with them. So when they got the call to come here and were ordered to bring along a videographer, I was elected."

"What's the situation?"

"Under control," Samuels said wearily. "There's no danger now. They used hydrogen cyanide with a gaseous cloud dispersion method. There was very little ground contamination. So it evaporated pretty quick, I guess. That didn't help these people."

"How many?"

"Still counting. No survivors if that's what you're

asking. There was no wind until 6:00 a.m. The cloud just sat here."

Bolan nodded and went to find his contact. Air Force Colonel Arnold Rail knew who he was before he presented his Belasko ID. He nodded to Bolan and ushered him into the kitchen, where the night before a villager had eaten his dinner and then died.

"Damn peculiar, my having to cooperate with one of you guys like this," Rail said. "But I'm not complaining. If the Company can track down the filth that perpetrated this..." Words failed him.

Bolan didn't bother to correct Rail's assumption that he was with the Central Intelligence Agency. He got straight to the point. "Found anything useful yet, Colonel?"

Rail shook his head as if in a daze. "No. Not a damn thing. Just a bunch of old Iraqi canisters of hydrogen cyanide and what's left of these spray devices. I doubt what's left of them will tell us anything, certainly not in the short-term. All but one of them blew themselves up. Maybe when that last unit is dismantled and analyzed..."

Bolan nodded. He had feared as much.

"My guys aren't supposed to be doing this job," the colonel said, suddenly looking Bolan straight in the eye. "They have a strategic mission—consequence management and force protection. And they have an operational mission—to turn victims into patients. They're not supposed to be goddamn coroners. Any grunt can tag a bunch of bodies."

Bolan nodded. "Thanks anyway, Colonel."

He walked back to the Land Rover and couldn't help but notice that the rows of bodies in the square had grown by ten in just a few minutes.

Samuels was running the camera without looking through the viewfinder. He was staring away into the distance, out over the scrub-covered, arid land that made up much of the Azerbaijani topography. But he really wasn't looking at anything. Just away.

Astara, Azerbaijan

A SIGN WAS POSTED on the side of the road, in Azeri, and it was so faded that even had he been literate in the language Bolan probably wouldn't have been able to decipher it. It didn't matter. He knew where he was.

He was at the starting point.

A new game was beginning.

At least, this was where he entered the game, a hostile player, for sure, and a contestant that the other players didn't know about and wouldn't welcome if they had known about him.

He didn't care about the other players. In fact, he was determined to beat them so badly they would never play again.

All he cared about was the stakes, which were high. They were counted in hundreds of innocent lives. As far as the Executioner was concerned, he had already been cheated out of some of his rightful winnings. The other players would pay for that.

He stopped the car in the middle of the decrepit village on the north coast of Azerbaijan and trod across the rocky ground to a shack made of ribbed pieces of aluminum. The old paint was so weathered it was almost impossible to read the decade-old pro-Communist message that had once been emblazoned there. The door was chipped, battered, unfinished pressboard with only a dirty, rude round hole where the knob should have been.

The Executioner nudged it open with his foot and walked into the tavern, and the five men slumped at the wooden tables looked away from his piercing blue eyes. They muttered, quietly, to themselves and each other.

Bolan stopped in the middle of the bar and spoke loud enough for everyone present to hear him. "I'm looking for Ali Hajiyev."

The man behind the short counter never met his eyes, just shook his head slightly and turned back to the man he was conversing with.

Bolan had been thinking hard during his flight from Lipetsk, Russia, considering the enemy he was up against. He had thought about the cowardly murders of all the innocent people in the poor, small villages. He wasn't going to let another catastrophe like that be perpetrated.

Which meant he had to move quickly and decisively. The last thing he had the time or patience for was uncooperative locals.

He withdrew the mini-Uzi from inside his black bomber jacket and squeezed the trigger, firing 9 mm slugs into the corroding steel ceiling and creating an echoing racket that seemed to go on and on. The patrons jumped and pushed and fell away, grabbing at their heads to protect themselves from the onslaught of noise. The bartender held his head as if trying to squeeze his own brains out, and he was shouting, but his voice couldn't be heard until the magazine cycled dry.

"—nough! Enough!"

Bolan asked again, "I'm looking for Ali Hajiyev." This time he got the answer he wanted.

BOLAN HAD ARRIVED in Azerbaijan on a flight chartered for him by Stony Man Farm within an hour after the first reports started rolling in. His business in Lipetsk was far from finished, but there was also far less need for immediacy.

Alexander Akhmedov and his drugs-and-guns smuggling operation weren't going anywhere. Bolan treated any call for help from Stony Man Farm with the utmost seriousness.

All those people. Innocent families. And the horrible agony of chemical death. Bolan had watched it occur in the deserts of Egypt and elsewhere. It wasn't a death he would wish on anyone. He would do what he could to prevent the use of more chemical weapons against innocent human beings.

Still, he had arrived in Azerbaijan with almost no place to start.

Then he had received word from the Baku airport flight control via Stony Man Farm intelligence-gathering resources about a mysterious blip that had appeared over their traffic control radar for a few minutes in the middle of the night. It might have been the helicopter that attacked the *Tuscany II*. It appeared to be landing in Azerbaijan, near the coast. The landing point was just outside a village called Agstafa.

Bolan didn't have what could be termed a wealth of contacts in Azerbaijan, but it turned out that Hal Brognola could put him in touch with an internal security man. And that man gave Bolan a name.

"If there is activity in Agstafa," he told Bolan, "then Ali Hajiyev knows all about it. He's a petty crook, but inside Agstafa he's like a king."

It was an old story. The petty crook shared his wealth with the local civilians, and they swallowed their pride and their sense of decency to play fawn to the petty crook.

Bolan didn't care about the locals. He really didn't even care about Ali Hajiyev. But his instinct told him he was at the start of the trail that would lead him to the people he did care about—the people who were willing and able to inflict chemical death on villages full of innocent people.

At the edge of the town the ground swept down a long incline, and in the sparsely vegetated valley below was a building that had the look of a barn. Nearby was a house, large by the standards of the village, or by any standards in the ex-Communist satellite nation. A pair of aged BMWs sat in front of the house, and a figure with an AK-47 who had been idly patrolling the front of the house had stopped and was watching Bolan approach.

The soldier slowed the Land Rover and parked it between the house and the large barnlike structure that stood nearby. The purpose of such a structure was hard to fathom. There was no evidence of crops being grown nearby, or of any livestock. He yanked on the emergency brake and stepped out of the vehicle, giving the guard a slight wave.

The guard spoke sharply in Azeri.

"Speak English?" Bolan asked.

"A little."

"Is Ali Hajiyev here?"

"He is not home now."

"Okay. I just need to take a look in the barn."

Bolan started for the building as if it were the most normal thing in the world.

"Stop. Who are you?" The guard jogged up behind him.

The Executioner turned suddenly and disarmed the guard with a swift chop, then grabbed his empty hand and twisted it behind his back with a lightning-fast move that snapped the bone. The guard started to scream, but suddenly his feet were swept from under him and he was propelled to the ground at a tremendous rate. He slammed facefirst in the hard-packed soil and lay still.

The guard was still breathing but he wasn't going anywhere soon, and behind the Land Rover he was out of view of anybody in the house. Unless the altercation had been witnessed, Bolan guessed he had a few minutes before reinforcements arrived.

He stepped quickly to the wide double doors to the barn and pulled at them, finding them immobile. A smaller entrance nearby was locked as well, and he thought he heard voices.

The soldier knocked.

He heard the sound of chairs scraping the floor, then a figure opened the door slightly. Hajiyev didn't train his men well, Bolan decided. He had ripped the door out of the man's grip and cracked his skull against the steel doorframe before the man had finished demanding to know who the hell he was. Another man heard the impact, said the unconscious man's name and came to investigate. As Bolan stepped inside, the man came out of the gloomy darkness of the interior with a furrowed brow. He stopped cold when he faced the menacing Beretta 93-R in the Executioner's grip.

The soldier said nothing, but the slight movement of the muzzle of the automatic handgun told the man to put his hands in the air and back up.

The man complied and, as his eyes adjusted to the dim illumination from a pair of grimy skylights, the Executioner saw that the barn didn't house a Russian-built helicopter. It did, however, contain a large number of palleted cotton sacks, tightly bound and unlabeled.

He moved sideways, the determination in his gaze telling his prisoner no good opportunity for a sneaky move was forthcoming. With his free hand he withdrew a thin stiletto from its sheath on his calf and chopped at one of the cotton sacks. The stiletto came out covered with white powder. Bolan shook off most of it, then touched the blade to his tongue, quickly spitting out the residue. It was uncut heroin, thousands of dollars' worth on the streets in the U.S. Bolan didn't know or care what its value was in Azerbaijani *manats*. He knew the true cost of the drugs, in these quantities, could be measured in many lives.

Still, it wasn't what he had come for.

"Where's the helicopter?"

"What helicopter?"

"You tell me where the helicopter is, or I'll kill you right now."

The man looked troubled, and his eyes moved wildly as if searching for a way to save himself. "It is not here," he said finally.

"Very helpful—"

There was a shout from outside the barn. Bolan's prisoner cried for help in his native tongue and bolted for the door. The soldier tracked him as he ran and allowed him to yank open the door, then triggered the Beretta 93-R. The big handgun fired three 9 mm Parabellum manglers that cut the prisoner down in the doorway. As the corpse toppled, Bolan was sighting his next target. Two surprised-looking gunners stood over the first downed guard, and two more were heading for the barn. They didn't react fast enough at the appearance of their shot comrade, and when he went down another tri-burst rocketed into their midst, taking them both out of play.

Bolan withdrew into darkness as the other two gunners came to their senses and moved out of his line of sight. If they wanted him, they would have to come and get him.

Although the barn was cleared out in the middle where the Russian gunship might have been hangared, it also contained the remains of several ancient cars and rows of barrels of oil and fuel. Bolan chose a hiding place among the corroded machinery. He didn't want those barrels getting blown up with him in the vicinity.

Crouching in the darkness, he waited for his pursuers. The gunners outside would get impatient before the jungle-trained soldier did. As it was, he didn't have to wait long at all.

They came to the door, and he heard them whispering as they checked the collapsed figures at the entrance for signs of life. Then they stepped inside, sweeping the dark interior with their Kalashnikovs. Bolan allowed them to move inside and separate. One of the men closed in on the Executioner without even realizing it.

The gunner peered between the barrels and peeked into the obvious hiding places, but was getting more nervous as he realized the vulnerability of his position. He stepped away from the rows of barrels, eyes wide, as if convinced his opponent was waiting for him there. As it was, he nearly backed into Bolan's arms.

The soldier stood, as silent as a shadow in the darkness, and withdrew a garrote from its place on his web belt. The lethal instrument, made up of nothing more than piano wire and a pair of wooden handles, weighed just a few ounces and, in the right hands, killed silently.

The Executioner looped the wire over the gunner's head and pulled hard to cut off his croak of surprise, then twisted the handles with merciless speed. The wire bit through the skin and embedded in the flesh. By the time Bolan lowered the gunner to the floor it was impossible to say if strangulation or loss of blood from the massive wound had killed him.

The other searcher called the dead man's name, then repeated it seconds later. When there was no answer he shouted it a third time, frantically, and raced for the door. Bolan had only to aim at the well-lit entrance and await his target's arrival. As soon as the man entered the doorway, the soldier fired another tri-burst from the 93-R, driving the newcomer to the floor.

The Executioner grabbed the unconscious guard in the doorway and dragged him outside, flopping him on the ground beside the first guard, the one with the broken arm. Securing them both with plastic cuffs at their wrists and ankles, Bolan entered the house and performed a quick search, finding nothing helpful.

He was quite sure none of them he had faced was Ali Hajiyev, which meant the man might be returning with reinforcements at any moment.

He jogged back to the barn and located a crowbar, then opened and tipped four of the fuel barrels, soaking the floor of the barn. He found a smaller canister of oil and used it to wet the pallets of heroin.

By the time he reached the Land Rover, the prisoner

with the broken arm was moaning and begging to be turned on his back.

"I need you to tell me who Ali Hajiyev is mixed up with," Bolan demanded.

"I do not know what you mean," the prisoner sobbed. His left eye was swollen shut and blinded with blood; his right eye was wide and wild.

"What about the helicopter. Where is it?"

"The helicopter! Yes! It is in Samkir!"

"Will you show me where Samkir is?"

The idea of accompanying Bolan didn't seem to appeal to the prisoner.

"Or you can stay here with the others. In the barn. When I burn it."

"I will show you where the helicopter is."

CHAPTER ELEVEN

Samkir, Azerbaijan

The guard's name was Osman.

About an hour after becoming acquainted with the Executioner, Osman was wishing he had never been born.

He had been hauled to his bound feet and pushed into the passenger seat of the Land Rover, where he was belted in. Tightly. His wrists were still in the plastic cuffs behind his back, which meant they were being crushed by his body. He couldn't sit straight, and the position was the worst possible one in terms of coddling his broken arm—whenever he leaned back slightly on the arm it seemed to pull at the broken section of bone and send pulses of pain rippling through his entire side.

All these factors were compounded by the less-than-smooth roadways of backwater Azerbaijan.

Osman leaned into the corner between the seat and the door, which gave his arm some relief, and kept him as far away as possible from the American at the wheel of the vehicle.

He'd never met or heard of a man so thoroughly efficient at murder that he could quietly kill all the men at Ali Hajiyev's estate and set fire to the barn and the house without hesitation. He left just one guard alive in the entire place—and that guard had still been unconscious in the dirt when they left the village.

How Osman wished he was that guard.

Because he was certain this quiet, dark American would kill him soon.

An hour passed on the road to Samkir. The American didn't say a word after getting directions to the place. The tension in the Land Rover became unbearably thick.

Then the shock wore off and the real pain came. The Land Rover slammed through a crater in the road and Osman, despite his best efforts at self-control, squeaked in pain.

"Is that it?"

Osman was now blind in one eye, and it took considerable effort to get his uninjured eye to focus. Was he losing his sight in the right, as well? Then the distant buildings came into focus.

"That is Samkir," he managed to say.

"The hangar?"

"It is on the north side of the village. You will see the trucks."

"And the hangar belongs to—?"

"I told you again and again I do not know. I came here just once to see the helicopter."

Bolan drove on, going off-road on the bare, rocky soil to give the village a wide berth and circle around its north side. Soon the large building he knew was the hangar swung into view.

The wounded guard had managed to stutter out most of the story as he knew it. Ali Hajiyev had been contracted to play a part in the attack on the *Tuscany II*.

His payment was a substantial shipment of heroin, to distribute as he saw fit—the heroin that was now reduced to ashes in Agstafa, courtesy of Bolan. Hajiyev's only responsibility in the operation was to allow his storage building to serve temporarily as a staging point for the helicopter.

The Russian helicopter had been trucked into Agstafa and readied for flight inside the barn. It wasn't launched until after dark, and it returned before dawn. By the time the sun rose over the grimy Caspian the gunship had been reloaded onto the truck trailer, covered and trucked out of the village. It had never been flown over land; it couldn't have been seen by any Azerbaijanis.

Bolan parked the Land Rover a couple of miles from Samkir.

"Get out."

Osman thought that the time had come to die.

The Executioner stood at the front of the Land Rover and examined the small town through field glasses, which brought the hangar close enough to see that there were no more than a couple of guards stationed within view. They were on the east side of the building, standing at the wide front entrance. The north side was long, featureless.

The cuffed guard was straining to maneuver his hands so that he could open the door, but he wasn't succeeding. Bolan yanked it open and the guard tumbled out.

Bolan slammed the door and drew his fighting knife, and Osman screamed. The soldier chopped at the guard's ankle cuffs, severing them, and got back into the Land Rover, driving another few hundred yards to bring the west end of the hangar into sight, then stopped and examined it through the binoculars. Another pair of guards leaned against the wide aircraft doors. Bolan could clearly see the large padlocks.

The only way to approach was directly from the north, trying to keep himself out of the sight of the guards. Approaching in the vehicle was out of the question. He'd be heard and seen long before he reached the hangar. And he had long-ago dismissed the notion of driving through the small town and hoping he wasn't noticed.

His only option was to approach on foot and stay out of sight as long as possible. He knew, also, that it would be wise to wait for nightfall so the dark could hide his approach.

He simply didn't have that kind of time.

To his left he spotted Osman stagger to his feet and walk a half-dozen paces before collapsing.

A new strategy materialized in the soldier's brain.

He quickly opened the rear of the Land Rover and unloaded the substantial hardware he'd been provided, via Stony Man Farm contacts, upon arrival in Astara. He took just what he needed and stowed the rest in a shallow ditch surrounded by low scrub. He left the rear window open. Next he wrenched off the rearview mirrors and two side mirrors of the Land Rover and flung them away. Finally, he turned up the radio loud.

Then he drove back to the wounded guard, who was sobbing in pain against the hard earth.

"Get in. I'm giving you the vehicle. You can drive into town."

Osman twisted his head to stare at the jaundiced sky and the dark, malevolent figure standing over him. "No more torture. Just kill me and be done with it."

"I'm not going to kill you. What I want is not here.

I'm leaving. You can use the vehicle to get back to town and get some medical attention.''

"Where will you go?''

"I'm going to be picked up right here—'' he glanced at his watch and looked at the sky "—in about half an hour.''

Osman rolled onto his stomach and pushed against the ground with his upper body but was unable to muster the strength to get to his feet until the Executioner grabbed him by the belt and hauled him up. Then he drew a large fighting knife and quickly severed the plastic cuffs on Osman's wrists. His broken right arm hung limply. Bolan pressed the keys into his left hand.

As Osman got into the driver's seat, he watched the soldier walk away. He didn't trust that man. Not for a minute. Maybe the Land Rover had been rigged to explode....

But there was little chance he was getting back to the village on foot, not in the weakened, pain-filled state he was in. He really had no choice.

Pressing the clutch to the floor, he reached through the steering wheel and twisted the key. The Discovery XD's 4.0-liter, V8 engine hummed to life. The radio was squawking with a newscast from an AM station out of Astara. It was an even longer reach to shift into first gear, then slowly he released the clutch. Maybe that would be the move that triggered the bomb.

But nothing out of the ordinary happened. The Land Rover moved forward slowly, bouncing gently in a depression. The pain rocketed through Osman and he eased upon the gas a little. Nice and slow would be just fine. He'd just cruise into the village in first gear. It still beat walking. He wished he could reach the radio to turn it off, and he noticed that the mirrors were gone, which struck him as odd. But he was simply too relieved to care.

He had escaped the American killer for sure.

BOLAN WALKED until he was sure he was out of Osman's field of vision, then cut to the left and circled in a jog directly behind the Land Rover as it moved. Grabbing the rear window opening, he stepped onto the rear bumper, taking care to keep the automatic rifle on his shoulder from banging against anything, and he kept a close eye on the back of Osman's head. The driver couldn't have seen him unless he turned his head all the way around, and any noise Bolan had made was masked by the radio. He adjusted his feet. It was a tenuous position at best, but he could hold on for a few minutes, which was all he needed.

He watched the hangar come closer. Osman was driving directly at it, and the guards at the east end were clearly in view. They noticed the approaching vehicle and watched it curiously. Surely they had to have thought it odd to see the vehicle coming out of the middle of nowhere at just a couple of miles an hour.

The Land Rover drove past another low clump of shrubs in a depression, and Bolan dropped from the back of the vehicle, landing flat on the ground and crabbing behind the shrubs. He wasn't as close as he would have liked to be, but he was as close as he dared. The guards didn't exhibit any alarm, which told him he was still unnoticed.

He'd announce his presence soon enough.

The guards had their guns ready when the Land Rover came into the bare grounds around the hangar and braked to a slow stop, but their aggressive stance disappeared as Osman got out of the vehicle and slumped against the hood. One of the guards shouted at the nearby building, and more men emerged. Bolan saw the men peering into the distance, at the spot where Osman had left him.

In minutes a pair of topless military-style jeeps were pulled to the front of the hangar and men jumped in, three in one vehicle and four in another. To the last man they carried AK-47s. The jeeps rushed into scrub land, and Bolan burrowed into the shrubs as they passed within ten yards of his hiding place, but they never even glanced in his direction.

Osman was being helped into the nearby house by one of the guards. The second guard had gone with the jeeps. The front of the hangar was suddenly emptied.

Time to move.

Bolan got to his feet and sprinted for the hangar, fully cognizant that a stray backward glance by one of the gunners in the jeeps or a quick look out the window by someone in the house would blow his clandestine approach.

He reached the hangar and pressed his back against the blank north side, now hidden from the building but in plain view of the jeeps. They soon would be reaching the point where Osman had left him. They'd be getting out and looking around. They'd see him then, he was certain. He estimated that he had less than a minute to get into hiding.

He moved east to the front of the hangar, leading the way with the suppressed Beretta 93-R. The area was still empty, and he bolted across the open ground to the low building.

The front door opened and the guard who had helped Osman emerged. He halted abruptly as the door slammed behind him, making a grab for the Kalashnikov slung on his shoulder. The 93-R coughed discreetly, and Bolan allowed the natural rise of the triburst to drive up his aim, so that the rounds took the guard in the stomach, chest and face, and he went down silently.

The Executioner grabbed the door and yanked it open, finding himself in a small, richly appointed vestibule, a stark contrast to the dismal exterior. The floor was shellacked flagstone, the walls gleaming, hand-painted porcelain panels. A hand-knotted runner stretched for almost twenty feet, and a marble fountain glistened in the corner. The sun, shining through the expansive skylights, seemed brighter than the daylight outside.

Bolan followed voices up the stone stairs and came to a series of rooms separated by wood-framed rattan walls, colored a rich burnt purple that seemed to give the place a quiet, cool atmosphere.

Time to heat it up.

He tracked the voices to a room where Osman was stretched out on a long, low cot. A guard was splinting his arm with a piece of wood, and a well-dressed Azerbaijani man with a heavy black mustache was leaning over him, speaking urgently. He did an almost comical double take when Bolan entered, and he grabbed for his pistol in a shoulder holster. The 93-R, now set at single-shot mode, sent a 9 mm subsonic round into his arm, followed by another to his lower rib cage. The gunner flopped over the cot, then fell to the floor, and the medic made his move, grabbing for the AK-47 he had leaned against the wall. A single round crashed into his skull, and the medic dropped hard and didn't move again.

The first downed gunner was still conscious, and still trying to get at the gun under his left shoulder. Bolan snap-kicked his hand. The gunner grunted and his head hit the floor, eyes staring wide at the ceiling, unable to vocalize his agony.

Bolan emptied the shoulder holster himself, tossing the pistol into the corner and kicking the AK-47 after it. He grabbed the wounded gunner by the collar and dragged his upper body a few inches off the floor.

"You're going to answer some questions."

The man was in a Western-style suit coat and jacket with an open collar. But the jacket was stained and rumpled as if it hadn't been cleaned in months. The shirt had been white when new, which was long ago. It was now dingy, threadbare in patches and stained. Still, none of the other men Bolan had observed in the compound were dressed with an illusion of formality. This man had to be someone of importance.

But he wasn't in a talking mood. He rolled his eyes at Bolan and tried to spit. The 93-R cracked into his cheekbone and spittle and blood flew across the room.

"Have it your way."

Bolan released the Azerbaijani and he hit the floor hard, groaning again. When the man opened his eyes, he saw the soldier holding the intimidating Beretta in two hands and aiming it directly at his skull.

The man chuckled. "I don't think you'd kill an unarmed man in cold blood."

"Guess again. If you don't talk, I have no need for you, and I can't allow you to live to cause me any further delay."

"You won't fire. I know you won't."

Bolan fired.

CHAPTER TWELVE

He screamed and felt something shatter and blast into his head. A moment later he realized he was still alive. The bullet had slammed into the floor at a proximity of just inches and sprayed him with flying debris.

"All right! All right! Whatever you want."

"Start talking."

"I am Ali Hajiyev."

"I don't care who you are. Who owns this facility? Who procured the helicopter? Why did you use it to murder those people aboard the oil ship?"

"I can answer just one of those questions. This place is controlled by Arif Oguz. That is all I know."

"Tell me about the helicopter or you're a dead man without a head."

"I don't know! It came here two days ago by truck. We did not even know to expect it. We have always just served as an import staging area...."

"Smuggling heroin, opium."

"Yes—and cannabis," the man added helpfully.

"The pilot?"

"He came with the helicopter and he left as soon as the mission was done."

"Why was the oil ship targeted?"

"I don't know. You'll have to ask Oguz that question."

"And Oguz is where?"

"That I do not know. He has more homes than anyone in the Azerbaijan. He stays mostly in Astara, I think."

Bolan felt he didn't have time for further questioning. Precious minutes had already passed. He grabbed the man's lapels and spun him onto his stomach with a sudden twist, then grabbed his arms and secured them with plastic cuffs. A quick check showed him Osman was in no way a threat. He was flying high, an empty hypodermic on the table next to him. He gave Bolan a sickly smile.

The empty bottle was labeled in English as well as Azeri. It was propoxyphene, a powerful opiate-related painkiller. Two more bottles were sitting at the end of the cot and Bolan grabbed one without hesitation, filled the ampule with the entire contents of both bottles and stabbed his prisoner in the buttocks, squeezing the contents into him. The man began muttering savagely in Azeri, but his voice began slurring before Bolan had even left the room.

His clock told him he had wasted nearly five minutes inside the building already. No telling how long the search party would waste looking for him out in the scrub land. No telling how many more men were still on-site. And he had a helicopter to attend to.

He sped silently down the stairs and searched the ground floor, finding nothing but living quarters and a kitchen that stank of rotting food. No paperwork, no computer, no log books to give him further direction.

The opening of the front door caught his attention as he was completing his on-the-run search, and he headed for the vestibule in a trot, the conversational tone of the newcomers telling him they were oblivious to trouble in the house. He never even slowed his stride but stepped around the corner and approached the three grimy arrivals with a raised weapon. They cried out when they saw him, then the first man in the trio found the suppressed muzzle of the 93-R pressed into his sternum.

They froze for a moment, then the front man made a foolish bid to take the advantage from the soldier, sweeping the 93-R away from his torso in one swift move of his arm and grabbing at the AK-47 hanging from his shoulder. With cries of triumph the others imitated him, but they didn't see the stainless-steel, serrated dagger that had appeared in Bolan's other hand. The instant the 93-R cleared the first gunner's body, the dagger homed in on him, slicing through tissue with terrible force and plunging directly into the heart muscle, bringing it to a spasmodic halt.

The 93-R was redirected to the other targets with a flick of Bolan's wrist. He achieved point-blank target acquisition on the right-hand gunner, triggering a single 9 mm subsonic round that took him down simultaneously with the knife victim. The final player saw death coming in a handful of milliseconds but, compelled by his aggression, tried to bring his AK into play, triggering the weapon into the floor at the same time the Beretta blasted a pair of rounds through his cranium.

The sound of the autorifle filled the house, and Bolan could only assume it would reach any others in the compound. He tucked the 93-R in its holster and swung his lead weapon into play as he kicked open the front door. He was using an M-16 A-2/M-203, the assault rife chambered for a 5.56 mm round, the grenade launcher loaded with a 40 mm high explosive.

The facility was empty at the moment, but he assumed the west-end hangar guards hadn't been accounted for yet, and in seconds he was rewarded with the appearance of a gunner around the north corner of the building. The soldier swung his weapon across the guard's path, triggering deadly full-auto fire that caught the man in the legs as he skidded to a halt. He fell on his back, moaning, and Bolan delivered a mercy round that ended the guard's agony. He covered the ground to the front of the hangar in several long strides, watching both corners, knowing a second gunner was bound to appear at any moment.

He came into view at the south corner, trying to trigger an effective barrage at the soldier while exposing almost none of his body. Bolan returned fire with so little reaction time the guard jumped back, startled, and was gone from sight. The Executioner landed with his back against the front of the hangar and watched the corner for a ten-count, assessing his options.

A rumble of engines changed the scenario—the jeeps could be seen raising dust in their return across the scrub and their urgency was apparent. They might have received radio warnings about the trouble in the camp.

He had no time to wait for the guard around the corner to make a mistake, so he went on the offensive, running into the open with the M-16 A-2 on full-auto, directing the rounds first into the metal sides of the building, raising a racket to disorient and frighten the guard. When he stepped into the open he found the guard retreating along the side of the building. Upon spotting Bolan, he knew he was a sitting-duck target.

Up against the wall like a prisoner before a firing squad, there was nowhere to hide, and he fell into a crouch. Bolan's autofire clanged into the metal wall of the hanger inches above his head, and he raised his Russian-made automatic rifle with speed born of desperation. What his desperation couldn't conjure was precision. His flawed fire cut the air to the soldier's right.

Bolan corrected his aim before his adversary could, and the gunner took the last several rounds in the M-16 A-2 magazine.

Sprinting to the front of the hangar, Bolan rammed home a fresh mag. He spotted a face in the only window, which was five feet off the ground in the wide hangar doors, and he fired at it. The face disappeared before the short burst of 5.56 mm rounds shattered the glass.

Bolan yanked on the door, counting on the speed and aggression of his attack to keep his enemies off guard, and fell back from it. A rattle of AK fire cut through the doorway an instant later.

He waited it out. The soldier had seen all he needed to see in a glimpse of the interior—the partially dismantled Russian-built helicopter with Iraqi military markings sat inside on a truck trailer. There was no mistaking it.

It had to go.

The Executioner inserted an HE round into the breech of the M-203, angled the weapon into the interior of the hangar and fired. The 40 mm explosive hit the trailer underneath the nose of the gunship. Bolan couldn't have placed it more accurately by hand.

The soldier put distance between himself and the hangar as soon as he saw where the grenade landed.

He heard and felt the explosion behind him as he jumped for the abandoned Land Rover and heard the distant cracks of autofire from the approaching vehicles. They were just coming in range of the AKs, but their bouncing, on-the-move fire didn't worry Bolan yet. He put another HE round into the M-203 and stood in the driver's seat, targeting carefully. The unit could launch a grenade approximately 375 yards, but the aim suffered as it pushed its limit. Bolan fired and watched the tiny projectile cross the gray sky in an arc, knowing his aim was less than perfect. The explosion occurred five paces in front of the nearest jeep, creating a crater that the startled driver was unable to avoid, and he skidded as he plowed through the freshly loosened soil. The other two jeep drivers slammed on the brakes. One of the front passengers had been standing in order to fire over the windshield, and he tumbled over the hood and crashed to the ground.

Bolan had exhausted his supply of HE grenades, but had three antipersonnel buckshot rounds remaining. He readied one as he landed in his seat and stomped on the gas. The Land Rover's finely tuned suspension gave him an advantage as he sped over the uneven ground, four-wheeling over patches of scrub grass and through tiny gullies. He sped at an angle, first crossing in front of the lead jeep, hitting its occupants with a barrage of 5.56 mm manglers that took one of them in the abdomen and sent the others jumping for cover on the opposite side of the vehicle. He steered next directly toward the right-flanking jeep, where the gunners had time to get protected behind the jeep and pepper the oncoming Land Rover with fire. Bolan accelerated as if to ram them, putting down a barrage of fire that sent the gunners ducking, then turned off when he was within twenty paces of the jeep. The gunners reappeared and managed to take another handful of potshots at Bolan as he barreled by, nearly sideswiping the jeep, and triggered the buckshot round almost in their faces.

The effect was devastating carnage. The blast of fifty double-aught lead pellets was the equivalent of the fire from an oversized sawed-off shotgun. The middle gunner took the worst of the blast, his skin flayed from his face in a heartbeat, his companions dying in a mass of ripped flesh and sudden blood.

The left flanking jeep was starting up, but there was something wrong with the lead jeep, and the driver was wrestling to get the engine to turn over. Bolan swerved to the right and allowed the moving jeep to tail him momentarily, then twisted hard and zeroed in on the lead jeep. The passengers jumped for safety behind the vehicle but the driver waved frantically—he'd started the vehicle after all—and two of the men jumped back in as he spun his tires at high revs in the loosened soil. The last man went down in the spray of soil and made a grab for the rear bumper, missing it by inches and landing on all fours. The jeep left him behind.

The abandoned gunner didn't waste time feeling sorry for himself. He crawled fast to his fallen weapon and rolled on his side, bracing the barrel of the AK-47 against his chest and swinging it at the Land Rover as it bore down on him. He fired, and the recoil slammed into his chest, throwing off his aim and pounding the air out of his lungs. White light filled his vision, then he felt the stinging impact of rounds, so many of them they felt like ants biting his chest and stomach. Then blackness.

Bolan veered away from the dead man and followed the trail of the fleeing lead jeep, which was lurching away. Then it stalled suddenly. The Executioner homed in on the vehicle, cut a tight turn to put him broadside with its rear end, and faced two gunners and a screaming driver just a few paces away. They fired together, and Bolan felt the singeing heat of 7.62 mm rounds around his face and arm, but his well-honed concentration didn't allow it to distract him. He triggered the M-203, and the buckshot round tore into the occupants of the jeep, obliterating them in blood.

Bolan stomped on the gas, taking the 4.0-liter Land Rover powerhouse to near-redline rpm and swung the wheel to avoid the next staccato burst of fire from the last jeep. The driver was full of rage and accelerated to keep up the pursuit, but when he attempted to follow Bolan through the high-speed turn, his vehicle wasn't up to the task. His inside wheels left the ground, forcing him to brake swiftly and steer into a slalom. The jeep landed on all fours, but by the time he started up again Bolan was completing a three-sixty and homing in for the kill.

The driver sank into his seat and covered his head, but his two gunners stood up to the attack with a hail of deadly fire that Bolan couldn't hope to outmaneuver—he sank low and shifted up, accelerating to highway speed that turned even the highly engineered Land Rover suspension into a roller-coaster ride. The 7.62 mm AK fire drilled into the hood and smashed through the windshield, and Bolan again turned the wheel as sharply as possible without sending the four-wheel-drive into a roll. Then he triggered his last buckshot round from a greater distance than he had hoped. The gunners nevertheless bailed from the vehicle like skydivers from a doomed aircraft.

The only casualties this time were two balding, Polish-made tires.

Bolan put distance between himself and the three survivors, who stood and watched him curiously as he turned and headed back in the scrubland, back where they had been sent to search for him.

When they saw him stop, just a mile away, they started to approach on foot, busily reloading their weapons.

Bolan took the rest of his hardware from its hiding place, stowed in desert-camouflage packs of waterproofed canvas, and returned them to the rear of the Land Rover. He could hear the three Azerbaijanis shouting threats, but their voices sounded less than truly threatening over the distance.

They would approach within range of their weapons in minutes.

With the skill and efficient speed of an expert gunsmith he opened the case containing the sections of a Walther WA2000 sniper rifle, nestled in sculpted rubber pockets. The bullpup-design weapon was fitted with a Schmidt and Bender telescopic sight, ten-power, and a front-mounted bipod for added stability. The weapon was assembled, 6-round magazine in place, in under a minute.

The soldier walked to the front of the Land Rover and placed the sniper rifle across it, then carefully lined up his shot. The trio was still far off, well out of AK range but close enough for the powerful .300 Winchester Magnum cartridge to reach out and touch.

He peered through the telescopic sight and watched them pause. They were appraising his behavior, slowly coming to the realization that maybe their adversary had some hardware they didn't.

Bolan fired, aiming high, and watched one of the Azerbaijanis topple. His cry of pain carried across the vast scrubland. Then, in a hurry, his companions grabbed him off the ground and hauled him away, back to the burning ring of their base of operation.

The Executioner disassembled the sniper rifle and allowed them to flee. He had bigger fish to find. And fry.

CHAPTER THIRTEEN

Johnston Atoll, Pacific Ocean

Johnston Atoll is a U.S. territory located in the Pacific Ocean some nine hundred miles from the Hawaiian Islands, putting it effectively in the middle of nowhere. The total land mass is less than two square miles. It was a dry tropical bit of real estate, mostly flat, with no natural freshwater source. In the late 1990s, despite the fact that it was managed by the U.S. Defense Nuclear Agency and the Fish and Wildlife Service of the U.S. Department of the Interior as a part of the National Wildlife Refuge system, it was used for little outside of the storage and disposal of chemical agents belonging to the U.S. military.

The small collection of buildings on the atoll had the less-than-glamorous portable look of a U.S. military outpost, like a hastily constructed town that was, against all odds, turning out to be a permanent settlement. The Army-slum appearance of the town was in direct contrast to the tropical vacation feel in the Pacific air.

"Well, the weather is here. I just wish it were beautiful," muttered T. J. Hawkins, as he and the rest of the Phoenix Force strolled off the Army aircraft that had brought them to the atoll from Oahu.

"Gentlemen," said the young officer approaching them, "I'm Captain Kiekhofer."

"Al Eveland," said David McCarter, leader of Phoenix Force. He shook Kiekhofer's hand.

"I'll be your liaison while you're on Johnston," the captain stated. "Have you been informed of my clearance?"

"Yes, I have," McCarter answered. Kiekhofer did have some limited knowledge of Phoenix force's purpose for being on the atoll, as did Colonel Steindl, who was in charge of the operation. But Stony Man Farm didn't make it a habit of telling people the true names of its members. Even—and especially—those who worked for the same government. The freedom of the Stony Man teams to operate outside the strictures of politics required it.

"I'll take you to meet the colonel, then to the quarters we have set up for your men," Kiekhofer said.

"We'd rather check out the JACADS," McCarter stated. "After meeting the colonel."

"Sure, Mr. Eveland. Whatever you'd like. In fact, I believe the colonel is about to go inspect the JACADS himself. But I have to be honest with you— I think you guys just made a long trip for nothing."

Kiekhofer led the five men to a trio of jeeps that was waiting for them. They made quick work of piling their gear into the vehicles, then started across the atoll to one of its concrete docks. Kiekhofer drove one of the jeeps himself.

"Why do you think we're wasting time, Captain?" Rafael Encizo asked.

Kiekhofer chuckled. "JACADS is secure."

"I'll bet Aberdeen felt the same way."

"Yes, but Aberdeen's incinerator was accessible. The JACADS isn't."

"Then how does the staff get to it?"

"Obviously it is accessible to the Johnston staff who run it...."

"If the people who run it can get to it, then somebody else can get into it," McCarter declared. "If they're intelligent enough, with the right knowledge and resources."

"They'd have to have knowledge that's restricted to CADS staff," Kiekhofer protested.

"Which they did in Aberdeen," Encizo said.

Kiekhofer shook his head. "You guys just don't get it. In Aberdeen they could just drive up and take what they wanted. This is a different part of the world, and we run our operation differently." He braked the jeep on the concrete pier looking out into the crystal-blue waters of the Pacific, and gestured out into the open water. "That's our CADS. There's not going to be anybody driving up and helping themselves to our chemicals."

McCarter and Encizo stepped out of the jeep and peered out over the turquoise Pacific waters. The rest of the team joined them.

"Is that what we just flew twelve hours to defend?" Calvin James asked incredulously.

"Yeah," Encizo said with a wry look.

The Johnston Atoll Chemical Agent Disposal System was a fat, unpainted steel cylinder jutting out of a landscape of shattered concrete about a mile from the shore.

"Looks like a grain silo," Hawkins observed. "We came all this way to protect some livestock feed?"

"There's the colonel," Kiekhofer said. A small, gray motorboat was cruising to the pier from the incinerator. Kiekhofer grabbed the rope as it came to halt and saluted the colonel, who ignored him and approached the Stony Man team, appraising them frankly.

"You're not military," he stated by way of greeting.

"No, Colonel," McCarter said. He introduced himself using the Al Eveland alias, but didn't go so far as to introduce the rest of the team.

"I'll have you know I have no interest in having you involved in this operation," Steindl said to McCarter, ignoring the others.

"I understand, Colonel."

"No, you do not, Eveland. You can't possibly understand. We've been developing and building this chemical disposal system for the better part of this decade. It hasn't been easy. Nothing is easy about living on this barren piece of coral a thousand miles from the real world. And we've done a damn good job. We've succeeded in creating the largest, safest CADS on the planet. We have a lot of personal pride in that system. We know its purpose is to rid the world of some of the most insidious substances man has ever created in its blackest moments. And now, at our moment of triumph, when we're scheduled to perform our inaugural full-scale start-up, we get this."

McCarter nodded. "We're not here to interfere with your operation, Colonel."

"I sure hope not. The last thing I need is to have to baby-sit a bunch of bureaucrat's representatives."

"We're not part of a bureaucratic organization—"

Steindl's voice lowered to a mutter. "I'd have refused on the spot if I hadn't received this order from the highest level."

"Colonel, let me promise you that we'll be here for just a few days, tops. If things go as planned for the JACADS, then we'll just fade away. If trouble starts, well, I think then you'll be glad we're here."

Colonel Steindl regarded McCarter and nodded. "I guess that's the best offer I'm going to get," he said, then turned to Kiekhofer. "Give these gentlemen the tour, Captain, and keep them out of my hair."

KIEKHOFER TOOK THE HELM of the small motorboat and steered them into the ocean, making a wide circle around the CADS incinerator.

"We built the island using scrap concrete and coral mostly," he explained. "That was five years ago, when the program was initiated. Then it sat there empty until last year. The program was delayed several times. There's a lot of political concern about the disposal of chemical weapons. There have always been political factions that have insisted that incineration of chemicals is too inherently dangerous to be permitted."

"My understanding is that incineration has always been the preferred method for destroying large quantities of chemicals like nerve gas, hydrogen cyanide, mustard gas, whatever," Gary Manning stated.

"You're right," Kiekhofer said. "But there have also always been alternative methods of neutralizing them. They're mostly very expensive, they're usually impractical, and they're often just as dangerous as incineration is perceived to be. Anyway, every time we were about to start construction on the incinerator, one of the political factions would stall the project while another nonburning method was suggested and researched. They were all eventually overridden, proved to not be feasible. Then the CADS program got started.

"The JACADS is the largest incinerator of the new CADS systems developed in the U.S. This is where we tested the technology, including the new software and protective systems."

Kiekhofer pointed the watercraft toward the makeshift island, and they could see the loading ramp and entrance to the building. "The CADS incinerator island is usually downwind of the atoll. It's also positioned where the water currents flow away from the island. That was an extra assurance built into the design so that, even should we experience a major malfunction and compromise of the system during incineration, the airborne and waterborne contaminant will flow away from the island. Even massive releases into the atmosphere and water will dilute to safe levels before reaching large-scale human habitation."

The boat pulled to the concrete pier that led directly through a large set of double steel doors, guarded by a pair of soldiers armed with M-16s. They nodded as Kiekhofer led the group into the interior of the incinerator. The room was a vast four thousand square feet, stuffed with containers and lined with specially racked and motorized burners.

"Those burners bring the temperature inside this room to over three thousand degrees Fahrenheit," Kiekhofer said.

"What are these containers made of?" Manning asked, kneeling before one of the containers, which was a milky, almost translucent blue. The contents of the plastic was a dark, liquid mass, ominous, like something evil frozen in a block of ice.

"Specialized thermoset plastic of some kind. Developed just recently. It's stable enough for short-term storage of many of the materials we're bringing here. It's turned out to be a pretty convenient way to encase the materials for safe transportation from the mainland to the atoll. It gets encased at its storage point and it never sees the light of day again. We just burn the whole thing, container and all."

Kiekhofer looked around nervously, realizing that, while he had Manning's attention, the rest of the team had spread out through the facility, carefully examining every corner of it—the controls embedded in wall panels, the racks used to hold the containers, the ducts to the atmospheric distillation system, even the seams in the walls and the ceramic sealant used to caulk where the floors and ceilings met the walls.

They were obviously a cautious bunch. They didn't touch anything. But, not for the first or last time, Kiekhofer wondered who in the world this bunch of guys was, why they were here and why Johnston Atoll had been ordered to give them its full cooperation by none other than the President of the United States.

Arlington, Virginia

"THEY OUGHT TO CALL THIS the Stony Suite," Akira Tokaido said to nobody, nodding with satisfaction as he looked around the large sitting room of the Hilton Hotel suite. The hotel staff had brought in extra tables, and they were covered with computer equipment. On the low end of the spectrum was a daisy chain of PCs, feeding information to and from a pair of computer towers under the table. These were hardwired to a series of displays on the opposite side of the room. A server was on-line with the rest of Tokaido's cybernetics lab, wired to a T-1 Internet connection, but this served strictly as a backup system to the satellite linkup, which had been dedicated to the operation. The satellite linked the cybernetics operation at the Hilton and the Computer Room at Stony Man Farm with the CADS system at Johnston Atoll.

The most important piece of equipment in the impromptu computer center—at least in the mind of Akira Tokaido—was the black boom box resting on top of a Hitachi monitor. He pushed off, rolling in his seat to the boom box, and booted the PC with one hand while starting the CD player with the other, spinning through the selection until a simplistic, almost silvery guitar chord started, transforming swiftly into a thunderous instrumental. Tokaido nodded in time to the thrashing music as he directed one computer after another through a progression of systems checks.

Glenn Willott emerged from the rear bedroom of the suite looking bleary-eyed. He rubbed his face, which was creased with worry.

He hadn't slept much since the nightmarish raid on his home in Minneapolis. He knew he'd come close to death in those moments. Now he was in custody. Despite his cooperation, he knew he was in a hell of a lot of trouble.

The only thing he could do was to keep cooperating, as best he could—help these people put a halt to the raids on the CADS.

He had underestimated the young Japanese man the government had paired him up with. What he'd first assumed was a punk hacker had turned out to be one of the brightest and most intuitively brilliant computer experts he had ever worked with. The kid was some kind of cybernetics genius.

"Do you mind?" he asked. Well, the guy did have his annoying quirks.

Tokaido nodded in time to the music and, grinning, spun down the volume.

"Are we about ready?" Willott asked, surveying the field of hardware Tokaido had erected in just a few hours that afternoon, like a kid with a big box of Lego building blocks.

"We're ready when they are," Tokaido said, jabbing a keyboard. "And we're on-line."

He nodded to the bank of extra monitors, which glowed to life with five separate black-and-white views of the scene half a world away. There was a shot of the entrance to the Johnston Atoll Chemical Agent Disposal System incinerator. Willott knew the view. He'd spent six months on the atoll as part of the development team.

Other monitors showed the makeshift island incinerator from various views.

The screens of the PCs, most of which had been in standby mode, started coming to life, mimicking the displays seen by the on-site staff at Johnston Atoll.

"They're initiating," Tokaido said. "Let's rock and roll."

Stony Man Farm, Virginia

"THEY'RE INITIATING the computer checks," Hunt Wethers said.

Carmen Delahunt took her seat, and Aaron Kurtzman hung up the phone with a few quick words as the computer systems throughout the room came to life. The displays showed the screens that were being seen in the control room on the Johnston Atoll.

But the staff on Johnston Atoll didn't know they were being watched from afar. And they would have been very surprised to learn that, half a planet away, a bunch of strangers were getting accurate readings on their system. And were, in fact, more in control of their systems than they were.

Wethers was looking at a pair of monitors, showing two displays that appeared to be identical. In fact, the windows showed identical graphs and digital readouts. The only difference between the two displays were their titles, in black letters at the top. On the left the display read JACADS. On the right the display read, ACTUAL.

This was what the Johnston operators would never see, if and when the incinerator was compromised using Glenn Willott's subversive software. It would show, at all times, what was really happening inside the Johnston incinerator.

"Akira, ready?" Kurtzman asked.

"Ready, here," Tokaido replied from the speaker-phone.

"Are we ready?"

"We're ready, Aaron," Delahunt answered.

Without looking away from his twin displays, Wethers said, "The question is, is Phoenix ready?"

Johnston Atoll, Pacific Ocean

"THEY'VE STARTED, Phoenix One," Barbara Price said. "You staged?"

"Affirmative, Stony," McCarter answered. "We're ready to move on your go."

"Okay. Let's hope it's a boring afternoon for you guys."

McCarter said nothing. If he'd given an answer to Barbara Price, it would have been something along the line of, "I don't think it will be."

But he couldn't have explained why he thought that way. Nothing tangible suggested trouble. But trouble was brewing, he could feel it in whatever part of his body was responsible for his warrior's instinct.

Phoenix Force hadn't been forced to hide during their few hours on the atoll, despite the fact that only two of the senior officers on-site were supposed to know who they were and why they were there. They were passing themselves off as a Washington, D.C.-based team of video journalists. That was easy enough. There were plenty of journalists on the atoll, hoping for a scoop should trouble emerge during the first running of the JACADS.

But now the team was in hiding. They had been granted use of a high-speed watercraft. The Mark V Special Operations Craft was the boat often used by SEAL teams for insertion and extraction. It wasn't a small vessel, by any means. At eighty-two feet in length and seventeen-and-a-half feet at the beam, it was meant to carry large numbers of SEALs and tons of equipment and still manage to get to speed approaching fifty knots. It had been delivered to Johnston for emergency use. Now it was parked in an enclosed boathouse on the pier, hidden from the bright afternoon sun in a concrete bunker of a room lit by a pair of fluorescent lights. It was tied into the same security system Stony Man was monitoring, and now the screens showed empty water and the abandoned front door to the incinerator.

McCarter's gaze was locked on the monitor, although the more he looked at it the more he was convinced it would show them nothing when the infiltration started. It was too out in the open.

But they would be coming. He knew it in his gut.

"The computer is stepping the system through a primary security check," Hawkins was explaining. He had been on the phone with Tokaido and Kurtzman during the flight to the atoll and had been briefed on the system. "It'll go through a proximity check first, just to make sure there's nobody nearby the incinerator. It's got motion and thermal sensors designed for the process. It'll even check inside the incinerator for movement or thermal activity that doesn't fit the profile of the contents. It's easy to do, since a human being gives off heat and the chemicals don't."

"Phase one of the preparation is completed," Kurtzman's voice said over the monitor speakers. "Moving into phase two."

"The computer performs a level one self-diagnostic. Of course, there's already been at least one level one self-diagnostic performed on the system today, but this one makes sure that the entire system is running optimally prior to the start of the incineration process."

"Phase two completed," Kurtzman said. "Entering phase three."

"Now the computer is evacuating the interior of the incinerator and filling it with helium," Hawkins explained. "Helium has very small molecules. If there's a leak in the system, the helium will get through it. The outer casing of the incinerator is filled with electronic leak detectors. They'll alert the system if it detects helium in parts per million greater than one. That's a pretty small leak.''

The wait now was longer, but minutes later Kurtzman reported the successful completion of the third phase.

The monitors in the small concrete boat shelter showed no activity at the incinerator.

"Incineration's beginning," Kurtzman said. The tension was tangible in his voice. They knew that, if the infiltration was going to come, it would come now.

Stony Man Farm, Virginia

HUNT WETHERS WAS WATCHING the twin monitors steadily, staring at them so long his eyes were starting to tear from the strain.

The third test phase gave way to the beginning of the incineration phases.

"Maybe we were wrong," Carmen Delahunt said under her breath, as if to herself.

The prefiring sequence of the sophisticated incinerator burners began, including the carefully controlled ramp-up of fifteen ceramic ignitors. If a single one of the delicate ignitors failed to reach temperature, the process would shut down.

The ignitors took three seconds to get from room temperature to over one thousand degrees Fahrenheit.

"Maybe you're right," Wethers agreed.

"It could still happen," Kurtzman almost whispered from across the room, watching his own readouts.

"Nothing going on yet over here," Tokaido said over the speaker, from the Hilton where he and Willott, the designer of the software, were watching the same displays.

"How long till we call this thing?" Delahunt asked.

"Not yet!" Tokaido said. "It could still happen."

"We're at temp," Delahunt announced. "Gas is starting."

"Nothing yet," Wethers said. "Everything is going to specification—wait!"

Johnston Atoll, Pacific Ocean

"WAIT! I'VE GOT SEPARATION!" Wethers declared, his voice exhibiting rare excitement.

"Confirm that!" Tokaido said. "The system is being jammed from inside the incinerator. The readouts in the control room on Johnston are being fed a dummy program. The gas is being turned off inside the JACADS."

McCarter's eyes never left the monitor, where the incinerator was still silent and undisturbed, and he felt slightly as if he were bearing witness to the activity of a ghost. "You sure about that, Base?" he asked.

"Yes," Kurtzman declared. "The incinerator is being taken through a controlled shutdown. The gas is being vented—the new control protocol was instituted just prior to the actual ignition of the gas. Fresh air is being vented in. The ignitors are down to two hundred degrees each. Phoenix, we've got intruders."

"We're on it," McCarter said. "Let's go."

The front end of the concrete boathouse started to open automatically as Calvin James hit the button and started the engine. He fed the throttle to carry the ship into the water just as the door was up high enough to allow it to exit, then accelerated into the open waters in the center of the great ring of coral that made up the atoll. The boat crossed the open lagoon at high speed and arced to the north as it left the narrow opening, heading around the curve in the coral that took it out to the island of concrete.

"We're approaching, Base," McCarter said into his radio. "Tell me again we don't need gas masks when we break into that thing."

"You don't need gas masks, Phoenix One," Kurtzman said. "The air inside is clean. The burners never lit, and none of the containers experienced any heat."

"What are the sensors telling you, Base?" Hawkins asked over his headset.

"We've got normal temps inside, T.J.," Delahunt answered. "What little combustible fuel was released into the atmosphere inside the incinerator has been vented off. There's no more chance of combustion. Also, we've got thermal surges, and motion has been detected."

"Can you tell how many players?" McCarter asked.

"Negative, Phoenix One."

"Price here. What's it look like over there?"

"About the same as your monitors are showing you. We've got no activity on the outside. They must have come in underground and under the water."

The craft came to a halt at the concrete pier, and the men of Phoenix Force jumped out, scanning the flat rubble that made up the surface of the island, and the open sea. The closed, sealed doors to the incinerator looked ominous.

"Price here. They've apparently spotted you guys on the island. They're trying to initiate an emergency shutdown. We're not letting them. We don't want to tip off whoever it is inside."

"Got that, Base," McCarter said. "Be prepared to blow the front doors for us."

"We're ready when you are."

The entrance to the incinerator was three yards wide, with double swing doors to allow entrance of large loading carts. McCarter stationed himself, Encizo and Manning at the entrance, keeping ex-SEAL James and ex-Ranger Hawkins on either side of the door. They heard nothing inside. The sirens from the atoll, as the staff reacted to the trouble, reinforced the lack of activity at the incinerator. It was almost peaceful here, and McCarter experienced a rare moment of doubt in the abilities of the people he trusted at Stony Man Farm. What if they were wrong? What if they were putting too much faith in Willott's "simulation" software and the incineration process was proceeding right now? If that was the case, the environment inside this building was one of the most toxic on earth. Phoenix Force would be dead within the minute.

There was only one way to find out.

He said into the radio, "Go, Base."

The door seal broke with a clang, and all hell broke loose.

CHAPTER FOURTEEN

The men inside spun to the opening doors, but their surprise didn't last long. They triggered Kalashnikov rifles, and McCarter, Manning and Encizo returned fire, aiming their bullets around the heavy steel doors as they pulled back from the opening. The gunmen weren't experienced under fire and they stood their ground, counting on the power of their weapons to protect them. But the Phoenix Force commandos were on the move and firing simultaneously, and the two gunners with the AKs were each cut in two.

McCarter and Encizo stepped boldly into the short entrance and flattened against either wall, looking into the room as best they were able. The interior of the incinerator was at least forty feet long, with a low six-foot ceiling. It was wide open, except for a small, three-sided enclosure at one end, its open side facing away from the entrance.

A volley of fire cut across the entranceway, coming from a gunman to the left of the entrance, behind the wall. Encizo was about to step into the open to peg him off when McCarter held up a hand, urgently motioning him to stop, then pointing to the right. He suspected there was another gunner hidden around the corner, this one to the right.

They heard the sounds of activity from the enclosure on the opposite side of the vast room. McCarter knew they had to move fast. He gestured quickly, indicating Encizo should take the right and he would take the left. Encizo nodded. The Briton held up three fingers and counted down silently. Two fingers, one finger and, on go, he and the little Cuban stepped halfway around the corner together, both lowering their weapons on the move and achieving target acquisition.

McCarter spotted a man flattened against the wall, ramming a fresh clip into his AK-47. He tried to use it and never got the chance. The Phoenix Force leader triggered his M-16, spraying a burst across the gunner's chest. He stiffened, fell back against the wall and slid to the floor.

Encizo faced a more-prepared gunman, who managed to get off a single round from his automatic weapon. The round flew wide, and the Cuban cut him down with a quick burst from his M-16.

"Clear," McCarter called.

Manning jogged in behind them, James and Hawkins just seconds later.

"Check it out—they took it all," James said.

McCarter saw it for the first time himself. The entire store—every last container of deadly weapons-grade chemical—had been stolen from inside the incinerator.

They heard more movement behind the alcove at the end of the room and started toward it, splitting into two teams that approached the alcove from either side. A man appeared just briefly around the right-hand corner, looking out fearfully, then was gone again. A moment later a hand reached around the corner and fired an Uzi, the rounds punching into the interior walls. James adopted a shooter's stance and triggered his

M-16. The precision-fired rounds bloodied the guy's gun hand and knocked the Uzi to the floor.

McCarter and Encizo approached the corner. The little Cuban stepped around it, finding the wounded man staggering for protection behind a pair of gunmen with furrowed brows. They didn't know what their next move should be until Encizo decided it for them. He targeted them and fired, sweeping his weapon in a figure eight that quickly bloodied the enemy at hip level, punching them crashing to the floor. The wounded man made a grab for a fallen AK-47. Calvin James had just stepped around the corner, and he took out the man the moment his hand touched the cold metal of the fallen weapon.

"Check it out," James exclaimed.

At the rear of the alcove, which had been solid concrete floor when they investigated the building just a few hours earlier, there was now a wooden ramp leading down into a lower level. Below was darkness.

Manning took the point without being asked, crouching and starting down the ramp, a dangerous exercise, in which the enemy would see him before he saw the enemy. He took just two steps onto the ramp when he was seen from below. A series of shots erupted from somewhere beneath them.

The big Canadian jumped down and out, into the darkness at the end of the ramp, finding himself in another room with a claustrophobically low ceiling, and darkness so absolute it hid the walls in most directions. He was a sitting duck, having landed in the middle of the room under the light from the incinerator above. The only other light in the place came from forehead-mounted lights on the figures huddled against the far wall, in the darkness. Manning rose to his knees and triggered a trio of bursts at the incongruous figures as they directed blasts of automatic fire at the ramp where he had just been. One of them collapsed to the ground while the others fell back, and Manning took the opportunity to launch himself behind the less-than-ideal cover of the wooden ramp.

"How many?" Encizo called from above.

"Unknown!" Manning shouted.

"Give us cover."

"Hold on." A flick of the switch sent the M-16 into full-auto mode, and a crack of metal took out the half-depleted mag. He inserted another as a fierce salvo came from the headlighted men on the other side of the cavernous room, cracking into the wooden ramp. Manning was thankful it was sturdily made as he listened to the rounds pound the surface.

"I'm getting rid of the ramp," he shouted, giving the wooden structure a shove. The legs were set on rubber wheels so that it could be maneuvered into position, and there was nothing securing them to the crushed concrete surface of the floor. The ramp rocked forward as Manning pushed, and he allowed it to rock back again, then gave another tremendous shove with a grunt. The ramp's lip scraped the ceiling above, then poised for a minute on one side. The gunners on the far side of the room renewed their fire, sending a torrent of bullets into the ramp as it fell onto its side with a crash. Manning landed on his knees behind it. Now the toppled structure made a much more effective barrier. He chose his moment, then shouted up to the team, "Come on down!"

He rose over the side of the barrier and unleashed withering full-auto fire from the M-16, aiming at the forehead-mounted lights. At least two of the lights snapped back under the impact of the rounds.

Encizo was the first to jump from the floor above, allowing his body to descend into a squat as he hit the floor at Manning's side. He came up firing, taking a cue from the big Canadian and targeting the lights on the far side of the room. James landed next to him and added his firepower. The last of the lights leaned forward and fell onto the concrete floor. Then the firing stopped and the cavern was silent.

Manning got to his feet and moved across the floor to the side wall, then inched up on the nearest corpse, ripping off the strap holding the forehead flashlight and using it to illuminate the end of the room. There was a total of five corpses in scuba gear. A single remaining canister of chemicals was sitting on the crushed concrete floor. Against the wall was a black pit of open water at least five yards wide.

MINUTES LATER McCarter was swearing quietly as he paced on the concrete pier of the JACADS island, ignoring the concerned and confused Marines who were milling around, trying to look useful. After the Briton had radioed Colonel Steindl, they had stormed onto the island expecting to take down Phoenix Force, only to discover the team was actually the good guys, and the ones they were after were already long gone.

James had to be almost physically restrained from jumping into the water in pursuit of the infiltraters. McCarter wouldn't hear of it.

"You don't know what's down there, mate," he'd declared. "It's black. You'll be unarmed. You don't know the way."

"I'll find my way," James said, holding up one of the underwater lights the infiltraters had been wearing.

"And if there are ten of those guys, waiting with spear guns? They'll make bloody quick work of you, Cal."

"I've been in underwater combat situations," the ex-SEAL said quietly, but he knew the question was moot now.

McCarter wasn't happy when he was caught in any situation unprepared. Like he was now. They didn't have the equipment to pursue the infiltraters on their escape route, which obviously led from the entrance point under the incinerator into the ocean. As the minutes ticked away, the infiltraters were getting farther and farther away.

The next boat that roared from the atoll to the makeshift island included Colonel Steindl and Captain Kiekhofer. They left the watercraft with obvious reluctance.

"Relax," McCarter said. "None of the chemicals are left."

Steindl looked at the Briton as if he'd sprouted a second head. "None?"

"Well, one of your plastic containers. They must have heard us coming and abandoned it below."

"What do you mean, below?"

The last thing McCarter wanted to do right then was to stand around talking about Phoenix Force's discoveries. As far as he was concerned, they were in the middle of a battle. "Are we getting gear or not?"

"There's none to give you," Kiekhofer said. "We don't have SEAL gear here."

"Spear guns. Anything. We've removed scuba gear from the guys they left behind."

"We've brought over a couple of spear guns. That's all we've got. It wasn't anticipated we'd ever need..."

McCarter didn't listen to the rest of it. He grabbed the two spear guns from the boat and headed back inside the incinerator, followed by the captain and the colonel. The interior was now filled with soldiers and the JACADS emergency crew, who were merely standing around. There was nothing for any of them to do.

"Have you got the search boats out?" McCarter asked as they strode back to the rear of the incinerator.

"I deployed them myself," Kiekhofer said. "We've got every spare vessel searching the area."

"Have you called in for help?"

"Yes. The Navy and Air Force are seeing what they can come up with."

The colonel stopped and stared at the new trapdoor in the bottom of the incinerator. "This is where they came in?"

"Yeah. And it's how we're going to follow them out," the Briton said. "Cal, you're with me."

James had expected as much. He was ex-SEAL, and had been extensively trained in underwater maneuvers. He quickly stripped to his shorts and dragged on scuba fins and mask, then grabbed a few extra lights from the corpses in the basement cavern. Lastly he took one of the spear guns McCarter offered him and stepped into the water.

CHAPTER FIFTEEN

The black surface of the water inside the basement cavern was the size of a small pond, but as James walked into it he found a long shallow area, finally stepping off into an entrance well that was no wider than eight feet. He tread water as McCarter followed him in, then put in his mouthpiece and allowed himself to descend into the murk.

The light on his forehead was feeble against the murk in the water, which was a rusty color that James realized had to be mostly silt. But in seconds he discovered the source of the reddish tinge in the water. At the bottom of the well-like opening was one of their antagonists. He had been stitched across the throat with gunfire from one of Phoenix Force's M-16s, and his jugular vein opened. Sunken by a weighed diving belt and his air tanks, his body rested at the bottom of the well and much of his blood had leaked out, filling it. Without an active current, it had gathered there, staining the water. His eyes were open wide, looking at James in silent terror, as tiny clouds of blood continued to ooze from the wound and air bubbles spluttered from the corners of his mouth.

The corpse rested at about fifteen feet below the surface of the basement, at which point the tunnel made a ninety-degree turn, heading horizontally, more or less, to the west. James examined the framework of the tunnel as he went, curious as to how it was built. The frame was composed of steel girders that had been bolted together in a triangular shape, then linked for a three-sided tunnel framework. The frame had been placed secretly underwater at some point during the construction of the concrete island, then covered with the scrap concrete slabs and chunks that formed the base of the island. If the concrete overlay was performed carefully, the inside of the tunnel would have been filled with only small chunks that could be cleared by hand. Not a bad plan, James had to admit.

Once he swam a few yards into the tunnel he began to feel a tinge of claustrophobia. The tunnel was about five feet wide at its base, and the jagged walls closed into a point at his head. He became conscious of being buried under untold tons of shattered, broken concrete. The concrete walls contained jagged edges and dark gaps and chasms, like open wounds heading up into the bowels of concrete. The water was filled with litter, which was about all their lights could illuminate, and James felt as if he were swimming in muck. He wondered how in the world he would be able to see an enemy before the enemy saw him. It was the kind of nightmarish scenario that sometimes got even experienced SEALs trembling, and he wondered how well McCarter was doing, just a few feet behind him.

They came to a wall of concrete, covered in brown mold, where the tunnel's integrity had given way under the weight of a massive concrete slab that penetrated inside it. The tunnel descended underneath the slab, and the litter of chips on the floor and the carved aspect of the concrete walls told James that the tun-

nelers had been forced to carve out this passage,
maybe by hand. But they performed a less than first-
rate job, chopping out a passage that had to have
scarcely allowed them to drag the plastic containers of
chemicals through. James twisted and laid on his back
in order to maneuver himself through the opening and
still be able to see where he was going. The shaft
curved up again like a horseshoe, reentering the
framed tunnel. Another of the infiltraters was waiting
for them there.

The man had been shot as well, but only wounded
and had made it this far during his flight. Getting past
the tunnel blockage had to have taxed all his strength,
because he was floating in the tunnel just beyond it,
sucking his air and looking desperate. He recoiled
from James as the black commando snaked around the
blockage. He was holding on to one shoulder with all
his remaining strength, but the blood was seeping out
from between his fingers.

James reached out and extracted the dying man's
knife from his sheath, and continued on. The man tried
to grab onto James's arm, and the commando shook
him off.

He grabbed James again, and this time McCarter
wrenched off the man's hands. The swimmer was startled by the newcomer and glared at him, then tried to
grab McCarter. It was clear he didn't have the strength
to swim any farther himself. He wanted them to get
him out.

McCarter shook his head and threatened the man
with the spear gun. The figure crowded away from
McCarter, fear visible in his eyes through his mask.

McCarter wasn't about to compromise their search
by dragging along the survivor. The swimmer had

sealed his own fate, and the Phoenix Force leader didn't feel all that sorry for him.

Still, he'd help the guy out if he was still alive when they came back this way.

James led them down a long, steady slope as the tunnel seemed to be heading into the depths of the ocean, and James was listening to his heart pound in his chest from the exertion. The infiltrators had to have been physically fit to be able to traverse the tunnel while dragging their cargo of chemical containers. He paused when he noticed a faint luminescence above him, and turned off his light. McCarter did the same, and they hung there in the darkness for a moment until they realized they were seeing a faint light coming through gaps in the shattered concrete slabs that covered the tunnel.

They swam on for another ten yards before reaching the end of the tunnel, then continued out onto the floor of the Pacific Ocean at a depth of about forty feet.

There were no more of the infiltrators waiting for them, but they had left one of their vehicles behind.

It was an underwater transport unit, an electric, propeller-driven device like those used by scuba divers for rapid underwater locomotion. James recognized it at once. He had trained on and used SEAL versions of the unit, specially designed for rapid, silent, underwater maneuvers. He had seen units of this size before, with an extra-heavy-duty powerhouse for towing large underwater loads.

This one still had its load attached to it—a mass of blue nylon-rope netting, containing eight of the plastic chemical containers.

Johnston Atoll

"THEY'VE BEEN RUNNING perimeter sweeps around the atoll for the last—" Kiekhofer checked his watch "—eighty-eight minutes, and they've come up with nothing."

"I know those guys aren't going far without getting some surface transport," McCarter said. "What about our friend in the tunnel?"

"We extracted him," Kiekhofer said, his face showing obvious distaste. "But he's no help. He ran out of air about fifteen minutes before we got to him."

"Bloody hell. All right. Give us a few minutes, will you?"

Kiekhofer seemed ill at ease with Phoenix Force's use of the colonel's office. He frowned as he left the room reluctantly.

"Base?" McCarter asked.

Barbara Price's and Yakov Katzenelenbogen's voices came over the speakerphone in the colonel's office.

"There are a couple of Navy craft coming in to help with the search, but they're not going to get there in time to do you any good," Price said.

"Well, they can't get that far using those transports and in scuba gear."

"Yeah, but they don't really have to," Katz said. "They just need to get as far away as they can and then sit there until they can get picked up by a surface vessel after dark."

McCarter nodded, thinking hard, and couldn't help looking out the window. Dusk wasn't that far away.

"We could still get lucky. Maybe one of our search craft will happen on them during their pickup," Hawkins suggested.

"Maybe," Manning agreed.

Encizo gave them both a look that indicated he didn't share their optimism, but he remained silent.

"Base, we could use some suggestions."

"We're working on some, Phoenix," Price replied.

"Like what?" James asked.

There was silence from the phone for a moment, then Katz said, "Well, Aaron's checking out the ship traffic in your vicinity."

"What good will that do us?"

"I'm not sure," Katz admitted.

"Yeah, those guys won't need a commercial freighter to move those containers," Manning said. "They could fit them into a fishing boat. Even a big pleasure craft or several different boats."

"That's the best we can give you, Phoenix," Price stated.

"Dammit!" McCarter growled after the line was disconnected. He slammed his fist onto the surface of the desk, causing the framed photos of the colonel's family to jump and topple.

The rest of the team said nothing, but they all felt the same way.

The phone rang again.

"Stony Man here," Price said. "Now that didn't take long, did it?"

"You've got something?" McCarter asked.

"Bear?" Price prompted.

"Hey," Kurtzman sounded from the speaker. "I just located an ocean cargo vessel called the *Pride of Vancouver*. It's a freighter used by Dualistic Dynamics Limited, based in Vancouver, apparently for special import-export jobs. It's never been implicated in anything illegal, nor has Dualistic Dynamics. But it's another subsidiary of a subsidiary of the Pollari Corporation, and it's steaming across the Pacific Ocean right now. Less than twenty-nine miles northwest of your position."

"Could they get there underwater using their towing devices?" Manning asked.

"Unlikely," James answered. "But they could certainly be meeting up with some sort of surface vehicle, as we hypothesized before, a few miles from here, which could tow them to the *Vancouver*."

"After all," Price said, "they have to be going somewhere."

THE MARK V Special Operations Craft was powered up on one of the Johnston Atoll piers minutes after Phoenix Force arrived, fully prepped. They boarded the SOC in a hurry, and McCarter shouted for immediate cast-off. The Navy driver complied, and they left the atoll behind in minutes.

"How long since their estimated departure from the incinerator?" he asked.

"Just under two hours," James replied, then anticipated the Briton's next question. "We know they won't travel all the way to the *Vancouver* underwater, but we don't know when they'll choose to surface. That will make all the difference in determining if they'll have reached the *Vancouver* yet. They'll travel at just a few miles per hour below the surface. Once they move onto the water, their speed might be better."

"It seems it would definitely be better," Hawkins commented.

"Not if they continue to tow their weapons cargo," James replied. They might decide it is easier and safer to continue towing it behind their boats rather than load it up for the remainder of the return to the *Vancouver*."

"How are we going in?" Manning asked. "Hard and loud?"

"Too dangerous," McCarter said, shaking his head. "The ship is an unknown entity in virtually every sense. We'll make this a clandestine probe and go hard once we've mapped the layout and defenses. We'll have to use our heads on this one, mates."

As THE SOC closed in on the *Vancouver*'s position, the engine speed was reduced, bringing the craft's throttle to a quiet rumble that wouldn't reach the shipping vessel. The moon had replaced the sun, a perfect orange half-circle on the horizon. Enzizo was scanning the ocean with a pair of thermal-imaging binoculars and was the first to spot the ship.

"There's our baby," he said.

Soon they were all able to see the lights of the vessel on the ocean, while Encizo was watching for additional activity on the ocean, and not finding it.

"We'll have to keep in mind that this boat could be just what it says it is—a shipping vessel, engaged in no sort of illegal activity," McCarter reminded them.

"Not likely," Manning said. "She's stopped. Why else would she anchor here, of all places?"

"Let's be bloody sure before we start shooting up the place."

"Got it."

They parked the SOC and inflated the black rubber SEAL insertion raft, piling in and leaving the Navy driver with instructions to move himself away from the *Vancouver* by at least another few miles and wait for their call for extraction. The sailor was a young, quiet man named Glasby, who was taking his ask-no-questions orders seriously.

The *Vancouver* was quiet, as if waiting for them. Waiting for something. As they approached, they slipped their oars into the water carefully to avoid the sound of splashing. The rumble of the engines was the only sound they heard from the ship. But as they drew near they spotted movement on the deck—four men watched from the starboard side of the ship, peering into the night with thermal binoculars.

"Uh-oh," Hawkins said as they circled and approached the craft from the rear.

They saw one of the watchmen waving over his companions and pointing out into the ocean.

"They see our boat?" Encizo asked.

Manning was looking where the watchmen were indicating. He saw their SOC sitting still in the water.

"Glasby didn't move out far enough. Dammit!"

"Get on the radio," McCarter said. "Tell him to get the hell out of here!"

James was already raising the Navy driver on his radio. "Glasby, you're too close!" he whispered. "Get out of here now!"

"How far out do you want me to go, sir?" Glasby asked.

"Just go!"

They heard the rumble of engines from the port side of the craft. The crew of the *Vancouver* was wasting no time investigating the strange boat.

"They're launching!" Hawkins whispered.

"Damn, they're going to come around this end of the ship," Manning said.

The others started rowing hard to move the black

raft against the ship, while James radioed to their Navy driver. "Glasby, you're going to have company. Head back to the atoll at once."

"I can't strand you guys here," Glasby retorted.

"Go right now and that's an order!"

"Right."

They fell into the black shadows that lay close to the rear hull of the *Vancouver,* where even the starlight didn't reach them. Dressed in matte-black combat clothing and webbing, and painted with oily black combat cosmetics, the five members of Phoenix Force managed to go unseen. But the men in the vessels being launched by the *Vancouver* had their attention on the Navy Mark V—two Kawasaki 1100 ZXi personal watercraft shot out from the cargo ship and accelerated through wide circles that pointed them in the direction of the Navy boat.

"Is he moving?" Manning demanded.

"Yeah. He's moving," Encizo said from behind his thermal binoculars.

"Those PWCs are pretty fast," James said with a mounting sense of dread.

McCarter heard the concern in his voice. The Navy boat was fast, but the tricked-out Kawasakis, with 1,071 cc displacement providing 120 horses, were lightning. Ignoring inertia and water friction as if they didn't exist, the powerful twin one-man boats sped over the nighttime ocean. Although they couldn't see the Navy SOC, the white spray of the wave-runners was hard to miss even in the darkness.

The leader of Phoenix Force felt a rising tide of helplessness. There was absolutely nothing he could do, nothing any of them could do, to help that innocent Navy driver.

"Encizo?" he said.

The Cuban had a front-row seat to the drama. The field glasses made him the only one who could see the progress the Navy boat was making. Glasby had it at full throttle, and it was churning up the ocean. But the other craft had at least an extra 15 or 20 mph capability advantage.

"He's not going to make it," Encizo said grimly.

He saw the first vessel close in on the Navy boat, pulling alongside for a moment, then arcing away and accelerating to distance itself from the craft. Encizo knew what had just occurred. Maybe Glasby never did. He never slowed the SOC. A three-count later the Navy boat became a mass of fire and light that illuminated the vessels as they turned and headed back to the *Vancouver*.

"They're going to see us," McCarter stated, noticing the headlights on the watercraft. "Let's get wet. Sink this raft."

The five men stepped over the side without hesitation, sinking into the tepid waters of the Pacific Ocean, buoyed by flotation pads built into the combat harnesses they were wearing. James and Hawkins were knifing the rubber raft repeatedly, and the quiet electric motor that they had intended for use when they left the ship soon dragged the spluttering rubber pieces below the surface.

They stayed low in the water, dog-paddling easily to stay afloat, until the vessels drew near, then they sank into the dark water and hovered against the hull of the vessel, just a few feet beneath the surface. Above them the dark surface turned light as the headlights from the watercraft passed above them. The churning sound of their engines increased as the runners moved around the port side of the vessel.

They waited where they were as the watercraft drivers circled the vessel, searching for them, descending below again as the runners motored overhead, finally returning their dock on the port side of the vessel.

McCarter was the first to creep around the rear of the hull, watching from low in the water as the two watercraft drivers pulled the Kawasakis into their slots. They were shouting to the crew of the ship.

"There'll be others! It wasn't just that one fucker! Watch the water and shoot on sight."

McCarter raised a hand and signaled the approach. Silently, stealthily, the five members of Phoenix Force moved alongside the hull of the cargo vessel to the watercraft slots. From the shadows they observed the drivers climbing the rope ladders onto the deck. They listened to the sounds of running feet above them as they crept onto the slot.

They had the Navy SEALs to thank for providing their hardware. The raft they had just sunk and black battle gear they were wearing had arrived with waterproofed Heckler & Koch MP-5 submachine guns, as well as waterproofed harnesses for their suppressed handguns. Each man was also armed with a combat knife, useful for absolutely silent kills.

The knives and suppressed handguns would help keep the probe clandestine for as long as possible. Then the MP-5s would help clean up.

Encizo was the first up the ladder, and he reached the top of the deck rail without noise, looking over the side onto the deck. He drew back suddenly, and Manning, directly beneath Encizo, could hear footsteps on the deck. They paused, then approached. The

Cuban was holding the ladder with one hand and had drawn a stiletto in the other.

A man holding an AK-74 close to his chest suddenly appeared at the rail, frowning, and he didn't have time to react when Encizo lashed out viciously, stabbing the stiletto through his adversary's throat just below the Adam's apple. The gunner made a croaking noise, eyes flying wide open, and Encizo allowed the stiletto to remain where it was, grabbing the gunner by the shirt and pulling him over the rail. The Kalashnikov rifle tumbled through the open air and entered the water with a small splash, but its former owner dangled from Encizo's grip, twitching limply as his lifeblood soaked his shirt and trousers and dripped from his shoes. When he was still, Encizo passed him down to Manning.

"Thanks," the big Canadian said, passing the corpse down the line. Hawkins was still waiting on the watercraft slip, and he wedged the corpse into the narrow space between the slip and the hull.

"Now that's teamwork," he muttered, but the others didn't hear him.

Encizo now found the deck clear. He launched himself over the rail and raced across the open area, ducking into the shadows under a set of stairs next to a large electrical box. Manning had to wait while a man on the top deck passed by, then sprinted to his side. In minutes the entire team had assembled on deck.

"James is with me," McCarter said. "We'll go fore and check out the bridge. I don't want this ship going anywhere until we're finished with it. You blokes go aft and see what you can determine in regards to our plastic pods from Johnston. Remember what our captain friend told us about those containers. One bullet hole could release enough of that stuff to finish everybody in the vicinity. So be careful.''

''What about transportation off this rig?'' Hawkins asked.

''Your radio survive the dunking?'' McCarter asked James.

James whispered swiftly into the mike and listened through his headphones. ''I'm getting us on-line with Stony Man via Johnston's uplink,'' he said.

''Report the death of our Navy friend,'' the Briton said somberly, ''and request extrication.''

''No matter what they send it'll take our ride awhile to arrive,'' Hawkins said.

''Good point,'' McCarter replied. ''Let's try to keep our presence a secret as long as possible.''

There were nods of agreement and understanding. Then the two factions of Phoenix Force separated and moved in opposite directions.

The probe began in earnest.

CHAPTER SIXTEEN

James and McCarter crossed in darkness, pausing long enough to watch the activity on the opposite side of the ship through a narrow passage to the starboard side. The crew seemed to assume the approach would come from starboard and was concentrating its efforts there. Not that they were ignoring the port side, they were walking regular search patrols along it.

"The crew's not that large," James commented. "Won't take them long to figure out they're missing a member."

"Yeah," McCarter agreed, then fell silent as a guard walked past them. He remained oblivious to the Phoenix Force warriors and disappeared around the front end of the ship.

James quickly updated Stony Man Farm on their situation, including the loss of their Navy driver. Price paused when she heard the news. James knew how she was feeling. He understood that the death of a team member, however peripherally allied to her action teams, never failed to affect her. But she buried her emotions.

"Hold on, Phoenix Three. I'll arrange other transportation," she said, returning after fifteen long seconds. "There's a Sea Hawk coming to you out of

Johnston. It'll reach your position within twenty minutes, then hang around outside of weapons range until you call for extrication.''

"Got that, Stony Man," James said, then relayed the information to McCarter.

"We can inflict a lot of damage in twenty minutes, right, Cal?"

"Better believe it.''

ENCIZO TOOK THE POINT, leading Manning and Hawkins among the shadows in quest of an access into the cargo holds of the vessel. They crossed paths four times with the constant patrols that were walking the port side of the vessel, but the lookouts were convinced their attackers were yet to arrive. They kept their eyes peeled for movement on the ocean without bothering to look into the shadows just a few paces behind them. Silent, the trio went undetected.

Arriving at an open area on the deck they found a pair of doors to a wide cargo hatch. The double doors were propped open with half-foot-long sections of two-by-fours. Inside was darkness. Standing nearby was a hatch that clearly led into the belly of the *Pride of Vancouver.*

"Here we go," Encizo said quietly as he turned the handle. He swung the door wide and leveled his handgun into the darkness, then nodded to the others, who followed him inside. Hawkins, with a last look around to insure they had gone undetected, closed the door behind him.

They descended the steps to a landing, where Encizo surveyed the cargo hold. It was full of something, which was all he knew for certain. Most of the floor space was filled with some sort of unstacked containers underneath a tarpaulin that was tightly tied to the steel supports in the walls. The huge hold was lit by just three dim fluorescent light fixtures set up high in the ceiling. Enxizo continued to the floor of the cargo hold while Manning and Hawkins followed cautiously. All of them were very aware that there was just the one way into the hold.

"Check it out quick, Rafe," Manning said. "This is making me nervous."

"You? Nervous?" Encizo asked in a whisper that still managed to carry throughout the hold. "We've got to be sure of this."

"I know, man, just hurry." Manning looked at Hawkins and gestured to the door. His teammate nodded and retreated up the stairs to guard the doorway.

Encizo quickly untied the knot holding one of the tarpaulin corners to the wall and drew it back. Several familiar translucent, sky-blue plastic shapes were revealed, plastered with ominous black-and-white decals showing a skull and crossbones that read: Warning! Extremely Hazardous Material! Exposure is Fatal! The message was repeated in several languages.

"Bingo," Encizo said with a nod.

"Good. Now let's get out of here," Manning stated.

Hawkins approved of that plan. But the plan went bad suddenly. The latch on the door he was guarding turned, and he stepped to one side to be out of the field of vision of whoever was entering. The door swung open and Hawkins made a grab, snatching at the wrist of the new arrival. With a heave he dragged the figure inside with one hand while swinging his suppressed Beretta 92-F into target acquisition on the man standing behind him. The figure made a grab for his own weapon but never had a chance. The Beretta coughed out a pair of tumblers that crashed through his chest and shut him down with a quick gurgle.

But the first man crashed down the stairs with a clang and a yell, and in response, Hawkins heard a shout from somewhere beyond his field of vision. He tucked the Beretta into its armpit holster and took the dangling MP-5 from his shoulder.

He alerted his teammates with a shout. The time for quiet was over. "Company's coming!"

McCARTER AND JAMES moved from shadow to shadow to the fore of the *Pride of Vancouver*.

"If they were smart, since they know we're coming, they'd turn on the lights," James commented.

"If they were smart, they wouldn't be in this business," McCarter added.

"Uh-oh."

McCarter saw it too. A single guard stood at the bottom of a set of steps leading to the bridge. He had an AK-74, one of the Kalashnikovs that had replaced the old AK-47s among the Russian forces a decade earlier. The autorifle was chambered in 5.45 mm. It didn't have the long-term reputation enjoyed by its predecessor, but had started making a name for itself as it gradually proliferated among terrorists worldwide.

This terrorist was holding his on his shoulder like a Marine standing at attention, oblivious to the intruders aboard the ship.

"We could take him out, but that would be risky," McCarter said. "Shall we try to find another way in?"

"Such as?" James asked.

"There's got to be another companionway on the other side of the ship."

"Probably guarded like this one."

"Maybe not, with all the activity going on over there."

"You want us to just go strolling through all those people?"

"Got a better idea?"

"No. But how're we even going to get to the other side of the ship from where we are now?" James asked. "That guy's not going to let us past, and it's a long way to go back."

"There's that passage that cuts through the deck-house—ten meters back," McCarter suggested.

"Doesn't seem safe, man," James said.

"Got a better idea?"

He shook his head, and they started back to the passage.

THERE WAS A RATTLE of autofire, and a torrent of rounds bounced off the floor in front of the entrance. Hawkins edged out of the entrance to spot the shooter and targeted the first moving shadow he saw, triggering a short burst from the MP-5. The shadow ducked behind a black pile of deck machinery, then reappeared a second later, leveling an AK-47. Hawkins fired first and cut across the faceless gunner with a barrage that sent the man sprawling, the AK unfired.

A shuffle from the other direction motivated Hawkins to pull back inside the doorway, which saved him from taking a volley of 7.62 mm rounds that passed through the empty air where he had been standing. He waited for a pause, then leaned out the entrance, triggering into the point where he believed the fire had originated. He spotted three men crouched behind a pair of ventilation flues, two of them waiting for him.

He fell back at once, his rounds wasted, return fire keeping him pinned.

Manning had rendered the stairway diver unconscious and tossed him to the floor of the hold.

"We're in trouble," Hawkins declared.

"What's the situation?" Encizo asked, joining them in a hurry.

"Three players to aft, well-protected. I took out a player to the fore, but there's probably more coming to replace him."

"Let's cut them down to size," Manning suggested, extracting a shrapnel grenade from his combat webbing. "I'll take aft."

"I'll take the front," Hawkins said.

"Just be damn careful not to send that thing through the cargo hatch," Encizo warned. "Even a blast that small might ignite the cargo."

"Gotcha," Manning said. "Let's do it."

They stepped back to back out of the doorway. Manning spotted movement behind the exhaust flues and tossed the grenade in an arc that deposited the bomb almost on top of them. Hawkins threw his into the darkness behind the machinery where more figures were gathering. They retreated into the cover of the doorway.

A shout of terror erupted when one of the victims spotted the grenades coming, but at the same instant his companions were opening fire on the movement on the companionway. The twin blasts loosed a cloud of deadly shrapnel that ripped into the trio of gunners tucked behind the flue, tearing through muscle and organs.

Manning and Hawkins stepped out of the doorway again, covering themselves to the front and rear with

their H&K subguns. Encizo joined them for a quick
march across the deck, covering themselves in three
directions like a three-pointed star. They made their
way to the machinery, where they were against the
rear wall of the deck and had adequate protection from
the front.

"Phoenix One, we're catching fire," Encizo said
into his headset mike as the others watched for more
arrivals.

He was answered with a quick pair of beeps from
McCarter, meaning the Phoenix Force leader was in
no position to reply verbally.

"The guys can't talk at the moment," he told the
others.

"Should we stay put?" Hawkins asked.

"I don't see us finding a better spot to hole up in,"
Manning stated.

A rattle of AK-fire came from the rear end of the
deck and the rounds bounced off the wall several feet
over them.

"See that guy?" Manning asked.

Hawkins stood on one of the mounting bolts of the
loading crane they were hiding behind and peered into
the shadowy landscape of machinery and metal boxes
that covered the deck. There was another rattle of gunfire, and he spotted the barrel of a weapon.

"I've got him! Corner!" he shouted suddenly as a
man with a leveled AK-74 appeared around the corner
and fired into their midst. Manning and Encizo pulled
back against the wall to avoid the gunfire, but Hawkins
was on display in his vulnerable position. Encizo triggered his SMG as the deadly hail of 5.45 mm hollowpoint rounds sought his teammate. The 9 mm manglers
cut into the gunner and sent him stumbling backward,

the last of his rounds firing into the night sky. His spine cracked against the ship's rail and he dropped to the deck, motionless.

Hawkins targeted the aft gunner and triggered into his position. The wounded man screamed with pain, then scrambled to his feet, his face a mask of rage. His AK-74 chattered angrily, seeking out Hawkins's position. The Texan's subgun chugged out an answering call, easily torpedoing the gunner's abdomen and ribs and sending him slamming into the deck.

"Phoenix One here," Encizo heard in his headphones as Hawkins stepped down from his perch on the minicrane.

"Go ahead."

"What's your situation?"

"We've got the aft deck to ourselves, now," Encizo answered.

"The cargo?"

"It's here."

"The crew molesting you blokes?"

"Not anymore, they're not, but we've raised a ruckus and we're sure more will be along soon."

"Hang tight. There's a Sea Hawk coming out of Johnston to give us a ride home."

"ETA?" Encizo asked.

"About ten minutes. Can you hold out?"

Another pair of gunmen raced around the corner, their AKs chattering in their hands, laying down a fire cover.

"Maybe!" Encizo shouted to the Briton as he fell to the ground to avoid the crash of rounds peppering the wall and the crane. The two new arrivals made it to safety behind a narrow, steel-encased control console mounted on the deck, where they paused to reload.

"Watch those guys!" Encizo said, his attention riveted to the corner of the building, where more reinforcements might appear at any moment.

"Let's light them up and flush them out," Manning said, making a grab for a flash-concussion grenade.

"Not a good plan," Encizo said. "They're too close to the hatch."

"My aim is better than that," Manning stated.

"We can't take the chance. You ignite the cargo and we're all dead."

"I can keep it out of the hold!" Manning exclaimed.

"I don't want to take that chance!" Encizo said. "T.J.?"

Hawkins triggered a blast of 9 mm tumblers from the MP-5, hemming in the two gunners before they could move into firing position, then fell back to allow them to empty their magazines into the steel walls.

"I'm with Rafe—let's save them for a last resort."

MCCARTER AND JAMES heard sudden shouts and went hard, falling back against the wall of the narrow starboard-port corridor they had been traversing, each aiming their MP-5s in either direction.

"This was a stupid idea," McCarter muttered. "Sorry, mate."

"It was the only option," James said, watching a handful of men run past the opening to the passage, all of them carrying rifles. But none of them noticed the Phoenix Force pair.

"The guys must have caused a stir," McCarter said. "Let's go."

James backed along the corridor as McCarter led them ahead to the starboard side of the vessel. They emerged into an area of the ship that was more brightly lit. Light equaled danger in the constricted confines of the *Pride of Vancouver*. But there was no one in sight, and they made their way boldly to the front of the ship, in search of the bridge. When they found it, the companionway leading to it was empty.

"Not bad," James said.

"It's going to be tight if we have to defend ourselves on those stairs," McCarter observed. "Let's stay sharp."

"You don't have to tell me."

McCarter started up the steel companionway in a crouch, keeping an eye on the glass windows in the bridge above him, unable from his low angle to see any of the sailors he knew were there. James stayed close with him, watching the deck in all directions.

"Phoenix One, we're catching fire." It was Encizo sending over the radio. McCarter reached for the button on his set, sending back a pair of beeps to Encizo that told him he was indisposed.

There was a volley of gunfire from the rear of the ship, and McCarter spotted a shadow of movement in the window of the bridge. The door opened and a man with a wrinkled brow stepped out, looking for signs of the chaos occurring at the rear of the ship. He spotted the commando crouched on the companionway in the same moment McCarter reacted with a savage thrust that sent the muzzle of the MP-5 stabbing into his gut. The sailor doubled over and staggered down the steps. James grabbed his collar and directed his skull into the steel railing with terrific force, dropping him unconscious on the steps.

McCarter was already moving, bounding forward and triggering into the first of two men on the bridge to draw his weapon. The small automatic never cleared its shoulder holster, and the man flopped to the floor. His companion grabbed at a shotgun stowed underneath the bridge controls and wrenched it free, but the stuttering MP-5 chopped into his hip and stitched up the side of his torso. His face slammed into the control panel, then he fell in a heap.

"Company!" James said, pushing McCarter through the door, saving him from a vicious blast of fire that crashed into the heavy glass of the bridge windows. They rolled over the pair of corpses while another blast finally shattered the window and the big shards collapsed inside the bridge.

MANNING COLLAPSED into a sit and snapped out the magazine that fed his MP-5.

"Newcomers," Hawkins said. Encizo fired as a band of gunmen came into view from the side of the deckhouse, and Manning was on his feet in a flash, triggering his subgun into the army of newcomers, who withdrew under the ferocity of their fire. The 9 mm rounds cut across the group, Hawkins and Encizo instinctively taking the outsides of the group and Manning traced a figure eight in their midst. Two of them leaped frantically for cover, both severely wounded, but the remainder of the team went down.

The gunner hidden behind the control console got up his nerve and fired on the Phoenix Force trio. Before he got off more than a half-dozen quick rounds, Manning loosed a sustained burst that ended in a scream of pain.

Manning watched the gunner sprawl on the deck

then try to get to his feet, screaming still. The Canadian rammed a fresh clip into the MP-5 without looking and aimed a mercy shot at his victim, who disappeared a second too soon behind the console.

All at once the wounded man let out a banshee wail and ran into the open, his face covered in blood. He stumbled to his knees and weakly aimed his AK-74 directly at the rear of the vessel, where a five-hundred-gallon fuel barrel was mounted on a steel frame four feet above the deck.

Manning saw his intention and achieved his target in a flash of movement, but not before the AK triggered a pair of rounds into the barrel and a flash of liquid streamed out, drenching the wounded gunman.

Manning swore softly under his breath, pulling back the MP-5 before he could fire. The last thing he needed was a stray spark from a ricocheting bullet.

Encizo was too busy watching the corner for more reinforcements.

"What is it?" Encizo demanded.

"Fuel spill," Manning said.

"Is it reaching the cargo?"

"Not yet. It won't be long."

"Relax. It hasn't ignited," Hawkins said.

The dying gunner was moving weakly on the deck, apparently unable to lift his fallen Kalashnikov rifle.

"It hasn't yet," Manning said. "I don't want to be around when that happens. Cover me, T.J."

As Manning bolted into the open, dragging out his fighting knife, Encizo shouted, "Gary, get down!"

Encizo fired at the new pair of gunners who had spotted him and stepped into the open to trigger their autorifles. Manning hit the deck and the rounds sailed over his head. The pair retreated hastily before one of Encizo's rounds could get at them.

"What's he trying to pull?" Encizo demanded, wishing he could tear his eyes away from the corner for just an instant.

"The guy isn't dead yet!" Hawkins exclaimed.

"So what?" Encizo demanded.

"I think he wants to take us all with him."

Manning jumped to his feet and launched himself into a long dive, falling heavily to the ground behind the control console. The wounded man heard the impact and turned weakly to look at Manning, oblivious to the storm of rounds flying over them both and the return fire from the Phoenix Force commandos. He grinned maniacally through his agony and held up his hand. Manning saw a small silver object.

The boat swayed gently, and the growing lake of fuel tumbled over the dying man and streamed through the open hatchway into the cargo hold.

Manning tried to move, and the top of the control panel—just inches from his head—deformed under the barrage of fire.

The dying man's head fell and hit the deck with a heavy thump, but his hand was still raised toward Manning, and his thumb moved in a last agonized act of bitter vengeance.

The spark turned to a ball of fire in a fraction of a second, turning the dying man into a screaming, withering yellow shape and blasting Manning's face with a wave of heat. He got to his feet and ran back to the cover he and his teammates had chosen. The sudden surge of flame had brought the autofire from the *Vancouver* crew to a sudden halt.

Hawkins was already on the radio. "Phoenix One!"

he shouted. "We've got to get out of here! We got to get out of here right fucking now!"

McCARTER HADN'T KNOWN Hawkins as long as he had known the rest of the men who made up Phoenix Force, but he knew the man was a courageous warrior. And right now that courageous warrior was expressing some kind of panicked fear. It wasn't a reassuring sound.

"T.J., what's going on?"

"We've got a big fire! It's going to engulf this end of the ship at any second. Where's that Sea Hawk?"

James was already switching frequencies. He spoke quickly to Price, who patched him through instantly to the Navy Sea Hawk that was heading in their direction.

"What's your ETA?" James demanded.

"Three minutes," the Navy pilot replied. "I see the *Vancouver* now—you guys trying to burn the thing up?"

"We'll be dead in three minutes! We need to get out of here right now!"

"I hear you. Where will you be?"

McCarter was speaking rapid-fire on his own frequency to the other Phoenix Force members, and he jabbed at the sky.

"On the roof," James stated.

"Get to the roof!" McCarter said to Hawkins.

"Phoenix—" Hawkins was cut off by a staccato blast of fire that pierced McCarter's skull through the headphones "—taking heavy fire! We can't go anywhere, let alone the roof. This thing's going to blow!"

McCarter tried to speak, but a barrage of AK rounds blasted into the front window of the bridge and crashed into the ceiling. The corner of the front window shattered, and glass rained on them. McCarter squeezed his eyes shut to keep out the flying crystal splinters, feeling tiny nicks of glass against his face.

Time was running out.

He snatched a grenade from his combat webbing and shouted a warning to James. "Hang on! I'm going to clear the playing field!"

He opened his eyes long enough to make sure he actually got the grenade out through the gaping windowframe, then shut them again and hid his face. The shrapnel grenade erupted with a roar. Metal shards flew out of it at flesh-shredding velocity, and suddenly the gunfire stopped.

"Let's move." McCarter jumped to his feet and headed for the door, barely glancing at the mess of human flesh and blood on the deck below that had once been, he could only guess, two human beings. He climbed onto the rail of the companionway and stepped into the windowframe, kicking out the last remaining blades of glass, then hauled himself onto the roof of the deckhouse. James was right behind him.

The two men raced along the length of the roof to the rear of the vessel, the clouds of oily smoke drifting past them, and McCarter found himself struggling not to breathe despite his exertion. His mind was racing. Had the fire reached the cargo? How long until the chemicals ignited?

The Briton saw the tongues of flame before he and James reached the edge of the roof, and he thought for sure his three teammates were dead already.

Then a barrage of rounds pelted the wall below him and he spotted two caches of gunners, tucked behind machinery and firing on a spot just beneath him.

Painted orange by the lake of fire that now covered half the deck, three grim-faced figures faced off with the gunners.

James immediately unleashed a deadly volley of rounds into the nearest cache of gunners, who didn't spot the newcomers from above until it was too late. His 9 mm hollowpoint rounds chopped them to pieces like the teeth on a meat grinder, and none of them were alive when James and McCarter pulled back from the edge to avoid the sudden gunfire from the second cache.

"Where's that Sea Hawk?" McCarter demanded.

"There!" James replied.

The heavy Navy helicopter was rushing at them at what looked like an impossible speed just a few feet over the ocean. For a moment McCarter thought the pilot would never be able to avoid crashing headlong into the *Vancouver*'s hull, but he swept off the surface of the ocean with a throaty roar of the rotors and came to a sudden halt above the ship.

"That's us on the roof!" James shouted into his microphone.

"I see you," the pilot answered, and gave them a wave out the window.

"The three just below us are also with us. We need to take out the gunners toward aft before we can extract them! The moment that cargo starts to burn, we're all dead!"

"I'll see what I can do," the pilot said, and the Sea Hawk swept suddenly over the rear of the ship. A gunner appeared in the side hatch, and he unleashed a brutal volley of .50-caliber machine-gun fire. The solid wall of metal slammed into man and machinery alike, chopping down the gunners who'd tried futilely to re-

turn fire. Just three men managed to avoid the onslaught and retreat along the side of the deck, and
McCarter and James let loose on them with a fury of
submachine-gun rounds. The three gunners were
caught in the open and attempted in vain to stand their
ground. A half second after the stream of 9 mm hollowpoint rounds drilled into them from the front, the
massive destructive power of the .50-caliber machine-
gun rounds hit them in the backs. The three gunners
went down in a mass of tattered flesh.

The Sea Hawk veered over the roof and extruded
its long flexible rope ladder. McCarter and James
grabbed at it, and James yelled for the pilot to lower
them to the deck to pick up the other three. But in that
instant, the five-hundred-gallon barrel of fuel broke
open with a muffled burst of an explosion and a gush
of flaming liquid sloshed across the deck, pouring like
a burning river of lava through the cargo-deck doors.
The pilot fed fuel to the rotors and lifted the Navy
chopper into the air to avoid the sudden ball of su-
perheated air that lifted off the deck, and James and
McCarter found themselves hanging with all their
strength to keep from being flung a hundred feet
through the air onto the doomed ship or into the black
sea.

"Go back! Go Back!" James ordered into his radio,
but McCarter wondered if it was too late already. Even
in the darkness of night they saw the thick clouds of
black smoke billowing from the cargo hold, and the
stench of burning plastic was suddenly overpowering.
The intense heat being generated below had to be penetrating those containers. Any second the smell would
change just enough to signal the presence of nerve gas
in ultratoxic concentrations.

The Sea Hawk veered back the way it had come and descended rapidly, sending the two men on the flexible ladder plummeting to the deck through the clouds of smoke. A hand reached out of the smoke and grabbed the ladder.

It was Manning. He hauled Hawkins, coughing violently, to the rope ladder and McCarter grabbed him. The ex-Ranger reached reflexively out and they clambered up together, then Encizo appeared out of the smoke and grabbed hold.

James shouted into his mike, "We're on! Go! Go!"

The *Vancouver* spun wildly beneath them as the Sea Hawk's rotors raced and grabbed at the air, swinging the helicopter away from the ship. There was a burst of orange flame from the cargo hold as they sped away, and the black clouds suddenly became a putrid gray color.

McCarter climbed into the belly of the Sea Hawk and helped hoist the others in after him. He watched the flaming, belching ruin of the *Pride of Vancouver* grow smaller behind them, not so far away that he couldn't see the survivors stumbling out onto the deck from the interior. He couldn't count them in the chaos but guessed there were at least fifteen men, grabbing at their throats and staggering. In seconds they had all fallen to the deck or thrown themselves into the ocean.

In a few more seconds, the flames and lights of the ship were lost in the fatal haze.

CHAPTER SEVENTEEN

City Wharf, Astara, Azerbaijan

Economically, in theory, things had been looking up for the Azerbaijani Republic for nearly a decade—ever since the signing of its first major oil deal in the mid-1990s with a Western consortium of oil companies, worth eight billion U.S. dollars.

More oil deals had come. At the speeches presented during the celebratory ceremonial signing of each agreement, it was pointed out that the money would help fund industrial development. Industrial development would raise living standards in Azerbaijan to the standards of the most successful of the former Soviet bloc nations—eventually even to the living standards of the West.

Judging by what Mack Bolan observed on the streets of its major port city of Astara, those political promises had yet to be realized.

The colorful advertising that was painted on buildings and propped up on billboards didn't come close to masking the ancient automobiles, the decrepit industrial-grade housing, the gray squalor of a former Communist nation.

Bolan had spent plenty of time in the USSR when

it was still the evil empire. He'd returned to Russia, Poland and the former East Germany several times in the past decade and watched them make true progress toward Western standards of living and comfort. He didn't see that progress here.

He had also watched as the former Soviet bloc nations gave rise to the worst perversion of capitalism—organized crime. Syndicates seemed to spring up overnight and entrench themselves in the fabric of the developing economies and political systems.

Few people understood the destructive nature of organized crime as well as the Executioner.

He was seeing that familiar structure here in Azerbaijan. The syndicate of shipping facilities, the well-defined system of ranks. He'd tangled with some players low on the totem pole, and now he had the name of one of the crime bosses. His driving concern was putting a halt to more chemical-weapons attacks before they happened. But he didn't mind doing some damage to the local crime lords along the way if that's what it took.

He'd traded the Land Rover first thing when he entered the city. As beat-up as the vehicle was, it still would stand out. Especially since reports of his incursions at Agstafa and Samkir had doubtless been dispatched throughout the crime system by now. He got a Moskvitch, a Russian car dating from the early seventies. It wasn't pretty, but Bolan's five-minute test drive and under-the-hood evaluation told him it was in good shape.

The owner was delighted to get the expensive European four-wheel-drive vehicle. He knew he was getting the better end of the deal.

But Bolan knew he was much less visible in the

Moskvitch, and when he pulled to a stop on the Astara wharf outside a decrepit building that belonged to a front company owned by Arif Oguz, none of the dock workers gave him more than passing notice.

Bolan was wearing a bulky, well-worn black leather bomber jacket, zippered to the collar, and he kept his hands in his pockets. When he entered the building he found a large suite of cubicles and several desks piled with old paperwork. Several creaking ceiling fans stirred the air. A computer monitor, obsolete by at least a decade, sat on the nearest desk, illuminated but blank. The place looked like someone had gone to the effort many months ago to arrange it to appear to be a real business office, but then had never bothered to touch anything again.

A stout woman in an outfit that was a mixture of Western professional and Muslim traditional came out of the back room frowning, and, in Azeri, asked him his business.

He smiled. "Do you speak English?"

She stopped at five paces. "A little."

"I am looking for a friend of mine." Bolan strolled forward another few steps, making the woman nervous.

"Yes?"

His hand came out of his coat to run his fingers through his hair, distracting her, and an instant later the Beretta 93-R appeared in the other hand leveled at her chest. Her jaw dropped, and she was about to flee when Bolan snatched at her scarf and pulled her close. "Arif Oguz. Ever heard of him?"

She screamed and a figure burst from the back room, drawing a Makarov handgun. He spotted Bolan and aimed the gun, despite the fact that the woman blocked his view of the soldier. Bolan shoved the woman out of the way without releasing her scarf and fired at the gunner. His suppressed tri-burst knocked the man into the wall. He slid to the floor, leaving a trail of blood.

The woman moved suddenly in Bolan's grip, a small .22-caliber pistol emerging from the folds of her loose, heavy top. Bolan knocked it away with the 93-R and targeted her again from point-blank range.

"I asked you a question."

"Hotel Astara Royale. Oguz owns it. It is where he stays."

Bolan dropped the scarf and picked up the pistol, unloading the ammo and pocketing it before returning the weapon to the woman.

"Oguz will kill you! He'll send you to hell, and I will be joyful when you are dead."

"You won't be the only happy person."

Bolan left.

WITHIN A MILE of the airport was a city block that had been gutted and remade, the streets repaved, the building facades resurfaced. Shops, restaurants and hotels had been refurbished and there the politicians and VIPs of the city could entertain themselves without being forced to see the poverty that permeated much of the rest of the city. There they would bring their international guests, who would pretend to believe that this was what Astara was really like. In that area, where money talked, Arif Oguz had built his hotel.

It angered Bolan when he found drug merchants living in luxury, insulating themselves from the horrors of the street—horror they helped sustain through their trade. When the soldier entered the lobby of the hotel, he realized Oguz had insulated himself very well, indeed.

It was a magnificent lobby, with a marble-tiled floor draped at virtually every step with expensive hand-made rugs, with potted plants growing in hand-carved wooden boxes, with uniformed wait staff lingering at every corner. The atmosphere was cooled, cleaned and dehumidified so thoroughly one could forget this was in a city sweltering in the fumes of one of the most polluted bodies of water on the planet.

Bolan was a changed man from the one who had stormed Samkir. Parking his Moskvitch blocks away, he'd changed into a fresh white shirt, suit and tie—courtesy of a Stony Man contact. The suitcase was expensive but looked appropriately well used.

"Do you have a room? I'm afraid I don't have a reservation." Bolan, a Massachusetts native, could affect the accent of the New England upper crust when the situation called for it.

"Yes, sir." The clerk's English was perfect.

"Actually, I'd like a nice suite, if you've got one."

"Of course, sir."

Bolan registered and presented an American Express Gold Card with the name Michael Belasko, an alias he had used off and on over the years. The clerk gave him the Prince of Astara suite at an exorbitant rate, even by Western standards.

"Does the television get CNN?"

"Of course, sir."

He'd been watched closely by two of the superfluous bellhops since he entered the hotel. Bolan figured they were probably paid to keep an eye on anyone who came and went. He felt their eyes on him as he crossed to the stairs and stepped into an elevator decorated with hand-polished brass and ostentatious weavings. It took him to the fourth of five floors. The controls required a room key-card for operation, and an actual key to get to the fifth floor.

He entered a suite the size of a small house, with a bedroom, sitting room, parlor and kitchen with a stocked bar. Vast stretches of pale ivory porcelain tiles were softened by more hand weavings from throughout the Middle, Central and Far East. A handful of lazy rattan ceiling fans and draperies hung from the ceiling throughout the suite to separate the rooms.

Bolan wasn't the type to be impressed by rich surroundings, especially when the taint of crime and drug trade was potent in every evidence of luxury. What he was most interested in was the map of the fourth floor, its intent to point out fire-escape routes. Bolan examined it, attempting to determine what was on the floor above him. That was where Arif Oguz would have his private rooms, which probably filled the entire floor.

But the hotel was rectangular, architecturally uninteresting, and the map told Bolan little.

He had several windows to choose from, and a walk-out balcony that looked onto the avenue below, crowded with foot traffic. Above him was another balcony, made of mortared brick. An easy access point to the suite once night fell.

Dusk was still several hours away, and the soldier was loathe to waste them. He wondered how he might fill his hours in a productive way.

He dialed the Julliard Restaurant on the first floor.

"Mr. Belasko, in 404. Can I still get lunch at this hour?"

HE TOOK THE STAIRS down, straightening his tie as he reached the ground floor and stiffening his stride. The suit routine was one of the easier roles he'd ever played. He had *The Financial Times,* which had been placed in his room and was only twenty-four hours old, under one arm.

The restaurant was designed to look as exclusive as the hotel, with just nine tables in a raised area at the rear of the lobby. It was hung with a crystal chandelier and upholstered on nearly every surface with burgundy finished leather. He took a booth, the only patron, and ordered a vodka. The waiter was dapper and silent, and disappeared like a shadow. Bolan propped the newspaper on the table and watched over the top of it. He had a feeling he wouldn't be alone for long.

He waited for less than five minutes before a man in a Western business suit exited the elevator and exchanged glances with one of the bellhops Bolan had noticed earlier. The suit approached in an easy stroll, adopting a well-practiced smile as he mounted the steps into the restaurant.

"Mr. Belasko?"

Bolan lowered his paper and looked up curiously, then got to his feet. "Yes?"

"How do you do. I am Hajy Abilov, personal secretary to the owner of this hotel." Abilov, a tiny, wiry figure with a vast smooth forehead and a heavy graying mustache, extended a hand and Bolan took it in a firm grip.

"Good afternoon."

"Forgive me for intruding. May I join you?"

"Certainly."

"My curiosity got the better of me, I'm afraid." Abilov crossed his legs in a relaxed pose as he sat across from Bolan. "We don't get many visitors from

America, and I couldn't help but come over and welcome you to Azerbaijan.''

"Thank you. To be honest, I hadn't planned on coming to Astara, but I was in Baku for a week and felt like I had enough time to spare to check out the situation here too.''

"On business, I assume.''

"Yes. I'm with Investing International Consultants.'' He withdrew the wallet Stony Man Farm had prepared specifically to fulfill the needs of his Belasko alias and withdrew a business card with the IIC company name and address. The phone, fax and E-mail were all functional. Even the URL listed on the business card would pull up a functional World Wide Web site. Abilov took the business card in both hands, giving it careful attention.

"In New York?''

"Yes.''

"You specialize in Central and South American opportunities for U.S. and European manufacturing investors?''

"Yes, currently. But we're trying to expand our expertise into the Central Asian states. We see tremendous opportunities here for manufacturing.''

"Really? We don't have much manufacturing in Azerbaijan now. Our economy is driven largely by oil and other raw materials.''

He shouldn't forget raw opium and heroin, Bolan wanted to add, but he smiled easily. "Right now, this is true. But we see great promise for expanding manufacturing here—consumer electronics, plastic goods, automobile components. All those products that have been instrumental in helping grow the economies in Southeast Asia could have the same benefits in Azerbaijan, Tajikistan, Turkmenistan, and so on. If we feel the opportunities are real. We plan to create a division to facilitate its development.''

"You work with the people with the money...."

"As well as the companies looking for low-cost manufacturing opportunities.''

"That would be a great benefit to the people of this city. You know Astara is not a wealthy city.''

"All of Azerbaijan would benefit from the added employment, of course.''

Abilov nodded with well-acted, but obviously false sincerity. "My employer knows municipal leaders throughout the region. I'm sure he would be able to make some appointments for you. How long will you be in the city?''

"A day or two at the most. As I said, I'd never even planned to visit more than Baku. I don't think I caught your employer's name?''

"Mr. Oguz.''

"I'd love to meet him. Get his perspective on the regulatory climate for business in Astara.''

Abilov's fake smile grew icy despite his best efforts. "That may be possible.''

"Actually, I have nothing planned for this evening, outside of sitting in front of CNN. Would he be available this evening?''

Abilov was wrestling with his suspicions and was taken somewhat off guard, and Bolan wondered if he had pushed too far, too fast.

"That may be possible, Mr. Belasko.'' Abilov pursed his lips, clearly clamming up to further probing, and got to his feet.

Bolan got to his feet briefly to be polite, playing the

business executive etiquette act to the hilt. "You know how to find me."

"Enjoy your lunch, Mr. Belasko."

Bolan ordered a full meal, finding it excellent, and ate it thoughtfully, taking his time. Maybe his instincts were off, but he got the impression that Oguz was, in fact, in the city, which meant he might be in the hotel right now.

Which meant that, as soon as the darkness closed in, Bolan and Oguz were destined to meet.

Whether Oguz wanted the meeting or not.

CHAPTER EIGHTEEN

"Of course I'm interested in meeting him. If he is what he says he is, then it will make for excellent public relations. If he isn't what I think he is, then it will be the best possible opportunity to slip him up and identify him."

Hajy Abilov nodded. "I would be much happier if I were able to make that determination prior to the meeting. Then we would know what kind of reception to give this Belasko."

Arif Oguz was sitting at a wide dining table in his suite, with newspapers from around the world spread out before him. With a speed and efficiency that might have been mistaken for compulsion, he scanned the pages and flipped them, piling them in a basket on the floor when he was done with them. He didn't give Abilov his full attention. The man didn't require it. The men had known each other for decades and were the closest of friends. There was no formality between them.

"It has to be him," Abilov muttered.

"Why do you say so?"

"To me it is obvious. One man attacks Agstafa and the report says he is an American. The same man attacks at Samkir and the survivors say he is an American. Then there is an attack at our wharves. Again, an American. They say he is trying to find you. Well, he found you.''

Oguz had sat back in his chair to listen to the explanation, and he laid his pen carefully on the spot where he had stopped scanning. He was a hideous-looking man, with a hawk nose and face that had been ravaged by a skin condition when he was younger. His black hair was combed as well as he was able but was naturally wild. His brows were heavy and too low on his forehead, giving him a Neanderthal look. But his physical appearance was made incongruous by a neat tailored suit and stiff posture and mannerisms that were so careful they were almost exaggerated.

''I do not see it as obvious,'' Oguz said, his voice level. ''Coming here, to this hotel, to seek me out? Too bold, especially for an American.''

''I see nothing less than obstinate boldness in any of his previous attacks.''

''Those were infiltrations. That's the kind of clandestine behavior I would expect from a CIA agent. Coming here and presenting himself to us is not.''

''I disagree,'' Abilov said fervently. ''Surely the CIA would be clandestine, but the CIA would never wreak havoc like we saw in Agstafa and Samkir. Trust my intuition here, Arif. The man I met in the restaurant was as cold as death. I could see it in his eyes. He was the one.''

Oguz looked away, across the richly decorated suite through the open doors of the balcony that looked out onto the rooftops of Astara. Oguz's city. Distantly he heard the sounds of the street traffic and milling people. Those were his people, to command and profit from.

"I will meet this man. If he is the man who we want, then we shall make the determination and simply shut him down. After we convince him to identify his support staff in-country. The general would be very happy to get such information."

THE EXECUTIONER DIDN'T often get invited to formal dinner parties. They weren't quite his speed. He didn't own a dinner jacket, and wouldn't take one on a mission even if he did.

Just the three of them attended the dinner party anyway—himself, Abilov and Oguz. The crime lord tried to hide behind cultivated European manners and dapper dress. He stood stiff and tall with one hand in his jacket pocket as if he were the Prince of Wales, shaking Bolan's hand stiffly, gesturing for him to make himself comfortable.

As Bolan had expected, the suite covered the entire top floor of the hotel, and he was taken through a large vestibule decorated with fresh-cut flowers, through a small sitting room, finally to stop in a large parlor abutting a huge dining area on one side, with a kitchen glimpsed beyond that. A closed set of double doors headed into what Bolan assumed was personal rooms—bedrooms, dressing rooms, bathrooms.

His soldier's intuition kicked in as he was led to the sitting area. He had the distinct impression he was entering a trap. He had expected it, naturally. He had deemed the risk worth the opportunity to get face-to-face with Arif Oguz.

"Drink, Mr. Belasko?" Oguz asked as he waved Bolan to a seat on a large, stiff sofa made of dark wood with burgundy cushions.

"Single-malt Scotch, if you have it." Bolan was still playing the American business executive role.

"Of course," Oguz said, waving at a small man in formal but traditional Azerbaijani dress who appeared to be serving as a butler. Abilov was also in non-Western attire.

The drinks appeared, and Bolan sipped his and nodded appreciatively, but his real concentration was on listening. Not to the chitchat coming from Arif Oguz, but to the ambient noise from elsewhere in the suite. There was a small sound of metal clicking metal from off to the right, but Bolan realized it sounded like pots on a stove top more than firearms. There was a small heavy sound from the dining area, and a quick glance showed him it was the butler, who was now setting a large platter on the table in preparation for dinner. There was something else, so quiet and muffled he wasn't even sure he heard it. Maybe it was just his instincts on high alert.

But he trusted those instincts implicitly.

"...hope you find the city of Astara has much to offer in terms of manufacturing opportunities. We have plenty of intelligent people—and in the city they are all literate. They want to work. Azerbaijanis want the opportunities."

"I've certainly seen that, Mr. Oguz. My company knows there are the people here to do the work. We're more concerned with infrastructure issues."

"Such as?"

"Manufacturing facilities, for instance. There's not much in Azerbaijan in terms of modern plants. Nearly all the plants I saw in Baku were from the Soviet era."

"Yes, and you will find the same is true here in

Astara—but new plants can always be built, Mr. Belasko.''

"At substantial cost."

"I think you will find that the city of Astara will be more than willing to help fund the construction of new plants if it means new manufacturing business can be convinced to locate here."

"I'm also dealing with the civil war issue."

"Ah!" Oguz dismissed the idea with a wave. "The civil war is far away from Astara. None of those people have made their presence known in this city. Even if they do succeed in breaking away from this country, it will not affect us. They add little. Their departure will mean little."

"But if protracted fighting occurs?"

"Neither side can afford it, and neither side has anything to offer foreign partners that would motivate them to lend support to either side. So any war would be brief and benign."

Bolan had to grimace at that. He leaned back into the corner of the couch and sipped his drink. "A benign war, Mr. Oguz."

Oguz chuckled ironically. "Maybe I'm playing it down a little. My point is, though, that any war by the independence groups can't go far and its outcome will have little effect on this part of Azerbaijan."

"The recent gas attacks in this country make me wonder about that." Bolan watched his abrupt shift in the direction of the conversation affect both Arif Oguz, who stiffened, and Hajy Abilov, who was sitting silent in a chair with an untouched drink. "My partners in New York got somewhat panicky when they started seeing the reports splashed across CNN. They wanted me to return home at once and forget the whole thing.

It took some doing to convince them I was far from the vicinity of the terrorist attacks.''

Oguz nodded and seemed to be searching for a correct response. There was another clink of pots from the kitchen and a metallic click from the bedroom that told Bolan all he needed to know. Gunmen were positioned there, waiting for the moment Oguz decided to give the orders to take Bolan out.

Bolan had come unarmed, save for a calf-sheathed fighting knife. A firearm would have been detected and blown his cover immediately.

He had accomplished the most important initial goal of this subterfuge, which was to positively locate Arif Oguz. He would react as soon as the opportunity presented itself to get Oguz under his control, find out what Oguz was up to, then find out who his partners were. Because Bolan knew this man, as powerful as he might be in his direct sphere of influence, wasn't calling the shots on this operation.

Oguz had started speaking again—nonsense about how the attacks in Azerbaijan and the Caspian Sea were isolated incidents by Iraqi instigators and would come to nothing. The people responsible would be ferreted out and jailed. He spoke with such confidence Bolan wondered if he half-believed his own lies.

Bolan smiled easily, nodding as if perfectly satisfied with the response.

The butler appeared in the wide entrance to the dining room.

''I believe we're ready for dinner.'' Oguz stood.

''I'd like to clean up before we eat. Can you direct me to the washroom?''

Abilov silently gestured to a short hallway just off the sitting area, and Bolan found a spacious washroom with an earth-colored ceramic tile floor and a wide window covered by wooden lattice shutters. He opened the shutters and evaluated his situation—the window was about fifty feet from the hard ground, and a few feet above it was an iron railing that surrounded the roof. In the dark of early evening there was some foot traffic on the street, but no one was noticing him.

He flushed the toilet and turned on the water faucet, then quickly crouched on the windowsill and stood, holding onto the top of the window as he made a grab for the roof railing with the other. The stretch was too great and he had to let go of the window and trust that the rail would hold his well-muscled two-hundred-pound frame. It wiggled slightly as he transferred his weight to it.

Highly attuned to the passage of time, he swung along the iron rail, his forearms scraping against the concrete lip of the roof, and stopped at the next window. He guessed it was one of the bedrooms, and the window here was larger.

He watched the sheers for a few seconds and saw the movement of shadows. That didn't tell him who was in the room, how many of them were there, or how well they were armed. And he was running out of time. Oguz and Abilov were going to get suspicious in a hurry when he didn't emerge from the bathroom.

He had to make a blind entrance.

The soldier held onto the rail with one hand and extracted the fighting knife with the other, using it to slowly draw the sheers away from the window. He spotted a pair of gunners, one pacing, the other stretched out in a chair near the window, both with Russian-made Stechkin machine pistols held close to their bodies. They were watching the closed door, but either of them was bound to spot Bolan at any second.

He stepped silently on the sill and grabbed the top of the windowframe as he released the roof rail above, unavoidably making a scraping noise and instantly alerting the gunners, who turned on him but were too stunned by his arrival to fire their weapons. Bolan leaped to the floor and lashed his foot savagely at the man in the chair, hitting him square in the face with the solid heel of his wing tips. Bone cracked, and the chair and its occupant toppled on their sides as the Executioner sprang across the room, directly into the barrel of the Stechkin as the gunner brought it into firing position. But the battle blade slammed into his stomach before he could pull the trigger, and then he made a long sighing sound as he clutched the knife handle and withered to the floor. Bolan turned to his first victim and found him gripping his face, moving drunkenly. Another sharp snap-kick twisted his skull hard and sent him to the carpet, where he lay unmoving.

Bolan grabbed both machine pistols, tucking one in the back of his pants, under his suit jacket, as he heard shouts from elsewhere in the suite. There'd been no cry from the gunners when they went down, which meant it was the absence of dinner guest Mike Belasko that was causing the alarm. He heard pounding footsteps as more men emerged from another room and rushed past the door, then he opened it and stepped out behind them.

One of the gunners happened to glance back before he rounded the corner to the large living area, and when he saw the stranger standing there he gave a shout. Bolan had already leveled the Stechkin and replied with a ripping burst of fire that caught the gunner's exposed arm and shoulder and twisted him 180 degrees before dropping him to the floor. The soldier strode quickly to the corner and leveled his gun into the living area, where a collection of armed gunners were still dealing with the confusion of one of their own going down at their rear. That confusion turned to sudden terror when the Stechkin pointed at them and they stared into the steely eyes of the Executioner.

In defense they raised their own machine pistols and automatic weapons, but the Stechkin fired faster that they could move, cutting a deadly sideways figure eight into their ranks, making them dance like marionettes in the hands of a spasmodic puppeteer. Two of them collapsed, dead from massive internal shutdown, while the third steadfastly refused to believe his own death for a few precious seconds. He turned and staggered to the sitting area before flinging out his hands and collapsing on his face.

Bolan followed and stood over him as he dropped the first Stechkin and swept the now-deserted living area with the second. There was a shadow of dark movement from the dining room and the butler appeared, triggering a Makarov pistol held in both hands. Bolan darted to the left to avoid the fire that homed in on him at shoulder level, blasting into the wall behind him, and sent a swift burst from the Stechkin into the dining room, slamming into the butler, who tossed the Russian handgun away and cracked his head against the dining table he had been setting just minutes before.

The kitchen door moved and an arm appeared, then a face. It was Hajy Abilov, who tossed a small, heavy object in Bolan's direction. The soldier didn't have time to fire before Abilov was gone again. Leaping over a small ottoman he dived to the floor, landing in a somersault on the far side of the parlor behind the solid wooden couch just as the grenade detonated. The shock wave slammed the couch into him while he was still rolling, and he was crushed against the wall.

He pushed the couch away and struggled to his feet, dazed by the impact, his ears ringing from the blast, feeling like an ant under a brick.

Abilov appeared around the corner looking for his body, then pulled back in a rush when he spotted the soldier coming to bear with the machine pistol. Slowed by the lingering effects of the blast, the rounds Bolan fired impacted uselessly into the wall.

Abilov's hand again appeared long enough to fling another grenade into the living area, and Bolan knew he had time and opportunity to send enough machine-fired 9 mm rounds into the Azerbaijani's arm to sever the hand at the wrist. It would have been his last act, because then he wouldn't have time to save himself from the blast.

There was just one avenue of escape and he took it, running for the balcony at the end of the sitting area as he listened to the solid steel sound of the tumbling grenade. As he stepped on the balcony he dropped the Stechkin, leaned over the rail at the waist and grabbed the rail uprights, ignoring the wildly swinging view of the ground five stories down. His upper body swung over the rail and the blast came. The shock wave missed his body, but turned the contents of the sitting room to dust and shrapnel. Bolan's hands felt like they were suddenly on fire. He used all his will to ignore the searing pain, to force the muscles of his hands to keep working despite the trauma.

Then the pain ebbed slightly and he slowly pulled himself along the uprights to the top of the railing. His hands were covered in black soot, burned in some places and glistening red in others. Somehow he managed to lean over the railing and tumble inside the balcony.

Inside the penthouse a lazy drapery fire burned and clouds of dust were starting to settle. But there was no sound. Hajy Abilov and Arif Oguz had successfully escaped the Executioner.

CHAPTER NINETEEN

The Dualistic Dynamics Limited logo came up on the screen for the fifteenth time in an hour and Aaron Kurtzman began stabbing the keyboard furiously, ignoring the tension headache resulting from hours of clenched teeth.

"Go, Carmen," he said.

Delahunt was already going. She was pounding commands into her own computer, displaying a different screen bearing a smaller Dualistic Dynamics logo. She entered the three levels of password protection, using the words the team had hacked over the past twenty-four hours, and paused as she reached the fourth level.

"I'm in," the redhead said.

"I'm not," Kurtzman answered.

Carmen Delahunt was torn between the urge to see what was holding up Kurtzman and the impossibility of ripping her eyes from the stopwatch graphic that had appeared on her own screen. She'd been here before. She knew she had the opportunity to make two attempts, at thirty seconds each, and then they would be locked out again for another five minutes.

The animated graphic switched from twenty seconds to fifteen, and Delahunt announced it almost under her breath.

"Working on it!" Kurtzman retorted. Neither of them noticed the door opening behind them.

"Ten," Carmen stated. "Decoy."

"Hold up," Kurtzman said.

Delahunt breathed, her eyes burning from not blinking. "Five!"

"Decoy!" Kurtzman said. Delahunt's fingers flew over the keyboard, snapping out nine arbitrary characters in under two seconds and hitting the enter key. The Internet connection fed the entry to the server in Vancouver in the basement of the Dualistic Dynamics building, and almost at once it responded with the expected screen-filling red letters: *Password Failed.*

Delahunt closed her eyes heavily for a few precious seconds, then opened them again. The new stopwatch graphic had appeared. "Twenty-five seconds," she announced. She was peripherally aware of someone standing in the door. Whoever it was had the good instincts to read the tension in the air and keep quiet. "Twenty."

"I think I'm getting there," Kurtzman said.

Despite her best intentions, Delahunt couldn't help but look at Kurtzman's screen. His fingers were flying, feeding data into a backup system in the less secure section of the Dualistic Dynamics server and responding instantly to the information it was feeding him. She watched the characters scrolling over his screen and saw the sweat on his brow. Personally, she felt ice-cold.

"Fifteen, Aaron."

"Be ready."

"I'm ready. Ten!"

"Here it comes!" Kurtzman paused, the silence coating the room like a thick, poisonous cloud.

"Five!" Delahunt said miserably.

Chemistry.

Delahunt didn't even think about the meaning behind the word as she snapped it out as quickly as her fingers would move and stabbed the enter key at the instant the stopwatch graphic turned to 0:00:00. She was sure she was just a fraction of a second too late....

Then *Welcome to Dualistic Dynamics' Secure Files, Mr. Pollari,* scrolled onto her screen.

"I'm in," she breathed.

"Good work, Mr. Pollari," Barbara Price said, resting her hand on Delahunt's shoulder.

"It was Aaron's talents that did it. He was able to develop a piece of software that was structured on the UNIX-based system Dualistic runs. He actually had to program it dynamically during the hacking process in order to compensate for the firewalls they'd built between their computers. But those walls still were not as tough as those built against external hacking. He actually had Dualistic's own Internet server break into its secure server and find Pollari's password."

"Now we'd better see what we can find in here before they notice they've got a stranger snooping around," Kurtzman said, wheeling up beside Delahunt.

"What's this?" Price asked as she leaned over them, indicating the first line of the screen, which read *Progress—Pacific.*

"Let's find out." Delahunt clicked on the word and the screen linked immediately to a screen of time-coded entries:

06:07 CST: Attempt to contact Vancouver fails.
06:05 CST: Attempt to contact Vancouver fails.
06:03 CST: Attempt to contact Vancouver fails.
06:01 CST: Attempt to contact Vancouver fails.
05:59 CST: Attempt to contact Vancouver fails.
05:57 CST: Attempt to contact Vancouver fails.
05:55 CST: Attempt to contact Vancouver fails.
05:53 CST: Attempt to contact Vancouver fails.
05:51 CST: Attempt to contact Vancouver fails.
05:49 CST: Attempt to contact Vancouver fails.
05:47 CST: Attempt to contact Vancouver fails.
05:45 CST: Attempt to contact Vancouver fails.

"I guess Pollari likes regular reports," Price said.

"I guess he got some bad news recently." Kurtzman added as he scrolled back three hours of repeated messages and found:

03:43 CST: Vancouver reports hostile boarders.
03:31 CST: Vancouver reports all is well.
02:39 CST: Vancouver reports return of retrieval team.

The messages continued backward, briefly and dispassionately reporting on the murderous activity of the Pacific team. Kurtzman hit the back button again, and a new column of time-coded text started to scroll into place. The first line Price was able to read was:

00:41 CST: Hudson reports all is well.

The screen went blank, then a new message appeared:

Tracing attempt detected and obstructed.

Delahunt swore. "They caught us. They cut the wires and tried to figure out who we were by tracing us to our source. The Stony system stopped them automatically, but the link to Dualistic is gone."

"Can you get it back?"

"Doubtful," Kurtzman said. "If they figured out snoopers were in their private files, they'll shut the whole thing down until they can figure out how we got in and how to fix the weak link. But we can give it a shot."

"Can you recover that last screen, at least?"

"That we can do," Carmen answered. "Every bit scrolls onto the hard drive at the same time it goes to the screen, just in case something like this happens." She moved to a different terminal and quickly accessed the emergency backup file. The laser printer hummed and extruded a printout a minute later.

All the time-coded entries were about the *Pride of Vancouver* except for the top line Price had spotted on the screen. "What, I wonder, is the 'Hudson?'" she said. "Sounds like another ship."

"The *Pride of Hudson*, perhaps?" Kurtzman said. "You think Canadian cities or bodies of water are Pollari's theme when naming his ships?"

"Why not?"

Kurtzman rolled to an Internet terminal, fed by Stony Man Farm's multiple secure T1 connections. A search yielded him results from several maritime databases almost instantly. "*Pride of Hudson Bay*. Commissioned April, 1997. Owned by Pollari subsidiary Dualistic Dynamics and supposedly working the West

Coast of North America. I'll bet a little detective work will show she's not where she's supposed to be."

Price nodded. "Good. Then start detecting."

Johnston Atoll

PHOENIX FORCE HAD new orders before they were all out of the showers.

"Where now?" Manning asked, feeling just somewhat refreshed after what had been an unexpectedly dirty job.

McCarter laid an 8-1/2 by 14-inch gray-scale printout on the table in the living area of the room that had served as their very temporary quarters on Johnston Atoll. The printout showed a ship sitting at dock, a near-twin to the cargo vessel they had just left stranded and death-filled in the middle of the Pacific Ocean. The name on the bow was similar, too: *Pride of Hudson Bay*.

"You're yankin' my chain," Hawkins said in disbelief.

"Is Stony Man trying to kill us?" Encizo demanded, still drying his hair and wearing nothing but briefs. "Do they know what we just went through?"

"This'll be different," McCarter said calmly. "This time the operation won't be clandestine. We pull her over with the help of the Navy. If she resists, we pull back and let the Navy bring her to stop. From a distance and downwind."

"So what do they need us for?" Encizo demanded.

"Stony Man wants us on the Navy ship, anyway, for full med checks. Just in case any of us breathed in some of that stuff on the *Vancouver*. We're to make sure the *Hudson Bay* is emptied and secured if it turns out to contain the cargo Stony Man thinks it contains.''

''And then?'' Manning asked.

''Then we wait, mate. Unless Striker's come up with something. And by then I think he will have.''

THE SEA HAWK SET DOWN heavily onto the deck of the USS *Mistral* in the late afternoon under grim skies. The *Mistral* was a Cyclone-class ship, assigned to Naval Special Warfare. The Bollinger Shipyards-made vessel operated on four Paxman diesel power plants, providing four shafts with 3,350 horsepower, enough to propel the 170-foot-long, 330-ton ship at speeds to thirty-five knots. Typically, Cyclone-class ships were found on coastal patrols. The *Mistral*'s captain approached in a hurry and spoke loudly over the rising wind, introducing himself as Captain Smithie.

''Glad you made it when you did. We've got a storm brewing, and it would've made it nearly impossible for you guys to put down.''

''I'm glad, too,'' McCarter said, ''because we would have attempted the landing no matter how bad the weather was. What's the situation with the *Pride of Hudson Bay,* Captain?''

Phoenix Force had heard only brief reports during the hours-long trip from Johnston Atoll aboard the Sea Hawk, but what little they had heard indicated a change in plans. ''We can't seem to find her,'' the captain admitted.

''How can you lose a five-hundred-foot cargo vessel?'' Hawkins demanded.

The captain smiled easily, and McCarter got the impression he was a man who had himself under control, who would be hard to rub the wrong way. ''Let me promise you that if I had personally located the *Hudson Bay* it wouldn't have been lost. As it was, I was proceeding under secondhand intelligence, including intel coming in from your friends stateside, whoever those people may be."

"I appreciate your efforts, Captain Smithie," McCarter said, playing his cards right, whether he needed to or not.

"I don't have room for all of you in my bridge office, so I've set up a makeshift office in our mess. We've got communications there to patch us into your friends at home. Unless you need to get freshened up, we'll head there immediately and get everybody up to speed."

"I don't think we need to 'freshen up,'" McCarter replied.

"I didn't think you would," Smithie said. He waved at the bridge, and an officer waved back briefly. As the captain took them below deck, they felt the engines thrum.

"Where are we headed, Captain?" Encizo asked.

"West."

"That narrows it down."

"You'll get a better idea of the situation in just a few minutes, gentlemen. Here we are."

The mess was cramped and stark, but well-lit, and the aroma of cooking stew floated from the nearby galley. A stack of maps was laid out on the tables, and the orange light on the face of the coffeepot glowed invitingly.

It took less than two minutes for the team to pour cups of coffee and gather around the table where Captain Smithie was arranging the maps. He checked his watch and pointed to a spot on the map. "Here we are. Last reported sighting of the *Pride of Hudson Bay* was here, about one hundred miles to the west of us.''

"Who sighted it?" Hawkins asked.

"There was a Navy chopper sitting on top of it until almost two hours ago. The weather got dangerous, and it had to head off. An hour ago a reconnaissance aircraft covered the area and failed to spot the ship.''

"How hard did he look?" Hawkins asked.

"I've got a lot of faith in our people, and they knew the stakes here. I'm willing to bet they were pretty thorough.''

Hawkins nodded. "Yeah, I'm sure you're right. Had the storm started then?''

"No. Low clouds but decent visibility and no rain. There's no reason they should have failed to sight the *Hudson Bay* if nothing else.''

"She couldn't have left the area too fast. I don't care how well-rigged she was, she's not going to outrun reconnaissance aircraft," James said.

"And the search plane took into account the fact that she might be rigged for quick-running. It searched the entire area, including flyovers of the landmasses in the area. No sign of the *Hudson*.''

"Could it have sunk?" Manning asked.

"It could have. Is there a chance the ship was attacked?" Smithie looked pointedly from man to man, looking for confirmation of that supposition. The captain knew he was being given information on a need-to-know basis; he wasn't sure what the situation was with the ship he was tracking. All he had been told was that it might contain a large store of chemical weapons, which meant it could have something to do with the stuff stolen from Aberdeen or the surge in military activity in the past twenty-four hours around Johnston Atoll.

He didn't even know who these guys were. Maybe some UN team. Their leader was a Briton, which meant they probably weren't even U.S.-sponsored, although they had American members and certainly had impressive U.S.-based resources. Smithie didn't really care who they were. He'd been told to cooperate with them, and he would do as ordered. And he had no reason to doubt their abilities.

"It's possible they were attacked and sunk. Or sank themselves after off-loading their cargo, specifically to throw us off their trail," McCarter said.

"If that's the case," he mused, "they'll probably have opted for smaller watercraft. They'll be virtually impossible to track."

"They can't get too far in small watercraft. And their options for a landing are pretty slim."

"How slim?"

Smithie pulled out a broader-scale map of the vicinity. "You're looking at about eight hundred square miles of the Pacific Ocean. We've got three landmasses in the area. I told you their options were slim. These two are just patches of sand and coral. No flora to hide in. So I guess that if they make landfall in the area, it'll be here." He tapped his pen on the third small circle. "Garden Island. It's got some vegetation, although the name is a gross exaggeration. There is even freshwater and a small natural bay."

"Big enough for the *Pride of Hudson Bay?*"

"No. And the Navy reconnaissance aircraft checked out the island, regardless. They would have spotted the ship if it was anywhere near the island."

"But the reconnaissance vessel didn't see the ship

anywhere," Hawkins protested. "And the *Hudson Bay* couldn't have gotten far in the hour after the chopper left it."

"You're right," Smithie said with a shrug, leaning back in his steel chair and tapping his pen on the edge of the table. "We have to consider that the Navy pilots missed the *Hudson Bay* or that the ship went down."

"Maybe Pollari sank it," Manning suggested. "He's clearly willing to toss away some expensive resources to accomplish his goals. What if he off-loaded to Garden Island or to smaller watercraft based out of Garden Island, then sank the *Hudson Bay?* It would look like it disappeared without a trace."

"If either of those scenarios is true, then I'm betting your guys are still sitting on Garden Island. If all they have is small watercraft, they'd be pretty foolish setting out in the mess that's closing in on them right now."

"How much of a mess are we talking about?" McCarter asked.

"Big enough to have a name," Smithie said, grimacing. "That's tropical storm Thurmond."

"Thurmond?" James repeated. "Who thinks up those names, anyway?"

"How bad is Thurmond going to get, Captain Smithie?" McCarter asked.

"Well, it's not going to turn into a hurricane, they think. But it's still bad enough that my ship is going to get out of here as soon as we figure out what to do with you cowboys."

McCarter tapped the small green circle that was Garden Island on the map. "We cowboys are going to shake hands with Thurmond."

CHAPTER TWENTY

The USS *Mistral* slammed into the swell, levitated and fell as if plummeting from a cliff. When it hit the water the spray shot from the prow for several yards in both directions.

"Getting rough," Captain Smithie said. "Thurmond's moving in fast."

"How risky is it for you to be here?" McCarter asked.

"Pretty damn risky. We'll be getting out of here the moment we drop you guys off. You still sure that's what you want us to do?"

McCarter nodded. "Yeah, I'm sure. If our guess is correct, they've sunk the *Hudson Bay* and holed up on Garden Island with several smaller boats. Once this storm eases, they'll head out. In small watercraft they'll be hard, maybe impossible, to find. We have to hit them now."

"You guys seem to know what you're doing. But I can't help thinking that you're going to get yourselves killed in this," Smithie said, raising his voice to be heard over the whistling wind.

"What I'm more afraid of is letting these men get away with those weapons. They could wipe out hun-

dreds, maybe thousands of innocent people. I don't
want that on my conscience, Captain.''

''I understand.''

They watched the roiling sea in silence for another
five minutes. Belowdecks the rest of Phoenix Force
was simultaneously getting checked out by the ship's
doctor, who, it turned out, had experience dealing with
pneumatic trauma, and prepping for off-loading at
Garden Island. So far the Navy physician's examina-
tions of the team showed no evidence of exposure to
the deadly mixture of gases that had poured out of the
burning *Pride of Vancouver*.

Now they were preparing to put themselves right
back into that situation.

McCarter wondered silently if Captain Smithie was
correct. Maybe he would be leading his men to their
deaths on the island.

But, as he had told the captain, he really had no
choice. Letting those chemicals slip through his fingers
wasn't an option.

''In ten minutes we'll be as close as we can get
you,'' Smithie said.

''We'll be ready.''

McCarter left the bridge.

''YOU SURE it's out there?'' Manning asked.

''It's there. We're less than two klicks from the island,'' Smithie replied.

Manning stared out into the darkness, through the
steady pour of blowing rain, and thought he could,
perhaps, detect a mass of darkness sitting on the black,
nighttime Pacific. But maybe not.

''We'll find it,'' James said assuredly. The ex-

SEAL was the most at-home in this type of operation. "What's the weather situation, Captain?"

"Thurmond's moving in fast. In fact, the worst of it is going to be on top of us in less than two hours. I hope to have the *Mistral* as far away as possible by then."

"I get the hint. We're ready to take off."

"Remember, once you leave this ship you're on your own for at least twelve hours. Anybody gets hurt or you get into a situation where you need backup, you're not going to get it. We'll be the closest vessel, and there'll be no way for us to get close enough to be of assistance until after Thurmond has passed through."

"Understood," James said.

"Understood," McCarter echoed.

Manning shrugged.

Smithie stood there watching the storm-tossed sea as if he felt he ought to say more to dissuade the team.

"Thanks for the help, Captain," McCarter said. "I know you're putting your ship at risk for this operation. We appreciate it."

"You can show your appreciation by still being here when we come to pick you up in the morning."

"You got it."

Smithie felt slightly helpless as he watched the team scramble to the edge of the craft and quickly don the last of their water-infiltration gear, which they had carried with them from Johnston Atoll. They disappeared over the side into the inflatable motorized craft that would take them to the island.

He heard the roar of their engine, but it faded almost instantly and the team was swallowed by the rain and darkness.

He wasted no time, jogging up the companionway to the bridge.

"Let's get the hell out of here," he said.

The *Mistral* powered up and headed away from Garden Island at full speed.

THE STORM'S INTENSITY escalated during the twenty minutes Phoenix Force was on the water.

The *Mistral* had actually carried them in a wide circle around the north end of the island, to avoid crossing the southern end of the island where the small bay was located, then dropped them off at the closest point allowed by subterranean reefs on the west end. This offered another advantage in that the island's densest growth of plant life was on the western side. It was their best bet for an undetected landfall.

Still, McCarter brought the boat to a halt on the rolling waves when they were still a hundred yards from the shore. From their unsteady position they watched the dark jungle onshore. They saw no light, no movement other than the windswept tossing of the vegetation. Only when he was sure there were no signs of life did he give the go-ahead for landing.

James and Hawkins were the first out, stepping into the surf up to their waists and spreading out on either side of the inflatable raft, scanning the jungle and covering their teammates as the raft was dragged onto the beach. They followed the others onto the shore when they were safely under the cover of the jungle, crouching in the darkness.

"We made it in unseen as far as I can tell," James said.

"I feel like we're the crew of the *Minnow*," Manning said. "Except we don't have a Mary Anne."

"Yeah, but you'll do as Gilligan," Hawkins replied.

"They'd have been off that island in a week if they'd had an African American SEAL on that three-hour tour," James declared.

"Can it," McCarter said sternly, putting the banter decisively to rest. "We've got our targets. Let's go. Stay in contact, but let's keep the conversation down. I don't think we should assume that Pollari's men are going to stay under shelter, despite the rain. They know they had a Navy chopper watching them this afternoon. They know we're probably going to pinpoint their location, and they're going to be waiting for us. Stay focused."

Without further word the team broke into two groups and separated. Encizo and James started down the shore, hugging the tree line. Hawkins, Manning and McCarter penetrated the jungle.

THE TRIO SPREAD OUT, putting five paces between themselves, and alternated taking point, counting their paces through the sparse palm jungle. Hawkins was in the lead when he raised a hand that silently brought the march to a halt. After a moment of waiting, he gestured to the others to join him.

They could barely make out the forms of a wall of palm fronds ahead of them in the trees, and between the loose palms there seemed to be occasional glimpses of an orange glow.

Approaching at a near-crawl, they moved to the right far enough to see beyond the shelter, finding an open, flat area. In the darkness and the rain they could just make out boats anchored in the small bay.

"They're pulled up pretty close to avoid damage during the storm," Hawkins stated.

"Which means they're probably not loaded," Manning said. "That's good news."

"Yeah, but they're also sitting out in the middle of nowhere," McCarter observed. "It's going to be a bloody difficult move for Rafe and Cal to get at them unseen."

"So let's create a distraction," Manning suggested.

They moved to the northeast, slowly and silently, finding four more palm shelters erected in the trees, their roofs reinforced with black plastic sheets to keep out the rain.

"We could take these guys down pretty easy," Manning said. "Roll in a few grenades and be done with it."

"I think securing the chemical store ought to be our first priority, don't you?" McCarter asked.

ENCIZO AND JAMES FOUND the going quick, even stopping occasionally to scan the way ahead for a guard. They circled the southwest quarter of the island before they found the shelter of trees on their left that fell away at the bay. They came to a halt, crouching among the trees and scanning the bay that opened up before them.

It was small and shallow, and the land around it was white coral sand empty of growth. A collection of small pleasure and fishing boats rode in the water so close to the shore that James would have guessed they were scraping the bottom, especially when the storm-tossed waves receded suddenly.

"They're riding pretty high," he observed. "Probably not loaded yet."

"Probably?" Encizo asked.

"I'm not going to be sure until I look inside," James said.

"That's a long way out into the middle of nowhere."

"Yeah."

They could make out a series of huts constructed under the shelter of the trees well away from the shore. They had been tossed together out of palm fronds hacked from the island's trees and lashed into place with cords on crude wooden frames. Black plastic sheets had been added to the roofs to keep out the water. They had probably been tossed together in just a few hours as the men realized they were going to have to ride out tropical storm Thurmond here.

"You think they took the chemicals inside the huts with them?" James asked.

"Would you want to sleep with that stuff?"

"Guess not."

Their earpieces hissed and McCarter spoke. "Phoenix One here."

"We're in position at the mouth of the bay, Phoenix One."

"We're behind the northernmost shelter, making our way east. We're looking for the containers."

They knew that the eastern end of the island grew sparse vegetation. Encizo and James could see little of the island in that direction, hidden by the boats and masked by the escalating curtain of rain.

"I'm heading into the bay to check out the watercraft."

"Watch for guards."

Encizo quickly looped a length of blackened nylon rope around a tree while James stepped out of some of his gear. He took the water-resistant MP-5 and, over one shoulder, a pack containing a supply of plastique and radio-controlled ignitors. He grabbed the rope and walked into the thrashing ocean.

James was the ablest member of the team in the water. As a SEAL, he had been trained to treat water as the safest place to be in a crisis situation. But he had rarely interacted with an ocean like this. The wind and waves were pounding and thrashing, rising and falling like mountains. The rain was picking up, falling in windblown torrents, so that even on the surface it felt as if he were submerged. With the rope tied to his belt he swam strongly through the chaotic currents that came and went, trying to pull him in all different directions, and it seemed as if he were helpless for a moment. But his powerful strokes drew him through the water toward the storm-tossed watercraft.

The Pollari team was taking a chance leaving its boats at anchor in a storm this close to the shore, but the alternative was putting them to anchor at a distance from the island, which they probably considered too risky. James wondered as he grabbed the first vessel's anchor chain, a forty-five-foot pleasure yacht, if they also considered putting a guard on the ship too risky.

There was only one way to find out.

He grabbed the rail, pulling himself to eye level with the deck, which was dancing with frantic raindrops.

The cabin was dark. There was no sign of movement, but the darkness inside was blurred by water. There might have been a gunner standing in that darkness, training a weapon on James without his even seeing it.

He clambered over the rail, torrents of seawater pouring off him, and moved across the deck in a hurry, getting out of the sights of the could-be gunner. A burst of lightning filled the night with sudden illumination and James rode it out, then entered the cabin. The interior was dark, still and dry, oddly homey and comfortable considering the circumstances. It took him thirty seconds to explore the crowded rooms and storage areas and determine there was no dangerous cargo aboard. What he did find were stacks of plastic fuel containers. They were planning on using this boat for a long-distance run.

It took him another minute to mold a block of C-4, then insert a radio-controlled detonator. A flick of the switch armed it. James crouched and pressed the plastique into the underside of the control panel.

It would be unnoticed if anybody entered the craft. When it blew, it would take out the controls and the radio and would blast through the hull. The boat would be very definitely out of business.

"Cal?" Encizo asked in his headphones.

"Boat one is empty and I've left them a present. Proceeding to number two. Anything going on out there?"

"It's raining."

"Thanks."

He crawled onto the deck and to the rear of the boat, where he slid into the water and found the rope to shore, which he'd left looped on the anchor chain, then paddled as best he was able through the storm-tossed sea to the next craft.

It was the smallest of the five ships, a pleasure boat with a diminutive cabin that had been cleared of fixtures and furniture, presumably to make room for cargo and for the extra plastic fuel containers it held. But the chemicals weren't onboard, and once again

James left a hidden chunk of plastique rigged for radio-controlled detonation.

At the third boat he found the door to the cabin locked. He picked it, then went through the search-and-booby trap process a third time.

As he descended into the water to head for ship number four, he heard more cracks of thunder, and lightning illuminated the sea in flashes. James's strength was being tested by the heavy seas. He could feel his muscles aching. Tropical storm Thurmond had to be sitting on top of them, blasting the island with its full fury.

As he reached the fourth vessel, an errant wave picked him up and slammed him into the hull, and he barely had time to cushion the impact with his hands. As it was he hit the hull hard. A flash of light rocked through his brain as he collapsed into the water, and he flailed to bring himself upright in the waves, reaching out at the same time to prevent himself from being carried into the hull again. Gratefully he found the ship's anchor chain and used it to haul himself to the surface, gasping for air, at the same time feeling the give in the chain as the boat dragged it to the shore.

This boat, at least, wasn't secure enough that it was going to survive the storm. Thurmond's fury was dragging it to the beach. If the storm didn't pass quickly, all the boats would be on the sand in the morning.

James boarded it anyway, finding it empty like the others and rigging it with plastique. As he slipped into the water again, he could feel the muscles all over his body straining and aching from the stress. His head and shoulder were throbbing from the beating against the hull.

Four down, one to go.

CHAPTER TWENTY-ONE

Hawkins, Manning and McCarter left the makeshift camp behind, trudging on top of the vegetation when they could to keep their feet out of the water and mud. The lightning was beginning to flash over their heads, slashing at the ocean, thunder rumbling in the low-lying clouds.

As the downpour worsened, McCarter brought the trio to a sudden halt with a quick raise of his hand. With a flick of his fingers, the three men descended into a slight ditch.

In front of them was a low rise in the land. At about six feet, it was probably the highest point on the island, and the Pollari team had chosen it as the driest storage place in the storm. Feeling no need to protect the plastic, sealed containers, they had only built two small shelters on the rise for the guards stationed there.

In the darkness and low visibility of the storm, the three Phoenix Force warriors had nearly walked into the middle of it all.

But the guards had failed to spot them. There was no sign of movement from the pair of crude huts, although the nature of their construction allowed them to see the guards within clearly, facing in opposite directions, but not toward the rear of the island. Maybe they expected that was the least likely origin of an attack, or else they thought no one would bother attacking them in the tempest.

Lying flat on their stomachs, the three commandos observed the guards.

"The poor saps are miserable," McCarter said. "They're not putting their full concentration into the task at hand. Do we see anybody else hanging about, mates?"

"That's a negative," Manning replied. "The shelters are totally obscured from here. So are the boats."

"Then let's take them down. And let's do it altogether. We don't want one of them getting the chance to call for some help. I'll back you guys."

Hawkins and Manning produced their 9 mm Beretta 92-F handguns from their weatherproof holsters and laid their firing arms on their forearms. McCarter rose into a crouch and readied his own pistol.

Hawkins gave a three-count, then the two warriors fired simultaneously. In the rush of the downpour the discreet coughs from the suppressed weapons were drowned and wouldn't have been perceived by the guards had the shots missed. But both rounds reached their targets. Hawkins's victim simply leaned over on the sand and was still, cored through the brain, but Manning's victim staggered out of the shelter with a ghastly wound to the neck. The massive flood of blood attested that the artery had been severed, and even the torrent couldn't wash the crimson tide from his shirt as it flowed from the vein. The dying man opened his mouth, but Manning's second round hit his chest dead-center, stopping him in an instant. He pitched down the rise near their feet.

McCarter never had to fire a shot.

They quickly dragged the corpses to the far side of the rise, then checked the chemicals. The stacks of plastic containers, mixed with a few metal hermetically sealed receptacles, seemed intact and safe.

"Let's just hope they don't get struck by lightning," Hawkins said.

As if mocking them, Thurmond sent a thin, slashing blade into the ocean less than a mile from shore, and the brilliance illuminated the island. For a fraction of a second the mask of rain seemed to be cut away, and the three warriors found themselves seeing clearly to the makeshift huts a hundred yards away. At the same moment one of the Pollari men was standing underneath a palm tree away from the huts, urinating into a rivulet while draping one arm over his forehead to keep the water out of his eyes.

His gaze locked with McCarter's and his mouth flew open, then he stumbled into the nearest hut. They didn't need to hear him shouting.

"We're made, mates," McCarter said. "Back the way we came."

They jogged down the rise and headed for the trees to the north of the huts, each choosing a tree for shelter.

"Keep them from getting to the rise," McCarter said. "Rafe, you there?" he radioed.

There was the start of a reply, then a crackle of lightning turned the signal to static that lasted for precious seconds. Manning and Hawkins were firing at the gunners who were trying to emerge from the nearest hut. The rattle of automatic fire cut through the storm.

The static was gone. "Rafe here."

"We've been spotted and we're trading fire," McCarter said. "What's your situation?"

"I've lost contact with Cal. He's getting banged around out there pretty good."

"You anywhere near the huts?"

"Negative. I'm still positioned on the south end of the island at the lip of the bay."

"We might be driving some players in your direction. Be on the alert."

"I will. But I can't do much about the boats until I locate Cal."

An angry buzz of autofire cut the ground inches from the tree that was protecting McCarter, and he cut off the conversation.

Hawkins had caught sight of the gunner who was targeting the Phoenix Force leader. The young commando's rounds cut up the side of a palm tree, slashing into the arms of the gunner, creating a spray of crimson that was washed out of the air by the pouring rain. The automatic rifle dropped and the gunner staggered out from behind his tree, looking stupidly at his tattered arms, giving Hawkins a clear shot. He stitched his victim from thigh to collar with a quick burst from his MP-5 and turned away before the dead man fell.

He searched for more hardmen and spotted Manning taking down a nearby shotgunner who was making an aggressive approach. A gunner from the second hut made a break for the rise, covering himself with a magazine-draining burst of automatic fire that made toothpicks out of Manning's tree. The Canadian ducked for cover and McCarter was trapped as well, but Hawkins was far enough away he judged he had time to snap off a few rounds before the runner could target him. He stepped halfway out and ripped out a burst that chopped into the gunner's thigh. As he twisted to take out Hawkins, his leg ceased to function and he slammed to the ground. The Phoenix Force warrior zapped him with another volley of manglers that entered his torso at the top of his abdomen and cut through his chest cavity.

Through the palms of the nearest hut he spotted more hardmen.

"I'm fragging them," Manning said, and Hawkins took cover himself as the Canadian stepped into the open long enough to launch a fragger at the hut. It crashed through the palms, and the ensuing scream and blast seemed to meld into a single sound. The grenade's ragged metal shrapnel ripped the hardmen and most of the palms of the hut itself into tattered remains of their former selves.

A screamer staggered into the open from the second hut, where he'd caught a good part of the blast in the face. He was holding his eyes, rain-diluted blood pouring down his bare chest, and he fell to the ground when McCarter targeted and fired a quick pair of mercy rounds.

More hardmen from the other huts were taking flight, doing their best to keep the huts between them and their assassins.

"Rafe, they're coming to you. You found Cal yet?"

"Negative! And his safety line's gone slack. He's in one of the boats or in the water."

"You see them coming?"

"I see them, Phoenix One. I'm going to go in after Cal."

"Do not, repeat, do not go into the bay, Rafe."

"Cal's in there, man!"

"You're not going to do him any good."

The radio issued an expletive, and McCarter heard the retort of Encizo's MP-5 cutting through the jungle. Hawkins and Manning were making quick work of checking the huts.

"Empty," Hawkins announced, emerging from the last shelter.

"Cal's gone missing."

They jogged after the fleeing horde, taking what cover they could in a slight rise at the edge of the bay shore, where the survivors were rushing through the water to their boats as best they could. Several gunners were in the water up to their knees, facing the shore and trying to cover the others.

ENCIZO, WELL-PROTECTED by a small copse of trees inside the lip of the bay, was pegging them. Two had already gone down.

Manning, McCarter and Hawkins reached over the top of their rise and triggered their water-resistant MP-5s into the enemy, going for the gunners first. Three went down in the next brief instant, and the mob panicked. Only two gunners kept their stance, but they were helpless under an attack that came from two directions. One of them emptied his magazine at Encizo as the Cuban warrior waited him out patiently, allowing his palm tree to absorb the deadly rounds. The gunner's companion took up the barrage then, but was helpless to attack from the front. His companion was desperately scrambling for a fresh mag when Hawkins cut him down, paused for a microsecond and cut Encizo's gunner across the waist.

The stronger swimmers were clambering aboard the boats. One of the engines fired up, and then another.

Encizo made a mad dash to join the rest of the team.

A figure on the first in the line of boats spotted him and raised an AK.

"Down, Rafe!" Hawkins shouted, and triggered his SMG at the same moment the gunner squeezed the trigger on the AK, but the waterlogged Kalashnikov never fired. The moisture-hardened MP-5 operated smoothly, depositing four rounds into the gunner's body and sending him flopping to the deck.

The boat rumbled and tried to maneuver, but a huge swell of water rose against it, and it couldn't turn. One of the men made a try at the anchor, and Manning cut into him with a quick burst from the MP-5 that sent him into the water himself, disappearing into the tide.

"There's Cal!" Hawkins raised his subgun and directed a withering torrent of fire at the farthest watercraft. McCarter couldn't see his missing team member, only a bunch of men on the craft diving for cover from the Texan's 9 mm barrage. Then Hawkins paused and a gunner appeared at the rail with an automatic handgun, which he aimed directly into the water.

McCarter fired and watched the rounds impact uselessly against the side of the boat as it rose unexpectedly in the tide, but the same movement threw off the handgunner on the boat and he never fired, retreating below the rail for shelter.

"Cover us, Manning. T.J., with me."

McCarter and Hawkins got to their feet and sprinted down the beach while Manning rose into a kneeling position and triggered a steady volley of rounds that traveled the length of the five anchored boats.

The Briton now spotted James bobbing to the surface and gasping for breath as another wave crashed on top of him and obliterated him from sight for a moment. Then he was there again, looking clearly dazed and weakened, but heading in their direction with steady strokes.

There was more movement from the boats as the crews tried to get the anchors up and the engines started, and their gunners tried to cover them. Many men were still swimming around the boats, having a difficult time just clambering on board. Manning paused just long enough to change magazines, and McCarter took over with a volley of his own that cut into the first two moving figures he saw. The Pollari team was doing a pathetic job of making an escape. The seas were simply too rough to make even the simplest operation easy.

A large wave rumbled through the bay, lifting the boats high into the air before carrying them down into a deep trench.

"Get Cal!" McCarter ordered.

Hawkins dropped his MP-5 and broke into a run, trudging into the shallows. One of the gunners sighted him and tried to aim, but McCarter triggered a short blast that compensated for the rise in the sea. The gunner was cut down before he could trigger off a round. McCarter adjusted his aim enough to cut through the front window of the boat and shatter it with a volley of rounds that took the pilot to the floor.

Encizo and Manning were moving leapfrog fashion in his direction, keeping each other covered. McCarter dared a glimpse in James's direction and couldn't see the black warrior anywhere. He only saw Hawkins plunging into the waves.

A puff of smoke materialized inside the nearest watercraft and McCarter glimpsed a fiery projectile headed directly at him, accompanied by shouts from Encizo and Manning. He dropped and felt the heat of the missile as it burned through the air where he had been standing and traveled for another thirty yards almost parallel to the ground before hitting one of the huts and exploding with a burst of orange fire.

McCarter was on his feet again, his face a mask of fury.

"Those bastards have rockets!" Manning roared.

McCarter clamped his jaw tight and pulled at his trigger, cutting a zigzag pattern across the bow and cabin of the ship and sending its occupants scrambling into its bowels. But when the mag was empty he was sure he hadn't scored once.

"How's Cal?" he demanded, not daring to look as he changed out the mag.

"I still don't see him," Manning said. "I'm going to help T.J."

"Go."

Encizo arrived at the Phoenix Force leader's side as Manning hurried into the water, and they delivered sporadic bursts at the line of craft. None of the boats were going anywhere until they could get their anchors up, and none of them could do so while Phoenix Force kept them under constant fire.

McCarter glanced at the water. Manning was under. Hawkins was snatching a gasping breath, and then he descended again. James was nowhere to be seen.

"Bloody hell," he growled.

"Rocket Man is back," Encizo stated and targeted the figure behind the LAW as he tried to come to the deck of the bucking boat. The burst from the MP-5 punched him over the deck and into the stormy sea.

There was a tinkle of shattering glass and the muzzle of the LAW protruded through a porthole on the side of the ship. It couldn't possibly aim from that angle at the warriors on the shore, and McCarter watched with grim fury as it aimed into the water and a puff of smoke signaled a launch.

He fired hopelessly at the boat and watched the rocket streak through the downpour at Manning and Hawkins. Both men sank into the water, and the rocket seemed to skim over the surface where they had gone down with just inches to spare and impacted on the beach, blasting a crater in the soggy sand.

Hawkins surfaced with the limp form of Calvin James draped in his arms. The warrior's head drooped over the sea, streaming water, but McCarter thought he saw movement.

Encizo started firing as another LAW appeared, jutting from the porthole, and more figures with weapons were crawling to the decks of the ships. They spotted the helpless three as they were crawling from the water. Manning had joined Hawkins, but the waves and the weight of the water seemed to have slowed their progress to a tortoiselike crawl.

McCarter fired at the LAW and watched it disappear inside for a moment. He triggered at the gunner on the roof and saw him duck.

Encizo spotted a gunner with an AK-74 jump onto the deck of the neighboring craft and fire briefly at the men in the water, then pull back before Encizo's fire could reach him. Another shooter appeared from inside the next boat, fired his weapon, then disappeared.

"They're sitting ducks," Encizo shouted over the roar of surf and storm.

"We're all sitting ducks," McCarter replied, then shouted, "Get down!" An unexpected gunner had appeared on the deck of the last ship with a massive machine gun dangling from his neck. The shadowy figure cut loose, and a volley of rounds chopped into the water and the beach, eating a path to the three warriors. McCarter fired and watched the gunner pull back.

The three men had nearly reached the shore and were standing in knee-deep water when a fresh storm-tossed wave slammed into them from behind and sent them staggering. James's feet were dangling in the sand, and his weight almost brought the other two to the ground. They were a long twenty paces from the nearest cover.

The LAW appeared again from the porthole and was aimed at the Phoenix Force trio. As the gunner waited for a fraction of a second for the swell to deflate under the craft, the machine gunner in the last boat reappeared. There was an endless fraction of a second in which McCarter saw the two powerful weapons aimed at his three teammates and knew there was very little his cover fire could do to stop the inevitable from happening.

Then he saw movement out of the corner of his eye that he hadn't expected.

Calvin James raised his head.

His eyes were red and cloudy, but he was smiling. He raised his hand, holding a remote control device with a tiny red light that seemed to cut through the gray mist of the storm.

The swell deflated and the LAW was staring them in the face. The machine gunner was coming to bear when James touched the button on the remote control unit, activating the five radio-controlled ignitors aboard the five watercraft. The boats exploded with a single sudden eruption that shocked the island and seemed to dwarf the fury of the storm. The ships disintegrated in seconds, and massive temporary craters formed in the ocean surface. McCarter and Encizo were knocked onto their backs. James crumpled to the sand when Hawkins and Manning collapsed under the impact of the shock wave. Wood and metal shrapnel rocketed in every direction, driving into the exposed skin of the Phoenix Force warriors and covering the tiny island with debris.

Then the ocean craters filled in under the onslaught of the pounding waves and nothing was left but the smoking rubble, washing toward the shore. The surface was coated with spilled fuel and human blood, but of the Pollari soldiers not a living soul remained.

CHAPTER TWENTY-TWO

Azerbaijan

Astara emergency services couldn't be well-known for their response times, Bolan decided. He got out of the hotel with minutes to spare before police and fire units arrived on the scene with sirens pulsating. By then the small blaze had turned to a conflagration encompassing the entire top floor.

He returned to his Russian-made Moskvitch automobile, removed a carryall from the trunk and wrapped his hands in bandages. Then he headed for another hotel, this one belonging to a French chain. He had already checked in under a different alias. He headed for the room and tossed the carryall on the bed.

In the bathroom he treated his hands well enough to satisfy any medical doctor. The splinters of wood—those that weren't completely buried in his flesh—he extracted. The minor burns he disinfected. The wounds he bandaged carefully, with an eye toward continued mobility as much as toward protecting the damaged flesh.

Those hands were going to see a lot more action in the coming hours and Bolan wanted full use of them.

He changed out of the suit he had worn to Oguz's

failed dinner party, which reminded him he could use more nourishment. Who knew how long until he saw another opportunity to eat? He ordered a meal from room service, and, as soon as the order was placed, dialed through to the U.S. It took a full two minutes for his call to click through various lines and scrambling devices to Stony Man Farm, half a world away on the East Coast of North America.

"Striker here," he said, identifying himself.

There was no answer except for another click and the ringing of another line, followed by a gruff, "Hello, Striker. How are things progressing in your corner of the world, my friend?" Yakov Katzenelenbogen asked.

"Not as well as I would like. A guy by the name of Arif Oguz ruined my evening."

"Barb had me put together a file on Oguz." Bolan could hear the flipping of the pages. "This one the world can do without."

"Tell me."

"He's got farmers up and down the east coast of Azerbaijan growing poppies for him. He's also organized drug retailing organizations in virtually every city in six *rayonlar*, which are Azerbaijani administrative divisions, kind of like U.S. counties. Looks like he has heavy influence on the government in each area. They get a cut, he gets to operate."

"Same old story," Bolan growled. "Where'd we get this information?"

"There's been an investigation into Oguz at the national level for years. This all comes from them. Aaron got access to it somehow. There's never been enough evidence to go after him. In fact, if I'm reading between the lines accurately, every attempt to seriously shut down Oguz has become bogged down in bureaucracy—surprise, surprise.''

"Do we have his home address?''

"Yeah. His primary residence is at the Hotel Astara Royale in Astara—''

"Not anymore.''

Katz thought about that for a second, then said, "He has a number of secondary residences. We've also got locations for suspected operations of all kinds—poppy fields, drug-processing facilities, smuggling distribution centers. We know the names of some of his most important dealers and smuggling partners. He ships major amounts of heroin into Russia, Turkey, other Central Asian countries.''

"I'll want all that intel.''

"You got it. There's something else you should know.'' Bolan heard more paper rattling and Katz continued. "Oguz employs a team of enforcers called the Killers.''

"Sounds like a British rock group.''

"Nothing so mundane. These guys are all KGB-trained agents who found themselves unemployed when the Iron Curtain came down. It's my impression these men were too corrupt to make a go of it in a kinder, gentler world, so they turned to the newly organized crime syndicates developing to take advantage of the new democracies. They were hired by Oguz, and now serve as a kind of roving enforcement squad. According to these reports, they are known to travel from town to town, anywhere Oguz's operations are running into trouble of whatever kind.''

"They roll into town, deliver the solution and move on to the next problem,'' Bolan said. "Very efficient.''

"Right. Oguz doesn't have to pay for on-site enforcement in each city as long as he has these guys. It sounds like the Killers are vicious enough that their lessons stay learned. You need to watch out for these guys, Striker.''

''I will.''

''I've got a lot more to give you,'' Katz continued. ''This guy sells guns on the streets and runs several brothels. He's been tied to child prostitution rings—a newly flourishing business in some CIS states.''

Bolan had seen it all before. He had witnessed young people's lives ruined by heroin. He had seen children in chains and had known women forced into prostitution. A face appeared in his thoughts—that of an innocent girl who had died in Massachusetts a long time ago.

''You were right,'' Bolan said. ''The world would be a better place without Arif Oguz.''

THE LIST OF POTENTIAL TARGETS filled several pages of Mack Bolan's war book, a small black notebook he carried with him when he could. In it were the names of many of his targets. Some were men he had faced down years ago, and nearly all of them were dead. Bolan wasn't the kind to cuff them and send them to jail. He preferred to permanently cut away the human cancer.

Other names in the war book were mere hints, the result of rumors and hearsay. There were times when Bolan disappeared into some part of the world to put a face to the names in his book, to find out if the rumors he had heard were true.

One of those names was Alexander Akhmedov, the Russian drugs-and-guns smuggler, whom Bolan had been hot on the trail of just twenty-four hours ago.

He'd carefully assembled a list of Akhmedov's operations. They were all in the book.

He would get to them eventually.

At the moment the new name of Arif Oguz had achieved the highest level of priority in the war book. And he had a new list of targets.

He thought about that list as he fieldstripped the cache of weapons he carried up from the Moskvitch. By the time he had carefully disassembled, cleaned and reassembled the Beretta 93-R, he had ranked his targets.

He cleaned and repacked his weapons carefully, as if he had all the time in the world. He heard the halls of the hotel grow quieter, and by the time he was preparing to leave, most of the guests were going to bed. It was after 11:00 p.m.

It was just the beginning of what the Executioner hoped would be a long, productive night.

It was the beginning of what he hoped would be the longest night of Arif Oguz's life.

HE CHOSE the first stop for its convenience.

It was the apartment building of one of the highest-ranking figures in the Oguz chain of franchise operations. Boz Akram had been working for Oguz for four years, and had renovated a former apartment building in the center of the city as his personal living quarters and a center for his operations. Bolan didn't even dare drive past it. The city was too quiet as midnight approached. Any vehicle would stand out. He parked several blocks away and made his recon on foot.

He was armed for all-out, close-quarters war. Going in quiet meant he would start with the Beretta 93-R. Sound-suppressed and firing subsonic rounds, it produced a coughing retort that was unfortunately nowhere near as quiet as the squirting noise a "silenced" handgun made in the movies.

When things started getting intense Bolan planned to change over to the mini-Uzi, which was positioned under his right arm for easy access. Harnessed on his back was another piece of Beretta hardware—an M 3-P police shotgun. Tucked into his combat webbing were extra magazines for all three weapons, along with a selection of grenades.

He was ready to do some harm to the Oguz crime syndicate.

Bolan crossed the street in the darkness and approached the building from the shadows that hugged the base of adjoining buildings, then sprinted along the brightly lit sidewalk that took him to the front door of Akram's home. He stopped there and waited for sounds of alarm. There were none. The street was deserted.

The Communist-era concrete brick building had a solid steel door and a pair of glass windows that flanked it, just four inches wide, three feet tall and a warm orange color. Inside was a small entrance area and a hallway, brightly lit but devoid of life.

Bolan wasn't going to waste time trying to find an alternate entrance. But he wanted to get inside without raising more noise than he had to. He had brought a hotel towel along and used it for the task at hand.

He wrapped up one hand and pressed against the glass, leaning his weight into it, building the pressure. The glass cracked, and Bolan eased the pressure quickly. A long web of three cracks had appeared where the base of his palm had rested. The crack had been muffled and, it seemed, unheard.

Bolan applied pressure to one of the newly created sections in the glass and it came off, falling to the floor inside the vestibule with a tinkle. The soldier saw a shifting of the light and stepped out of sight of the window.

He heard the steps and listened to the man enter the vestibule. When the guy seemed to have stopped, the Executioner stepped into the open again. Through the narrow window he saw an enormous walrus of a man standing very close to the window so he could look up and down the street for any sign of the disturbance that had caused the glass to break. When Bolan materialized just eighteen inches from his face he pulled back in alarm. Too obese to have easy access to a shoulder holster, he had the gun on his belt that was pulled up over his distended stomach, and he grabbed for it with beefy hands.

But Bolan inserted the muzzle of the 93-R through the hole in the glass and fired three rounds in rapid succession, each one ripping into the huge belly. The walrus stumbled against the entrance to the vestibule and sank to the floor in a sitting position. His eyes remained open, looking at Bolan, but all movement had ceased.

The Executioner reached through the glass and found the doorknob, opening it quickly and stepping inside. He paused long enough to press his fingers into the folds of the walrus's neck and found no pulse.

He searched the ground floor and found nicely appointed but simple rooms. Akram lived well by Azerbaijan standards but didn't go in for the opulence his boss enjoyed. The rest of the ground floor was devoid of life.

Bolan ascended the steel stairs to the second floor

and faced a hallway full of closed doors, realizing there might be as many as twenty men stationed here. How was he going to target Akram?

He heard movement and descended the stairs quickly and silently until he was just starting over the top of them. A dark-haired woman walked from one of the rooms, looking sleepy, wearing a short red silk robe. She entered a washroom and flipped on the light, closing the door behind her.

Bolan moved quickly to the rest room and stepped inside, grabbing the woman's mouth and putting the 93-R to the bridge of her nose before she had time to scream.

"Speak English?" Bolan asked. The woman shook her head, eyes wide beyond his hand. "Speak Russian?" he asked and this time she nodded slightly.

Bolan was well versed in the Russian language, and knew that many of the Azerbaijani spoke some. "Where is Akram?" Bolan demanded in Russian, slowly pulling his hand away.

The woman rolled her terrified eyes to the ceiling. "One floor up," she stuttered. "First bedroom."

Bolan nodded and removed the 93-R from the bridge of the woman's nose and showed it to her. "I'm going to kill Akram and everyone else who tries to stop me."

She began to tremble violently, her lower lip quivering.

"You," Bolan added, "leave now."

It was a threat and a command at the same time. The woman knew precisely what would happen if she didn't do as told. Bolan stood up and stepped back, his finger to his lips as a signal for silence. She raced out of the bathroom and down the steps. Bolan's only hope was that she didn't scream at the sight of the corpse in the vestibule.

AKRAM HAD BEEN a minor drug dealer on the streets of Astara in the mid-1990s, young, tough and ambitious. When Oguz moved in strong to consolidate his hold on the city, Akram had fought back viciously, personally leading battlefield-like attacks on Oguz's street soldiers.

His audacity and courage caught Oguz's eye. When the day finally came that Akram walked into a battle he couldn't win, he stood his ground and prepared to fight to the death rather that beg for mercy.

Oguz was even more impressed. He made Akram his first franchisee, giving him a healthy share of the profits and a free hand in running his operation as he saw fit. Akram quickly came to realize he could make more money operating under the low-overhead system Oguz had developed, and joined his former enemy as a business partner, fully intending to someday bring Oguz to his knees, usurp control of his business and kill him through long slow torture for daring to put him in a subordinate position.

Boz Akram tended to dream about the day he would have Oguz under his control. Sometimes he had Oguz tied to a table and was slicing off segments of his flesh in small pieces, making him scream and scream and scream....

Akram awoke with a start and found himself staring into the bright glare of his bedside lamp, positioned to shine directly into his face. Beyond the glare he saw a black shape standing over his bed.

"Who are you?" he demanded in Azeri.

"I'm looking for Arif Oguz." The figure spoke in

English, with an American accent. Akram knew he was in the presence of the American who had stormed through Oguz's operations all day, causing chaos.

"Who are you?" he repeated, this time in English.

There were shouts from outside, and the sound of feet pounded toward the door.

"In here!" Akram shouted.

The door burst open and a gunman stood in the door, looking bewildered at the helpless plight of his employer. Before the new arrival could use the large 9 mm automatic in his hand Bolan triggered a stuttering burst from the mini-Uzi. The gunman pitched to the floor, never knowing what hit him.

Akram pushed the light away and rolled to the other side of the bed. In the darkness he never saw the 93-R trained on his lower torso and when it fired he thought the strange blast came out of nowhere. Two of the rounds crashed through his legs and propelled him over the edge of the bed in a bloody mess of tangled sheets and blankets.

Bolan let him lay there screaming, and advanced to the door and stepped into the hall just long enough to target more approaching gunmen. The burst of rounds from the mini-Uzi cut into their midst, striking at least two of them. They all went down seeking cover.

The Executioner slammed the door to the bedroom and approached the writhing form on the floor. Akram gazed up through blazing eyes. He'd knocked over the light, so the area around him was illuminated, but it still seemed as if he were staring into blackness when he looked at the figure above him. For the third time, and now pleading and terrified as he had never been terrified, he said, "Who are you?"

"Tell me where Oguz is, and I'll let you live."

"Oguz is in hiding."

"Where?"

"I will never tell."

"You are dying, Akram." Bolan pointed to the massive soggy puddle of blood soaking the sheet around his legs. One of his 9 mm rounds had ripped through the artery in Akram's leg. "You want to protect Oguz with your dying breath."

Akram could feel the heavy spurts of blood pouring out of his leg. He knew the shadowy killer was right. He had moments to live. Did he want to spite his killer or Oguz in his final moments? He considered his options for a moment.

And by then he was dead.

Bolan cursed under his breath and turned to the door as it burst open. The foolhardy gunner shouted Akram's name and swept the room, and in the same instant he spotted the crumpled form behind the bed, he felt the impact of 9 mm rounds. He fell to the floor, kicking, and a mercy round to the head turned him off.

The Executioner rammed a fresh magazine into the mini-Uzi, then tucked away the Beretta handgun and reached over his shoulder to withdraw the M 3-P police shotgun. He unfolded the stock and jammed it tight against his stomach, marching into the hallway like a living, walking modern-day incarnation of Death.

A wounded man was rising from the pile of bodies and trying to make his fingers operate an automatic handgun while another gunner came up the stairs behind him with an automatic rifle. Bolan triggered the 12-gauge, and the blast slammed into the wounded man like a sledgehammer. The gunner on the stairs tumbled backward and scrambled to his feet again, covered in his own blood and that of his comrade. The mini-Uzi cut into him before he could get his bearings, and he was crashed to the stairway landing, this time for good.

Panic-fired shots filled the landing, and when there was a pause in the action, Bolan stepped into the open long enough to trigger the M 3-P and a short burst from the mini-Uzi at the three men he spotted at the bottom of the stairs. Then he pulled back quickly. He couldn't be sure his burst would stop all of them. He heard grunts and the sound of falling bodies, then the rattle from a single automatic rifle. It was magazine-draining desperation fire, and when it came to an abrupt halt he stepped onto the landing to find one man, bloodied and trying to crawl up the steps in his direction. The gunner had just retrieved an AK-47 from one of his dead companions. He swung it onto the stairs in front of him and tried to raise it from the ground to sight Bolan.

The soldier stood on the landing, waiting for it to happen.

The wounded gunner failed to muster the strength to raise the autorifle, so he crawled up another step and this time managed to hoist his body onto his knees. He lifted the AK-47 into a wavering firing position, aimed it at Bolan and made a grab for the trigger.

Only then did Bolan issue a final burst from the mini-Uzi, and the gunner's final efforts were cut short.

CHAPTER TWENTY-THREE

Etibar, Azerbaijan

Bolan hit the brakes and pulled the Moskvitch onto the shoulder of the road, throwing up gravel as he flipped off the headlights. Ahead of him, sooner than he had anticipated, appeared the lights of Etibar.

He jumped from the vehicle and grabbed his packs out of the rear, heading overland into the darkness of the semiarid brushland that seemed to make up much of the Azerbaijani landscape. He sped up a peak on foot and then paused, looking back on the Moskvitch. Alternately he searched without amplification and through a pair of infrared field glasses that showed nothing alive for hundreds of yards in any direction. It looked as if he had avoided being seen.

That wasn't his most important concern.

Right now he had some farming to attend to.

The leads he was following had gone through any number of human agents, and he hoped they could be counted on. The first had panned out, and with luck so would this one.

Traveling overland on foot, he counted his paces and converted them to kilometers. The instructions Katzenelenbogen had relayed told him to go one and a half kilometers north-northwest of the small water tower in the corner of the small town of Etibar in order to locate the entrance to a narrow gorge where he would find a field of poppies.

He closed in on the small village, watching for signs of life. He saw none. No guards were in evidence.

But then, none were needed to protect the village. The guards would be needed at the fields. In the dark they would have the advantage of knowing the terrain intimately. The advantage the soldier possessed was an instinctive ability to read the land and adapt his behavior to it. Another advantage was less intangible—the infrared field glasses, which could read the heat signatures of human beings as if they were flares in the darkness.

He moved north-northwest at a steady pace, watching the potential hiding places ahead of him by continually alternating between field glasses and bare eyes. The path he was following led to a small opening in the sudden steep hills that rose without warning from the land. Bolan decided that taking the direct route would be unwise, so he cut away from the path to the left, slowing to climb the incline as quietly as he was able in the almost pitch blackness of the night.

At three-quarters the way up the side of the hillock he halted, alerted by a sound he couldn't have described. It was a distant murmur, perhaps, or foliage being gently stirred by the wind.

More probably it was the night guards camped in the fields, watching against local rivals intent on stealing their crop. Bolan didn't know if those guards would be on a hill above their crop or camped out in it, so he approached the hilltop with great care.

He reached the top in a crawl, making his way to the edge and peering into the gorge.

It was an ideal spot for growing opium poppies. The natural rise in the land was ragged and meandered, gorged in the middle, where acres and acres of the plants could flourish without being visible from any angle except directly above.

The whisper of sound reached him again, and he saw the night guards. They were on the hilltop opposite him, just a hundred feet away and almost eye to eye with him. A small, permanent tent had been stitched together out of sheets and cloth scraps. A pair of armed guards crouched outside the tent, talking in low voices. Their campfire smoldered in front of them, orange coals winking lazily in the night, while the great clear sky stretched out behind them.

Getting at them would be a challenge, and it was unlikely that they would be able to provide the answers he needed. Better to get access to the man in charge of the fields. He was the one who could tell Bolan where to find Oguz.

He kept an eye on the gunners across the divide as he primed the M-16 A-2/M-203 with the first of many incendiary grenades he had packed. He targeted the far end of the poppy field about 250 yards to his right—well within range of the M-203. He triggered the 40 mm grenade and instantly turned his attention to the gunners across the divide.

They jumped to their feet at the sound of the grenade launch, shouting in confusion. The bomb exploded, the flames engulfing a massive swath of the plants. The gently moving sea of plants suddenly took on definition in the burst of yellow light.

Bolan knew the light was enough to bring him into

focus to the gunners, and they grabbed for their rifles. He fired the M-16 A-2 as the first rifle pointed in his direction. A gunner cried out and clutched his chest as he fell into the smoldering fire. His companion screamed, and the Executioner realized it was a woman. But he didn't discriminate against drug propagators by gender, and certainly not when they were attempting to kill him. When she stepped to the edge of the precipice and aimed a large-caliber hunting rifle across the divide, he didn't hesitate to trigger a burst of 5.56 mm rounds. She didn't make a sound when she pitched forward into the gorge.

Bolan began the serious destruction of the field below, sending one incendiary grenade after another into the gorge, placing them two hundred feet apart as he moved along the ridge. By the time the ridge began to descend, Bolan could hear shouts coming from the village and realized he was at a loss for effective cover other than the darkness of the night.

He would have to make the most of it.

The soldier reached the bottom of the ridge when he was caught in the glare of approaching headlights, followed by quick shouts and gunfire from the vehicle. He raked the front of the oncoming truck with a sustained burst, which brought it to an abrupt halt. Bolan ran into the gorge.

The wall of flame of his own creation was a hundred feet away. Bolan ran toward it, evaluating his position. It would take a few minutes for anyone to reach the northwest ridge, and if he hugged the southwest ridge none of his attackers would be able to spot him. At his back were acres and acres of burning poppies, a conflagration that was still escalating.

If a sudden wind didn't start up to drive the fire into

him and push him out of the gorge, Bolan had several minutes of solid cover from which only a front assault could be staged.

The pickup's headlights were shot out, but the truck was bathed in orange when it took the corner at high speed and aimed at Bolan, a handful of men in the rear shouting and hanging on as they tried to sight him down the barrels of their rifles. A wild plan popped into the soldier's head. He broke from the wall and hurried into the middle of the gorge, in the direction of the fire, weaving as he ran to avoid the sporadic fire the gunners were attempting. The truck accelerated directly at him until he skidded to a halt, spun quickly, and fired a savage burst into the windshield of the truck. The driver was dead before his head slammed against the back of the cab. Bolan bolted for cover as the out-of-control vehicle sped at near highway speeds in his direction, and sudden terror distracted the gunners in the rear. Without a driver to apply the brakes the truck barreled at full speed into the endless burning field of poppies.

Bolan headed back to the base of the hill and ducked when the explosion came, sending metal chunks flying throughout the gorge.

He tucked an HE round into the M-203 and changed magazines in the M-16 A-2 a half second before another attack. This time a hunting party came through the gorge entrance on foot, armed with rifles and shotguns, and Bolan laid a line of automatic fire at their feet, bringing them to a halt. They became distracted by screams from behind their enemy. The faces of the villagers went open-mouthed and ashen, and the soldier chanced a look back to see one of the truck occupants emerge from the conflagration. During his race through the landscape of fire, his clothes and hair had ignited and now he was completely ablaze. He whirled into the open like a horrible dancing fire god. Bolan sighted on the screaming man and deposited a pair of mercy rounds into his skull, ending his agony.

A rifle blast came from the end of the gorge, and the Executioner responded with another withering blast, cutting at shin level into the gathered, utterly inexperienced band of fighters. The one man who didn't fall at once made a hasty retreat until Bolan cut him down with a burst to the back of his knees.

Bolan watched the others carefully as he closed in, and as soon as one of them overcame his pain and snatched at his weapon, Bolan dispatched him with a sharp tri-burst aimed at the chest.

The wounded trio of survivors glared at him, faces ashen with pain and terror.

"Where is Arif Oguz?"

Their expressions transformed to bewilderment. Then one of the men nodded and spoke in rapid-fire Azeri. The others answered, and the first man responded in broken English that required much concentration. "We do not know where Oguz is. Oguz hiding."

"You're lying," Bolan stated without hesitation. "I kill liars." He withdrew a hand grenade from his combat webbing.

"No lie, no lie!"

The translator pleaded with the others in Azeri, and they finally nodded and replied, "We think he is in his villa! In Davaci!"

Bolan said nothing more but replaced the grenade. The fire was getting hot at his back, and he realized the intensity of the flaming poppies was igniting even the scrubby dried weeds that made up the normal vegetation in the gorge. The fire was creeping inexorably toward them.

There was a sudden buzz of startled voices, and he turned to see a gathering of villagers on the northwest ridge. At their feet was the dead guard and the burning ruin of their poppies, now engulfing the entire crop, and the blackened hulk of the flaming pickup truck were below. One of them trained his gun on the Executioner. Bolan stared the man down, motionless, over the hundred yards that separated them.

The gunner had second thoughts. He couldn't possibly hope to take out Bolan without the very high probability of hitting the wounded men scattered at his feet.

Bolan walked away from the scene, leaving the wounded trio desperately dragging themselves away from the encroaching consuming blaze.

More villagers—the women and children, mostly— were huddled halfway between the village edge and the ridge.

Another ancient work truck was waiting nearby and Bolan helped himself to it, leaving the agricultural community of Etibar a much more humble place than when he had arrived.

CHAPTER TWENTY-FOUR

Stony Man Farm, Virginia

Barbara Price stared at the printout. She tucked her hands between her thighs, suddenly feeling cold.

Human beings never failed to amaze her.

And to give her nightmares.

All those dead people. Personalities. Families—loving husbands and wives and children. Snuffed out. And now they knew why.

Aaron Kurtzman rolled into the War Room in a hurry, the first to arrive, and he was about to speak but stopped short. He knew Barbara Price very well and counted her as one of his dearest friends. And he could sense when she was feeling overwhelmed.

Rolling to her side, he looked at her silently. She put a hand on the table and he took it.

"Greed," she said quietly. "Money."

He didn't know what she was talking about, but he saw the SMF Top Priority Security label on the report sitting in front of her.

BROGNOLA CARRIED his briefcase and had a cigar clamped in his teeth, jutting almost directly to the side, and he adjusted it expertly so that he wouldn't take it off in the doorway. Price and Kurtzman were waiting for him, and Yakov Katzenelenbogen was behind him.

Price slid reports across the table to the newcomers. Kurtzman was pouring coffee and held up the pot with a questioning look. Brognola was tired and he nodded. He needed caffeine, even if it meant choking down Kurtzman's swill.

"What's going on?" Katz asked. He'd been catching some sleep and didn't know the purpose of the meeting.

"I was just briefed by Striker," Price said, leaning back in her chair. "He's been successful in tracking down Arif Oguz and convinced Oguz to give us the whole story. We've got names, places, motives, all of it." She tapped her pen on her own copy of the report.

"We were right about Edgar Pollari's involvement," she continued. "He's the mastermind behind the entire operation. He allocated funding and equipment from various entities of his own business empire, as we already know. There's another major player that we don't know about—Tariq Ramadan."

Katz gave a long low whistle. "There's our Iraqi connection."

"Yes. For the rest of you not so well-read as Yakov, Tariq Ramadan is an upper-echelon general in the Iraqi army. At least he was until very recently. He quit to join Pollari."

"What's Ramadan's story?" Brognola asked.

"Nothing outstanding as far as I know," Katz said. "He joined the Iraqi army in the late 1970s. He's ambitious, and he's been kissing the right Iraqi army ass throughout his career. He joined the upper ranks during one of Hussein's shake-ups. As far as I know, he's still serving Iraq."

"He was until just days ago," Price explained. "Apparently Pollari got to Ramadan somehow and talked him into throwing in with him. Pollari wanted to make use of chemical weapons, and he had a feeling Ramadan could get them for him. He was right. Ramadan knew the location of several stores of chemical weapons inside Iraq, some of which have been hidden for years. Ramadan carefully cultivated a network of loyal supporters among the Iraqi army, and a few days ago he and his supporters, including Colonel al-Duri, the one high ranker we do know about, just up and left the country by various routes. When they left they took Iraqi hardware—transport equipment, aircraft and an unknown amount of Iraqi chemical weapons."

"Dammit," Brognola muttered.

"That explains the use of the Russian chopper with Iraqi army markings in the *Tuscany II* attack," Kurtzman said. "It certainly threw the world onto the wrong track."

"It's also pretty easy to see why Iraq has been less than willing to defend itself in the eyes of the world," Price said. "They'd lose a lot of face if they had to admit to not only the defection of one of their most important generals but also the loss of many men and lots of equipment. It's embarrassing."

"Yeah," Brognola said. "The Glorious Leader would just as soon pretend it didn't happen at all. Especially since it would mean admitting he still has extensive stores of chemical weapons in the country."

"Okay, fine, all that makes sense to me. But I'm still not clear on what's driving these guys," Katz said.

"Greed is driving these guys," Price stated bitterly. "Nothing more than greed. Namely, the rights to new oil fields under Azerbaijani soil worth maybe tens of billions of dollars."

"But Pollari has worked dozens of oil fields around the world," Brognola said. "Why couldn't he just cut a deal with the Azerbaijanis?"

"He tried to," Price said. "In fact, a deal was thought to be in the works as recently as sixteen months ago. The land had been privatized by the government of the Azerbaijani Republic. It is now owned by thousands of Azerbaijani citizens scattered throughout forty-three villages and towns in four administrative districts. Pollari went in and staged a campaign among the people, promised them more money than they had ever seen before in their lives, and had the people and the government ready to sign over the oil rights.

"Then trouble started. A consortium of smaller oil companies came in, did some testing, and realized Pollari was trying to rip off the Azerbaijanis. Using new techniques for measuring the field, the consortium, which is eighty-percent U.S., was able to get a handle on its true size and realized the flat fee the Azerbaijanis were being paid by Pollari was a small percentage of its worth. The people and the government were furious with Pollari for trying to trick them—although he played dumb—and signed a preliminary agreement to have the consortium come in and pump the oil. The Azerbaijanis will get a cut of every barrel that comes out of their ground. All very equitable."

Katz nodded. "But that's not going to happen now."

"Not if things keep going the way they are. The people of Azerbaijan are convinced Iraqi oil interests are furious that the Azerbaijani fields will decrease the importance of their fields, which they were counting on to help rebuild the Iraqi economy and infrastructure," Price explained. "They see the hand of the Glorious Leader behind every chemical attack."

"Despite the robberies of chemical weapons from the U.S.," Kurtzman continued, "the Azerbaijanis don't believe there is a connection—in fact, news of the U.S. robberies is getting very little media play in Azerbaijan."

"Meanwhile, everybody else on the planet is blaming the U.S.," Brognola added. "Which is keeping my boss up nights."

"So what's Pollari's plan now?"

"He's already started a new news campaign in southeastern Azerbaijan," Kurtzman explained. "He claims to have Iraqi inside connections. The morning Baku paper, which will be on sale on the streets within the hour, is running this photo."

Kurtzman displayed a black-and-white photo of Edgar Pollari deep in conversation with Saddam Hussein, surrounded by several decorated army leaders. "He actually tried to play diplomat at one point in order to free up some of the Iraqi oil. The backlash in Canada was so bad he dropped the attempt. But the inference of the photo and of his entire campaign is that he has the influence with Iraq to bring its violence to a halt."

"Is he coming out and saying that?" Katz asked, amazed.

"Not in those words, but pretty damned close," Kurtzman said.

"He's blackmailing ten thousand innocent Azerbaijanis," Brognola said. "Are they going to go for it?"

"Of course they are, Hal, if it means their families will be safe," Price replied.

The big Fed nodded. "So what are we going to do about it?"

Qusar, Azerbaijan

BOLAN DECIDED to stop in and see the Killers.

Unable to go barging into Ramadan's compound in the middle of the day, he had to wait until darkness closed in. And the small city of Qusar, where Oguz's band of enforcers was currently deployed, was on his way north. It was a good investment of time.

The Killers were the kind of men who got their own special mention in the Executioner's war book. They were ruthless, smart, aggressive. One of them would take over when they discovered Oguz was out of the picture.

Bolan wanted to be certain that didn't happen.

He reached the city limits during the morning hours, looking for the hotel that was home to any Oguz operatives who might be passing through, finding it in the small downtown area of the city. He entered and found the place had little more class than a transient hotel in any major U.S. city. The grizzled old man working the front desk was on the phone, speaking Russian and jotting notes on a piece of paper. As he hung up he said a Russian name, which Bolan recognized from his list.

The soldier took the piece of paper from the old man, who protested in Azeri.

"Don't worry about it," Bolan answered in Russian. "I'll take care of their breakfast order."

The room number was on the slip of paper. It was a top-floor room and Bolan headed for it, striding up the three flights of stairs.

It sounded like a party was going on. Maybe it had been going on all night. If that was the case, these Killers would be tired, perhaps still drunk and slow to react. But Bolan wasn't going to count on that.

He knocked and a harsh voice shouted for him to enter.

The door to the bathroom was open, and Bolan saw a large man standing in front of the toilet. The woman on the bed had the heavily painted look of a prostitute. She sat up when she saw Bolan instead of the old hotel proprietor, but a quick finger to his lips and a gesture with his gun kept her quiet.

"Put it on the desk!" the man in the bathroom shouted in Russian.

Bolan stepped to the doorway and waited for the ex-KGB agent to emerge. When he spotted Bolan he reacted instantaneously, slamming a powerful fist at the soldier's hand and knocking his arm away as he triggered the 93-R, then sent a powerful roundhouse at the Executioner's skull. Bolan ducked and pulled back, hitting the wall and firing again. This time the round connected, drilling into the Russian's shoulder and tearing at the flesh. The wound was deep, but it only infuriated the man, and he tackled Bolan with a roar.

His weight crushed Bolan to the floor, but the soldier propelled himself in a roll that pushed his adversary onto his back. Then Bolan shoved away and was on his feet. The Russian roared again and sat up, coming directly into the path of the 93-R, which triggered one time into his skull. The Russian's eyes rolled back into his head, and he wavered for a second before falling back and slamming his head on the wooden floor.

The hooker on the bed had been screaming since the fight began, and she was now standing naked on the bed.

The door flew open and a tiny, wiry man stalked in, spotted Bolan and raised his Makarov PM pistol. Bolan leveled the 93-R in a two-handed shooter's stance and fired it twice. Both rounds found their target. The wiry Russian staggered into the hallway and hit the opposite wall.

Bolan put away the Beretta and drew the Desert Eagle. The stopping power of the .44 Magnum rounds was formidable. Obviously his need for silence was over. He had three of Oguz's Killers left to take out.

He aimed the big handgun squarely at the hooker and she stopped screaming at once. Bolan heard activity at the other end of the hallway, which could have been innocent guests—or more Killers. He stepped into the hall with the Desert Eagle ready to fire and evaluated the man walking in his direction.

The man wasn't armed and was talking to someone inside an open doorway.

The person saw Bolan and snatched at the air, grabbing a handgun that had just been tossed to him. The Executioner triggered the Desert Eagle once, and the gunner's chest imploded, sending him to the floor. Racing to the doorway, Bolan suddenly came to a cold stop. The tiny red dot of a laser sight poked at his chest, and he saw a Heckler & Koch SP-89 autopistol, with an H&K Model 100 Laser Aimer, in the hands of a pinched-faced woman with short, shaggy hair. With a dour grin she assessed the warrior.

"You're very good," she said.

"And you're very bad, Wilhemina Solomin."

She nodded slightly. "You Americans were always

very well-informed. I should know. I personally killed several of your compatriots.''

"That was during the cold war. Americans and Russians are friends now.''

She barked a short laugh, but the laser dot didn't waver. "Whatever. I don't consider myself anybody's friend. And I'm getting very rich using my KGB talents in this filthy backwater country.''

"Getting rich through exploitation and murder,'' Bolan said.

"Like I said—whatever.''

"I've killed plenty of your kind, myself, Solomin.''

She nodded, now looking serious. "That is what I thought. You're very skilled at what you do. You are the man who has caused my employer no end of trouble over the past few days. You've slipped in and out of his properties like you were walking through the park on a Sunday afternoon. You've killed many of his men. There are not many men who have this kind of skill and daring. Certainly not many Americans.''

Bolan said nothing.

Solomin spoke loudly. "Dmitri! Come out here.''

A younger man emerged from the bathroom where he had been laying in wait. He held a SIG-Sauer P-226 DA autopistol, which he pointed at Bolan.

"Say hello to a true warrior, Dmitri,'' Solomin said. "He waltzed into Azerbaijan and started wiping out Oguz's operations single-handedly—that's the signature of a true warrior. We don't see many of his kind.''

"In fact,'' Bolan added, "just a few hours ago I killed Oguz himself.''

Solomin smiled slowly and broadly. "Really? Oh, I don't disbelieve you, and I'm very happy about it.

That means there's a vacancy at the top of Oguz's organization.''

"You think you can fill it?" Bolan asked.

Solomin shrugged. "The Azerbaijanis are used to taking orders from Russians. I'd offer you a place on my staff if I thought there was the slightest possibility you would take the job. But I know you will not.

"Dmitri." She gestured for her lackey to remove Bolan's gun.

The Executioner didn't move.

Dmitri came to him from the side, careful not to block the tiny red beam of laser light touching Bolan's chest, and took the Desert Eagle from the soldier's hand.

Bolan made his move, fast and precise, grabbing Dmitri by his gun hand and propelling him with all his strength at Solomin as he moved out of the path of the red beam. The woman uttered a small sound as she adjusted the laser aimer and fired, directly into the stumbling body of her Russian comrade. He fell against her body, and she pushed at him to get her hands free.

Bolan had already extracted the mini-Uzi as Solomin leveled her weapon. As the tiny red light traced a red-hot path along the wall, homing in on his body, he squeezed the trigger and held it down, weaving the muzzle of the weapon in a pattern of loops that cut into both Russians at chest level until the magazine was dry.

Wilhemina Solomin and her young ex-KGB cohort fell in a pile of tattered flesh and flowing blood.

CHAPTER TWENTY-FIVE

Mangghystau Oblysy, Kazakhstan

Less than an hour's drive from the Kazakhstan port city of Aqtau was the private fortress of former-General Tariq Ramadan. He was a civilian now, and a capitalist, and loved every minute of it.

He had found the local people more than passingly receptive to his presence and to Edgar Pollari's massive infusions of unregulated cash into the local economy. Not that he asked much of them. Just that they ignore him and his growing staff.

The compound, established five kilometers outside the Aqtau city center with the help of Pollari subsidiaries, consisted of large storage buildings that had been shipped into the nearest port and trucked to the scene as steel girders and aluminum sheets. Even the heavy equipment, including cement mixers, was shipped in for the construction and pouring of the building foundations.

Next had come the people. Pilots, mostly, and some trusted support staff, followed by an influx of one hundred Iraqi soldiers and officers, all commissioned by Ramadan personally. Several days of intensive training gave them the knowledge to efficiently operate the dispersion equipment that had been erected in Irkuk and Heydar, in nearby Azerbaijan.

Ramadan liked working with these men. He liked knowing he was making them all, like himself, very rich.

But suddenly all their efforts had ground to an abrupt halt. There was nothing more for them to do. Ramadan blamed the Americans.

Pollari's American contingent had been charged with taking tons of chemical weapons containers out of the Aberdeen and Johnston CADSs. Their initial strike, in Aberdeen, had been compromised, but at least had netted them most of the containers they had been after.

But following Aberdeen, every step of the operation the American teams attempted ended in failure. Their software spy was tracked down and apprehended. Their processing and distribution centers were shut down decisively.

The pattern repeated itself on the atoll. The containers were successfully stolen, and Ramadan had thought the actual theft would be the most difficult part of the operation. But the ship carrying the entire store of Johnston containers had been attacked and the containers burned, with one hundred percent loss of life aboard the ship. Finally, the last of the Aberdeen shipment was tracked down in the middle of nowhere in the Pacific Ocean. Despite drastic attempts on Pollari's part to keep the containers, including the scuttling of a ship worth millions, the containers were retaken by agents that could only have been working for the U.S.

Instead of having a warehouse packed to the brim with chemical containers, Ramadan had nothing. He was impotent, a situation he didn't enjoy.

And one he was planning to rectify.

The twin TL 6 transport aircraft waited on the dirt runway within a few yards of each other, and Ramadan shouted last-minute instructions to the flight crew of the first aircraft. They understood the strategy and saluted smartly, assuring the general they were up to the demands of the mission.

He gave the wave his assembled troops had been waiting for and headed to the aircraft. A flight crew of just two men, a pilot and copilot, entered the first TL 6. Fifteen Iraqi soldiers crowded into the second.

The planes were Pollari-owned and had been flown in by Canadian pilots. But this was to be an all-Iraqi mission. The Canadians, after starting the aircraft and taking them through a preflight check, handed over control to the Iraqi crews.

Minutes later the transport aircraft took off from the packed-earth runway one after the other and headed out of Kazakhstan. Once over the Caspian Sea they turned due south.

By afternoon they were entering Iraqi airspace.

"GET INTO POSITION," Ramadan ordered his pilot, then barked the same command over the radio to the second vessel.

"Affirmative, General," the first aircraft radioed back.

Ramadan watched the other TL 6 start to slow and carefully home in on his plane. It seemed to float over his aircraft smoothly, but as it came closer he thought he saw the wings wiggle. He wondered if the pilot was nervous.

The pilot in his aircraft certainly was. He was craning his neck to keep an eye on the other TL 6. Ramadan had sworn to the Canadian pilot teams that his men possessed the flying skills—and the iron nerves—required for the exercise, but now that he was in position and sitting just a hundred meters directly underneath the other aircraft, he was having a rare case of doubt. One errant move, one occurrence of localized turbulence, could result in a collision that would bring down both planes.

And Ramadan planned to crash only one of them.

His pilot stayed highly alert but seemed to lose some of the tension after several minutes of flying in the strange sandwich formation.

"We're entering Iraqi airspace," the copilot announced.

"How's our heading?" Ramadan demanded.

"We're on target, General," the pilot assured him.

"Any idea of our ETA?"

"No more than seven minutes."

In fact, it was just six. Ramadan saw the familiar landmarks swim into his field of vision and he ordered landing maneuvers to begin.

"Just to the east of that circular formation of rock ridge," he pointed out. "Take us down there."

"General, are you sure the sand isn't too deep for us? We need to be able to take off again," the pilot asked tactfully.

"It was no more than a fine layer on the soil last time I was there," Ramadan answered. He didn't add that his last visit had been fourteen years ago.

He radioed the second aircraft and the descent began. The upper aircraft slowed to pace the descending TL 6 for as long as possible, coming almost to stalling speed as the TL 6 containing the fifteen Iraqi soldiers touched the arid desert surface and slowed to stop.

Ramadan, courtesy of his rank, had high levels of security clearance to Iraqi intelligence for years, but what Iraq still didn't know about the capabilities of the Western forces monitoring the northern and southern Iraqi no-fly zones would fill volumes. He was counting on—and hoping—that his trick flying would cause the two transport aircraft to show up on radar as one, and, most importantly, that the now-landed aircraft wouldn't show up at all.

The airborne TL 6 accelerated to a more typical cruising speed and picked up altitude. The automatic pilot would be engaged. With her fuel precisely dumped over the Caspian, she would fly for another one hundred to 125 miles before slamming into the desert. There it would certainly attract attention—and draw attention away from Ramadan's position.

As Ramadan exited the front hatch he saw the pilots jettison from the airborne aircraft one after another. Their blue stealth-type parachutes were virtually invisible against the sky.

Already the small motorcycle with its wheeled sidecar was being driven out of the ramp of the TL 6.

"Go get them and get back here quickly," Ramadan said to the driver. "We'll need every body to dig."

He led the rest of the men into the jumble of nearby rocks, which formed a sort of natural oblong shape in the desert. The earth here was less smooth, still showing the signs of the digging that had been conducted on this spot fourteen years ago.

Within minutes they were shoveling at the dirt. The motorcycle with the two crewmen from the doomed TL 6 returned and added their backs to the labor.

The Iraqi army had long ago hidden caches of

chemical weapons at the command of the prime minister, which had been another of his impulsive strategies for war preparedness. At the time Iraq was being harshly criticized for its use of chemical weapons. Photos of dead Kurdish children were exposed regularly in the global media. The prime minister had feared the possibility of attacks aimed at wiping out his supply of such weapons, and he had ordered the caches placed around the country—in homes, schools, hospitals and pits dug at strategic points through the vast desert nation. Ramadan had long considered that his knowledge of this northern cache, in an area long ignored and quite possibly forgotten by the army command, in an area totally inaccessible by air due to the Western enforcement of no-fly zones, would someday prove useful.

The steel boxes were beginning to see the light of day, still gleaming, showing no corrosion. He had little doubt the steel pressured canisters inside were as good as new.

"Start loading at once! I want to be off the ground in one hour."

He glanced at his watch and realized the other TL 6 ought to be running on empty about now.

Andersen Air Force Base, Guam

THE U.S. AIR FORCE BASE in Guam filled end to end with the whine of the quartet of engines on the massive Lockheed C-5 Galaxy. McCarter heard the sound even through the closed hatch and slowing engines of the smaller transport jet that had taken them that far. When the hatch was opened the assault of sound magnified fivefold.

An Air Force major waited impatiently at the bottom of the steps with three chauffeured jeeps, and he practically accosted the Phoenix Force leader.

"I'm to get you in the air immediately, sir." He exhibited the curious awkwardness of military people who simply didn't know the protocol for dealing with members of what they suspected was a special operations group.

"Where are we going?" McCarter demanded.

"Yeah, we haven't been told a thing," Manning added.

"You'll be briefed on board sir." He gave a wave in the direction of the great black hulk of the C-5.

"We're going in that?" Manning asked.

"Please, sir. We're running behind because of the *Mistral*'s delay in getting you off Garden Island. There is an extreme sense of urgency here."

"All right, all right." McCarter sighed. "Let's get our gear into the jeeps and let's get going."

"Why weren't we radioed on the passenger jet?" Encizo asked as he yanked the belly hatch on the jet and lunged at a sea-dampened equipment pack.

"Probably didn't have a secure enough line."

"We're set up for a full briefing on board the C-5," the major offered again helpfully, hoping it might hurry them up.

"At least tell us where we're headed, Major," Manning said.

The major looked around quickly, as if expecting to see a spy in an overcoat and sunglasses trying to listen in on the conversation. Then he hissed, "Kazakhstan!"

Ramadan Compound, Kazakhstan

BOLAN HAD BEEN monitoring the compound outside Aqtau for almost five hours. He had watched the furious unloading of the TL 6 aircraft into a low building, using his field glasses to bring him in close enough to read the faded red-painted legends adorned on the steel boxes. The writing, it turned out, was unreadable Arabic. But the lurid skull and crossbones told the tale plainly enough.

A new shipment had just come in.

A few minutes later, the first heavily loaded cart was pulled from the opposite end of the low building and transported to a waiting aircraft.

Another pair of Iraqi gunships were parked there, as well as three small transport aircraft bearing Iraqi markings.

The rest of the transport aircraft were obvious impostors. There was an assortment of small, prop-driven planes of various colors, all emblazoned sloppily with Iraqi flags and markings.

It wouldn't matter to the people of Azerbaijan. They would doubtless be convinced it was truly the Iraqi army that was sending them to their deaths.

The few who survived would spread the misconception, unless Bolan and Phoenix Force could stop the attacks before they could start.

With that many aircraft, how many targets could Ramadan hit simultaneously? The rough calculations Bolan performed in his head pointed to hundreds, maybe thousands dead within the space of an hour if he staged coordinated assaults.

The sun was going down, and the timely arrival of his backup force was looking less likely. He was out of contact and didn't know where they were—en route from Guam, he had last heard.

The weapons were hefted quickly into the aircraft. Processing of these chemicals into weapons wasn't required. Ramadan had come into a shipment of Iraqi weapons that were already configured and ready to use.

Bolan saw no reason why Ramadan would delay his ruthless attacks. As soon as the night closed in the chemical strikes would begin.

Unless, somehow, Bolan could stop them on his own.

CHAPTER TWENTY-SIX

He moved as soon as darkness closed in. But the compound was being operated on a generator that enabled enough high-powered lights to keep the buildings, the aircraft and the runways brightly lit. He made the generator shed his first order of business. Not only would darkness give him extra freedom to maneuver, it would keep the planes from leaving the ground—for awhile.

He crept along the west side, where his presence could at least be partially concealed from the main section of the compound by one of the aircraft. Crossing open ground to the airplane parking area, he was tempted to stay and begin sabotaging the planes. But staying was too risky with maintenance and loading crews coming and going.

He broke for cover in a crouched run when he judged no one was there to spot him and made it to the side of one of the huge hangarlike buildings where the aircraft had been kept out of sight until the loading started. He was in safer territory. Less windows and activity were on that side of the compound, and a final burst of speed took him to the shed from which the power cables that webbed the complex originated.

His target was a diesel tank standing next to the

shed. The pipe fittings on the underside of the tank required a large wrench to loosen them. He gave it a try by hand without getting them to budge.

The buildings throughout the compound were designed for quick erection and protection from sand and the curious. The thin extruded aluminum panels were screwed into steel beam frames. Bolan used his multitool screwdriver and his fighting knife to remove five screws and bend back the rear corner of the shed, the creaking of the metal drowned in the rumble of the generator inside. He crawled quickly through the open corner.

The shed was lit by a single bare one-hundred-watt bulb. The generator was a large diesel unit and was paired with an emergency-use twin that was currently silent. The tools Bolan was looking for were piled on the hard ground just inside the door.

He slithered outside and had the pipe fittings loosened in seconds, spinning them until the trickles of spilling diesel turned into a gush. He tossed the wrench through the opening into the shed and forced the bent panel back into position.

Falling back away from the compound to escape the lights and the widening lake of diesel fuel surrounding the shed, he stayed low, biding his time. It was just minutes before the steady rumble of the generator turned to a sputter. Seconds later the lights began to dim throughout the camp. He boldly got to his feet. In a blacksuit, his face painted with camouflaging combat cosmetics, he was a half-visible wraith come to haunt General Tariq Ramadan.

RAMADAN JUMPED TO HIS FEET. "What's going on?"

"Generator failure," Colonel Muhyi al-Duri said,

his eyes searching the bare bulbs dangling from the ceiling in their command building as they faded to darkness.

"Brilliant," Ramadan snarled, stomping outside and shouting orders to his men, who were suddenly standing around, motionless and perplexed. "Break out the flares and stage them by the runway. I want to be ready to make use of them to mark it if we don't get the power back. Where's the mechanic?"

"Here, General," said a man who was jogging by with a tool kit. "I was just on my way to the generator."

"Go," Ramadan snapped, relieved that at least one member of his army had taken initiative. "The rest of you, start lighting barrel fires throughout the camp to provide light. I want this place fully illuminated in five minutes. Colonel al-Duri!"

The colonel had emerged from the tent directly behind Ramadan and was watching the activity as if from an opium haze. What had happened to the man? Ramadan thought. He had exhibited every evidence of being an energetic and capable leader when they were in Iraq. He had certainly showed no signs of passivity. But ever since his bold, perfectly executed escape from Iraq with his load of chemicals, he'd seemed to have lost all his drive, mired in some sort of lethargy that rendered him all but useless.

"Go to the generator. I want a report from the mechanic as soon as you have it. I must know if it was sabotage."

"Sabotage? You think one of our men...?"

"Of course not. I'm just wondering if Oguz's friend might have arrived."

The colonel trudged off glumly, considering that

possibility. He wondered if it would be true. They knew little about the death of Arif Oguz. Their contacts in the local police force had reported that the house had been transformed into an abattoir, the dead strewed about the place as if they had been attacked by an invisible maniac. They were knifed and shot, some exhibiting no signs of resistance, as if death had come out of the very air to attack them. Others had shown contortions proving they had fought their attacker viciously, but in vain. Not a man was left.

Al-Duri had first felt the presence of a black spirit of death days ago, during his terrifying flight across Iraq with his stolen cargo of chemical weapons. Despite the fact that his mission was a perfect success, the dark terror that descended on him had refused to be shaken.

He thought about the wife and daughters he was leaving behind. His wife had become obstinate and saggy in her middle years, and he had grown weary of her. He had told himself over and over that he wouldn't miss her, that he didn't care that she would suffer hideous torture at the hands of the Iraqi high command as they tried to determine where he had escaped to. She would most likely be put to death when they finally convinced themselves that she didn't know where he was.

His daughters would be orphans. But it didn't matter. They were only daughters. They would find work on the streets when they came of age.

He told himself he didn't care about the countless faceless foreigners who would be struck dead due to his successful plundering of the Glorious Leader's chemical stores.

So why was he haunted by this dark spirit? Was the

dark spirit real, embodied in the merciless killer that had wiped out Arif Oguz and all his men in one horrible hour of violence?

Was the dark spirit here? Now, come to take down him, the general and all of them for their crimes against humanity?

He tried to shake the thought as he stomped across the camp, sidestepping to avoid the blundering soldiers who were dragging empty barrels into position and dumping scraps into them for fire. Ahead of him the mechanic with the toolbox had opened the generator shed.

The mechanic looked oddly at the ground, then raised one foot. The earth clung to his shoes like mud.

Then he dropped his toolbox and took one step before erupting in flame.

BOLAN TOSSED an incendiary grenade at the generator shed and turned to put distance between himself and the bomb before it hit the ground.

The burst of flame turned to a bonfire instantly, igniting the fuel that covered the ground inside and outside of the shed. Bolan glanced back to see a figure step out of the building engulfed in flame, flapping his arms like one of Satan's angels, then crashing to the ground.

Much of the fuel had soaked into the soil, and the light of the fire wasn't as bright as Bolan had feared it might be. Nevertheless, his cover of total darkness was gone. More lights would come on as soon as the camp organizers got their act together. In the light, a single man against a hundred gunners, he would be highly vulnerable. He had to slow them down as much as he could, as fast as possible.

His first stop was the aircraft.

THE COLONEL STARED at the unholy flaming apparition that the mechanic had become, as if he were looking at the embodiment of his own doom, as if he were seeing the face of Satan himself in the flames. He was frozen by fear until the burning man stumbled in his direction. The colonel stepped away and the mechanic fell to the ground, writhing as the flames devoured his life. His cries turned to a long, pathetic wail.

Al-Duri's fears of a few moments ago were transformed into a horrible certainty—the killer was in this compound. He had struck his first blow, and he would strike again soon. He would cut everyone without mercy.

For the first time in days his head cleared and he experienced a burst of energy. It was time to fight or die.

He marched away from the burn victim—he would be dead in seconds anyway—shouting at the gathering crowd of soldiers.

"The generator is out of commission so we need to light the airfield using flares. I want the entire strip lined with flares every ten paces, and I want it done now. The rest of you, your five minutes are up! Why don't we have this camp lit?" He shoved the nearest soldier, sending him into the dirt. "Get going!"

Al-Duri charged back to the general's tent, feeling an invigoration born of near-panic. "General, you were right. The generator has been deliberately destroyed. We have an enemy on the premises."

"You are sure of this?" Ramadan asked.

"Yes."

"What evidence is there that this was not an accidental explosion?"

"No evidence, General, but I am sure."

Ramadan saw the fire had returned to al-Duri's eyes, which was something positive anyway. "All right. There can't be many of them, or they would have shown themselves. We're working with a few men, or just one man. I want the guards around the aircraft doubled. I want orders to shoot to kill any stranger. And I want our aircraft to start getting off the ground immediately."

The colonel saluted quickly and headed for the parked aircraft, calling for the soldiers to join him. Their fires were appearing now throughout the camp, but the orange glow coming from the wood scraps and paper burning in the barrels was a poor substitute for the cold white floodlights they replaced. The soldiers were just shadowy shapes moving in near-darkness and any one of them might be the killer.

"Get all the planes powered up—I want their lights on," he shouted. "I want all the vehicles not being used for the loading of the planes to be parked in a circle around the aircraft. Keep the engines running and the lights on. I want the entire vicinity lit up."

He called for the pilots and started shouting for them to prepare their aircraft for takeoff as soon as they were prepped. "All loaded aircraft will get into the air right now. You've all got plenty of fuel. I want you sitting in a holding pattern above the complex until we are all off the ground and ready to go. The rest of you are to be loaded as quickly as possible. Have your crews ready and get off the ground the minute your cargo is stowed."

"When's the runway going to be marked?" one of the pilots demanded.

Al-Duri turned to the runway, which was now marked with flares for some fifty meters of its length. No more flares were appearing. There was no sign of the men who had been sent to put out the flares.

The colonel knew instantly what had occurred out there in the blackness. His fear was so cold he was numb, and he calmly issued instructions. "I want ten armed men to get out there and finish the job."

There was a crowd full of averted eyes and al-Duri reacted furiously. "You!" he said, shoving a man. "You! You! You!"

He soon had ten men stumbling nervously into the black airfield.

BOLAN STOOD IN THE MIDDLE of the airstrip, cloaked in darkness, and watched the two soldiers walk directly at him.

They were carrying large sacks of flares, and every ten or fifteen paces they would grab one, light it and toss it on the ground next to the packed-earth runway. They didn't know they were strolling to their deaths.

The Executioner stood sideways and braced the hand holding the suppressed Beretta 93-R across his other arm to give him exceptionally precise aim. He waited until the soldiers were close enough to talk to, until he heard a burst of shouting from the camp, loud enough to guarantee the cough of the handgun would be masked. Then, coldly, emotionlessly, he fired.

The first round hit the first soldier in a virtually foolproof killing pattern, slamming into his gut. Allowing a specific gradation of the natural rise of the gun, Bolan sent the next round into his chest, piercing his heart. The third round cut through his skull and into his brain.

Before he had even witnessed the soldier's reaction to the deadly triple impacts Bolan turned his fire on the other soldier, who had never heard the fire of a suppressed handgun and was trying to figure out what the sound was. His thought processes came to an abrupt halt after just a single second.

Bolan continued the large circle he was making around the busy compound, distancing himself from the landing strip and contemplating his next move. Fully half the men in the camp were gathering around the aircraft. Was there any way he could get at those aircraft in time to shut them down before they took to the skies?

One thing was certain—if they got a fix on him he was in deep trouble. There was nowhere for him to run, nowhere to hide. They would swarm over him with their vehicles and automatic weapons, and he would surely go down.

There was no question that he would make that sacrifice if it would keep those chemical weapons from getting off the ground. But how to keep them all grounded?

The answer was simply one at a time.

He saw a group break off from the planes and head to the landing strip to take up where the dead soldiers left off. More were heading in the direction of the motorcade, and some were climbing into the aircraft. They were going to power everything up, get the place as well lit as they could using headlights.

He wasn't going to have a better opportunity than this. He headed for the aircraft, his M-16 A-2/M-203 primed with an HE grenade, which he launched from about three hundred yards out. He did his best to place the lethal egg on top of the most distant aircraft from his position, one of the gunships. It hit the ground under the slow-moving rotor canopy of the idling Hind and detonated with a clap. The next he guided to the left, aiming for the twin-engine TL 6, and the round transformed it into a ball of flame.

Already a handful of foot soldiers was running in his direction, sporting AK-74s as a man behind them frantically shouted orders. Bolan triggered a steady burst of 5.56 mm rounds at the line of gunners and sent a few in the direction of the man in charge, then thumbed a CS grenade into the M-203 and deposited it at the feet of the gunners. It erupted in a cloud of smoke that sent the enemy reeling back. Bolan faded into the darkness and continued his counterclockwise circle of the camp.

As the aircraft started motoring away, Bolan risked sending in one more round. The chain reaction he had counted on hadn't occurred, and he was hoping for it before the planes dispersed. He sent another HE round into the path of an Antonov An-32, a Russian-made transport aircraft. The Antonov sped up as if the pilot knew the grenade was coming for it, and the bomb detonated a few yards behind its tail without causing any visible damage. Bolan cursed and kept moving— the CS cloud, even in the stillness of the desert night, was dispersing quickly.

The gunners formed ranks as a pair of jeeps appeared from within the compound. The man in charge, dressed in an Iraqi army uniform, stood in the passenger seat of one of the vehicles and barked orders to his soldiers. Flanked by the jeeps, the soldiers marched into the scrubby desert to where Bolan had been.

The Executioner realized his tactical error—although they were looking for him in the wrong place, the small army had effectively cut him off from returning to the landing strip. And the aircraft weren't just being moved, they were staging for immediate takeoff. Already the second Russian-made helicopter was powering up and tilting into the air. The fixed-wing craft would be ready to go as soon as the runway had been fully marked off with flares.

Bolan spoke into his throat mike. "Striker to Phoenix. Come in Phoenix." The earplug he was wearing on the right had been silent all evening. It remained silent.

He'd have to fend for himself for a while longer, simply do whatever he could do.

The Iraqi-marked Hind gunship flared to life with a giant belly-mounted searchlight that gave it the look of a UFO searching for an abductee. It swept forward over the heads of the soldiers and the jeeps, illuminating acres at a time, then turned in Bolan's direction in a hurry.

The soldier bolted toward the nearest building, knowing that as soon as he appeared in the helicopter's spotlight he would be the target of a barrage of automatic riflefire. The searchlight veered crazily over the ground as if trying to trip him up, take him by surprise.

Bolan almost felt the heat of the giant light searing his back as he reached the nearest prefab field building and slipped around the corner, hugging the wall. The searchlight hit the roof, illuminating only his feet as it passed over him and headed back into the desert.

The soldier's mind was going at warp speed, assessing the situation from every angle, strategizing, discarding ideas one after another like a computer assessing every possible progression and outcome of a chess game. But every scenario he was coming up with ended with himself in checkmate. The problem was, he was a single king on a board full of knights, rooks and pawns.

And one other king.

If he could somehow, some way, slip past the pawns, locate the enemy king and take him, the game would be over. Suddenly and completely.

Bolan didn't know what the other king looked like. But he knew the king's name.

Tariq Ramadan had to be somewhere on the game board.

"PROGRESS," Ramadan demanded.

"We think we've got them on the run, in the desert," al-Duri shouted through the small radio, his voice almost drowning in the rumble of the jeep and the roar of the overhead gunship.

"How many aircraft were disabled?"

"Two or three. One Hind, the transport plane, and maybe the Antonov."

Ramadan almost choked when he heard that—the Antonov An-32 was prepped to carry him personally. "Is the Antonov being checked out? I need that aircraft at one hundred percent."

"I know, General. I ordered it in the hangar at once and put the Canadian mechanic in charge of assessing it for damage. I deployed a ten-man guard around it. Wait!"

"What? What is it, Colonel?"

"I thought we'd spotted one. It was nothing."

"I want that man brought down!"

"It's got to be more than one man, General."

"Then bring them all down, Colonel."

Ramadan hooked the radio on his belt and started grabbing up the maps and diagrams on this desk, stuffing them into his large battered leather briefcase.

"We're moving to the hangar, into the Antonov," he announced to the two majors who served as his personal bodyguard. He looked around the makeshift office for anything else important or incriminating. "We'll get airborne as soon as it has checked out."

One of the majors turned his head sharply, displaying a bloody scalp, and pitched on his face. Ramadan snatched at the radio on his belt.

"He's here, Colonel!"

CHAPTER TWENTY-SEVEN

Bolan crashed through the door and targeted the second guard, cutting him nearly in two with a heavy blast of fire from the M-16 A-2, then swept the room and recoiled as Ramadan jumped from behind the desk spraying fire from an AKSU. The rounds slammed into the wall at the soldier's back, and he spun into the doorway again as the magazine came up dry on the AKSU, only to find a Stechkin machine pistol aimed at the space he now occupied. Bolan twisted away as the Stechkin chattered savagely.

Overhead the screaming whir of the Hind's stressed rotors increased in volume, and it appeared over the center of the compound. A crowd of gunners appeared from the door of the nearest building, then fell back as they spotted Bolan. Suddenly, he was the center of attention. He triggered an incendiary that exploded directly inside the door and mangled the doorframe, then snatched two more grenades from his rapidly dwindling supply. One was a multiprojectile round—the buckshot round that turned the M-203 into a shotgun. He thumbed it into the breech and pulled the pin on the second device, a grenade that he lobbed underhanded through the door of Ramadan's HQ. Almost instantly he heard the sound of shattering glass, followed by the explosion of the grenade. Bolan stepped inside just after the shock wave bulged the building.

No one was home.

The desk was kindling and the furniture was in splinters. There was no place to hide, the human remains didn't belong to Ramadan. The breaking glass had to have been the Iraqi general making a quick escape.

As Bolan exited the building a pair of gunners appeared, hungry to take him down with their AK-74s. But the blast from the M-203 peppered them with buckshot and slammed them both to the ground.

A Hummer shot out from behind the HQ building with a gunner protruding from the passenger window, laying on the trigger of his automatic rifle. Bolan responded with lightning-quick reflexes and cut him off with a quick burst from the M-16 A-2, but he was too late to target the driver—it was Ramadan, and he propelled the Hummer away from the soldier, toward the far end of the hangar.

Bolan changed the mag on the M-16 A-2 and followed the Hummer in a run. He heard the clanking of a large automatic door opening, followed by the sudden accelerating whine of aircraft engines coming to life. Racing around the front of the building, he was targeted by a gunner stationed behind a makeshift steel shield and operating a tripod-mounted .50-caliber machine gun. He swept the front of the hangar, firing from the near side of the Antonov's wing. Bolan ran toward the nose of the aircraft, hoping the gunner would follow him with a trail of gunfire. A burst of .50-caliber rounds would probably disable the aircraft. But the gunner was alert, and he pulled back before the fire reached the fuselage or wings.

Instead he ran from behind his shield and made a bold approach, intending to take down the intruder with a close-proximity shot that wouldn't endanger the plane. Bolan stitched him across the abdomen first.

The Antonov lurched forward, the fuselage slamming bodily into Bolan's shoulder, tossing him to the ground. As he rolled, he glimpsed the pilot steering the wheels in an attempt to crush Bolan underneath them. He spun away from the tires and jumped to his feet as the wings cleared the hangar, only to crash back to the earth again to avoid a canopy of AK-74 fire cutting above his head. The gunner was Tariq Ramadan, standing in the open hatchway.

The 5.56 mm fire halted abruptly and the hatch closed as the pilot laid on the gas. The Antonov lurched away from the hangar and made a tight turn around a secondary storage building, on its way to the runway.

Ramadan was gone, slipped through the warrior's fingers.

More gunners were crossing the compound, targeting him, but Bolan kept them at bay with his burst of highly accurate fire. Overhead he could hear the thrum of the gunship, sitting above the compound, just waiting for him to appear.

He heard a rush of engines and watched with a sinking feeling of defeat as he witnessed the Antonov accelerate down the flare-lit runway and take to the air. Within a minute it was just lights in the sky, turning south and growing smaller.

The gunners staged around the hanger began dissipating, heading for their own aircraft. A second aircraft sped down the runway as the Hind kept its position over the compound, waiting to cut down Bolan if he appeared.

Bolan was trapped.

The Ramadan-Pollari strikes were going to proceed this night as planned. Hundreds more would die.

Bolan had failed.

"Phoenix One calling Striker."

Bolan grabbed at his microphone. "Striker here! What's your position?"

"We're a couple of miles out. We're watching your position and closing fast. Is that Russian helicopter giving you a hard time?"

"David, we've got to contain these aircraft. Every one of them is loaded to the gills with chemical weapons, freshly imported from Iraq. They've all got individual targets, and they're all on their way now. We can't let one of them get away."

"Read you, Striker. We've got a few aircraft ourselves."

"Suggest your first order of business be to render that airfield unusable."

"Will do."

Bolan heard the Hind turn tail, and the sound of its retreat was instantly matched by the roar of more helicopters closing in. A pair of Huey Cobra combat helicopters roared over the compound in close formation, and as Bolan emerged from the hangar they parted ways. One went after the Hind as the second headed for the runway, while one of the small twin-engine aircraft started on its takeoff run.

"Striker to Phoenix—keep in mind these aircraft can't be shot down near populated areas. If those chemicals start burning…"

"We know about that, Striker. We'll let the Cobras know."

The first Cobra had accelerated to its top speed of 150 mph and overtook the small twin-engine craft, sitting almost on top of the taxiing twin-engine plane when its M-157 launching pod fired two of its complement of 2.57-inch rockets. They slammed into the runway with twin cracks, leaving fresh craters. The twin-engine prop plane shuddered as the pilot slammed on the brakes. He failed to stop fast enough; the plane slammed into the ditch and upended on its nose, poised there, then collapsed back on its belly, snapping its landing gear. It looked like a half-deflated blimp.

Bolan liked what he saw. The crater and the wreckage were less than halfway along the landing strip. No more aircraft were going to be making it off the ground here tonight.

A troop transport chopper with stars and stripes on the fuselage appeared almost directly over Bolan's head, the side wide open. Ropes were flung out, and within seconds a handful of soldiers rappelled to the ground. Bolan gave McCarter a rare grin, which soured when he realized there were just four members of the Phoenix Force team present.

"Calvin?"

"He had a fight with a boat. The boat lost, but he's a little banged up so he's riding shotgun in that bird instead of running around with us grunts." McCarter gave a nod in the direction of the Cobra that was disappearing after the Hind. "What's the situation here, Striker?"

"Strictly cleanup. The important work will be

downing the remaining aircraft. Especially the Antonov. Tariq Ramadan is on board.''

There was a rush above them, and Bolan looked up in time to see two pairs of fighter jets rush over the compound at two thousand feet—nothing but fast-moving, noisy lights in the darkness.

"Two F-15s and two MiG-21s," Manning explained with a wide grin. "The central government of the Republic of Kazakhstan was convinced to cooperate, but they wanted the Russians in on it."

"What are their orders?" Bolan said.

"They're to force the planes down. They're under orders to shoot them down only if the planes are determined to use their chemical weapons," McCarter explained.

Bolan nodded grimly. That was about as good as could be expected.

COLONEL MUHYI AL-DURI WATCHED the two pairs of fighter jets streak over the compound with sudden dread.

It was all over.

Ramadan had escaped and he had not.

There was nothing left to do now but fight it through, and probably die in the attempt.

Giving the orders for his men to gather their arms and stand their ground, he grabbed a pair of AK-74 rifles for himself and exited the aircraft that could have taken him to safety.

There was no use for fear, he realized. There really wasn't any doubt he would die this night. Why not embrace it boldly?

Al-Duri strode through the men, who were clinging against the parked aircraft, and fired his weapon when he saw the first of the Americans appear from around the side of the buildings. The intruders recoiled as soon as he fired, and he knew he had wasted his shots.

Inspiring his men, they were emerging into the open, standing at his side. Two of the Americans stepped into the open just long enough to trigger rapid-fired bursts into his men and cut down two of them. One died, the other writhed and screamed.

They were in the open, and the Americans were protected. That wasn't fair and Al-Duri intended to do something about it. He broke for the building and sprinted around the corner, triggering his AK-74 at the spot where they had been hiding.

His rounds clanged into the wall of the structure. The men were gone.

He glanced to the left when he saw the pair of American gunners come out of the darkness from twenty feet away. They had been hiding in the shadows. That was an evil trick, he thought, and felt their simultaneously fired rounds cut through his body, one from the left, and one from the right, and then the darkness came over him.

McCARTER AND MANNING laid down heavy fire that sent the Iraqi soldiers and their comrades in arms scurrying back to the cover of the aircraft, demoralized by the death of their leader.

Hawkins and Encizo had been busy shooting out the tires on all the cars and trucks in the compound, and made a break to the Hummer nearest to the parked airplanes. Cloaked by the darkness and seeing their way with infrared glasses, they were easily able to discern the hot glowing shapes of several gunners as they also made a break for the Hummer. The enemy was laying down cover fire toward McCarter and Manning, oblivious to the other two Phoenix Force warriors until Encizo and Hawkins calmly laid their weapons on the hood of the Hummer, targeted the approaching soldiers carefully and fired without warning. The withering autofire cut down the Iraqis before they had even fixed its origin.

The remaining Iraqis withdrew farther into the cover of the aircraft, then into the darkness of the scrubland, falling back, prepared to flee.

Then out of nowhere came screams of terror and pain. Suddenly, they were being cut down as if by an invisible warrior. They heard faint retorts, but the wide open land was entirely without illumination.

One of the men became hysterical, firing his weapon blindly into the blackness until he collapsed on his back with a blasted ruin where his face should have been.

As if the thought had been shared by the entire army simultaneously, they broke and ran, fleeing wildly into the desert, anything to get away from a killer against whom there seemed to be no defense.

Suddenly, the sky above them became blindingly illuminated and the ratcheting sound of machine-gun fire cut through their midst. The Cobra swung over the desert and sliced through them viciously, using the 7.62 mm M-28 minigun mounted on its forward turret. The path of the Cobra turned into a wide circle, bringing the stampede of soldiers to a stop and herding them into a nervous circle. As one small group separated from the rest and tried to flee, the Cobra's 40 mm M-129 grenade launcher delivered an HE round that blasted the ground several paces in front of them.

Two of them dropped. The rest staggered back to the group.

Armed but helpless, they stood in their nervous group like a herd of cattle knowing they were destined for the slaughterhouse, awaiting their fate.

CHAPTER TWENTY-EIGHT

Stony Man Farm, Virginia

Mack Bolan wasn't a happy man, and he was getting less happy every minute the meeting dragged on without his hearing what he wanted to hear.

"There's an investigation already started on Johnston," Brognola reported to the gathering in the War Room. Kurtzman, Price, Grimaldi and Katz were also present. They were all feeling extremely uncomfortable. Only the big Fed was exhibiting enough self-control to hide it. "Somebody inside knew about the tunnel framework being put in place during the construction of the CADS island. Not to mention the trapdoor that was carved out of the floor. They're optimistically projecting that they have nailed down the ID on the guilty parties and will have court-martial proceedings filed within a few weeks."

"What about the Iraqi soldiers rounded up at the compound outside Aqtau?" Katz asked. "They'll get worse than court-martialed if they're sent back to Iraq."

"They all ended up in Kazakhstani jails," Barbara Price said.

"That won't be pleasant," Kurtzman stated.

"If they were sent back to Iraq, they'd be dead men. If they were brought to the U.S., we'd be able to insure a long-term stay in prison for each and every man. But we've been promised by the Republic of Kazakhstan that they'll be incarcerated for a long time."

"The Iraqi chemical weapons—all accounted for?" Brognola asked.

"As far as we know. The helicopter and the plane that managed to get away from the Aqtau compound were forced down on Kazakh soil, but the government wanted nothing to do with it. They were more than happy to hand it over to the U.S. for destruction."

"Ramadan?" Bolan growled.

"Landed in Istanbul," Price said. "His aircraft contained no chemical weapons when it landed, and we're sure it never dumped any. It had an F-15 and a MiG watching it every minute and every mile of its flight."

"Ramadan?" Bolan repeated.

Price looked at Brognola.

"The CIA got him," Brognola said.

"What is that supposed to mean?"

"He was arrested at the Istanbul airport and the CIA was on him like flies, Striker. They claim he's an intelligence gold mine. He can supply all kinds of inside information on the Iraqi high command. They—" Brognola hesitated, then continued "—they struck a deal."

"A deal," Bolan repeated.

"Ramadan sings. The CIA gives him preferential treatment."

"You mean he gets off?" Bolan's voice was steady and low, and potent with fury. "He slaughters hundreds of innocent people, and now he goes free?"

"Well, he'll be in the custody of the Company. He's not exactly free—"

"Don't insult me, Hal." Bolan sat forward and put his hands together on the table. His knuckles were white.

Brognola said nothing.

Every pair of eyes was on the table, except for those of the big Fed and the Executioner. Bolan said, "I want Tariq Ramadan."

"You can't have him."

"He can't go free. Hal, it's unthinkable."

"I'm sorry, Striker...." Brognola raised his hand, as if to illustrate the point, when he suddenly realized there was nothing more to say.

Bolan walked out of the room without another word.

Rhein-Main Air Base, Frankfurt, Germany

U.S. AIR FORCE AIRMAN First Class John Samuels sat bolt upright in bed. It was 5:32 a.m. and the phone was ringing shrilly.

He grabbed the receiver, and the voice he heard this time was definitely not his CO.

"You know who this is?"

Samuels put a face to the voice instantly, but he realized he didn't know the man's name. "Yeah."

"I need you to do me a favor."

SAMUELS WAS DOG-TIRED. The flight home had been cold and uncomfortable. The seats on the transport aircraft were little better than padded benches, and he hadn't slept a wink, even though he was exhausted.

But it never occurred to him not to do the favor the stranger on the phone had asked of him.

He drove five minutes from his apartment to the media center. The parking lot was nearly empty, and only a single security guard was on duty. The nighttime guy, Mel, was downloading a video feed from the States and running an old *Wheel of Fortune* rerun on the live feed. Even at this time of night the audience of television viewers out of the Frankfurt, Germany, station, through direct airwaves and indirect feeds, was in the tens of thousands.

"Hey, John, what's up?"

"Got to do a favor for a friend."

Mel nodded and went back to his *Sports Illustrated* magazine.

It took Samuels almost an hour to convert ten minutes of footage to high-quality MPEG video, compress it and load it onto the hard drive of his computer. Then he logged in to the stateside computer address the stranger had given him and began downloading the file.

He hoped the guy had a pretty good modem, or the download might take three or four hours.

It was done in less than one.

Stony Man Farm, Virginia

BOLAN VIEWED IT one time on the screen in Kurtzman's Computer Room, satisfying himself that it was what he wanted. Then he phoned Hal Brognola.

Brognola answered groggily, but he was lucid. In his position he was used to being phoned in the middle of the night.

"Striker here."

"What's going on?" The big Fed could count on one hand the number of times he'd been phoned by Bolan at home.

"I've got something you have to see."

Then the line was dead.

BROGNOLA ENTERED the War Room at Stony Man Farm and found his entire senior staff present. And looking grim. Barbara Price glanced at him with red-rimmed eyes, and Carmen Delahunt had a tear rolling down her face. Katzenelenbogen, Kurtzman and Grimaldi were sitting quietly around the table, staring at its surface. Wethers and Tokaido were in the back of the room.

Mack Bolan stood at the head of the table. A computer monitor was facing the gathering.

A chair was waiting for the big Fed at the other end of the table.

"What is this? Some kind of ambush?" Brognola asked.

"My doing," Bolan said. "I have something to show you."

Delahunt's chair scraped suddenly, and she strode out of the room. "I'm not looking at that again," she stated quietly.

Brognola took the chair that had been saved for him.

Bolan quickly clicked the mouse, and the screen flared to life.

The big Fed knew instantly what he was staring at. It was one of the Azerbaijani villages that had been decimated in the chemical weapons attacks. But this was hardly the footage that was released to the news agencies around the world. This was the true atrocity, up close and personal. The cameraman seemed to be

strolling through a small home. He came upon the
bodies of an old couple, somebody's grandparents.
The woman was half in and half out of the bed. The
old man was in a sitting position next to the bed, arms
around the old woman. He had been trying to help her
out of the bed when death took them.

The cameraman left the house and the video ran in
real time. Another small house, the doors standing
open. The camera came upon a man and a woman.
There was a small bundle in the woman's arms. They
were against the wall, as if they had fallen and dragged
themselves there to die.

Behind them was a girl of eight or nine, eyes wide.
The camera took her in, laying on the floor looking
into nothingness, arms holding a small stuffed animal
with orange fur.

The camera zoomed in on her, merciless to its viewers. She was beautiful. Bright eyes, even a touch of a
smile on her dead face.

The big Fed said, "All right. Jesus. That's enough."

But the video continued for almost five more ago-
nizing minutes.

When it was done the screen faded to a glow and
Bolan said, simply and directly, "The man responsible
for that is the man you are protecting."

Brognola had long ago realized that this *was* an ambush. "Goddammit, I can't give you Ramadan!"

"Why not?"

"I've been ordered not to!"

"It won't be traced to you or to the Farm."

"I don't even know where he is myself!"

"That's incidental, and you know it. Aaron can
track him down."

Brognola was silent, and Bolan knew he had won.

The big Fed got to his feet in a hurry. "All right, dammit. Do it."

Brognola stormed out of the room. He was in a foul mood. He sincerely disliked being manipulated and coerced, and Bolan had just done both.

Heading for the chopper, he realized that, coercion or no, he had made the right decision.

"Godspeed, Mack," he said quietly.

CHAPTER TWENTY-NINE

Dryhole, Arizona

The Browning Hi-Power was untraceable, and the Chevy Blazer was rented under the name of a man who didn't exist.

It didn't match the other name, the one on the United Airlines ticket for the flight from Washington, D.C., to Phoenix, Arizona.

Anyone who tried to trace his origins would come up with nothing but a handful of dead ends.

Bolan entered the old Route 66 tourist town of Dryhole in the early evening and spent a half an hour eating a meal at the old diner. It had flourished years ago, and still did okay business. Enough to keep it going. Americans loved their culture and were willing to go out of their way to reconnect with the history that towns like Dryhole and diners like Todd's Route 66 Stop-And-Eat represented.

He drove out of town at dusk and paced the Blazer to keep it away from the rest of the traffic, of which there was little. When he was alone in the desert he pulled off the road and drove until the vehicle was lost in the night. No one would see him from the highway.

Then Bolan grabbed a bottle of water and started walking.

He found the trailer at midnight after hiking, he guessed, about five miles. It was more or less where Kurtzman's intelligence, siphoned from the Central Intelligence Agency's secure computer system, had placed it. It was protected by at least four agents, two on either side.

Maybe they were CIA, maybe FBI, maybe agents from some military branch. Bolan didn't know or care. He only knew he wouldn't, couldn't, touch them.

Ramadan would have to be taken from under their noses.

He extracted an MM-1 multiround projectile launcher and quickly loaded its revolving cylinder with tear gas grenades, then dragged on the gas mask. Positioning himself at one end of the trailer, he carefully assessed his target points.

Then he began firing.

The weapon was capable of sending a round about 120 yards, and Bolan was well inside its limits. Functioning without muzzle-flash, it was able to deliver the 37 mm grenades to their destination unnoticed—until they hit the ground and started spouting gas.

Placing six rounds up and down either side of the trailer, he had thoroughly filled the area with an unbreathable cloud that sent the agents stumbling away, shouting into their radios and calling to each other. They'd be damn uncomfortable, but they'd suffer no permanent damage.

He raced for the trailer, which he had targeted from outside the spreading cloud, and pulled out the Hi-Power as he reached the door, shooting it without hesitation. The doorknob disintegrated.

Yanking it open, he stepped inside.

Ramadan was standing in the living area holding a cloth over his face. He had closed the windows to keep the worst of the gas out and stared at the gas-masked figure with frank amazement.

"Who are you?"

"Ironic, isn't it? Using tear gas to get to you?"

"Why are you here?"

"To avenge the death of two hundred innocent men, women and children of Azerbaijan."

Ramadan laughed, but he was a bad actor. Bolan knew he was faking his amusement and expected the lunge that came in the middle of the hilarity. He sidestepped the charging Iraqi general and pushed him to the floor. Ramadan twisted as he fell, landing on his back and raising his hands as if to push Bolan away. He uttered a single pleading word.

"No—"

But Bolan fired without hesitation. The crack of the six rounds filled the trailer and seemed to shift the clouds of gas that embraced it like a cocoon.

Bolan dropped the gun and disappeared into the night.

Pacific Ocean, 300 miles west of Acapulco, Mexico

EDGAR POLLARI SAT in the sun on the upper deck of his boat, trying to read but too distracted. He kept checking the horizon for strange watercraft. He kept an ear out for news from the bridge, but so far everything was peaceful.

By God, it seemed as if his strategy had paid off perfectly.

Not that the project was a success by any means. A

few million dollars down the tubes. Nearly two years of effort and planning wasted.

But really, it could have gone much worse. All the Iraqis were dead or imprisoned. Ramadan was a prisoner of the CIA. Many of the Canadians and Americans he had hired were dead. None of them would be naming him as their employer. None of them even knew who he was. He had gone to great lengths to keep himself uninvolved in the actual dirty work.

He would be tied to the operations, certainly, and Ramadan might name him as the money man behind the operation. And all the circumstantial evidence pointed to him.

But there was little in the way of solid evidence to link him to any of it. And he was rich enough to purchase the support he would need to bluff his way through should anybody try to lay the blame at his feet.

What more could they do, really, except cast aspersions?

He heard the roar of a motorboat and watched his armed patrol craft take off and circle his ninety-foot *Oil's Well That Ends Well*. Nothing was going to get past the patrol.

It was time for lunch and a little CNN International. See if there were any hints as to what had become of his Iraqi friend, or leads on the mysterious mass murders in Azerbaijan. The news media had stopped blaming the U.S. and were concentrating more on the Iraqis. After all, somebody had to be blamed.

As long as it wasn't him.

BOLAN LEFT THE NAVY SEAL scuba transport parked at the rear of the deck of the *Oil's Well* and watched the distant patrol boat until it circled the side of the ship and was gone. Then he slipped out of the water and crouched on the rear of the deck, pulling the Beretta 93-R from its waterproof case.

He climbed the ladder to the deck and strode into the bridge as if he belonged there. The captain took one look at him, and Bolan grabbed him by the neck, leveling the 93-R into the face of the mate, who stood at his shoulder.

"Make a noise and I kill you both. Cooperate and you'll both live. Sound fair?"

The captain nodded.

Bolan quickly secured them with plastic handcuffs, then, for good measure, tied them into their seats using a section of plastic rope from the deck's lifesaver. He gagged the captain with a four-inch piece of black tape.

The mate was more nervous. More likely to spill good information. Bolan needed very little. "How many crew?" he asked.

"Just us and the butler."

"Passengers?"

"Only Mr. Pollari."

Bolan grabbed the phone and dialed the kitchen. The butler answered, and the mate cooperated by requesting his presence on the bridge.

The butler turned out to be a young, sandy-haired man in crisp white shorts and linen shirt, over which he wore a cook's apron. He turned to jelly when Bolan dragged him inside the bridge and rested the muzzle of the 93-R on the bridge of his nose. He was quickly cuffed and gagged.

Bolan hurried downstairs, finding the oil millionaire sitting in a small parlor area off the main dining room, eating a small salad and watching the world weather report. He never even heard the Executioner's approach. His hand dropped his fork when an iron grip flashed out from behind him and grabbed his wrist, yanking it behind his seat back. He cried out and tried to turn, but his other hand was grabbed too, and pulled behind him with a fast yank that snapped his shoulder. He screeched and struggled vainly.

"Who are you? Stop this! Who are you?"

Something plastic went around his wrists, and suddenly Pollari couldn't move his arms. Then he was pulled away from the table, and a piece of plastic rope was wrapped around his torso and the back of the chair by a large, dark-haired figure that said absolutely nothing.

"Why are you doing this? Tell me who you are and why you're doing this!"

Bolan opened the waterproof pack he was carrying on one shoulder and withdrew a small blue steel gas tank. The fresh label was red and white, with a skull and crossbones. It was topped with a tiny mechanical device and a small LED readout. Bolan adjusted the mechanism and pressed the tiny glowing red button.

"You have twenty minutes," he said to Edgar Pollari.

Bolan walked away.

Pollari was sweating and stuttering but saying nothing of meaning. He leaned forward hard against the ropes, barely able to make out the sun-dimmed LED. It said 19:33.

The label on the canister was easier to read. It said HYDROGEN CYANIDE in large, bloodred block letters.

BOLAN PUSHED THE CAPTAIN, the mate and the butler down the steep steps to the deck and into the motorized lifeboat. He took off the captain's handcuffs and stepped back, covering him with the handgun. "In just over fifteen minutes this boat will be flooded with hydrogen cyanide gas. Every living thing on board will be killed. Everything that gets caught in the gas cloud before it dissipates will be killed. Since the wind is coming from the west I suggest you go west. And I suggest you tell the others to go with you."

The captain had something he wanted to say, but at that moment Pollari started screaming. It was a nightmarish, insane scream. The captain started the motor on the lifeboat and steered quickly in the direction of the patrol speedboat.

In a few minutes, they had transferred to the speedboat and it headed due west. Bolan and Pollari were alone on the *Oil's Well*.

Bolan stepped into the water, finding his scuba gear and the SEAL transport where he had left it. He started up the submersible motorized unit and maneuvered away from the ship. Jack Grimaldi was scheduled to pick him up at a location about six miles to the west.

He had business to finish with Alexander Akhmedov in Lipetsk, Russia.

EDGAR POLLARI'S EYES were watering from squinting at the tiny faded LED. His stomach, chest and wrists were ripped and bleeding from his desperate pulling against his bonds.

He got the idea of moving himself forward, chair and all, and somehow grabbing the canister and tossing it overboard. Sure, it was a long way to a rail from where he was sitting. And how would he grab the thing?

He flung his body into the air and managed to make a short hop. He had done it! He had moved a good three or four inches! He tried again and felt himself come to a sudden lurching stop. He craned his head wildly and was able to make out a length of rope tied from his chair to a wooden handrail. He could get no closer.

His mind cleared suddenly. He had been wild and maybe a little insane for a short while, but now he was perfectly calm, numbed by terror.

At least moving forward made the little LED easier to see.

The final minute was on him.

Maybe the mechanism would fail. Maybe this was all an elaborate hoax.

Just seconds remained.

That was it. It had to be a hoax. After all, who would have the guts to execute a man like him in this fashion? It was unthinkable.

Pollari felt momentarily jubilant.

The gas started to flow.

An old enemy poses a new threat....

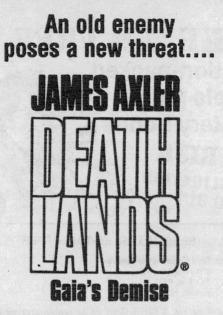

JAMES AXLER

DEATH LANDS®

Gaia's Demise

Ryan Cawdor's old nemesis, Dr. Silas Jamaisvous, is behind a deadly new weapon that uses electromagnetic pulses to control the weather and the gateways, and even disrupts human thinking processes.

As these waves doom psi-sensitive Krysty, Ryan challenges Jamaisvous to a daring showdown for America's survival....

Book 2 in the Baronies Trilogy, three books that chronicle the strange attempts to unify the East Coast baronies—a bid for power in the midst of anarchy....

TAKE 'EM FREE

2 action-packed novels plus a mystery bonus

NO RISK

NO OBLIGATION TO BUY

James Axler

OUTLANDERS™

OUTER DARKNESS

Kane and his companions are transported to an alternate reality where the global conflagration didn't happen—and humanity had expelled the Archons from the planet. Things are not as rosy as they may seem, as the Archons return for a final confrontation....

Book #3 in the new Lost Earth Saga, a trilogy that chronicles our heroes' paths through three very different alternative realities...where the struggle against the evil Archons goes on....

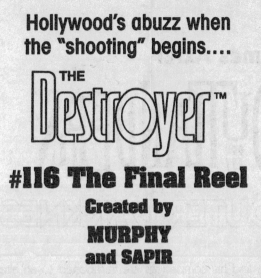